THE DRAGON HEALER

TIANI DAVIDS

To you: a dreamer, reader, lover of fantastical worlds and beasts.
May we one day find our own dragon.

CHAPTER ONE

ELINTA WOKE TO THE fierce howling of wind and heavy pat-
ter of rain slamming into the roof above her and pulled her
blankets close against the cool night air. A noise had woken her
from a deep sleep, a different sound sitting under the wind, just
low enough that she couldn't quite place it. She lay listening for a
moment, wondering what it could be. Then, when the wind died
down between gusts, the sound rose above the storm. Low, nervous whinnies, and, above them, a squeal she recognised instantly
as belonging to the new stallion. Throwing back her blankets,
Elinta rifled around in the dark for her clothes, stumbling over
her bed and the neat rows of bandages that she'd folded for Galen

earlier. A clap of thunder like the rumble of a large beast shook the house. Elinta laughed at the thought. There once was a day when it could have belonged to a monster. But that was a long time ago.

"Elinta!" Blaine's voice rose above the rain, along with a series of loud knocks on her door.

"I'm coming!" she yelled, slipping out of her nightdress and into a pair of pants and a shirt. Pulling on an old jacket, she opened the door to find her brother soaked to the bone and windswept, hair flattened against his face, standing in the doorway. Water dripped down his large overcoat and onto the wooden floor. His brow was crinkled in worry.

"What's happened?" she asked.

"The stallion got into the front paddock and bit one of the mares near the shoulder. He's torn a large chunk from her. And the older bay has hurt her leg." Blaine pushed a hand through his dripping blond hair. "I've got to get back down there. Father's having trouble with the new stallion. He doesn't like the storm."

As if to emphasise his point, another squeal echoed up from the stables.

Elinta ran back into her room, grabbed her satchel of herbs and cloths and tugged on her work boots. "Let's go."

They hurried from her room, the sound of their steps on the wooden flooring lost under the renewed gusts of wind and rain. Stopping by the front door, Blaine turned to her.

"Ready?" He reached for the handle.

The wind howled once again, louder than before, and rain hammered against the door. Elinta nodded, pulling her jacket tightly around her, the satchel hanging from her shoulder. Blaine shoved the door open, and they dashed out into the night. Freezing drops of water instantly soaked through her hair, and a burst of wind chilled her to the bone. Tucking her head down, Elinta followed her brother's strong figure in a run towards the stables,

THE DRAGON HEALER

sloshing through deep, muddy puddles and fighting to keep her feet under her. Through the heavy haze of rain, she could see the dim light of a lantern shining through the open door of the stables. She pulled her jacket even more tightly around her, but it did little to block the chill. Blaine picked up the pace as the stables loomed over them and they burst inside.

"What took so long?"

Turning, Elinta found her father firmly gripping the halter of the chestnut stallion who tugged away from his arm, ears back and eyes wide in terror. The animal snorted and kicked at the ground. Blaine hurried to take the halter and lead rope from their father, who stood an inch shorter than him but was just as muscled.

"This way," their father said gruffly to Elinta, grabbing a lantern from a hook on the wall.

Elinta followed him, wringing the water out from her hair. Passing several rows of closed stalls and earning themselves nervous whinnies and a nicker of greeting, Elinta's father led her to the back of the stables.

"How long since they were hurt?" Elinta called over the wind, tying her sodden blonde hair back from her face.

Her father shrugged. "Looks only recent but could be up to an hour. I knew I should have brought those three in for the night." He pointed to the two end stalls on the right and handed her the lantern. "They're in there."

Stepping lightly up to the door, she found the palomino mare turned into the back corner, water still dripping from her coat. The bite Blaine had mentioned wasn't in sight.

"Hey girl," Elinta called, watching as the mare's ears twisted towards her voice.

Slipping inside, she placed her hand on the horse's rump and pushed her around and away from the wall. The flickering light of the lantern slid over the bite as it came into view. The stallion had left a wound about half the size of her fist, but it wasn't as bad as Blaine had thought. Blood trickled down the mare's shoulder before mingling with the water in her coat and turning the hair a pale reddish-pink.

"Do you need Galen?" Her father called over the storm, referring to Elinta's master.

She studied the wound. The stallion's teeth had cut into the shoulder, but the damage seemed limited to the soft flesh. She shook her head, rubbed the mare's neck, and hurried back to her father.

"It looks worse than it is. It won't take long to treat." She hung the lantern off a hook on the back wall above head height and started rifling around in her satchel.

"Are you sure you can handle it?" her father said.

When will he stop questioning me?

Elinta bit her lip. Rather than responding straight away, she started pulling out cloths and jars of salve. She'd been an apprentice to Galen, the best healer in the village, since she was thirteen. That made it three years now.

Choosing her words carefully, Elinta said, "Yes. I've dealt with a lot worse."

"With Galen."

There was no room for arguing, even though he was wrong. She had dealt with much worse, without Galen and even with the horses before. Taking a deep breath, she reminded herself that he just wanted the best for the animals.

"Is the bay in the next stall?" Elinta asked.

Her father grunted in response, which Elinta took to mean yes. Retrieving the lantern and leaving her supplies by the door, Elinta stuck her head into the next stall. The other mare was waiting expectantly for her as the soft light of the lantern chased away the shadows. She nickered softly, ears flicking to listen to the storm, Elinta, and her father, but she appeared entirely relaxed. Elinta smiled at the old horse's docile nature. Nothing seemed to worry her.

Stepping inside the stall and absently rubbing the mare's muzzle, Elinta searched for any sign of a wound, but her left legs were fine. She ducked under the mare's neck and scanned her other legs.

"Ah," she said softly, finding a nick on the bay's lower back leg just above the fetlock. About the length of her little finger, the cut was shallow but continued to weep a small stream of blood.

"I don't see any inflammation," she said, checking the rest of the leg. Twisting, she placed the lantern on another hook, then ran both hands along the mare's leg to feel the muscles and tendons. "Or feel anything."

"No, the leg's moving fine."

That lined up with what Elinta was feeling, or rather, wasn't feeling. The cut hadn't damaged anything internally.

"She looks like she'll be fine." Elinta patted the horse's neck. "I'll see to her after the palomino and check on them both again tomorrow."

Her father nodded. "I've got to finish checking on the others," he said, then abruptly turned on his heel and disappeared. Elinta watched her father stride back to the front of the stables and sighed. If only he was as good with people as he was with horses. She shook her head and turned back to the bay, wrapping a piece of cloth around her leg.

"I'll be back," she said and left the stall. The wind had finally started to abate, though the rain continued to pound on the roof. Elinta fetched a halter and lead rope and went into the other stall.

The palomino had turned to watch Elinta working in the neighbouring stall and softly blew as Elinta entered with all her supplies.

"Hi girl," she said, replacing the lantern on the hook. "You gonna talk to me now?"

The mare shifted in place, ears twitching.

Elinta sidled up beside the mare and slipped the halter over her muzzle and into place before tying the lead rope near the door.

"Are you going to be nice for me, girl?" Elinta asked softly, fetching the supplies she'd left out. The mare didn't move, so she took that as a good sign. Elinta set to cleaning the wound, stopping regularly to reassure the mare, who shifted and tossed her head uneasily with each attempt to flush it. She covered the bite in one of Galen's special salves for infection and inflammation. Orange-yellow in colour, the salve came from flowers in the north that Galen bought. Rubbing the remaining salve from her hands onto her pants, she bent to pick up her supplies.

"Do you need any help?"

Elinta jolted in surprise and twisted towards the voice. "Blaine!"

The rain must have hidden his footsteps because she hadn't heard him approach. Her brother leant on his arms against the waist-high stall door, a grin spreading across his wet face. "Sorry."

Elinta rolled her eyes and gestured to the mare. "I'm finished with her, but you can hold the bay still for me, if you want?"

"Come on." He pulled the door open and stood aside for her.

Elinta took the halter and rope off the palomino, slung it over her shoulder, grabbed the last jar from the floor, the lantern from the hook, and followed her brother into the next stall.

Blaine slipped the tack from her hand and had the bay in position within seconds. "She's a good old girl." He gently patted the mare's neck.

"She is," Elinta agreed.

She set about flushing the cut while Blaine talked to the docile mare. The mare was naturally so calm that Blaine's presence wasn't needed, but he stayed anyway while Elinta worked. When the bleeding had stopped, Elinta opened the jar of orange-yellow salve, but their father reappeared by the stall before she could apply it.

"How's it coming?" he grunted. The light of the lantern hardly reached him, hiding his features almost completely from view. She could just make out the soft glow of his green eyes and the shadow of his salt and pepper beard.

"Fine." Elinta turned her back to him and bent to cover the wound in the salve.

"She's doing great," Blaine said.

"And the mare?"

"She'll be fine." Elinta kept her face turned away to hide her irritation. "Both of them."

"Check over the stallion when you're done, will you?"

"Sure."

Their father left without another word. After covering the cut with a thin, breathable cloth, Elinta straightened, wiping her hands on her pants.

"All done," she said, patting the mare.

Blaine slipped the tack from the mare's head and hung it outside the stall. Rubbing the mare's neck on her way out, Elinta smiled gratefully. "If only all the horses were as calm as her."

The mare nickered softly as they walked away from the stall, taking the light with them.

"She's a good one. Good mother too," Blaine agreed. "I'll hold the stallion for you. He'll have settled now the wind has died down." Her brother picked up his pace and turned into another stall. Elinta left the lantern on another hook to the side of the stall where the stallion couldn't kick it. It cast just enough light to see the horse.

"Come on in," Blaine called softly, just loud enough to be heard over the rain.

Elinta slipped through the door. The stallion's ear twisted to follow her as she moved around him, checking over his body for any bruising or cuts, but he stood perfectly still, at ease by Blaine's presence. Running her hands along the horse's legs, chest, and back, Elinta had a moment to be thankful for her brother's talent with the horses, because the stallion wouldn't have been as calm for her, or even their father.

"Well," she said, stepping back. "He's fine."

Blaine rubbed the animal's muzzle. "He was pretty riled up by the storm when we got down here."

Leaving the stall with her gear and taking down the lantern, Elinta smiled at her brother. "He obviously calmed right down when you took over from father."

Blaine hesitated, then nodded, following her out of the stall.

"Have you said anything about Culmar to him yet?" Elinta asked, instinctively lowering her voice even though their father had left. Blaine wanted to set up his own business in Culmar, doing the same breeding, training, and farrier work as their father did, but in the port city instead.

"No," Blaine said, scuffing his shoe as he walked. "I don't know how he'll take it, since I'd be moving the business there once he hands it over."

"You know it's a better place to be," Elinta said encouragingly. "And so does he. Even if he's never made the move, he's still had to travel to Culmar for better stock."

Blaine grinned. "Maybe you can make the argument for me, eh?"

Her eyes widened. "I don't think so."

They continued towards the main door in silence. Elinta watched Blaine from the corner of her eye. Even though he was four years older than her, he was her closest friend in the village, and she believed in him as much as he believed in her. If he wanted to go to Culmar, she'd support him even if it meant he'd be far away.

Pausing in front of the door, Blaine turned to her. "I am going to go. Just once I know where he stands on it, and if he needs me here, I can always make the move once he retires."

Elinta nodded at the familiar argument, then cocked her head, listening to the rain outside. It hadn't eased since they'd run down from the house.

"Let's go," Blaine said before they could change their minds.

"Oh, wait!" She was still carrying the lantern. Elinta blew out the flame, casting them into shadow, and hung the lantern on the hook by the door. "Ready."

Blaine threw open the door and ran into the night.

Following her brother, Elinta gasped as the cold water slammed into her body, plastering her hair against her face and trickling under the collar of her jacket within seconds. They sprinted back towards the house, kicking up even more mud than before and splashing through deep puddles of water. Firelight radiated through the front windows of the house. Elinta smiled gratefully at the thought of her father lighting a fire to heat the three of them up. She tucked her head down against the rain and ran harder.

Blaine reached the house first and ran inside, closing the door behind her when she joined him. They stood in the entryway, dripping onto the floor as a wave of heat and the smell of burning wood hit them from the living room. Peeling off her jacket and boots and leaving them in a pile by the door, Elinta hurried over to the fire. Their father was nowhere to be seen. Elinta looked around the house as Blaine, also out of his overcoat and boots, joined her by the fire. Their father's bedroom door was closed. He'd gone back to bed.

Elinta wrung out her hair, freely letting it drip onto the floor. Despite the coat she'd worn, her shirt was wet, as were her pants, so she stood as close to the flames as she dared to stop the shivering that had crept up on her. Beside her, Blaine stripped off his wet shirt and laid it on the floor.

"Cold," he grumbled.

Elinta murmured in agreement, her teeth chattering. "I'll be back."

Hurrying to her bedroom, she stripped out of her wet clothes, pulled on her dry nightdress, and slung a blanket over her shoulders, careful not to trap her wet hair under it. Now, much dryer and much warmer, she went back to the fire. Blaine eyed her blanket.

"Oh no," she said, looking at his wet form. "You're not sharing my nice, dry blanket."

"Please, Lin?" he asked, shivering.

"Go put a shirt on! That's why you're cold." She pulled her blanket tighter around herself.

He frowned. "It's too cold to leave the fire."

"Then run," she said stubbornly.

"You're horrible," he said, but he smiled anyway and ran off to find a fresh shirt.

Moments later, Blaine returned in dry clothes and Elinta let him huddle under the blanket with her. His blond hair was now starting to dry, though Elinta's own still hung in wet clumps past her shoulders.

"You smell like wet hay," she said, inhaling the smell of the wood-smoke from the fire and Blaine's own scent of hay underlined by leather and the tang of horse.

"So do you." He bumped her shoulder. After a pause, he spoke again, "Mum would be proud of you, you know."

"You think?" Elinta asked, trying to summon a picture of their mother in her mind. But most of her memories were second-hand, given to her by Blaine, who'd been seven when she died.

"I do. You're good at what you do, Lin," he said softly.

"So are you."

When the fire finally began to die down, the two went their separate ways and were back in their own beds just as the rain died back to a light shower. Tucked up in her blankets, Elinta rolled over and drifted back to sleep.

The light of the morning revealed the damage caused by the storm. As she walked through the village to Galen's hut, apron in hand, Elinta lifted the hem of her blue, ankle-length dress dodging puddles of water and trenches of mud. The people around her picked up knocked over signs and cleared away litter and branches that had blown through the wide streets in the storm. There didn't seem to be any major damage to the buildings she passed by, which likely meant there would be very few injuries, if any.

Elinta nodded greetings to those she passed on the street; some she had treated before, others she passed every day on her way to the healer's place. It was a bright, warm morning already, at odds with the cold of the night before, and Elinta was already thinking of the patch of sun waiting for her by the herb garden, which would warm up her bones. She turned off the main street and walked down a pathway weaving through the wooden houses and was cast into shadow. Just as she drew level with a small building with four cramped windows facing out onto the street, a tiny frame burst out in front of her.

"Tully!" Elinta caught the girl just before they collided.

"Sorry, Elinta!" Tully grinned up at her from under a mess of dark hair, fingering the satchel slung across her shoulder and chest.

"Brynne's got you running around pretty early today." Elinta dropped her hands from the girl's shoulders and nodded to the bag Tully still fiddled with. "More deliveries?"

Brynne was the only other healer in the village and had enlisted Tully to run errands for her while she started training her new apprentice. Tully was hopeful she'd be picked once she was old enough. The girl nodded. "Mr. Ivors needed something for a toothache. He was very insistent."

Elinta smiled. "Can you tell me what Brynne would have prescribed?" she quizzed, knowing the girl's enthusiasm to learn.

Tully scrunched up her face. "Flowers from the evening vine," she said triumphantly.

Nodding, Elinta asked her how Mr. Ivors would have taken it.

"He just has to chew it." She grinned toothily at Elinta.

"That's right. I better watch out for my job! You're getting good." Elinta laughed. "You better get going before you get in trouble."

Tully gave her another big smile, then ran off down the path in the direction Elinta had come from. Elinta watched the little girl as she disappeared around the corner. All arms and legs and a huge amount of enthusiasm. If she kept absorbing knowledge the way she was, Brynne would pick her up as soon as she finished with her new apprentice.

Elinta continued down the path to the outskirts of the village where Galen's hut sat. The forest loomed behind it, just a short walk through the grasslands. Knowing Galen probably hadn't risen yet, Elinta slipped around the back of the hut and to the herb garden. Bursting with as many medicinal herbs as would grow in a village garden, it contained a large percentage of the herbs that they needed to treat most common, and a large portion of uncommon, sicknesses and injuries. The rest of the herbs and plants could be found in the forest or ordered through the traders who worked their way through the villages, towns, and cities of

Eldras. Kethmere wasn't a huge village, but it was a common stop for traders moving through the south of the continent.

Tying the apron around her waist and pulling up the hem of her work dress, she knelt on the ground before the nearest garden bed and set to work. The storm had knocked some of the plants over, so she retied them to their stakes and tidied any damage. There wasn't much to be done after that, as she did a little work on the beds each day, but she let her mind wander as she soaked up the warm sun while weeding the bed and trimming the plants. It was her love of gardening that had singled her out to Galen from among the applicants for the apprentice position. Galen said that her already having a good knowledge of plants and a little sketchbook full of drawings of ones she'd discovered had done half the work for him, so he'd taken her on earlier than most apprentices. *He's a good teacher*, she mused, running her hands over the leaves of the young evening vine growing along a trellis. *And a good healer.*

"Elinta!" Galen's harsh voice sounded from inside, causing her head to snap up. Always one to skip formalities. No doubt he already had a job for her.

"Yes, Master Galen?" she called over her shoulder, continuing to work in the garden bed.

"We're out of black disc fungi. Go get some once you're finished in the garden," his voice returned, much closer than before. Elinta sat back on her heels and twisted, finding his thin frame in the entryway of his hut.

"OK." She paused, picturing the jars along the shelves lining the hut. She'd checked over them before finishing yesterday. "I think we're nearly out of weeping bark as well, sir? Should I get some more?"

Galen waved his hand. "No. It was a good thought, but I would have told you to get some if we needed it."

Elinta nodded and turned back to the garden. He'd probably send her to get some of the bark in a few days anyway. She finished by tugging out the last of the weeds sprouting up around the calendula, careful not to disturb its delicate roots. She brushed her finger against one of its soft petals and smiled. It was a sweet little flower, useful too.

She pushed off from the ground, dusted her hands on her apron and hurried back inside, ducking under the herbs hanging from the roof to dry. She paused at the entrance to let her eyes adjust and, slowly, the simple interior came into view. Galen sat at his desk in the corner, his grey hair hiding his face as he poured a thick paste into one of the many empty jars sprawled across the surface in front of him. A basket waited for her beside the front entry. Elinta crossed the room, picked it up, and hesitated. She quickly scanned the various jars of herbs, pastes, salves, and tonics, certain the weeping bark needed filling.

"Elinta ..." Galen said softly, but there was a warning in his voice.

"Just going now, sir." Without a backwards glance, Elinta stepped out into the morning sun and waded into the grasslands behind the house.

She pushed her way through the thick tussocks, grasses tickling at her elbows as she passed. Elinta beelined for the small path carved into the grassland by the rare traffic of the odd villager looking for wood and food. Elinta was the main contributor since she regularly walked to the forest for Galen. She emerged onto the path and flicked away some stray pieces of grass caught in the skirt of her dress and clinging to her apron. The path was, unsurprisingly, deserted. It was rare to come across anyone on her trips to collect herbs. Just the way she liked it.

Elinta followed the path, idly swinging the basket in her hand and enjoying being outside with no one looking over her shoulder. Herbs and healing were the one thing she was good at. She didn't need supervision so much anymore, especially since she was nearly ready to be on her own permanently. As in, full time. An actual healer. A flutter of nerves hit her stomach, but she pushed them away as she stopped in the long thin shadows cast by the forest. A soft gust of wind blew the sweet, yet sickly, smell of decaying leaves across her face. She inhaled deeply. Smelling the freshness of the dirt and the leaves after the storm.

Smiling, she stepped under the thin canopy of the outer trees and carefully picked her way further in, weaving around trunks, strangles of bushes, clumps of saplings and the odd branch knocked down from the wind overnight. Her eyes scanned the forest floor, locking onto each and every herb and weed that she found. She named each as she went, a habit she'd developed long ago.

Galen was after black disc fungi which would be deeper in the forest, in the darker, thicker parts of the woods, where the water clung to the earth. There'd been a patch near the lake only a week ago, about a twenty-minute walk away. Plenty of time to study the plants around her and listen to the birdsong as she went. Elinta passed trees whose bark could treat stomach cramps, flowers that when ground into a paste treated skin rashes, and leaves of a bush that made a tea excellent for the health of pregnant women. It was amazing what could be found in nature.

The temperature shifted the further into the forest she travelled. Goosebumps tingled up her bare arms. No matter the temperature outside in the grasslands, here, deep in the forest, was always cool. Head tucked down, rubbing a hand up and down her arm in an effort to reduce her chills, she didn't realise how far she'd travelled until she stumbled out of the trees and found the lake directly in front of her. No longer contending with the trees, warm sunshine beamed down onto the lake and reflected onto Elinta. She closed her eyes and soaked up the heat, finally dispelling the goosebumps, but when she opened her eyes, a shock of chills coursed through her again. And not because she was cold.

The trees at the far left of the lake were … flattened? They were broken, splintered, and knocked over in a wide line that appeared out of nowhere. It wasn't, couldn't be, storm damage. The odd branch here and there was normal. She'd seen enough of it on her way here. But *this*. This looked like some kind of … of trail. Into the *air*. Elinta stared at the destruction. What could cause something like this?

Swallowing the lump in her throat, Elinta hesitantly took a step towards the ruined trees, still holding her basket in one hand. She took another step. Then another and finally found herself in front of the trail, feet in the lake, the water gently lapping at her heels. Now she was closer, Elinta could see the height of the damage changed as it went further into the forest. The trees at the back appeared more whole, some only missing their very tops. As the damage grew closer to the lake, more and more of the trees appeared to have been knocked down or snapped until, by the edge, a whole patch of saplings had been demolished and huge branches had snapped off the larger trees. But that wasn't the strangest thing. At her feet was proof that it was indeed a trail. Deep ruts had been carved into the earth, spreading loose dirt across the ground, and disappearing at the edge of the lake as though whatever had flown off into the sky had come from the water.

All thought of the fungi forgotten, Elinta twisted her body, eyes following the path of the ruts to the water's edge. Her heart pounded in her throat and her skin crawled as she studied the calm water of the lake. What had come out of there? As if in answer, a low keen came from across the water. Elinta's blood froze. Her body froze. Jammed up. The noise sounded again. The cry of a hurt or scared animal, but it was like nothing she'd heard before. It sounded big. As though the noise reverberated in a large chest. She closed her eyes, all too aware of the damage behind her, steadied herself, then raised her gaze to look across the lake. What she saw there, barely twenty-five metres away, made her heart stutter. The basket dropped from her limp hands. What she was seeing— what she was looking at ... it wasn't possible. They hadn't been seen in Eldras in over a hundred and seventy years. But she knew what it was. Its name came out of her in a strangled whisper. "Dragon."

CHAPTER TWO

E LINTA'S KNEES SHOOK AND her jaw was slack. Her mind flashed back to every song and story she'd ever heard about this creature before her. One verse stuck in her head. The one where the dragons left Eldras and peace descended on the country. Her breath hitched. Every last egg was destroyed from that final clutch. The guardian dragon was killed, and every dragon had left. She knew that. Except ... there was one right in front of her. How was this creature here?

Elinta stared at the animal, trying to wrap her mind around its sheer size. Though its tail wrapped protectively around its hunched body, she guessed the creature to be thirty-five- to forty-feet long. Amber eyes stared back at her from a long face, its head topped by two horns above its ears. A few smaller spines jutted out by its jawbone, pointing towards its back. Raised bumps ran along the back of its neck, growing smaller until they tapered out. But what struck her most was the colour of its scales. They were white. Snow white. Clear and bright and more beautiful than the flowers of a yarrow.

Her heart thudded in her chest. She could taste her own fear in her mouth, but her body wouldn't move. She was locked in place, knowing this creature would soon kill her, just as the tales said. Seconds passed and nothing happened. Elinta stared at it. The dragon was *lying down,* tail tucked around its body, large membrane wings tucked against its sides, and its head was resting on the ground. Apart from a small flick of the tip of its tail, the dragon wasn't moving. Elinta frowned. It was the exact opposite of aggression. Of everything she knew dragons were.

Elinta's body slowly relaxed, allowing her to close her mouth, though her heart continued to thump loudly in her chest. She studied the holes that were the dragon's ears and wondered whether it could hear something like that. The fierce beat of her small heart trying to break free from her chest. She ran her eyes over the dragon's body one more time and finally noticed the bright red blood oozing from the wing closest to her. She shook herself and forced her mind to kick back into gear. How had she been so ridiculously unobservant? First, not to notice the dragon when she arrived at the lakeside, and now, not to notice its injury when moments before she had heard its sad call. No wonder the animal's behaviour seemed off.

The dragon raised its chin and tilted its head, eyes locked on her. As if *studying* her.

Elinta swallowed. She looked at its injured wing again, then cautiously flicked her eyes down to the ruts in the dirt beneath her and thought of the damage behind her.

"You must have come down in the storm," she whispered.

The dragon's head tilted. Elinta gasped. It *could* hear her from across the lake! The dragon blinked and rested its head back onto the ground, its eyes still burning into her. Elinta's mind was racing. How was she going to get away from the dragon? It seemed placid enough right now, but she'd been standing still for some time. What would happen when she moved? Would the dragon swoop upon her then? Her eyes landed on the animal's bloody wing again. Maybe it couldn't fly. She could sprint for the trees and hope it wouldn't follow her, hope it wouldn't fit among the closely knit trunks. But she already knew it could easily knock young trees down. The chaos behind her proved that. Elinta remained still. Unsure what to do. Even if she ran ... who was to say this beast couldn't move quickly across the ground? The songs always spoke of the way they cut through the air, masters of flight and fire, but they never spoke of their movement on the ground.

She couldn't wait for anyone to come looking for her. Even if she was still alive when Galen found her, what could he do against a dragon? There wasn't much to be done but find a way out of this herself. Leaving the basket where it lay, Elinta raised a trembling foot and slowly set it down away to her side. The dragon didn't move. She raised her other foot and took another step to the side, hoping to make her way back to the trees, inch by inch if she had to. Just as she raised her foot to take another step, the dragon let out another low, sad keen. And despite her fear, the sound tugged at Elinta's heart.

"No," she told herself in a whisper. "That is a dragon. Not some soft-hearted mare. It's not even some love-struck stallion. That's a *dragon*."

But its eyes were still fixed on her and its blood continued to trickle.

"You don't have your kit," she continued, now really trying to convince herself to leave. Why didn't she leave? She could turn her back on this creature. She knew, oh she knew, how dangerous it was. How evil this species was supposed to be. "The Ballad of the Slain" was on a never-ending loop in her mind: the king marching to kill the dragons.

But her heart whispered back to the logical arguments she'd made to herself. *It's hurt and you can help. It's not even aggressive. You passed half a dozen useful plants on your way here*. So Elinta moved her still hovering foot and placed it down in front of her. And then she took another slow, small step towards the dragon. It blinked. Its tail flicked. She took another step, but the animal didn't move. Slowly, ever so slowly, she edged her way around the lake, drawing ever closer to the animal, wondering when it would rise and snap her up in its huge mouth or cover her in a burst of fire. She tried to look as harmless as possible, keeping her hands open and motionless by her sides and her head down, though she couldn't tear her eyes from the beast. The dragon followed her every move with its eyes but, still, it didn't move. Elinta's heart continued trying to break free of her chest.

She stopped five metres from the beast, her shaking legs unable to carry her any closer. Its amber eyes were locked onto her own. Yellow and brown locked in a stare. Its eyes were beautiful. Deep swirls of amber surrounding a black, slitted pupil. It reminded her of the sun and the night all at once. Now that she was closer, she saw the bumps along its neck were not quite spines but more like large, raised scales that ended in a point. They dwindled away before reaching the beast's back. Elinta stared at the dragon, at a loss. Her mind flashed back to how she talked to her patients, even the horses, when they were injured. There was a hint of fear in the eyes looking back at her, but also ... intelligence? The creature seemed to study her as much as she was studying it. Maybe talking to it calmly would help. The horses always responded well to a gentle tone.

Elinta licked her lips. "Hello there," she said quietly.

The dragon blinked.

"You're not looking too well, are you?" She inched sideways, aiming to stand before its injured wing and trying not to focus on its massive, four-clawed feet.

"I'm meant to be collecting herbs for Galen, you know? Not treating injured dragons."

She took another step. Its head followed her movements. She continued speaking quietly to the creature, but internally she was screaming at herself. What was she thinking? This was a dragon! But she couldn't bring herself to turn around and walk away. Not when its blood had left tracks down its scales and dripped to the ground beneath it. Not when it looked at her so … knowingly. Finally, she stopped beside its wing, a mere two metres from the dragon.

Her eyes were still on the beast's. Fear kept her from taking her eyes away from its head and teeth and deadly breath. Its head had continued to follow her movement, twisting its neck around so it could watch her. She looked at the holes in the side of its head that were its ears. If only they were like a horse's, twitching and turning to show its mood. She couldn't read the small pits in its head. Only its wide eyes seemed to show any emotion. And though its tail twitched occasionally, she didn't know what that meant.

"OK, OK," she mumbled to herself. "I'll just check the wing."

The dragon lowered its chin to the ground and looked from her to its wing. Elinta frowned at the strange movement. Was its wing so painful that it would be this distracted from her? Tearing her eyes away from the dragon's head, Elinta studied its furled wing. There were cuts along the parts of the membrane that she could see, and along the bony framework of the wing. A bulge of veins sat under the white of the membrane. Held up to the sun, she thought an entire network of veins and tendons would be revealed within. But with the wing furled, she had no idea the true damage the dragon's apparent rocky landing had caused.

She looked back at the dragon. Its eyes were still on her. "I'm just going to get some herbs to treat this, OK?"

She looked back at the wing.

"And then hope you let me touch you," she muttered to herself.

Of course, the dragon didn't understand, but the tone of her voice seemed to have calmed it, so she continued talking as she edged away from it and disappeared into the forest. Under the shade of the trees and back in the cooler air, she took her first easy breath since she'd opened her eyes and seen the destruction wrought by the dragon. An *actual* dragon. She leant against the nearest tree, its rough bark digging into her back.

She should tell someone. The village needed to know there was a dragon nearby. But even as she thought it, she knew she wouldn't be able to bring herself to tell anyone. They'd kill it. Just as they'd been told to, just as they believed they had to. Like every other human in Eldras, the people of Kethmere celebrated the disappearance of the dragons. Celebrated the Eggslaying and the death of their protector as a holiday. Elinta closed her eyes. She did too, just not with the same amount of fervour as some. But she did.

Dragons were dangerous. Vicious beasts that wouldn't hesitate to burn an entire city to the ground. Yet, the one waiting for her by the lake seemed nothing of the sort. And hadn't the Asali, the only other race in Eldras, condemned the Eggslaying and ended the treaty between their peoples? Surely, they wouldn't do that because of the death of monsters? Elinta shook her head. It didn't matter what everyone else thought. Killing an injured animal that showed no aggression ... she couldn't condone it. She couldn't be responsible for it.

Opening her eyes, she came to her decision. She'd help it. She'd treat its wounds and then make sure it went on its way. And hope, desperately hope, no one found it in the meantime and provoked it into spilling its wrath upon Kethmere and its neighbours. Taking a steadying breath, Elinta switched her mind over to what she now had to do and find. She needed something to treat the wounds for infection and inflammation. And maybe some kind of poultice to help the wounds stay closed. Yarrow would be best. There wasn't a lot of the small plant around, but she'd found a patch in a small clearing not far from the lake several weeks ago. She hadn't bothered to take any since Galen grew his own.

"OK," she mumbled to herself, "you'll need something else to clean the wound.... That's easy, I'll use some of the black disc fungi." After all, there was a patch growing near the lake. That was why she'd been there in the first place. The little black fungi were used to clean wounds of dirt and other invasives and was quite efficient at treating infection too. She could make a tea from it, drawing out its goodness, and pour it over the wound when it cooled. Or she could mash it up and mix it in with the yarrow poultice.

With a plan in mind, and not allowing herself to wonder how she was going to get close enough to the dragon to treat it, she walked further into the forest and towards the patch of yarrow waiting for her. She fiddled with her apron as she picked her way among the trees, carefully stepping over roots and the uneven ground. Worry tugged at her, but she pushed it away. She was doing the right thing. She *was*. Glancing up, Elinta saw the small clearing she was searching for ahead of her and picked up her pace.

Emerging into the open, the ground blanketed in grass and leaves, her eyes landed on a small patch of yarrow on the border of the clearing. It was a many stalked, thin plant with deep green leaves that reminded her of tiny feathers. Its flowers were small, bunched into a single head with pure white petals. Elinta picked several of the long, thin stems, choosing ones covered in the leaves she needed for the poultice. Grabbing the bottom on her apron and holding it up to form a little dip, she dropped the stems inside, twisted on her heel and headed back to the lake, all the while thinking of the basket she'd left abandoned by the shore.

Elinta paused in the shadows of the trees by the lake. Her heart had started fluttering madly again at the sight of the dragon though it hadn't moved since she'd left. The beast's amber eyes had fixed on her as soon as she'd come within sight of it, but it didn't make a sound and it didn't move. It was as though it could sense the fear radiating off her. Tightening her grip on her apron, she forced herself to take a step out into the open. The basket and the patch of fungi were to her left, the dragon to her right. Her mind screamed objections at the idea of turning her back on the huge beast, but she had no choice if she wanted to help it heal. Besides, the dragon hadn't shown her any aggression yet, and looking at its giant mouth and terrible claws, it didn't need to wait for her to turn away to hurt her.

Taking a deep breath, Elinta turned towards the basket, her back to the dragon. She waited for several heartbeats. Her joints locked up. Everything she knew about the beast behind her screamed at her to turn back around, to keep her eyes on it, to run and hide, and hope it didn't follow her. But the seconds ticked by and still nothing happened. This beast wasn't going to hurt her. She was sure of it. But she couldn't work out why.

Elinta forced her legs to carry her over to the basket. She squatted to pick it up and tipped the yarrow inside. All the while she could feel the dragon's eyes following her, but she didn't turn. She hurried to the first patch of black disc fungi she could see. It was small, black and grew in clumps of three heads along a rotten log, the tip of which rested in the lake water. Elinta tore away several clusters of the mushrooms and put them in the basket with the yarrow. Now all she needed was something to mash the two plants into a poultice with, and something to keep the poultice in since it would just ooze from the basket. There was no way to make the tea from the fungi out here, but it didn't matter, the poultice would do the same job. She could use water from the lake to clean the wounds. The yarrow and fungi would treat any bacteria from that too.

Nodding to herself, she scanned the surrounding area for something with a dip in it to hold the poultice. She surveyed the damage the dragon had caused. Maybe there was something among the ruin she could use. Elinta rifled among the destruction, picking up potential pieces of bark and leaves before tossing them away. She glanced at the dragon every couple of minutes, reassuring herself that it hadn't moved while she searched.

Not having any luck, Elinta sighed and cast around further away. There! A large piece of bark had fallen away from one of the trees, dipped in the middle like a bowl. Hurrying over to it, she grabbed the bark. It was thick, sturdy, and as long as her arm. Perfect. Placing it inside the basket though the end stuck out, she looked around for a rock or thick stick for crushing the plants. She didn't have to look long before she found a suitable rock by the lake, smoothed over by the water. Now all she had to do was walk up to a live dragon and poke and prod at it.

"Easy," she whispered.

The pressure of the dragon's eyes on her back hadn't eased while she'd collected the fungi or while she'd found the bowl and rock. Now, she turned to face it again and indeed, its eyes were still on her.

"OK, then. We'll just take this nice and slow." Just as she had when she'd first arrived at the lake, she edged towards the dragon, small slow step by small slow step. It was only now that she realised she hadn't checked the dragon's other wing for damage. So, this time, Elinta angled to the beast's other side to get a glimpse of the other wing. Sure enough, there was a small amount of dried blood along it, but the injuries seemed lesser.

"I'm just going to have a look, OK?" she said, continuing along the length of the dragon. Drawing close, she found the blood along the wing was only from some minor scrapes that could be left alone. Somehow, most of the damage had happened to its other wing.

"Huh." She shrugged. That saved her a trip to fetch more yarrow. Backing away, Elinta sat a few metres from the dragon and placed the basket before her. It twisted its neck around and laid its head in front of her. This close to it, she could see small pits along the upper lip, like a snake. There were three on either side. Did that mean it could sense her body heat? She shivered.

"I'll just sit here, girl," she said quietly, rummaging in the basket. In truth, she wasn't sure if the dragon was a girl, but she wanted to call it *something,* and it seemed like a girl. While she set to work crushing the yarrow and the fungi together in the bark bowl, the dragon continued to watch her intently with those intelligent amber eyes.

"It's for the cuts on your wing," she told it, more to fill the silence than for it to hear her voice anymore.

The dragon seemed totally at ease with her sitting so close to it, but that didn't ease the nerves in her own stomach. With all the yarrow and fungi now crushed, she stirred it together, scooped a tiny amount of water into the bowl and stirred it some more. She didn't have any flour to add for thickness to help it stick, but it didn't matter. The fungi was doing most of the work the flour would have.

"Well," she said, looking up at the dragon. "It's done."

The dragon slowly stretched its wing out before her, covering the length of its tail so only the tip peaked out. Elinta's mouth dropped. The small visible piece of the tail twitched, and the beast's massive eyes blinked expectantly at her. She looked from its face and back to the wing.

Feeling silly, she whispered, "Can you understand me?"

It tilted its head and blinked again.

"I ..." Elinta shook her head. *This is stupid.* It was an animal. It couldn't understand her. It wasn't possible.

Picking up the bowl full of crushed plants, she shifted to a crouch in front of the wing, her feet just inches away from the water. Bright tracks of red glittered in the light, spreading across the brilliant white scales and membrane. With the wing spread out, she could see most of the cuts were focused along the edge of the wing, on the frame and membrane. Some were deep and short, others long and shallow. She'd take them one at a time and see what damage had been done.

"It's not too bad," she said, looking over at the beast's face. It had twisted its neck around again to watch her. She told the beast how gorgeous it was while dipping her hands in the water and scooping up a handful. "All right, girl. I'm going to pour this on your wing. Don't ... don't eat me, please." *It's just like a horse,* she told herself, *a really big, scary horse.*

She opened her hands and let the water trickle over one of the shallow tears in the membrane. A light shudder went through the wing. Her neck cracked as she whipped her head around to look at the dragon, sure that it was about to snap at her. But the animal hadn't moved, and its mouth was still closed. "Good girl." She breathed a sigh of relief and scooped up another handful of water, tipping it on the same wound. The wing remained still. "OK, this is good."

A low hum came from the dragon, the first sound it had made since she got back with the yarrow. Elinta smiled. It seemed like ... a happy sound? No, maybe like it was agreeing with her.

"As long as you stay happy with me, because I've still got to do all the others and use this." She gestured at the bowl beside her, then frowned. Why was she talking to it like it understood her?

Shaking her head, she dipped her hands into the bowl and collected a handful of the grey-black mess inside. Without warning the dragon this time, she pressed a large glob onto the wound. The tail twitched. With every passing second that the dragon stayed calm, Elinta's nerves continued to settle. So, she kept cleaning the wounds with the water and then covering them with the poultice. Elinta saved the largest wound for last, a deep cut along the membrane near the outer bone, stretching nearly as long as her forearm. When the time came to treat it, a nervous flutter had settled in her stomach again. For the most part, the dragon had remained still while she'd treated the wounds, though its wing had shuddered when she cleaned some of the deeper cuts. But would it stay that way?

"OK, then. This is probably going to hurt, girl. Just ... just don't hurt me. I'm trying to help." The dragon fixed its enormous amber eyes on her. Was it possible? Could it actually understand her? Those eyes seemed so ... intelligent, knowing. Like it understood every word she'd said since arriving. Like it was more than an animal. She scooped up some more water in her hands and trickled it over the wound. The dragon keened quietly, and its wing shuddered. Elinta sat back on her heels.

"It's OK, girl." Reaching out a trembling hand, she stroked the frame of its wing. It was the first time she'd touched it without the muck of the poultice in the way. She'd thought the scales would be rough but, running her hand along them, they were unbelievably smooth. She fingered one of the pristine, white scales. They were beautiful, the way they interlocked and overlapped. The way they glistened in the sun.

The wing shifted under her hand.

"You're right." She pulled her hand away and collected more water. The dragon didn't shudder or pull away again as she poured handful after handful of water over the long cut. Finally satisfied it had been flushed, Elinta began to press the last of the yarrow and fungi into the wound. Her hands were sticky with the mess of the plants and the dragon's blood when she scraped the bark clean and pressed the last of the poultice over the end of the cut.

"There you go." Elinta pulled back, holding her dirty hands away from her.

The dragon let out another low hum and raised its head from the ground. Slowly, it moved its head towards her, stopping so close Elinta could feel its warm breath blowing on her face and against her hair.

"Hello," she whispered and hesitantly raised her dirty, sticky hand. The beast didn't move, not even when she pressed her hand to its muzzle. Or when she pulled away, leaving a grey-black patch smeared across its white nose in the shape of her hand.

Her eyes landed on the colour of the handprint. The fungi! Galen was still waiting on her. She cleared her throat. "I should go." She grabbed the basket, leaving the bark behind, and stood, brushing off her dress.

The dragon fixed her with its eyes and emitted a soft rumble from its throat.

"I don't know what that means, girl." Although the sound had a distinctly friendly tone to it, she couldn't place what it meant. The horses sometimes whinnied in greeting to her, but she doubted dragons could make that kind of noise. The animal lowered its head back to the ground.

"I'll be back to check on you soon. If you're still here ..." she said, hurrying back to the patch of fungi to collect some for Galen.

"I hope he won't be mad," she whispered, tugging the fungi free and being careful to keep the stalks intact. Galen would use every part of the plant. She'd been gone for much longer than usual. The sun had almost risen to its peak, and her stomach had started to growl. But maybe, just maybe, Galen hadn't noticed how long she'd been gone. He could be like that sometimes, lost in his work for hours and not realising the day had passed. Basket now full of the fungi, she washed the muck and blood from her hands in the clear lake. All the while, she knew the dragon was watching her.

"I'm ... going now," she said awkwardly. She didn't know why she kept talking to the animal, more than she would with the horses, but she did. It felt right. And the dragon seemed to have some level of understanding ... but how much? She continued to think about her time with the creature as she walked back through the forest, hardly paying attention to where she was walking. It seemed impossible that the dragon should seem so calm and friendly, and yet it was. When it'd looked at her, she'd seen the intelligence in its eyes, and hadn't it seemed to respond to her words? She couldn't deny it. This dragon was more than just an animal ... if that was possible.

Tripping on a root, Elinta stumbled a few steps before righting herself. She tugged up the hem of her dress and continued on, much more carefully. There was one thing she was certain of: she couldn't tell anyone about the beast. They'd try to kill it and perhaps they'd be successful, but they'd be killed in the process.

Half an hour later, Elinta arrived back at Galen's hut and ducked inside. One glance told her he wasn't there. His satchel was gone, and his desk was abandoned.

"Must be with a patient," she mumbled, crossing to the desk and dropping the basket of fungi on it. Galen would want the fungi cut and dried so it could be crushed and put into a jar.

Elinta fetched a clean cutting board from beside the desk and a knife from a drawer near the sink in Galen's little kitchen and placed them on the desk. She washed the mushrooms carefully in the sink. The water was tinged with black as it went down the drain. Even as she worked in Galen's hut, her mind was back in the forest by the lake with a beautiful white dragon, shimmering in the morning sunshine. Elinta took the clean fungi back to the desk and cut each into strips. But she hardly saw her hands working, hardly heard the knife scratching along the cutting board. All she could hear was the low keen of the dragon in pain and its quiet rumble.

The knife slipped and pricked her finger. "Oh!" She'd almost stuck her finger in her mouth when she realised it was black from the pigment of the fungi. Sighing, she hurried to the sink and washed her finger in the cool stream.

"Silly," she grumbled at herself.

Turning the stream off, she sucked a bead of blood from her finger and turned back to the desk. "Focusing this time."

She shook her head and set back to work cutting the fungi, making sure to keep her mind on the work in front of her and not on the dragon.

Elinta was laying the pieces out to dry when Galen returned. He stomped the dirt from his shoes on the porch and dropped his satchel by the door.

"How much did you get?" Galen crossed the room to look at the tray of cut fungi.

"Enough for a couple jars," she said, laying out the last piece. She waited for him to ask what had taken her so long, but he just nodded and started cleaning his desk of the cutting board and remains of the fungi.

"Did you have a patient?" she asked, taking the trays out into the afternoon sun.

"Nothing you haven't seen before." He sat at his desk and pulled down another empty jar. "Carlie Abney cut her leg along her calve." He turned to face her as she came back inside. "What could I have used for infection?"

He was right. It was nothing she hadn't seen before or dealt with. But he liked to quiz her to keep the knowledge fresh.

She pointed at the fungi outside, then rattled off a list. "There's also yarrow, honey, or oil from thyme leaves. Although thyme shouldn't be used if the person has high blood pressure so that wouldn't work for Mrs. Abney." She hesitated, another thought occurring to her.

"Sir," she said slowly, "would all of these work on an animal? Like ... like a bat or something?" It was the closest example she could think of to a dragon, that and a lizard.

Galen frowned. "I see no reason why it wouldn't. We recommend honey and yarrow for wounded pets."

Elinta nodded as he turned to hunch over some evening vine.

"Have you eaten?"

"No, sir." She cleaned the knife and cutting board, then wiped the sink clean of the juice and dye from the fungi. What would Galen say if he knew she'd treated a dragon by herself? She almost giggled at the thought.

Galen twisted in his chair, holding a piece of the vine in one hand. "Go eat and come back in an hour."

Nodding, she breathed a sigh of relief when she emerged on the street. He hadn't asked about what happened in the forest. As far as she could tell, he wasn't aware she'd been gone for longer than usual. Maybe he'd left not long after her to see Mrs. Abney. Her mind safely returned to the dragon while she walked home. Elinta hardly noticed the people along the familiar streets and paths around her, going in and out of buildings and walking to and from their homes.

The nervous flutter had settled in her stomach again, but not from fear of the dragon. She had a secret to keep now, and things would be bad if someone found out. Someone like her father who celebrated the Eggslaying with fervour, or even Blaine who would be among the men sent to kill the creature. She shook her head. The dragon would be well enough to move on soon, and then all of this would be behind her. No one needed to know she'd helped such a hated creature.

Feeling slightly better, Elinta soaked up the midday sun as she drew closer to her home. The warmth drove away the last of her nerves and chills from the forest. Blaine and her father were out in the paddocks with the horses, though the two injured mares were noticeably absent. Blaine looked up from shovelling manure and waved. She smiled, returning the wave. Her father didn't seem to notice Blaine pausing in his work or her arriving home, and continued working. She pushed into the house, the fire from the night before in ashes, and set to finding something to eat.

CHAPTER
THREE

E LINTA SPENT THE REST of the day with Galen, sorting
through their supplies. It was mindless work, and just the
sort of thing she needed, because no matter how hard she tried,
and she did try, her mind kept turning back to the stunningly white creature waiting for her just outside the village. While
she worked, Elinta studied Galen's calm demeanour as he sorted
through his records. What would he say if he knew what she'd
really done this morning? Or that there was a dragon so close to
where he lived? He certainly wouldn't be so calm.

"Can I help you with something, Elinta?" Galen looked up
from the paper in his hand and met her gaze.

"Oh, no. I was just thinking ... about the," she looked at the jar in her hand, "wattle bark."

"What of it?" Galen straightened in his chair. Elinta grasped for something to say to mask her lie. She looked at the dark strips inside the jar.

"I know we use it in a tea, sir," she said, realising where to take the conversation, "but I heard one of the traders last market day mention that they all eat it as it is. I wondered whether it has any medicinal properties when taken that way or whether it's more for sustenance," she finished in a rush. It was something she'd heard just last week from one of their suppliers, but she'd dismissed their use of the bark as food rather than medicine. Galen didn't know that though.

Galen nodded thoughtfully. "There might be some minor benefits from eating it as it is, but the boiled water helps release the nutrients and properties we're after. I would stick to making a tea for now. When you're on your own, you can experiment with it."

He turned back to his papers. Releasing a sigh, Elinta put the jar back on the shelf. This dragon was going to be a problem if she couldn't keep her mind off it. How was she supposed to keep it secret if she kept spacing out? But it was just so ... unbelievable. That there was a dragon out there, injured, and it hadn't tried to eat her.

That night at dinner, despite her best efforts, even her father noticed how distracted she was. Snapping back to attention when he asked what was on her mind, Elinta found herself grasping for something to say for the second time that day.

"I'm sorry. Galen brought something up today and it had me thinking." The lie fell easily off her tongue even if there was a stab of guilt with it. She flicked her eyes from her satisfied father to Blaine, who spooned a heap of mashed potato into his mouth.

With a start, she realised even he, who had always read her well, seemed totally unaware of her lie. She quickly looked away so he wouldn't notice her gaze.

Her father pushed back his chair and stood, smoothing down his hair. "I have to see Mr Ivors about his gelding. I'll be back late." And without another word, he grabbed his jacket and left.

Elinta glanced at her brother. "When do you have to leave?" She faced having the house to herself for most of the night, and once Blaine left, she wouldn't have to risk anyone noticing her lack of concentration then.

"Soon," Blaine said around another mouthful.

Relief flooded her.

After dinner Elinta fetched a large bag from her room, brimming with cloths, and dumped the contents by the fire. She sat beside the huge pile with a heavy sigh. Another job from Galen, she had to roll every single cloth up separately for their bandage stock. And he wanted it all done by tomorrow. It was the second lot she'd done in only a few days.

"I'll be back later tonight, Lin." Blaine entered the room, buckling his belt on, a sword now in place by his hip.

Blaine had another training night with the other guards of the village. They were a group of young men, and a few women, chosen to protect the village and to act as a defending force if they were ever attacked. Sometimes bandits would prey on villages that were a long way from Nevira, their capital, or separated from other villages. Whilst Kethmere was often busy with traders, the nearest village was over a day's ride away, plenty of time for a group of robbers to come in and ransack the village before help could arrive. It hadn't happened in a long time, but the force was also used to deal with smaller crimes around the village itself. Elinta smiled at her brother as he tugged at the hem of his shirt.

"You could almost run those practice sessions," Elinta said, grabbing a cloth.

Blaine chuckled. "Not quite." Bending over, he picked his work jacket up from the floor beside the door and shook it out.

"Fine, but you're nearly equal with old Jareth," Elinta said, referencing the instructor, a retired soldier. Blaine shrugged into his jacket and Elinta wrinkled her nose. "Please put that with the washing tomorrow."

Blaine pursed his lips. "I'm *nearly* equal to Jareth," he agreed. "And what's wrong with my jacket?" Before she could comment on the overly strong horse odour, he winked and said, "I'll see you later."

Blaine straightened his collar and strode from the house. Elinta turned back to her pile and started rolling the next cloth.

🔥🔥🔥

The next day, Elinta rose early to check on the injured mares. She stood a moment in front of her house, breathing in the fresh morning air and looking unseeingly across the dew-covered paddocks. Her mind was already in the forest. She'd found a dragon yesterday. A *dragon*. She pictured its large form, its white scales. What was it doing now?

Elinta shook herself from her thoughts. She had a lot to do. Elinta pulled her jacket on over her dress, a simple dark green one with a skirt midway down her shins, and trudged down to the stables. The days were slowly warming up, but the nights were still cold enough to leave the grass wet and her breath as fog in the morning. Mud splattered on her hem as she walked.

Both mares were waiting for her and shifting restlessly in their stalls when Elinta entered the stables. The bay had spent half of the day in the paddocks yesterday, but Elinta had asked that the palomino be kept in her stall to rest.

She changed the dressings on their wounds and walked the bay out into a paddock. The palomino could go for a walk later but needed to stay inside for another day. After returning the bay's halter and lead to the stables, Elinta hurried back up to the house to discard her jacket. She collected her satchel and the bag of cloths she'd finished rolling, then continued to Galen's.

Since it was the first day of the weekend, most of the village was quiet, but there were others like Elinta who still had to start early. She passed a bakery with its doors thrown open, the scent of warm bread wafting out into the street. The markets would be open later today and there were traders scurrying around, hauling their wares early to the market square on the other side of the village to claim a prime place. Kethmere, though not a large place, really was beautiful.

Elinta watched the quiet, sleepy houses with envy. Many of the people within them had the day off and would spend it at the market. But she wouldn't have gone there. The forest was heavy on her mind. She could have happily spent the entire day out there by the lake. With a sigh, she hurried on to Galen's.

"See you on Monday, Master Galen." Elinta pushed through the back gate and instantly started across the grass field and towards the forest. It was early afternoon, and the sun was at its hottest and brightest, causing her to squint against the light. The shade of the forest was a welcome relief when she plunged in among the trees. She'd spent so much of the previous day and night thinking about the dragon, but now that she was drawing ever closer to the creature, her nerves returned. She wiped her palms on her dress. Would the dragon still be calm? Had it eaten since she'd seen it last? She didn't want to be near a hungry dragon. Elinta dodged a thicket of thorns, careful to keep her skirt away from the grasping prickles and continued on.

When she saw the sun glinting off the lake in the distance, Elinta refused to let her feet slow. The dragon would hear her coming, she reassured herself, and if she stopped now, she wasn't sure she'd get moving again. So, when she reached the edge of the trees, Elinta continued on into the open.

A small rumble greeted her from her right. The animal had moved since she'd seen it last. It wasn't crouched opposite its landing site anymore, having moved closer to where Elinta had emerged from the trees yesterday. It was lying on its side, curled up in a patch of sunlight. The sight of the creature had her breath catching in her throat. The sun was shining off the dragon's snow-white scales, just as it had yesterday. It was blindingly bright, but unbelievably beautiful. Elinta took a step towards the dragon, and it raised its head from its foot.

"Hi girl," Elinta said quietly, squinting against the reflection from its side. The massive creature rolled onto its stomach and pushed its head forward, closing the small gap between them. A smile lit up Elinta's face.

"I wasn't sure you'd be friendly," she said, reaching out a hand. The dragon tilted its head just as Elinta's hand rested against its muzzle.

"There you go again," Elinta mumbled, "like you can understand me."

The dragon pulled away and sniffed at the bag hanging by Elinta's hip. "I thought I'd have a look at your wing again," she said, walking around to the dragon's side. Had she really been nervous about seeing this beautiful animal again just moments ago?

As she stopped in front of the more damaged wing, it stretched out to reveal the entire membrane and frame. Elinta sighed. Quite a few of the poultices had rubbed off, or smudged, overnight, probably from the action of opening and closing the wing. But the deepest and longest cut was still mostly covered. It wasn't a total loss.

"Well, I'll give these a clean again, but I don't think there's any point doing another poultice." Elinta looked back at the dragon's head, which had turned to watch her again.

She had a moment to be thankful there wasn't anyone around. Apart from the fact she was treating a dragon, she was also *talking* to it. She couldn't help it. She'd thought long about this beast overnight and concluded that there was some kind of intelligence behind those amber eyes. And though she'd voiced suspicions about it understanding her, something inside her told her it could. So, abandoning any feelings of madness, she continued to talk to the creature. Because it helped her as much as it seemed to help it.

Fetching the bowl-shaped piece of bark she'd used the day before, Elinta collected some water and washed the crusted remains of the poultice from the dragon's wing. The creature stayed still while she worked, but Elinta was aware of its eyes following her every move. Checking all the cuts, which had all closed overnight, she left them open to the air. She doubted the dragon would be able to fly, or whether she should, for another couple of days.

Sitting back on her heels, Elinta ran her hand along the dragon's wing, feeling the smooth membrane and the rough scales of the wing frame. She lightly ran her fingers along a network of tiny ridges showing through the leathery skin of the membrane, the dragon's veins. The wing shifted under her hand and a soft burst of warm air ruffled her hair. Turning her head slowly, Elinta saw the dragon's head, just out of arm's reach. Those amber eyes were locked on her. Another burst of air blew her hair back from her face.

"Hello," she said, sitting back on her heels. "You're a gorgeous animal, aren't you?" It was then Elinta realised the sun was no longer shining off the dragon's scales and into her eyes. "What time is it?" she said in surprise, looking for the sun. It was no longer directly above the lake but hidden by the surrounding trees. She had to get home to help prepare dinner.

"I should get going. Someone's going to wonder where I am." Elinta glanced down at the wing and then back to the dragon. "Be careful around here. If anyone sees you, they'll kill you," she told it.

A deep grumble sounded in its throat. Elinta jumped to her feet, but the growl didn't seem to have been aimed at her, rather her words. She cautiously placed her hand on the dragon's nose. The beast seemed, *was,* worried, almost afraid, by her words. Elinta could feel it like a tangible thing, but when she removed her hand from its smooth scales, the feeling dissipated.

"Just be careful," she whispered, then hurried from the lakeshore and back to her home.

Elinta half-heartedly shoved her food around on her plate, hardly hearing her father and brother discussing their plans for the next day. Elinta's mind was on her own plans. Sundays were her day off and she intended on making the most of it by visiting the dragon again. The creature fascinated her. It was nothing like she'd been raised to believe it should be. She wanted to know what else was different.

Elinta tuned back into her brother and father's conversation just as it ended, and before she could stop herself, she was asking her father about dragons.

"Are there any stories about dragons where they don't kill anyone? Or ... or aren't killed?" she stammered.

Her father laughed. "Of course not. All they ever brought with them was death."

Elinta saw Blaine frown from the corner of her eye.

"You know the stories, Lin," her brother said, shovelling some food into his mouth.

"It's just ... I only wondered."

Her father frowned and lowered his fork to his plate. "You don't need to look any further than the Eggslaying. You know we only fought back because they killed Prince Tristan first. What happened that day has brought us lasting peace. And if they ever return, we'll do it again."

Elinta nodded. She knew all this, of course she did. But there had to be more. More than the stories of death and destruction that were told every year at the festival. Because if there had been one dragon given several opportunities to kill and it hadn't, there had to have been others.

"Are there any stories about their behaviour? How they communicated?" she asked. The white dragon had made several noises when she was around, and its eyes were certainly expressive, but it was so hard to read. If only it was more similar to a horse. She pictured the huge animal with massive horse-like ears and fought a laugh.

"They were animals, Elinta. What does it matter?" Her father picked up his fork, his frown deepening. "They weren't like the horses, where you could read them and anticipate their behaviour," he said, as if reading her thoughts. "All the dragons ever did was kill and destroy. You didn't get a chance to read them."

"I know. You're right." Elinta let the matter drop and returned to her food, but Blaine's hazel eyes lingered on her a moment longer before he deftly changed the subject, turning to their father and asking about Mr. Ivors's gelding. Elinta didn't bother to listen. Her father was wrong. Not all dragons were evil. Not all of them deserved to die.

CHAPTER FOUR

OVER THE NEXT COUPLE of days, Elinta continued to visit the dragon. She spent a couple of hours with it on her day off, then returned the following day during her lunch. She checked on its injured wings and stayed with it for a little while afterwards so that it had some company. When her lunch break came on Tuesday, Elinta arrived at the lake to find a smattering of white spread across the lakeshore. From a distance, they almost looked like shells, but she recognised them instantly. They were scales. Elinta picked one up in her hand.

"You shed," she said, amazed. She flipped the scale over in her palm. It was no larger than the gold coins they used at the market, but slightly ovular. There were a couple of larger scales by her feet, and even some smaller ones, but the one she held looked like it may have come from the dragon's leg. It certainly didn't match the size of the large, thick plates covering the dragon's back.

She brushed some dirt from its smooth surface. It was so *white*. She tried to imagine the colour of the dragon killed at the Eggslaying. They said it was blue or green, but she couldn't picture it. The brightness of this scale seemed perfect for it.

Elinta slipped the scale into her dress pocket. She wanted something to remember the creature by when it was gone. If her family found the scale, she could make something up about where she discovered it. Maybe she'd say she found it buried in the other side of the forest when she was digging for roots. Elinta tore herself away from the other scales and approached the dragon who was walking towards her.

"Hi," Elinta said, patting its forehead as it dipped to look at her. Happiness seemed to radiate from the dragon at her touch. She pulled her hand away and the feeling stopped. Elinta frowned. *"What?"*

The dragon snorted and cocked her head.

Elinta pressed her hand against the dragon's scales again. Confusion. That's what she ... felt? Sensed? Elinta gasped. "Wha—How?"

She felt the dragon's confusion. She didn't see it. Didn't read it in the animal's face. She *felt* it. Not quite like her own feelings, but in a corner of her mind. The feeling shifted as she expressed her own confusion. Humour. Elinta looked into the dragon's eye and saw a flicker of amusement there.

"What is this?" she whispered, tugging her hand away and stumbling back a couple paces. The dragon settled into a crouch and stared at her.

"What was that? I-I *felt* your emotions!"

The dragon didn't make a sound, but she was sure it understood her. This was not normal. No way was it normal. Not even the Asali could share their emotions like this, and the dragon was an animal, not some other race.

Elinta sat heavily on the loose dirt by the lake, her eyes glued to the dragon. None of the stories ever mentioned, ever *hinted* at, something like this. *What is going on?* Hesitantly, Elinta reached out her hand and touched the dragon's clawed foot. A whole mess of emotions jumped at her: confusion, humour, concern, and a hint of affection.

"This is impossible," she muttered.

Yet clearly, it wasn't. Fear rose in her chest and her mouth went dry. Maybe she was imagining it? Maybe there was something wrong with her? But she knew deep down that wasn't the case. She'd spent days with this creature, and every interaction had left her questioning its level of intelligence. But now she knew. This beast was more than an animal. Just what it was though, she wasn't sure.

Elinta released a nervous chuckle and folded her hands in her lap. She sat in silence by the dragon, her mind whirling, until it was time for her to leave and head back to Galen's. But the whole time, the dragon never looked away from her and the echo of its feelings seemed burned into her mind.

Wednesday dawned and Elinta rose before her family. She had an earlier start than usual at work, so she skipped breakfast and hurried to Galen's in the dim morning light. The village was sleepy, most people were only just stirring, and the quiet was peaceful. She looked out over the trees of the forest. She'd decided to continue visiting the dragon in her lunch breaks until it left, which could be any day now, to learn as much as she could about the creature. Hopefully Galen would give her a longer break today since they were starting earlier.

When she arrived at Galen's, he emerged with some fresh rolls from the baker.

"Mr. Willan brought these around. A thank you," Galen said.

She followed him inside where he placed the tray of bread on his small dining table. Her stomach grumbled as she caught the scent of the fresh bread.

"That's kind of him." She'd provided Mrs. Willan with some herbs to ease her morning sickness yesterday. The pregnant woman must have found them useful.

Elinta sat with Galen over a quiet breakfast. They ate the rolls as they were. Though no longer warm, they were fresh and airy with a slightly sweet flavour that made it perfect even without any fillings. What had the dragon been eating in the forest? Had it eaten at all? *How often does a dragon need to eat?* Elinta thought, taking a bite of her roll.

If Galen noted her distraction, and she was sure he did, he didn't say anything. She liked that about him. He often left her to her own thoughts, trusting she would ask if she needed more information. Sometimes, he would ask her directly, but usually he let her be. He liked silence, and in this instance, so did she. When they finished, Elinta covered the remaining rolls with a cloth and put them in a cupboard to stay fresh, while Galen went back to his desk.

She spent the next couple hours out in the herb garden, tidying up the beds and harvesting flowers and leaves ready to store. Her thoughts were on the dragon the whole time. Would she be able to see it before it left? Never in her life had she been so distracted from her job, but she couldn't help it.

"Elinta!" Galen called from the back door.

"Yes, sir?"

"I need you to go get some weeping bark. We're out."

Elinta climbed to her feet, almost sighing both in relief and exasperation. She'd mentioned it to him just days ago, when he'd sent her to retrieve the black disc fungi, but he hadn't wanted any. At least she had an excuse to go out into the forest now ... where she could make a quick stop to see the dragon.

"Sure. I'll go now." Elinta struggled to walk normally into the hut and through the room to the front door. She grabbed the door handle and started to turn it.

"Elinta?" Galen called, now back at his desk and not bothering to look up.

"Yes?"

"Don't forget the basket."

Her hand dropped from the handle. "Right. Of course," she stammered. The basket. It was by the back door where she'd left it after bringing in the herbs from the garden. Hurrying through the hut, she picked up the basket and strode back to the front door.

"I'll be back soon, sir." She left without a backwards glance.

"How are you today, girl?" Elinta dropped the basket full of weeping bark at the forest edge. It had taken her a quarter of an hour to collect it all, not helped by her distracted thoughts of the dragon.

The dragon rose to its feet and walked to her, wings tucked in at its sides and head stretched forward. Elinta met the creature halfway and rubbed her hand along its muzzle. The dragon had become familiar with the gesture and seemed to enjoy it, eyes half closing in pleasure.

"I was going to come see you in my lunch break if Galen let me leave, but he needed some weeping bark, so here I am!"

The dragon lowered itself to a crouch, and Elinta sat as well, dropping her satchel beside her. "You'll be able to leave any day now. I wanted to make sure I saw you again before you left."

The dragon rumbled in response, and Elinta stretched out her hand to the dragon's leg. She felt its happiness at her statement. Smiling, Elinta shifted her hand to its head and rubbed its cheek along the jawbone. She let her hand wander to the base of the small spines there before returning her hand to its muzzle.

She'd miss it when it was gone, but it was for the best. It would go home somewhere off the coast to the south and Elinta would continue as though nothing had happened. Besides, there was a wriggle of concern nagging at her mind. This creature was unnatural. The way it shared its emotions was not normal and would surely only lead to trouble. No, Elinta would see it on its way.

"Can I check your wings again?" she asked, thinking that she'd at least be sure it was healed enough to leave and hadn't reopened the wounds. She no longer felt strange asking this of the animal either. It had proven time and again that it knew what she wanted, and unfolded one of its wings, stretching it out across the ground. *If only people were this compliant.*

Elinta ran her eyes along the wing with a sense of satisfaction. She shifted to get a better look at the cuts on the membrane, carefully leaning over so as not to stand on the dragon's wing. All the cuts were healing well. Some wouldn't even be visible in a couple days. The largest cut in particular was looking great, covered in a thick scab.

When she finished, the dragon stretched out the other wing for her. It was in even better shape since there were only a couple shallow cuts there.

Still standing next to the dragon, Elinta twisted to look back at the damage the dragon had caused when it had crashed less than a week ago and gained the injuries. She recalled the moment she saw the creature and the fear that had clutched her. She looked back at the dragon and smiled. The dragon tilted its head in response.

Things have changed, she thought.

Elinta returned to sit where she'd been before and folded her legs, tugging at her dress to allow the movement. She pulled the full basket of weeping bark towards her. Maybe she could waste some time by preparing the bark here, then she could stay longer with the dragon. She started stripping the bark, first tearing it into smaller pieces and then separating the outer layer from the inner layer. "I guess you'll probably leave tomorrow, hey, girl? Maybe even today?"

The dragon tucked in its wings and lowered its head on to its front feet, its attention solely on her.

"Will you go home?" she asked, partly musing out loud. How had the dragon ended up in Kethmere? For that matter, how had it ended up in Eldras, so far from its home?

She dropped the bark she was tearing and tentatively touched the dragon's foot, wondering if she could glean an answer from it and tugged her hand away in surprise. She felt *fear* and a deep sadness, like grief.

Elinta frowned. Was it thinking about its home that made it feel that way? Or was it something else? Elinta sighed and looked into its eyes. Was it worth trying to learn more from it when all she had were guesses?

As she stared into its eyes, an odd, absurd, thought occurred to her. Here she was, asking it questions. But if this animal was so intelligent, if it could communicate in the way that it did ... what if it was closer to her or the Asali than it was to the birds and the animals that walked on the ground? *Are dragons another race?*

"Do you have a n—"

A stick snapped somewhere behind the dragon and there was a rustle of something moving away from them through the under-growth. The dragon pushed to its feet and, with surprising speed, whipped around to face the noise. Elinta leaned sideways to see around its bulk, but there was nothing there.

"Must have been an animal?" she said, watching the dragon's tense body. The muscles in its legs rippled and loosened, and the dragon slowly turned back to her. It settled into a crouch again. Elinta rocked back to sit properly, satisfied that the dragon didn't seem worried, but she'd lost her train of thought.

Looking at the light shining down on the lake, she judged she still had some time before Galen started to worry ... if he even noticed how long she'd been gone for. It was probably nearly midday. She should have been back by now, but her master hadn't noticed the last time she'd been late. She shrugged and looked out over the lake, steam rising off it in the sun. What did it matter if she got in trouble for being late today? *I'm a good student,* she thought, *he'll be mad but not for long.* Besides, she was still working while she sat with the dragon, by preparing some of the bark he'd asked her to collect.

She just wanted to spend some more time with the dragon before it left. Galen was proud of her, even if he didn't say it ... and didn't really show it. But he'd begun saying things like 'when you're finished with me' and 'soon you'll be doing this by yourself.' Just a few days ago, he'd talked about her being alone. She was ready for it. Between Brynne and Galen there was still room for another healer in the village, and some of the people she'd treated wanted to move over to her when her training was over. Yes, she'd be OK if she stayed out a little longer and returned with the bark ready for use.

So Elinta worked her way through the basket, chatting occasionally to the dragon. As she reached the last handful of bark, the dragon's head snapped up and tilted to the side. A deep growl sounded, its lips rising to show huge, pointed teeth.

"What is it?" Elinta fought the urge to stumble away from the creature's warning. It wasn't looking at her, but away into the trees behind her. Elinta twisted, but she couldn't see anything, couldn't hear anything.

"What is it?" she asked again, her heart thumping loudly in her ears.

Beside her own unexplainable fear was another, the dragon's. Turning back to the creature, she went to pull away from it, thinking she'd touched its scales unconsciously and could feel the dragon as she had before. But she hadn't. There was a gap of over a foot between them. Her eyes widened in surprise, but that was the moment she heard what the dragon had heard. The sound of heavy footsteps tramping through the forest and towards them. The sound of many, many sets of hurrying feet and the low buzz of angry voices.

"Someone's coming!" She spun back to the dragon, panic rising in her. She shoved the beast's chest. "You have to get out of here!"

Too late. Bodies appeared among the trees at the far end of the lake. The sun glinted off the steel and iron weapons in their hands. Dozens of them. A shout of alarm rose from the first of the men to break from the trees and stumble onto the sand. It was Jareth, the leader of the force Blaine was a part of. But Elinta could see other men from the village as well, their bodies tense with fear and anger. Some stared in open disbelief. Someone had roused the force and a huge portion of the menfolk.

Jareth swept his speckled grey hair back from his forehead and called across the clearing.

"Elinta? Is that you?" he called, concern and nerves tugging at his gravelly voice.

"Yes," she shouted. "I'm OK. Please, everything's fine. The dragon isn't here to cause trouble."

More men joined Jareth, the tension in their bodies clear even from where she stood.

"Hurry," she whispered over her shoulder, knowing the dragon would hear her.

Jareth stretched out a hand towards her. "It's OK, Elinta. Come here, slowly. You'll be fine. We're going to take care of this beast."

The dragon growled, stretching out its neck so that its head was beside her. Shouts of alarm sounded from the jostling group of men, more and more joining them by the second.

"Please," Elinta shouted. "You don't understand. This dragon is *good!*"

Angry shouts met her words.

"Good?" a husky voice yelled incredulously.

"The girl has lost her senses!" someone else shouted.

"You know the law, Elinta. We have to take care of it." Jareth took a step forward but didn't come any closer.

Elinta's heart hammered in her chest.

"No. You don't have to. Please, just let it go! Can't you tell she's afraid?" she called, still shoving the dragon's large head, but it wouldn't budge. Its fear was tangible.

Jareth frowned. "It's the law, Elinta. Don't stand in our way."

The threat was clear. She'd be in trouble if she tried to stop them, not that there was much she could do against the large group in front of her.

"Please," she quietly begged the dragon.

As one, the group of men edged forward, but another growl from the dragon stopped them in their tracks. There were swords and axes among the group, even the occasional pitchfork and loaded bow, though she doubted they would penetrate the dragon's scales. It had been an *illayas* weapon that had killed the last dragon seen in Eldras. But she didn't want to find out the truth of that story.

Somewhere among the group was her brother, but scanning their faces, Elinta couldn't see him.

"He must be somewhere at the back," she murmured, craning her neck, but it was no good.

Jareth was speaking again. "Get out of the way, Elinta."

She shook her head, but words failed her. What should she do? What could she do? Panic rose in her chest as Jareth bowed his head.

"Then you'll be arrested and taken back to the village to stand trial. If you're hurt in all this, I won't be responsible," he said in a low voice that carried across to them.

At his words, the dragon reared back its head and bellowed.

Elinta slapped her hands over her ears as the sound shook through her chest and down her bones. Hot air ruffled across her hair. Several of the men took an involuntary step backwards, but Jareth rallied them, and they took another few hesitant steps forward. They were taking their time closing the distance between them, but soon they would attack.

"You need to get out of here. They'll kill you!" she shouted at the dragon, turning her back on the villagers. Or the dragon would kill the villagers. Fear and concern sounded in her mind and ... the dragon's heart beat faster, her chest tightened, and her stomach knotted. Elinta sensed it all. *Felt* it all as she watched the dragon lower its head and gently push her with its nose. Despite the light pressure, she stumbled back, feet sinking in the loose dirt by the lake's edge.

"Please go," she said. Her voice sounded thick to her own ears. But the dragon pushed against her again and looked at its back. Elinta frowned.

"I don't know what you mean." She glanced behind her again, but the men were advancing only a few slow steps at a time, as though testing the dragon's response. "Just get out of here!" She'd face the consequences of helping the dragon, but she couldn't stand to see it killed. The steps behind her seemed to grow louder.

The dragon looked pointedly from her to its back, then repeated the motion.

Realisation dawned. "No, I can't lea—"

An arrow pinged off one of the pristine scales on the dragon's front leg and dropped to the dirt. Elinta jumped in shock and the dragon growled again. Its fear was suddenly tinged with an anger that rose in its chest. Elinta's eyes locked on the arrow. They could have hit her! Elinta thought over Jareth's words, that he wouldn't be responsible for what happened to her. He meant it. He really *meant* it. In fact, she wondered whether he didn't care what happened to her at all.

Turning to the angry crowd advancing towards them, Elinta realised that none of them cared. As she watched, a man nocked another arrow to his bow and took aim. Her decision was made for her. Gasping, Elinta swivelled in place and hurried to the dragon's side. It dropped into a crouch. Its belly was flat on the shore, but Elinta couldn't get a grip on its back to pull herself up, it was too tall. Flattening her hands on its side, she stepped onto the joint of its front leg and pushed herself up. Her chest hit the dragon's back, and she used her feet to scramble up and slung one leg over, now sitting astride the massive animal with its wing joints behind her.

The shouts from the men redoubled as they watched her climb the dragon. They were louder than ever, full of anger and confusion, but their words were lost, muddled together. Elinta clapped her hands over her ears, trying to block it out. There was just too much happening. Too many emotions bouncing around. Her own were more than enough for her, but now for some reason she had the dragon's, and coupled with the yelling and screaming around her, it was nearly more than she could take. Her breaths were speeding up from the panic. *I have to get out of here. I have to leave.* No one was going to let her out of this.

Hands still over her ears, Elinta scanned the group, searching for her brother. Blaine would have been one of the first called to arms by Jareth. Finally, she saw a familiar mess of blond hair. Her brother was at the far right of the group, a few ranks deep and staring in open concern. His sword wasn't in sight. Standing next to him was her father. His jaw tense and his eyes hard, his face was a picture of stone-cold fury. Elinta's heart ached at the anger she saw there, so she turned back to Blaine, feeling her desperation sprawled across her face. Her brother held her eyes and gave a simple, small nod. He was giving her permission to leave. Telling her it was OK.

She closed her eyes against the sight of her brother, father, and the villagers just as the dragon's wings unfolded and beat at the air. Wind rushed around her, tugging at her dress and her hair. The movement jolted her in her seat, and she watched as the men yelled and ran forward, weapons ready. She caught a glimpse of a familiar lean figure with grey hair and a satchel slung over his shoulder, but the wind stung at her eyes. Elinta flattened against the dragon's back and neck, below the point where the larger scales dropped off. She flung her arms out and against the dragon's neck, clinging on for her life, her fingers digging into the scales while tears clouded her vision and the pressure of the wind picked up.

Then they were shooting into the air, wind rushing over her and blocking out the sound of the yelling voices of the men. Galen and her family grew smaller and smaller until the lake dropped out of view and the forest passed under them as a sea of green. The sun was on their right, almost at its peak, casting the distant sprawl of Kethmere in a bright light. Elinta closed her eyes to the rush of the land passing under them and the sickness in her stomach.

She pictured the group they'd left behind by the lake. Her father and brother would soon be going home, likely defending themselves against sharp comments from the villagers about what she'd done. But, seeing her father's face in her mind's eye, she knew they would be fine. He'd recently made his opinion on dragons clear to her and now, his opinion of *her* was even clearer. He wouldn't welcome her back after what she'd done. Water dripped down her face. She'd just had her last view of Kethmere and Blaine.

"Goodbye," she whispered.

Elinta forced her eyes open and rubbed the tears from her cheeks. Cautiously, she raised her head, digging her fingers in tighter, and, buffeted by the wind, looked around her. They were no longer flying over the forest. It was now receding behind them, no more than a distant green line.

"Where are we going?" she mumbled. The sun was still on their right. "North?"

The home of the dragons was supposed to be in the south.

With a few beats of its wings, the dragon rose higher, and its speed grew until the land far below them was only a blur speeding by. Goosebumps raised on Elinta's skin. Fear and panic radiated from the creature, mirroring her own. Where were they going to go? Kethmere was long behind them now, and though she wanted to, they couldn't go back. The villagers had actually tried to kill them both! Maybe not her directly, but they certainly weren't trying to keep her safe.

Elinta lowered her head below the wind streaming along the dragon's body to rest against its warm scales again and absently stroked it. She was at its mercy now. Aside from her limited memory of Culmar away to the east, she'd never visited any lands beyond Kethmere. They weren't going near the capital, Nevira, also east of Kethmere, which was a good thing, though she'd love to see the royal city. There was the Bradfin Desert in the centre of Eldras, which they would pass over if the dragon continued on as it was. And after that, just more settlements and eventually the White Mountains on the north-eastern tip of the continent. But she couldn't guess where the dragon would take them.

The sun quickly reached its midday peak and began descending on their left, but the dragon's speed picked up rather than slowed. By afternoon, Elinta was growing stiff and struggled to shift her body to get more comfortable without losing her balance, nearly tipping over when she moved too far to her left. *How far are we going?* she thought once she'd rightened herself and fixed her grip on the dragon. She closed her eyes to the rushing of the land below, feeling the dragon's powerful muscles rolling and straining as it pumped its massive wings.

Elinta no longer cared so much where they were going. It didn't matter. Once the dragon landed, they could go their separate ways. She could slip into a new village and offer her services to the healer there. That was the way to go. No one would know who she was and what she'd done. She could start anew.

At dusk, when her stomach was growling and her bladder was ready to burst, the dragon started to descend. Elinta pushed herself up from the dragon's scales and, buffeted by the wind, looked around, wondering where the dragon had taken her. But there was nothing. Nothing to tell her where they were. Though long shadows sprawled across the land, its sparse coverage was clear. Even the yellowed vegetation was easy to see. Squinting, she looked ahead of them, searching the horizon. There! Away in the distance and slightly to the west was the empty yellow-brown lands of the desert. They were nearly halfway across the continent.

Why was the dragon stopping here? There was nothing here. She couldn't even make out a village or town. The dragon continued to descend. It had to be landing. Lowering herself back against the dragon, she spread her arms as far around it as she could and dug her fingers in. It landed with a rush of wings and a gentle thud.

As soon as its wings were tucked against its sides, Elinta slid clumsily from its back, needing solid ground under her feet. Her knees buckled as she landed, forcing her to catch herself against the dragon.

"What are we doing here?" she asked, looking at the empty land surrounding them and stretching out her legs. When her bladder twinged, an idea struck her and she looked at the dragon in realisation.

"Oh," she said, watching as the dragon turned its back to her and walked away. This wasn't their final destination; it was just a quick stop along the way.

A few minutes later, with her bladder feeling much better but her stomach still empty, Elinta stared up at the dragon's back.

"We're not stopping here?" she asked, turning to watch the sun dip below the horizon. The dragon blinked at her, then looked at its back.

She looked down at her aching fingers and sighed. Knowing there was nothing else for her to do, using the dragon's front leg, she climbed onto its back and settled in for a long night of uncomfortable flying and little sleep.

They stopped again in the early morning for a few hours of rest, and Elinta found a small plant she recognised from her learning as edible though normally used for treating liver diseases. She picked the handful of leaves that had sprouted and chewed them as she stretched her legs. It didn't do much to alleviate her hunger, but it was something. The desert was now behind them, but the land was still empty. There was nowhere for her to go, and despite how exhausted she felt, she couldn't sleep. Not out here. When the dragon gestured for her to return to her place on its back, Elinta did. They flew on, the sun on their right and the distant peaks of the White Mountains finally coming into view. There was little for her to do on the dragon's back other than dwell on her thoughts. Which also meant her memories of the day before came to the forefront of her mind. Though she tried not to think of her family and the village, she couldn't stop replaying the events in the forest over and over again. Especially the way the villagers, men she'd known her entire life, had looked at her.

Just after midday, the dragon had turned, putting the sun behind them. Elinta shook off her melancholy thoughts and, yawning, craned her neck to see over the dragon's head and started. The White Mountains rose before them, closer than she'd expected, and the dragon seemed to be aiming straight for them. Its snow-capped peaks ranged from jagged to slightly rounded and drew closer and closer with every passing second. They were definitely headed right for them. The wind bustling around her had raised goosebumps along her arms and legs, but she shivered, looking at the mountains looming before them. The only item of clothing she wore that might be suited to the snow and ice were her boots, and she doubted they would stay dry for long. Her dress certainly wouldn't keep her warm up there. The only reason she hadn't froze on the dragon was because of the warmth of its body and the wind streaming along the dragon's head and over her.

She opened her mouth to tell the dragon just that, but the wind snatched the sound away before she even formed a word. Neck aching, she lowered her head again and let the dragon carry her ever closer to the mountains. She wracked her brain for information on the snowy peaks. One thing came to mind. The Eggslaying happened somewhere among these mountains, over one hundred and seventy years ago. Did the dragon know that? Remember it? *Is that why we're going there?*

Other than the Eggslaying, a small group of Asali had once lived in the White Mountains, but whether they were still there, she didn't know. In general, the humans of Eldras had stopped keeping tabs on the Asali after the fallout of the Eggslaying. If they were there though, it'd probably be better to avoid them. The fewer people who saw the dragon, the better.

The dragon's speed slowed, and the surrounding scenery became clearer and closer. The creature was dropping. It angled its body downward and Elinta closed her eyes to the sight of the snow-covered peaks soaring towards them. The wind howled in her ears and then suddenly, and with a jolt, it stopped. There was a rustle as the dragon's wings shifted behind her. Cold air raced across her skin and raised fresh goosebumps, chasing away her tiredness. The sleeves on her dress combated some of the cold but couldn't stop her from gasping. Opening her eyes, Elinta found herself in a world of white.

CHAPTER
FIVE

T HEY'D TOUCHED DOWN ON the side of one of the peaks, surrounded by snow. The tree line was distantly visible below them as a grey blur. A cliff rose some way in front of them, dropping in a gentle curve to Elinta's left. Her eyes struggled to focus on the white dragon beneath her, the outline of its form blending in with the snow. Her eyes landed on its bent leg though, so she knew it had dropped to a crouch. Swinging a stiff leg over its back, she slid down its side and landed heavily in the snow. Her legs failed to catch her weight, and she sunk to her knees with a crunch. Ice-cold snow instantly soaked through her dress.

"Argh." Pushing herself to her feet, she dusted the snow from her knees and wrapped her arms tightly around her middle. Her stomach gurgled and, trying to ignore how little she'd eaten since yesterday morning, Elinta turned on the spot, taking in the snowy scene that seemed to be their final destination. The sun was continuing to drop, meaning that it was going to get even colder soon, and she couldn't see anywhere they could shelter. There were no plants at all for her to search among for food, and she couldn't hunt.

She turned to the dragon. "What are we doing? It's too cold here." Of all the places the dragon could have taken her, why did it need to be here?

The dragon grumbled softly and started walking towards the lower side of the cliff to their left.

Elinta frowned. "Where are you going?"

It grumbled in response and continued walking. Just as its long tail, raised inches above the ground, passed her, she sighed and trudged after it. Maybe some of the aching in her muscles would disappear the more she walked. Her legs sunk all the way to her shins in the snow and her boots soaked through within seconds. Her dress grew heavier as snow further soaked the hem within a couple of steps. Sighing, Elinta looked around for shallower snow, but there was none and the dragon's footprints, though full of compacted snow, were too deep and too far apart for her to walk in. She trudged on. The dragon stopped ahead of her and waited for her to draw alongside it. Once more it looked at her and then at its back.

Elinta shook her head, shivering. "No, that was more than enough."

It repeated the motion.

Elinta hung her head. "Fine."

Once the dragon was in a crouch, Elinta scrambled back up onto its back, wincing as she settled her aching butt back in place.

Though she was used to riding horses, riding a flying dragon was apparently a different matter altogether. It was more than enough to make her uncomfortable.

Elinta was instantly warmer against the heat of the dragon's body and out of the snow, though the wet fabric of her dress clung to her. The dragon started forward with a surprisingly comfortable gait though quite different to the horses. This time, she clung to the dragon with her legs and sat up straight to look around as the creature began climbing the far left of the cliff, which seemed only a small slope from where they were. They kept the cliff's edge to their right, and they moved higher, the land stretching away to their left in a seemingly never-ending sheet of white. The dragon seemed to be going towards a collection of large boulders pressed into the wall of another cliff-face rising in front of them.

Elinta could still feel the dragon's emotions, but it had shifted to a deep sadness.

"What's the matter, girl?" she called, but the dragon didn't make any sound in response. Not that it could tell her anyway, but the feeling was out of place. Frustration or anger would have suited the creature better given the situation, not the heavy ache sitting in its chest. It was strange, the way she both just knew what the dragon felt and could also tell how it was affecting its body. It was like another sense. *Why hasn't anyone mentioned* this *before?* Why didn't the stories talk about the dragons sharing their emotions the way that this one was now? It was such a huge thing to leave out. It didn't make sense.

Refocusing on the path in front of them, Elinta studied the cluster of boulders the dragon was still going towards but now at an angle. With each step, a sliver between the boulders grew wider and wider until, when they finally stood before it, it was revealed to be a cave entrance large enough for a dragon to pass through.

Elinta flattened against the dragon as it passed through the entrance, afraid they'd scrape the ceiling, but there was room to spare. The cave widened immediately, and Elinta found herself in a huge cavern that stretched far into the cliff-face. A large shelf was set into the back wall of the cave, large enough for a dragon to sit on, but below this, on the ground against the wall, were thousands of small amber and red ... things in a natural dip in the ground. Elinta was struck by a deep sorrow within the dragon.

"What is this place?" Her whispered voice echoed around the cave, throwing the words back at her.

The dragon tilted its head and keened, then shuffled towards the thick coloured layer on the ground, carrying Elinta with it. Absently, she stroked the creature's scales while she narrowed her eyes, trying to make out what they were heading for. They looked like fragments of flat stone? No, some of the larger pieces were curved....

They stopped at the edge of the thick layer of stone and the dragon nuzzled the fragments. A thought jolted through Elinta as she slipped from her perch upon the dragon and stretched out her legs. Elinta took a shuddering breath and tread forward, crouching beside the dragon's head, and looked down at the fragments. Now closer, her suspicions were confirmed. The inside of the curved surfaces were smooth, the outside was slightly grainy to the touch. And there were thousands of fragments of all different sizes, some smaller than her fingernails and others as large as her palm. All the same deep amber or red-maroon colour. The dragon keened again, a deep sorrowful sound, and it was all enough to tell her she was right. This was all that remained of the eggs destroyed in the Eggslaying.

Elinta twisted sharply, searching the rest of the cavern, but there was no sign of any remains from the dragon killed while defending these eggs. But there were signs the creature had been there once. Now that she looked, she could see scorched patches on the cavern floor and walls, blackest in the centre, some spreading out in a circle, others shaped like a comet or simply darker patches of stone. But what had happened to the carcass of the nest dragon? Dumbstruck, Elinta turned back to the white dragon.

"I'm sorry," she whispered, looking at the eggshells at her feet.

The stories and songs had never agreed on the number of eggs destroyed. "The Ballad of the Slain" said forty, other songs said twenty-five. Elinta couldn't be sure of either. There were just so many fragments. And they still looked fresh. As though they could have been destroyed only yesterday. With a rumble, the dragon gently nudged the shells.

Elinta stared at the fragments, the last evidence of a totally different time. These shells were over a hundred and seventy years old. What had it been like back then?

The dragon tilted its head and released another low, long keen that vibrated through the shells. A sorrowful tune, it lamented the loss of so many young.

"I'm sorry," Elinta said again, but it didn't feel enough.

She ran a hand over the surface of one of the larger fragments. She knew the story behind the Eggslaying. Why it had happened and why it was a good thing. But staring at the remnants of that destruction, she wondered if there could have been another way to get peace. A whole clutch had been *crushed*. A whole generation of young killed for something they hadn't done. Elinta felt a tear track down her cheek. She didn't know what to think anymore. But she stretched out a hand to comfort the dragon anyway.

They sat in silence beside the shells for several long moments before the dragon finally turned away. She followed and the dragon led her to the far-left wall before it turned towards the entrance again. Frowning, Elinta stepped after it, but the dragon grunted deep in its throat.

"I don't know what that means," she said, foot frozen in midair.

The dragon grunted again. Did it want her to stay here while it went somewhere else? Was it going to come back?

Right on cue, Elinta's stomach growled again. Aside from a handful of leaves, she hadn't eaten in over a day, and that time had been a rollercoaster of emotions. The dragon, though, stared at her stomach. Elinta's eyes widened. "Are you ... are you going to get some food? To hunt?"

The dragon blinked, then started to turn to leave. It hesitated, lifting its nose in the air, and sniffing deeply. After another moment, it shook its head and left, slipping out the entrance and disappearing into the snow-covered world that would be dark in a few hours.

"I guess that's a yes?" Elinta's voice echoed around her. "I hope that's a yes." What would she eat though? With a sigh, she sunk to the ground, feeling the pull in her muscles as she lowered herself, and rested her back against the cold stone wall. The dragon's emotions slowly faded but remained just on the very edge of her senses, unnoticeable unless she concentrated hard.

A shiver traced up her spine, but it wasn't just from the low temperature. The cave was eerie. Completely silent and full of reminders, thousands of reminders, of the loss the dragons had suffered there. Part of her wondered whether she only cared because of the connection she had with the white dragon, whatever that really was. But she knew if she'd come here alone, she would have felt some sadness at the sight of the shattered shells.

Alone as she was in the cave, her thoughts quickly turned to everything that had happened to her. Why had she gone to the lake? Why, why had she lingered there so long? *I was so stupid,* she thought, rubbing a hand across her face. She should have known someone would come looking for her and now, looking back, she realised someone had. That moment they'd heard something in the trees nearby. She'd dismissed it as an animal, but now, now she knew it had to have been Galen searching for her. She'd collected the bark not far from the lake, and Galen knew she preferred to go to the spot. And he knew it wasn't far from the lake. Maybe he'd thought she'd stopped for a drink, or a swim and come to check. Instead, he'd found a dragon. Whatever had happened, Elinta hadn't learnt from the previous time she'd been out too long and this time, Galen had noticed when she hadn't returned.

Her brother's face flashed before her. His confusion, his understanding. Did he miss her as much as she missed him? Another tear trickled down her face.

"I'm sorry," she whispered into the empty cave.

Her father's face appeared then, chasing away Blaine's. The stone-cold anger of it stabbed anew at her heart. *He* wasn't missing her. She'd helped a dragon. Protected it. Defended it. She was a traitor now, to him and to the crown. Would Blaine still think that their mother would be proud of her? Or would she have sided with her father? Elinta released a shuddering breath. There was nothing to do now but follow the brief plan she'd made on the dragon's back while they'd flown here. They'd go their separate ways, and she'd settle in a new village, far enough away that no one knew who she was, hopefully working for the healer there until she finished her apprenticeship. It was the best she could hope for. Even if it meant she'd be alone.

A soft growl broke through her thoughts. Her head shot up.

"Dragon?" she asked, but there was no sign of the animal at the entrance, only the now fading light outside. Running the noise over in her head again, she realised the sound had echoed.

Whatever made it was already inside the cavern.

Elinta's heartbeat immediately picked up as fear rushed through her system. She wiped the tears from her face and looked at the shell fragments again. For a moment she wondered if it were possible there was another dragon in the cave.

She immediately dismissed the thought as another growl reverberated around the large space. It didn't sound large enough to be a dragon. Her eyes flittered about the cave, checking every nook and crevice she could, but too much of the cave was now cast in shadow. She couldn't see what was making the sound. Pushing to her feet, all thought of her aching muscles gone, she decided she was better off waiting outside in the snow. Better to risk hypothermia than be attacked by whatever was inside the cave with her. Just as she stepped away from the wall, a large form appeared on the ledge of the back wall and jumped lightly to the ground.

Eyes widening, Elinta froze as she caught sight of the animal. It was a mountain cat, sleek, and with long white and grey speckled fur. It had to come nearly up to her waist in height.

The cat bared its fangs and uttered a long growl, then set to pacing a short way along the wall, then back.

Elinta's body shook with fear. Should she run? Stay utterly still? What did you do when faced by a large cat? None of its cousins lived near Kethmere. She'd never faced something like this before. She could see the cave entrance from the corner of her eye. If she could just get out, maybe the cat would leave her be? Maybe it had claimed the cave and was just being territorial? Maybe it was hungry. Her hands began to ache from clenching them, her fingers digging into her skin.

Lifting her foot slowly, she took a small step towards the entrance. The cat blinked its slitted eyes and widened its maw but continued its agitated pacing. Elinta kept her eyes locked firmly on its own. Some animals supposedly saw it as a challenge and would back off ... although she'd heard stories of such an action encouraging attacks. But she was too scared to look away now. She took another couple steps, her mind screaming at her to move faster, but it seemed to be working. The cat wasn't coming any closer. Then another sound carried through the cave, and Elinta understood the cat's pacing and aggression. It wasn't hunting her.

The sound she'd heard was a soft mewling. Cubs. Elinta's heart beat all the faster. *I'm staring down an angry mother.*

The sound of its young seemed to stir the cat into action. It immediately started forward, hissing at her as each quiet tread brought it closer. Its ears turned back, flat against its head. Elinta abandoned all thought of creeping out and sprinted for the exit, her dress pulling against her long strides. She hiked up her dress and ran harder. As she reached the huge hole in the wall and felt the freezing temperature swirling in the gap, she looked over her shoulder and saw the cat mid-pounce. It was nearly on top of her.

Elinta twisted sideways and threw herself into the snow, but the cat's claws raked across the side of her right thigh. Grunting, Elinta pushed to her feet and ran forward, stumbling as she pushed through the snow. She dared not look back. Her leg screamed at her to stop, but she kept running, half stumbling in the snow, feeling warmth seep down her leg. That's when she realised the cat wasn't following her anymore. Taking deep, gasping breaths, she turned to see where it was, expecting its claws to slice through her again at any moment. The cat had stopped in the entranceway, its eyes fixed on a spot opposite to Elinta. She followed its eyes and nearly sobbed in relief.

The white dragon had returned, and its anger and concern slammed into her all at once. It loomed out of the white surroundings, its outline blurring at the edges, making it even harder to see in the dimming light, but its amber eyes stood out. It jumped towards Elinta and roared at the cat. The sound went straight through Elinta and even shook the snow around them. The cat's ears turned back and with a final hiss it slinked back into the cave and towards its young.

The dragon twisted its neck and lowered its head level with Elinta. Heart still in her throat, Elinta's leg gave way, and she sunk down into the snow with a huge sigh.

"Thanks," she said to the dragon, but her eyes were on the dark patch spreading across her dress.

Already shivering in the cold, Elinta pulled her dress away from her thigh and twisted her leg to see the damage. Five dark slashes across her leg wept dark blood. The three middle cuts were the longest, starting on the front of her leg and stretching laterally across to cover the side. Her hand couldn't even cover the length of the smaller two. Rallying herself, Elinta took stock but there wasn't much to take stock off. She had no herbs, nowhere to get any, nowhere to shelter and only her dress to use as bandages.

"This is not good," she whispered.

She picked up a fistful of snow and dropped it onto the wound, shivering even harder, then picked up another and another until she'd covered the wound. It was the best she could do to clean it, but it wouldn't be enough. A mountain lion's claws wouldn't be clean. She needed something to fight the infection that was sure to come. She needed a needle and thread. But there was nothing. She had nothing.

"Y-y-you're fine," she told herself firmly, but the effect was dampened by her shivering. "Get a grip."

After dusting the snow away and trying to dry the site with her already wet dress, Elinta tore strips from her ruined hem, exposing herself even more to the chill but giving her crucial bandages. She folded one into a pad and, pressing it against the wounds, wrapped it in place with the other strips she'd torn. A small patch of blood seeped through.

"Wh-what are w-we gonna do n-now?" she stuttered, shivers wracking her body. The sun had nearly disappeared beneath the horizon now and the dragon was a dim silhouette. Soon it would be dark, and they had nowhere to go. No one to help them.

In response, the dragon dropped to its belly beside her and rolled to its side, body slightly curled and exposing its belly to her. Its wing, tucked under its body, was spread out across the snow. Elinta understood immediately and dragged herself over to the dragon, carefully moving across the strong membrane and pressing her back to its warm underside, but she continued to shiver. The dragon hummed and spread its other wing over her like a canopy, tucking its nose under the membrane and forming a block to the wind and freezing temperature.

The air around her immediately started to heat up. It was like being inside a tent or a room, except the wall she leant against gently rose and fell in time with the dragon's massive breaths. The shivers wracking Elinta's body slowly calmed and stopped until her exhaustion hit her in a wave. Despite the pain in her leg and the ache in her starving belly, her eyelids slowly drooped, her head dropped back against the dragon's scales, and she fell into a fitful sleep.

Images flashed before her mind. She was flying, diving, twisting, and turning in the air. She was alone, but she could feel them. All of them. So much happiness, enjoyment as they weaved through the air, the wind in their faces. She saw a trio of islands in the distance, saw the others soaring in the air above them, and felt peace. This was her home.

Emotions, feelings, soared through her body so fast she was only left with an impression of who she was. Kind. Intelligent. Regal. Until finally, a name burned into her being, her core. Zhayra. She was Zhayra.

CHAPTER
SIX

"WAIT! DO NOT MOVE."

"Wha—are you—we have to take it out before it attacks," a voice whispered.

"Put your weapon away. You do not know of what you speak," the first voice replied. It was a pleasant voice, deep and ringing with authority but also kindness. The two voices continued, drilling hole after hole into Elinta's mind and pulling her back from sleep. She didn't like that voice anymore, or the other one, the one that seemed confused and tinted with fear.

There was a crunch as though someone was moving through snow, but Elinta pushed the sounds away, unwilling to wake.

She just wanted to sleep, to return to the blackness or the flying dream, then she wouldn't feel the pain in her leg.

A deep rumbling growl sounded next to Elinta, beginning near her toes, and passing up through her body. *Zhayra*, she remembered vaguely, but her thoughts were slipping, slipping.

"Ra ayn nai lurai," the first voice said. Elinta frowned at the foreign tongue. Where was she? *"Ngasai ayn nai."*

"Friends?" the other man hissed, but the pleasant-sounding man shushed him.

The dragon grumbled again. Did she need to wake up now? Elinta fought to crack open her eyes, struggling to understand what was happening, and found herself pressed up against the dragon's white scales, a wing spread over her in the dark. Despite the wing under her as well, snow had gotten everywhere. It was pressed against her face, had melted in her dress and hair. A stabbing pain went through her leg, causing her to gasp and her eyes closed again. Zhayra's concern returned full force.

"Zearla, ra ayn nai eyan lurai eka."

The words bounced around Elinta's confused and aching head, and though she couldn't understand the words, she knew what it meant. The Asali were here.

After a long pause, there was a light fluttering and a sound like leather moving over leather. A burst of cold night air hit Elinta. She frowned and pressed harder into the dragon's stomach, but the sound continued, and the temperature dropped further. The wing under her pulled back, bunching against her. Shivering, Elinta fought to open her eyes again, but they were so heavy, so, so heavy.

"A girl?" the second voice said in disbelief.

There were loud crunches in the snow. A hand gripped her shoulder and rolled her onto her back. Elinta groaned and tried to turn away, back to the warmth of the dragon but the hands held her still.

"Lie still, *Zearla lurai*."

Elinta's eyelids fluttered, and she glimpsed the man kneeling over her in the darkness. There was a soft light from the moon reflecting off the snow and off him ... no, *he* was glowing. The light came from him. Elinta caught sight of luminescent light brown skin and glowing white pupils, ovular rather than circular, and surrounded by grey irises, before her eyes shut again and shivers wracked her body. The image of the shining man was burned into her eyelids.

"We need to get her somewhere warm," the other voice said.

Gentle hands pulled away the slick bandage at her leg. The last piece tugged at the gashes causing her to gasp. As she slipped into unconsciousness, a warmth started in the wounds and spread outwards, through and over her leg. Blood? Then all went black.

She was warm. That was the first thing she noticed. Then she realised that she didn't feel any pain in her leg. But her head was heavy as though she'd been in a deep sleep and her stomach ached with hunger. A flood of emotions hit her, emotions that weren't hers. Worry balling in a huge stomach, caution making it uneasy and then happiness. Zhayra. Wait. How did she know the dragon's name? How did she know she *had* a name? Yet she was sure that was the dragon's name. Elinta's confusion doubled as vague memories came back to her and her mind settled on the last thing she'd seen before she'd slept. Glowing ovular, white pupils. Grey eyes. Glowing skin. An Asali.

"You may open your eyes now. You are quite safe." She knew the voice immediately. One of the Asali that had found her and Zhayra, the one she'd seen, anyway.

Forcing her eyes open, she blinked in the light and the man finally came into view. His hair was dark brown, curled and cut short over a broad face and a strong jaw. His eyes, unlike anything she'd ever seen outside of a history book, were mesmerising and full of kindness. But his friendly manner didn't ease the tension in her body.

"You must be hungry," he said, holding out a small loaf of bread.

Ignoring him, she twisted her head, looking around frantically. Where was the other Asali she'd heard out in the snow by the Eggslaying cave? She was in another cavern, on a bundle of furs pressed into a corner and against a stone wall. The Asali man knelt beside her. A curtain spread between the two walls, obscuring her view of the rest of the cavern. But there were sounds of other people moving about behind the curtain. The clinking of metal, the rustle of fabric. There was more than one other Asali in the cave with them.

"Where am I?" she asked.

She tried to think of everything she knew about the Asali. Their races weren't on friendly terms with each other because of what happened to the dragons, but this man seemed to have helped her. What did he want? The dragon seemed to grow increasingly agitated as Elinta's worry grew.

"It is OK. You are safe here," the man repeated in his sonorous voice, still holding the bread out. If the common tongue was his second language, she could hardly tell. He spoke clearly and easily, if a little formally. "I am Ciar."

"Elinta," she said. "Where's Zhayra?" She focused on the man's jumper. It was made of grey and white fur, similar to the mountain cat that had attacked her.

Ciar's eyebrows rose. "You know the dragon's name?"

"I—" she stuttered, "I guess so."

The man smiled. "You are *Zearla lurai.*"

"What?" The Asalin words were completely foreign to her, just like the rest of his language. Was she meant to know what he meant?

"Zhayra is fine," Ciar said, avoiding her question. "She is waiting outside for you." He gestured to her leg under the thick fur blanket covering her. "Your leg is fully healed though there is a scar."

Elinta frowned. Her muscles were no longer aching either. "Wha—how long have I been here?"

The man chuckled, a deep musical sound. "We found you last night."

Head whirling, she sat up and pushed the blanket aside to find she was in a new dress.

"Your dress was ruined," he said, gesturing at the one she now wore. "You will need new clothes before you leave us, of course. These garments are for night only, when in shelter and under the furs."

That made sense, she thought, looking at the thin, white fabric covering her body. Curious, she started to bunch up the material. No way had the wound already scarred, but she couldn't deny the lack of pain there. When the dress slipped halfway up her thigh, she gasped. Ciar was right. Where her skin had been ravished by five deep cuts, now there were only thin silver-white scars in their place.

"How is this possible?" She ran her hand over the scars that would have taken weeks, months, to form.

Ciar's eyebrows rose. "It has been a long time since our races mixed, yet I am surprised you do not know this about us." Ciar gestured at her leg. "The Asali have the ability to heal, though the process cannot be completed on one of your race. Whilst we are similar, there are also too many differences."

"You mean, you don't have scars?" Her head was spinning. They could *heal*? Was that why they lived so long? She'd heard they could live for thousands of years, but how many?

"No, we do not." He smiled. "There is another who wishes to speak with you. I believe he means to help."

"What?" Everything was happening too fast.

A low rumble sounded in the distance. Zhayra.

"Of course, you may wish to see Zhayra first. She seems impatient and I am not one to deny a dragon." He laughed again, apparently delighted by the very idea of a dragon. Then again, it was probably the first he had seen in a long time.

Elinta had to agree with his assumption, based on the link she seemed to have to the dragon's emotions. Zhayra was impatient. And she was desperate to see the dragon and thank it for saving her from the cat. Elinta's mouth opened and closed a couple times, unsure what to say to the man before she settled on nodding. Zhayra first.

"I will get you some warmer clothes." Ciar held out the bread for her again, which she gratefully accepted. He ducked under the curtain and left Elinta to her swirling thoughts. Her head no longer felt heavy with sleep, but it didn't ease the confusion of her mind. Too much was happening. Too much had happened. Overwhelmed with homesickness, she rested her head against the wall behind her and waited for Ciar to come back, only nibbling at the bread and hardly tasting it. Who was it that wanted to meet her? Was it the other Asali that had found them? Or someone else? She closed her eyes to try to gather her thoughts, tugging her dress down to cover her feet.

Ciar returned a moment later and placed a stack of folded clothes on the end of her blankets.

"Thank you," she said, not bothering to ask what they'd done with her ruined dress. Ciar ducked behind the curtain again while Elinta took one last bite of the bread before putting it aside. She clambered to her feet and reached for the bundle. At the top of the pile was a pair of black pants, lined with fur so fine it was hard to see. She ran her hand along the smooth fabric. What animal had this come from? She pulled the pants on under her dress, marvelling at how soft it felt against her skin.

Next was a loose shirt; she wasn't sure what it was made from. It was surprisingly light for the climate. Slipping out of the dress, she pulled the shirt on and picked up the last item of clothing. Like the other two items, the jumper wasn't as bulky as she'd expected. It was white, lined with white fur on the inside, but it was the same unknown fabric as the shirt on the outside. She slipped into the jumper, which fit her perfectly just like the pants and shirt, and wondered at how warm she was. In fact, she was perfectly comfortable. Looking around, she found her boots sitting nearby and shoved her socked feet inside the now dry shoes.

She grabbed the bread, then tugged the curtain aside and found Ciar waiting for her. "What is this made of?" she asked, still marvelling at the fabric of her jumper.

Ciar winked. "That is a secret." He gestured for her to follow him. "Zhayra is this way."

Elinta strode after him, stumbling when she allowed her eyes to roam. Dozens of Asali men, women and even a couple children, stared openly at her from around the cave. Elinta stared right back, cheeks heating. Every single one of them had bright white pupils surrounded by grey irises, except they weren't all the same shade of grey. Some were light, so light to almost be white, while others were a deep metal grey and still some others were silver. Every one of them had a faint glow to their tan, light brown, or dark skin, and every single one of them looked just as curious as she felt. Elinta was so distracted by the people surrounding her that she hardly noticed her surroundings until she'd followed Ciar to a small opening in the rock face.

Following him outside, Elinta squinted in the morning sun. If she'd expected to feel colder outside, then she was pleasantly surprised. The clothing Ciar had given her kept her toasty warm, and the snow wasn't deep enough to cover her shoes here.

"I will come back soon," Ciar said and disappeared back through the small opening in the cliff-face behind her.

Elinta felt a rush of happiness from the dragon and peered at the surrounding landscape. Zhayra's scales matched the snowy mountains perfectly, but her movement gave her away. Several metres directly in front of her, a large, white mound shook, and a long neck slowly uncurled. Zhayra hummed, jumped to her feet with surprising agility and, in a couple long steps, was in front of her.

"Hello girl." Smiling, Elinta pressed her hand to the dragon's muzzle. They'd now saved each other. Zhayra from the storm and villagers, and Elinta from the mountain cat.

"Thank you," she whispered, a shudder going through her body at the memory of claws raking through her skin.

"So, what are we going to do now?" What was Zhayra going to do now? If they went their separate ways, where would the dragon go?

"I'd like to help you work that out."

Elinta whirled, nearly tripping over her feet in the loose snow and dropping the remainder of her bread, to find a young man standing at the entrance to the Asali cavern. He was, quite noticeably, human and only a couple of years older than her at most. His eyes were a deep blue, standing out against the grey of the rock behind him. His short, dark brown hair was uncovered, and only a small amount of his tan skin was left bare by the large cream jacket, black scarf and ankle-high boots that sat over his dark pants. A sword hung in a simple sheath at his hip. It was hard to tell, given all the layers of clothing he wore, but he seemed quite well-built.

"Who are you?" Elinta asked, recognising his voice. He was the other man who had found her and Zhayra last night. It wasn't another Asali after all. She stared at potentially the only other person to visit the Asali in over a hundred years, other than a representative of the royal family, and waited for his response.

He smiled, his eyes flickering briefly to Zhayra behind her, and then back. "I'm Lorrin Rey."

He smiled as though to put her at ease, but the effect was lost on Elinta. She blanched and quickly scrapped her last thought. He wasn't the only person outside of royalty to see the Asali ... he *was* royalty. What was the crown prince doing out in the middle of the White Mountains? And among the Asali? Her mind whirled with a million other questions and worries, but chief among them was the fact she was standing next to a dragon and the prince had, quite obviously, seen them ... twice.

Elinta's mouth opened and closed. Zhayra's feelings remained cautious, and Elinta was sure the dragon understood the implications of the presence of this young man. The man whom she'd betrayed by simply being with her.

The prince's eyes flickered between them again. "It's OK," he said to the silence. "I just want to know what's going on ... how you met." He paused, then took a cautious step forward. "The Asali told me that the dragons weren't—aren't," he corrected, "what we believe them to be. Seeing it protecting you last night ... I'm inclined to believe them."

Elinta didn't know what to say, to think. "I—" she stuttered. She couldn't deny the *prince*. "What would you like to know, Your Highness?"

"Don't worry about titles." He waved a dismissive hand. "I prefer Lorrin. I would like to know your name though."

Her name? She stared at him for a moment. This was the last person she wanted to be near, but what more did she have to lose? If he really believed the dragons weren't evil, then what did it matter if he knew who she was? She'd just left a village full of people who hated her, and every single one of them knew her name.

"Elinta." She gestured to the dragon behind her. "This is Zhayra."

The dragon hummed in pleasure at Elinta's use of her name. Elinta smiled. The name suited her.

The prince's eyebrows rose. "So, it's true? They aren't … beasts?"

Zhayra shuffled beside her, settled into a crouch, and slung her tail around her body and in front of Elinta. It was a question she'd thought over many times herself during her trips to the forest. She looked at Zhayra.

"No," she said. That much was clear to her, especially after her dream … thing last night. "But I don't know much about them."

He ran a hand through his hair. "No, I didn't expect you to. Ciar said they're self-aware … sentient." He shook his head, looking at Zhayra again.

Nodding, Elinta thought over his words. Sentient. Like another race. That actually made sense. Zhayra really did understand her, really could think. She'd been thinking something along the same lines before the villagers arrived by the lake just a couple of days ago.

The two stood awkwardly for a moment, surveying each other.

"What did you mean before?" she asked. "About helping us?"

"It's not hard to guess you're in a tight spot." He looked pointedly at the dragon. "But how did you two … meet?"

Elinta shifted uncomfortably. "She came down in a storm. Outside my village." She swallowed the name of her home from her tongue. "In the south."

"Did anyone else know she was there?"

Why did he want to know? To see whether they'd done their duty? Tried? But if he meant to help her … finally, she shook her head. "Not at first. They saw her later when I was with her. Then we left," she finished lamely.

"I see you two have met." Ciar appeared behind Prince Lorrin in the cave's doorway. Elinta almost sighed in relief for the break from the prince's questions. Her mind still hadn't caught up with what was going on.

"There is still much that needs to be discussed," Ciar continued. "Will you come inside?"

Zhayra grumbled with irritation, not that Elinta needed the sound to know when she could sense the feeling so clearly. Elinta could guess why the dragon was annoyed too. There was no way she'd fit inside the Asali cave, not even her head would fit through the entrance, and she wanted to be involved. Ciar bowed his head.

"Of course, perhaps we could stay out here where Zhayra may see us."

Lorrin nodded, looking nervously at the dragon. Smiling, Elinta watched Zhayra settle again, happy to be included.

"I will find us some chairs," Ciar said, ducking inside.

Elinta dropped her hand from the zip of her jumper, where she'd been fiddling with it unconsciously, and tried not to stare at the prince. A moment later, Ciar returned with three wooden stools stacked together. In a few minutes the three of them were seated in a small circle, with Zhayra included, her large body stretching away behind them.

"I am sure you have many questions, Elinta, but may I ask first what the two of you were doing at the breeding grounds?" Ciar said, looking between her and Zhayra. The breeding grounds. It sounded better than how she knew it. Hopeful, even. Like it still was that way, and not a graveyard.

"I don't know," she said honestly. "We were just trying to get somewhere safe, and Zhayra took us here." She gestured around at the mountains. *Why did Zhayra take us here?* But then she remembered the eggshells in the cave. Maybe the mountains were one of the few places the dragon knew of in Eldras? Had she been there before? Or did she know about it from those that had?

"Did someone attack you?" Ciar asked, drawing Elinta's attention back to the conversation. A hint of anger was in his pleasant voice.

"My village," she answered, pushing away the memory of her father and brother among them.

Understanding dawned on the prince's face.

"It has been many years since a dragon was seen in Eldras. It is a pity humans would still kill them," Ciar said sadly.

Zhayra lowered her head onto her front feet.

"What are you planning to do now?" Lorrin said.

Elinta glanced at the dragon beside her.

"I thought we'd go our separate ways," she said honestly, though the idea had lost some of its appeal to her. "I was in my final year as an apprentice to a healer in my village. I was planning on finishing my training somewhere else."

"And the dragon?" Ciar asked, face unreadable.

"I don't know." Elinta shrugged, trying to seem light-hearted. "I guess she'll go home. She doesn't need my help anymore."

"Help?" Lorrin looked between them.

"She was hurt when she landed in the storm."

Ciar was shaking his head. "I do not think it will be that simple. There is a reason Zhayra has left the safety of the dragons' new home, and I believe there is more between you two than you understand."

"What do you mean?"

"You can feel her, can you not?"

Lorrin's eyes widened, and she looked between the two of them, confused. Couldn't everyone?

"Yes," she said, slowly. "Her emotions."

Ciar nodded. "Something has brought Zhayra here, and you must help her."

"Why?" Elinta looked over at Zhayra, who was watching her closely with her large amber eyes. She wasn't sure what it was the dragon was feeling now. It was like a mix of curiosity and concern. Like she wasn't sure what Elinta would decide. Which was pretty accurate, since Elinta had no idea what to do. The dragon had seemed worried when she'd asked her about her home, but there was no way to learn why.

Ciar didn't respond, his white eyes thoughtful.

"Is that normal?" Lorrin turned to Ciar. "To feel a dragon's emotions?"

"For some."

Lorrin gazed at Elinta in awe. She shifted in her seat uncomfortably. Not everyone could sense the dragons the way she could? *What does that mean?*

"Can you?" Elinta blurted. The Asali man seemed to understand Zhayra, on some kind of level. Maybe he could help them.

"No." At seeing Elinta's surprise and disappointment, he continued, "My people had much to do with the dragons while they lived in Eldras. Though it's been nearly two hundred years since we have seen them, we remember their ways. I can read her body language as you might read mine, but I cannot feel her."

"You called me ..." she searched for the words, "'*Zearla lurai*' before. What does that mean?"

Ciar shook his head. "I am not the right person to speak to on this. I am sorry, but I cannot help you."

"Is there someone here who can?"

"No," he said. "We have not had a *Zearla lurai* among our number for many years."

Sighing, she shook her head. She liked this man, but he'd avoided a few of her questions now. Things weren't becoming any clearer ... if anything, some things were becoming more confusing.

Crossing his legs, the prince broke the silence. "Well, this at least answers one of the questions we've had for a while." He gestured at Zhayra. "Rumours of a dragon in Eldras have reached Nevira. No one believed them, but it must have been Zhayra."

Ciar nodded, but Zhayra seemed ... confused. Elinta frowned at the dragon. It seemed she wasn't the first person to see the dragon after all. How long had she been in Eldras? But what she really wanted to know was why the prince was here. What business did he have with the Asali?

Elinta's stomach rumbled, pulling her thoughts back to the loaf she'd dropped in the snow. When was her last proper meal? Two days ago? Her stomach gurgled again.

"I am sorry," Ciar said, smiling. "It has probably been some time since you ate. We can talk more later." He stood and started packing up the stools.

After patting Zhayra's muzzle, Elinta followed Ciar inside, Prince Lorrin trailing behind her. She felt his curious stare drilling into her back as they left the snow-covered mountain behind them.

Elinta took her first proper look around the Asali cave as they walked inside. It was huge, big enough to comfortably fit double the number that it currently housed. Beds of fur and material lined the walls where the inhabitants slept at night, now rolled up to give them more space. It seemed the three of them had been sitting on most of the stools the Asali had. Only a woman by one of the fires and working with some kind of material sat on a stool. Everyone else sat cross-legged on the floor. Elinta craned her neck to see the rounded ceiling and gawped. It was a dim grey colour, lined with silvery veins, reflecting the light of the small, smokeless fires heating the cave and the light of the Asali themselves.

"It's *illayas,*" the prince said over her shoulder.

"Really?" Elinta asked, gazing in awe at the rare silver-coloured metal streaking across the ceiling and down the walls. "It's beautiful."

She'd never seen the metal in its raw form before. She did see a sword made half from *illayas* and half from steel in Culmar once when she'd visited with her family, but the metal had been tinged with a faint blue. Apparently, the swords were mostly owned by old military families or descendants of a few advisors.

"Can it really only be forged in dragon fire?" she murmured.

"Indeed. It is what turns it blue," Ciar said, leading them to a spot by a fire in the centre of the cavern. Elinta sat by the warm flames. "I have some things to attend to. My wife, Raisa, will bring you some food in a moment. She is curious to speak with you."

"Thanks," Elinta said, surprised. Why would someone want to speak with her? She amended that thought, thinking of Ciar's excitement at the prospect of a dragon in the mountains. Maybe someone did want to speak to her after all.

"Can I sit with you?" the prince asked, standing beside her in the warmth of the fire. Yet again, she was surprised to notice the clothing she wore kept her comfortably warm and no more or less, even by the fire. The prince's didn't seem to maintain his temperature the way hers did, being human made. She watched as he loosened the scarf around his neck. He seemed more comfortable without Zhayra around.

"OK, Your—" she cut herself off, remembering his dismissal of titles. "OK."

He laughed lightly and sat beside her, leaving some space between them. Around her, Elinta noticed the occasional curious glance from passing Asali. It was hard not to return the stare. They were ... she grasped for a word ... strange, but beautiful. Everywhere she looked were the same glowing bodies and glowing eyes on very different people. It was amazing. And when she considered they could somehow heal wounds overnight ... they were almost unbelievable.

Sensing Lorrin's gaze on her, she turned to face him.

"It's something, isn't it? Seeing them for the first time," he said.

Elinta nodded, eyes flicking to a small Asali woman passing by on the other side of the fire. "I know it's not my business," Elinta started, her father's disapproving voice echoing in her head at the thought of questioning royalty, but she pressed on. "But why are you here?"

The prince looked into the flames, and she wasn't sure if he was going to answer. Maybe she'd gone too far. He shifted.

"I'm not supposed to be," he admitted, a faint grin shining through.

Elinta's eyebrows rose. The prince was sneaking around?

"I think it's time we started trying to mend things with them, and my trip to Tremass put me in the north. It was the opportunity I needed." He shrugged as though what he said wasn't important, but clearly it was. Tremass was somewhere on the far west coast, and the White Mountains were in the far east. But there was more to it than that. A new alliance with the Asali would change things, *fix* things. Trading could reopen between their peoples. The Asali could share their knowledge again, and with such long lifespans, the people had much of it.

Elinta opened her mouth to ask him more but was interrupted.

"Excuse me? My husband said you needed some food." A woman approached, looking to be in her early thirties though her real age was impossible to tell. She could be over fifteen-hundred years old and Elinta would never know. Her long blonde hair trailed over her shoulders, complementing her light grey irises, which were only slightly darker than her pupils, giving the illusion they were the same colour. The effect was slightly disconcerting. The woman was carrying a wooden bowl with meat and another loaf of bread.

"Yes, thank you." Elinta said, taking the offered bowl from the woman, Raisa she assumed.

"May I sit with you?" She had a light voice, clear too. She glanced between Elinta and Lorrin. The prince made no objections.

"Of course," Elinta said, trying not to stare at her eyes or the glow on her skin.

Sitting cross-legged across the fire from the prince, the woman fixed her bright eyes on Elinta. "My name is Raisa. It's a pleasure to meet you, Elinta."

Elinta laughed and shook her head. "I think it's more my pleasure than yours." She studied the loaf in her bowl, not having looked at it before, and wondered what they made it from. It was like nothing she'd had before.

"It's been a long time since we saw a dragon in these mountains. Ciar said he and Prince Lorrin found you by the breeding grounds?"

Elinta nodded, taking a bite of the grain loaf. It was a solid loaf but crumbled in her mouth. She nearly groaned in pleasure as its savoury taste washed through her mouth. Why hadn't she eaten more of it before?

"Strange," Raisa said.

Elinta's eyebrows rose, but she couldn't speak around the food in her mouth.

"What do you mean?" Lorrin asked, voicing Elinta's thoughts.

"We don't like to visit the breeding grounds. Since the Eggslaying, it has become a site of death and mourning. We prefer to remember it as it was." She gestured at the prince. "But you've also visited it with my husband, and there was another spotted there several weeks ago. Sometimes one of our people will go there to mourn, but this man was unknown to us."

"Could he have been from the Green City?" Lorrin asked.

Elinta took another bite of her food, unsure where this was going or why it was important.

Raisa shook her head. "Our kin in the west do not visit the Ash Mountains," she said, using the old human name for the mountains, from before the dragons left. "It is too strong a reminder of what was lost."

Elinta snuck a glance at the prince, wondering how he would take the comment. It was his ancestor who stormed the breeding grounds and expelled the dragons from the country after all. But the prince took the comment in his stride. He'd probably been proud of the fact before he'd learnt what the dragons were really like. Hadn't she supported it too?

"Elinta?" Raisa drew her back from her thoughts.

"Sorry, I was just ... thinking." She smiled apologetically.

"It's a lot to take in," Raisa said, looking around the cave and the many Asali engaged in various jobs around them. "You're welcome to stay here as long as you like, but I don't believe Zhayra will be happy here."

Elinta wondered if Ciar had told her Zhayra's name right before she'd come over.

"No, Ciar didn't think so," Elinta said, dejectedly. Her plans were looking more and more unlikely to happen, but then, she wasn't so sure that she wanted them too anymore. *What am I supposed to do with a dragon?*

Raisa moved to rise, but Lorrin interjected. "Who do you think it was? The Asali that visited the breeding grounds?"

"We do not know." Raisa tilted her head. "Why?"

Lorrin frowned. "There's been rumours spreading of an Asali man spotted in human towns recently. I wonder if it's the same man...."

Raisa's frown was deeper than Lorrin's.

"Some of our people recently left without a word. We awoke one morning, and they were gone. It could be any one of them, but it is strange that an Asali would walk among your people."

She paused, eyes shifting as she thought furiously. "Would you come with me to speak with Ciar?"

"Of course." Lorrin rose to his feet and followed Raisa, glancing at Elinta briefly over his shoulder.

Elinta finished her meal alone in silence, looking into the flames in front of her because the sights around her were so overwhelming. Not knowing what to think of all Raisa and Lorrin had talked about, she let it all drift away and enjoyed the last of her meal, only pausing to wonder whether Zhayra had eaten recently.

CHAPTER SEVEN

T HE ASALI LET HER sit in silence beside the fire. It was time she needed to collect herself. Elinta let the murmurings of their language wash over her, not hearing a single word in her own tongue. She studied the people around her. Every one of them was busy with one job or another. Men and women sharpened elegant wooden spears tipped with metal. A woman prepped a fresh fur to dry, a man cut meat to cook, while others arrived at the entrance with firewood, though where they got it from, Elinta couldn't guess. Among them all were only three children, their eyes the same colours as those around them, with the same luminescent skin. One little girl, Tully's age, with short brown hair and a curious stare tugged at the dress of the woman standing over the fresh fur. A boy, surely no older than three, slept in a bed of furs near the back wall and the other child, a young boy, stood in front of Elinta, blond hair tussled. His skin was a similar tone to Ciar's. His eyes matched Raisa's.

"Hello," Elinta said, smiling at the boy.

He stared curiously at her. "You are human."

"I am." She paused, then leant in. "You're Asali."

The boy nodded, hair bouncing. "Did you really come with a dragon?"

"I did."

"Can I see her?" The boy twisted side to side, his hands shoved in the small pockets of his jacket. Unlike his parents—she was sure he was Ciar and Raisa's son—the boy had a light accent to his words. His use was impressive; he'd hardly have reason to use the common tongue here.

"Sure," Elinta said, completely comfortable with the idea though had he asked her a couple days ago she would have blanched. But Zhayra would probably enjoy seeing them. Elinta glanced around the cave, but she couldn't see Raisa or Ciar. They must have been hidden by the cooking station. "Why don't you let your parents know and then we'll go see her?"

Nodding, the boy sprinted away, deftly dodging the people working around them. When he returned a few minutes later, the girl had followed him.

"Can I come too?" Her silver eyes stood out brightly against her dark hair. She had a gentle accent like the boy's.

Do they teach all the children the common tongue? she wondered, staring at the girl, *even though they have nothing to do with us?*

Nodding, Elinta felt the eyes of other Asali on her. For a moment she wondered whether they'd ask to see Zhayra too.

"I'm Elinta," she said to the two children.

"I am Eiran." The boy nodded at the girl who was studying her with a serious expression. "This is Laira."

"Let's go then." Pushing to her feet, Elinta led the way. Walking towards the entrance, the boy could hardly contain his excitement beside her. He was nearly jumping.

"First dragon?" she asked, hiding a smile.

He turned wide eyes on her. "Yes?"

She laughed. "Mine too."

Laira shook her head, but her excitement nearly matched the boy's.

They emerged into the snow-covered landscape, but this time the Zhayra-mound wasn't there. She looked around, aware of the children's disappointed faces and slumping shoulders. "Zhayra?"

A tickle of anticipation was her only response.

"Zhayra?" she called.

Huge wings beating at the air and the rush of wind reached her ears. The children's faces lit up and they eagerly searched the sky for the source. Their faces were open, excited, not a trace of fear. Elinta shook her head in wonder. These children must have been raised vastly different to her to have no fear of a dragon. Zhayra soared over the cliff to their backs and hovered in the air a moment, letting the children see her in flight and basking in the attention. Elinta had to laugh at the dragon, but she received the reaction she'd obviously hoped for. Laira and Eiran's faces were masks of pure awe. Their eyes, already naturally shining, were brighter than ever.

Battering them with air, Zhayra flapped her wings twice and landed lightly in the snow. Gasps of wonder sounded behind them, and Elinta twisted to see several Asali standing in and around the entranceway, grey and silver eyes glued to Zhayra. The children weren't the only ones desperate to see a dragon, though Raisa, Ciar, and Lorrin weren't among them. Whispers of '*zearla*' ran through the group, a word Ciar had used earlier, but she wasn't exactly sure what it meant. She supposed 'dragon,' but she wasn't sure how that related to her, since Ciar had been speaking about her when he'd used the word.

"Can we touch her?" Laira's high voice asked from beside her.

"I think she'd like that." Elinta nodded towards Zhayra, who had settled into a crouch, eyes bright and locked on the two kids. Her tail twitched behind her in excitement. Practically leaping forward, Eiran sprinted to Zhayra, Laira on his heels, and stopped right below the dragon's head.

"*Layzun!*" the boy called, perhaps in greeting, Elinta wasn't sure.

Lowering her head, Zhayra nudged Eiran, knocking the chuckling boy to his butt in the snow. Laira tentatively touched Zhayra's scaly brow, smiling wildly. Eiran pushed his feet under him and jumped onto Zhayra's neck. It was quite a large jump and the dragon grunted in surprise, but the boy didn't seem to notice, pulling himself up and sitting between two of the larger spine-like scales.

Laira gaped at the boy. "Can I do that?"

Elinta opened her mouth to respond but Zhayra lowered her head completely to the ground and allowed Laira to jump up below the boy. A light laugh drifted over from the cave. It was the woman Laira had been tugging at by the furs. She was still in the entranceway, but everyone else had returned inside.

The two children climbed down Zhayra's neck and onto her back with flawless balance, giggling when Zhayra twisted to watch them and blew warm air over their faces. Elinta couldn't believe how easily they moved about on the dragon. She'd just spent nearly two days riding on Zhayra's back and she'd hardly been comfortable sitting up, not to mention she'd almost fallen off. The kids were moving around like they'd been doing it for years.

Nearly an hour had passed before Prince Lorrin came out to see them, his hand resting on the pommel of his sword. His eyes were glued to the two children climbing on the massive dragon, an expression of shock on his face.

Elinta would have reacted the same way a week ago, no, even yesterday, before whatever had happened when she learnt the dragon's name. But Zhayra's name wasn't the only thing she'd learnt. She was pretty sure she'd seen the dragon's nature too. That was why she didn't feel any fear around her now, or any nervousness.

Why am I the only one who can sense her feelings? she wondered.

She shook off her thoughts. Turning, Elinta grinned at the prince, feeling more relaxed than she had in a while. "Would you like to join them?"

Horror burst into her stomach as soon as the words left her mouth. Had she really said that? Out loud? To the *prince?* But Lorrin just laughed, shaking his head as he crossed the distance to stand beside her.

"No, thank you." He tore his blue eyes from the children. "I wanted to talk to you."

Zhayra's head perked up at the prince's words, but she kept playing with the kids, beating her wings softly to send bursts of air over them, ruffling their hair and clothes.

"Oh?" Elinta asked, unsure what else to say.

"I meant what I said earlier about helping you. And I think you might be able to help me."

"Oh?" she said again. Unless he needed a wound treated, which was unlikely given what she'd learnt firsthand about the Asali's healing abilities, she didn't know what he could need. Her hand trailed to her healed leg.

"I want to mend things with the Asali, but things are still strained. With Zhayra and you around though, I think things might be easier. Now that I know the dragons aren't what we thought, things could change." He surveyed the scene before them, a hopeful spark in his eyes. "I know you won't be safe anywhere with her, but maybe that could change too. If I can prove it to my father. It might just ... take a while."

It was the only option anyone had actually given her, other than saying they couldn't stay here, and they couldn't go their separate ways. She stared at the dragon for a long moment. "What would we do?"

"Come back with me to Nevira." He plunged ahead before Elinta could point out the flaw in his plan, the dragon. "Zhayra wouldn't be able to come into the city, but you could. I need to check some books and talk to my father. It would be good for you. We have copies of nearly all the available books that mention dragons ... not that there's many anymore," he added as an afterthought.

Elinta stared at Zhayra for a long moment. Go to the capital? And the palace? Despite her own plans to leave the dragon, she felt a twinge of sadness at the idea of Zhayra having to stay away from the city. "Where would Zhayra go?"

"There's places outside the city she could hide."

Zhayra's eyes locked on her and Elinta sensed her acceptance of the idea, mixed with a twinge of hope. It seemed to be the best plan for them, whether they stayed weeks or months there. Elinta could learn more about the dragons, and maybe things could change for Zhayra. She could stay in Eldras and still be safe. Elinta thought of the islands in her dream last night and the dragons flying around them. Would the others come back too? There was so much wrapped up in what Lorrin was offering, but Zhayra seemed happy with it.

Nodding, Elinta twisted to face him. "OK."

He grinned, but his smile faded. "Do I—do I need to ask Zhayra?"

"No." Elinta laughed, "She's OK with it."

"OK. Good." He ran a hand through his already ruffled hair and watched Laira slide down the dragon's leg and into the snow. "This might take some getting used to."

"It does."

That night, Elinta lay wrapped in her fur blankets, staring at the ceiling, thoughts clambering in her mind. Though he was worried about someone finding Zhayra, Ciar had ultimately supported Lorrin's idea of them going to Nevira. He, like the prince, hoped that things could change. They were leaving the day after tomorrow. She just hoped she was making the right decision. Elinta sighed and rolled over, tugging at the furs, and letting her hand drift to the new scars on her thigh. Only two weeks ago she would have laughed if someone had told her where she'd be now. She felt a twinge of Zhayra's emotions from wherever she'd settled to sleep for the night. She'd have to get used to knowing the dragon's feelings. Was that what *Zearla lurai* was? What did it mean that she could sense them? And how had that happened?

She sighed and her thoughts turned to the previous night, when she'd fallen asleep pressed against Zhayra and dreamt that she was the dragon? Ciar hadn't said anything about dreams, only feelings. But she'd learnt the dragon's name, didn't it stand to reason then that she'd experienced something more than a dream? And what did it mean that she had? Maybe it was a strengthening of their bond, but how had it happened? She tried to focus on the images she'd seen, but sleep chased away her thoughts before she could linger any longer on her questions.

Elinta woke to the Asali rising for the day, their light chattering echoing as they clattered around the cave. With a rush, Zhayra's emotions returned to her. She seemed content. Elinta wondered what the dragon could be doing and threw back her furs, curiosity getting the better of her. She changed back into the clothes that

Ciar had given her yesterday and pulled back the curtain separating her from the Asali. Belatedly, she wondered where the prince was sleeping. Hers was the only curtain among the group, except for a changing area. He must have slept among them.

Nodding her good mornings and hellos, Elinta walked through the cave, past several freshly lit fires, and out into the bright morning, the sun reflecting off the snow and into her eyes. Squinting, she looked around for Zhayra, but she was nowhere to be seen again. A spike of alarm rose in her but was quickly squashed. The dragon still seemed content. She couldn't be in danger.

"Must be flying," Elinta murmured and having had her curiosity sated, went back inside.

Elinta sat awkwardly at one of the small fires, empty bowl beside her, the Asali bustling around her. She was the only one with nothing to do, something extremely rare for her. Even the prince was busy, having left early in the morning after insisting to join a hunting party. Surely, there was something she could do to help.

Seeing a familiar figure, Elinta jumped to her feet. "Ciar!"

The stocky Asali turned from the man and woman with him and crossed to meet her. "How are you this morning?"

"Good." She shifted on her feet. "Is there anything I can do? Everyone seems so busy and I'm ... not."

Ciar smiled. "There is not much more to be done." At seeing her crestfallen face, he continued, "But some of our people are going in search of a root beneath the snow soon. You may join them if you wish."

"OK. I'll do that."

He gestured to the opening where Raisa stood with some baskets. "Raisa is leading the group today. You can wait with her for the others."

"Thanks," she said, relieved to have something to do to keep her occupied and to help the people who'd helped her.

Elinta hurried to where Raisa stood. A tall, lean man had also joined her while she'd spoken with Ciar. He had a spear slung across his back.

"Hi Raisa," she said, stopping in front of the woman. "Ciar said I could join you looking for a root?"

Raisa smiled. "You're welcome to. We're just waiting on Eiran." She turned to the man next to her. "This is Illar."

"Hello." She held out her hand, then nearly took it back. Did Asali shake hands? Illar took her hand and shook it firmly.

"I'm Elinta," she said, relieved she hadn't blundered the introduction.

The man grinned, showing perfectly straight teeth. "I know who you are. We're very excited to see a dragon in Eldras once again. You have our thanks for bringing it here."

That was a bit of a stretch, she thought. The dragon had brought *her* here. She told the man as much, but he just laughed.

"It doesn't matter who did the bringing. We're glad for it."

"Glad I could be brought," she stuttered awkwardly.

Illar shared a grin with Raisa, but Elinta was saved from her embarrassment when a small boy appeared at her side.

"Ready!" Eiran practically shouted. He turned to Elinta. "Are you coming too?"

"I am."

His light grey eyes widened. "Is Zhayra coming?"

"No, I think she's out flying. I don't think she's hunted in a while." Unless you included the night in the Eggslaying cave, but she didn't think Zhayra had been gone long enough to catch anything. She certainly hadn't hunted during their long flight from Kethmere.

At her son's dejected face, Raisa touched his shoulder. "Besides, I doubt Zhayra would be able to help us today. Her claws aren't ideal for finding *rellaesi*."

Elinta assumed she meant whatever root they were going in search of.

"You'll probably see her later," Elinta offered.

Eiran nodded, slightly placated, as his mother handed around the baskets and they followed her outside.

Once again, Elinta was comfortably warm in the clothes Ciar had given her. Raisa led them along in the shadow of the cliff-face for half an hour, stopping occasionally to dust back a layer of snow, looking for signs that Elinta couldn't see. Curiosity finally got the better of her. She'd never gone looking for plants in the snow; it didn't fall near Kethmere even in the winter.

"What are we looking for?"

Raisa looked up from where she crouched, Eiran by her side. "The roots grow under the snow through the winter. In the spring, they send up small shoots which we look for to know where they are." She gestured at the cliff looming over them. "They only grow in the shadow of the cliffs."

Illar called from behind them. "Here's one."

Eiran jumped to his feet and ran back through the snow to drop next to the tall man. "Where?"

Illar laughed. "You're not the only one on their first trip out for *rellaesi*."

He gestured for Elinta to join them, lowering his spear to the ground with the other hand. Eiran scooted over to make room for her and Elinta crouched next to the boy who seemed to be in a permanent state of excitement. A small green-brown nub protruded barely half a centimetre from the snow. The crunch of snow announced that Raisa had joined them. She offered a small, flat-ended stick to Elinta. She glanced between it and Illar's spear. For a moment, she'd thought Illar's weapon was for digging, not defence, but the memory of the mountain cat chased that thought away.

With a questioning glance, Elinta took the stick and at a nod from Illar, started digging at the soil around the small bud. The ground was hard, packed solid from the weight of the snow and the cold. She hardly made a dent. After several more thrusts, she sat on her heels in exasperation. Hardly half an inch of soil had moved.

Eiran looked at her with open confusion. "Why are you taking so long?"

Elinta spluttered. If not for the boy's honest confusion, she'd have been slightly offended.

"The ground's frozen solid," she said, pointing at the soil, equally confused by the boy's reaction.

Eiran's frown deepened, as though that didn't really answer his question. "Can I do it?"

"OK?" She gave him the stick and shifted aside to give him space, but she couldn't see what he'd be able to do differently. The boy stabbed at the ground over and over, holding the stick in a two-handed grip. In even less time, Eiran had matched her effort and then continued on. Elinta's mouth dropped open. The small boy was stronger than her.

Illar chuckled while Raisa watched her son. "It's been a while since our people have worked together. I'd forgotten the differences between us."

"Differences?" Elinta asked. Sure, they looked different, but she hadn't noticed anything that could explain the boy's unusual strength.

"Our race is naturally more agile than yours. We have faster reflexes and are stronger." He nodded at Eiran. "It is a marginal difference in strength, but apparently it still makes a difference."

Elinta recalled the way the boy had jumped onto Zhayra's neck and moved along the dragon as though he was born to it. Is that what Illar meant about being more agile?

Eiran paused in his work and stared at her with his glowing eyes. Elinta couldn't stop herself from staring back. "What else is different about humans?"

Illar chuckled, drawing a smile from Elinta. Raisa ran her hand through Eiran's blond hair.

"You know, to Elinta, we're the strange ones," she told her son.

Eiran scrunched up his face and pulled away from his mother's hand. "I am not strange, *zhatin.*"

He continued stabbing at the ground. Elinta smiled, shaking her head at the boy, and watched as he uncovered a deep red root as thick as her fist and as long as Eiran's arm.

"Wow." Elinta took the weighty root from a smiling Eiran. "How do you cook these?" She paused. "They are for eating, right?"

With their healing abilities, Asali hardly needed medicinal plants. She made a mental note to ask someone about that one day, but maybe not today. She didn't want to overextend her welcome.

"We usually bake them in the fires like a potato," Illar said, filling in the hole they'd dug.

Taking the root from her, Eiran put it in his basket, and they continued searching along the base of the cliff. Elinta spent the rest of the morning searching for *rellaesi* with Raisa, Illar and Eiran, though she didn't do much digging herself. Now that Illar had told her of their differences, she spent time studying them, trying to catch the moments when their agility and strength were on display. But it wasn't the best setting to show it. She did notice that they didn't seem to struggle through the snow as much as her, though that could be put down to experience, and, of course, they had little difficulty in digging up the roots.

Just as they began walking back to the Asali camp with baskets full of *rellaesi*, an enormous shadow passed over them.

"Zhayra!" Eiran shouted, eyes wide as he watched the sleek white form come down to land in the distance.

Even Illar's face lightened when he saw the dragon. Their reactions were in stark contrast to those of her village ... except maybe Blaine. Would he have liked Zhayra? Reality crashed back down on her at the thought of her family. Sighing, Elinta continued trudging through the snow, the Asali in the lead. There was nothing she could do but continue down the road she'd chosen and see where it took her. Hopefully, things would work out. The prince seemed genuine in his offer to help her, but what would happen when they reached the palace in Nevira? She looked up from her feet to see Zhayra waiting patiently for them by the cave opening, crouched low and tail flicking behind her. She looked rather like a cat. Elinta cracked a smile at the sight.

Raisa fell into step beside her. "I know you're travelling to Nevira with the prince, but I hope one day you and Zhayra will find somewhere where you can be safe together." The woman touched her arm lightly. "Maybe your village will be ready for you when you're finished with the prince."

"Thank you," she said, quietly.

She was still so unsure of what she really wanted, but the longer she spent around Zhayra, the more sadness she felt at the prospect of leaving her. Would they both be welcomed together somewhere? Why did things have to be so complicated? Raisa didn't seem to notice her inner turmoil, her eyes fixed on her son who was hurrying towards Zhayra. It struck her then that none of the adult Asali had approached the dragon in the way the children had. They seemed to hang back, faces alight but respect in their eyes while the two children had been all over Zhayra. Eiran reached the dragon and snatched his hand back at the last moment.

"Can I pat you?" he stammered.

Raisa smiled at her son's politeness.

Zhayra lowered her head, amused by the question, and Eiran rubbed her muzzle. "Thanks!"

He ran inside, the basket of roots bouncing in his arms. Funny how he'd spent the previous day climbing all over the dragon but stopped to ask to pat her today. Elinta followed in the boy's steps, running her hand along Zhayra's cheek, and knowing she didn't need to ask. The dragon's eyes closed in pleasure.

"Did you get anything to eat?" she asked even though she knew Zhayra couldn't answer. She just hoped the dragon's contentment was because of a full belly. The others ducked into the cave, leaving Elinta and Zhayra alone and one of her many questions bubbled out.

"Why are you in Eldras?" she asked, but Zhayra's only response was a shift in her emotions, from content to worried, underlined by sadness. Just like she had when she'd asked her in the forest only days ago if she would go home. It seemed like a lifetime ago. The dragon pulled away from her hand.

Elinta sighed. "I don't suppose I'll learn to speak dragon, or you'll speak human?"

A low rumble was her only response. It sounded almost like a laugh. "Well, whatever it was, I hope it works out. For both of us." She scratched the dragon's chin, hoisted her basket into a better grip and followed the others inside.

CHAPTER
EIGHT

T HAT NIGHT ELINTA, PRINCE Lorrin, and the Asali all sat together around the fires, enjoying a meal of *rellaes,* Eiran had explained that *'rellaesi'* was plural. They ate the root with some goat meat from the hunting party Lorrin had joined. It was the first meal they had all eaten together. Ciar had arranged it to say goodbye to their guests, or two of them, since Zhayra couldn't fit inside. Other than Elinta and Lorrin sitting with Ciar and Raisa, everyone sat where they wanted, with no apparent order. The three children ran from fire to fire, their laughter echoing around the cave as they chased one another. The youngest eventually lay down in between two groups and fell asleep, *rellaes* still clutched in his glowing hand.

Elinta kept losing focus on the conversation around her, instead distracted by so many Asali sitting together. There were so many different shades of grey and silver eyes around her that she just kept looking at them. Some were so dark as to match the surrounding walls. Others' eyes, like Raisa's, were nearly as light as their pupils and sclera. It was amazing. The collective glow of the Asali was also distracting. She wanted nothing more than to put all the fires out and see just how luminescent the group was in the pitch black. As it was, there was hardly a shadow in sight. She couldn't be sure, but Elinta suspected the fires were more for warmth and cooking than for light. But she loved the way the flickering light reflected off the *illayas* above and around them. The beauty and strangeness of the Asali and the cave nearly took her breath away.

"You look like you're in another world," Prince Lorrin said from beside her.

She wrenched her eyes away from an *illayas* seam directly above them. The prince's sword sat sheathed across his knees, his plate beside him.

"I am," she said, looking pointedly around them.

Lorrin smiled. "It does feel like it, doesn't it?" he said, glancing around at the Asali.

She lowered her empty plate to the ground. "Have you been here before?"

"No," he said, "I doubt I will be again." At her quizzical frown, he continued, "The mountain Asali rarely stay in one place for long. There are so few resources around. They'll be moving on soon, so this area can recover."

"Really?" she said, but she wasn't all that surprised. Even today they'd only taken enough of the roots to last the group two weeks at most. They certainly weren't storing it up. "How are we going to get to Nevira?"

"I left my horse in Donlee, a small village at the base of the mountains. We're not too far up here, I hope you don't mind walking down?"

"That's fine, I'm not too keen on a repeat of the trip up."

Lorrin laughed, the fire reflecting in his eyes. "I can't imagine why not."

"It wasn't too bad," she said honestly, but then she thought about the stiffness she'd had in her muscles. "Not my favourite method of travel though." It was too cold, uncomfortable ... and high. A horse would be welcomely familiar. She looked forward to using a saddle.

Curiosity flooded his face. "How long did it take to fly here?"

Elinta thought about it. They'd left sometime around midday and flown through the night, slept in the morning, and arrived around noon. She told him.

"Really? Zhayra must have been really moving. It'll take us about two weeks to get to Nevira," he said, poking at the fire with a stick.

Elinta breathed a sigh of relief. She wouldn't need to fly to Nevira on the dragon.

As the night wore on, she found herself staring at the prince beside her more and more, trying to understand him. He'd snuck away from his duties to be here. To work towards a treaty, she assumed his father didn't know about, and the Asali wouldn't initiate. And now, he was helping a girl and a dragon. Who was this young man she'd be travelling with?

She rose early the next morning, finding a fresh set of clothes waiting for her next to her bed and some warm water to wash with. The clothes were identical to the ones Ciar had given her only a couple days before. She slipped into them after cleaning up, leaving her old ones on the furs, and quietly pulled back the curtain. A few Asali treaded lightly through the cave, rolling up their beds of fur and stoking fires. Lorrin was among them, stoking the fire they'd sat by the night before, sword at his hip again. Illar and three other Asali slipped inside the cave with a whirl of snow following them, carrying snow in what looked like buckets made of animal skin. The group dropped their haul by one of the fires. She hadn't thought about where their water came from up here, but it made sense to use the snow. There was plenty of it.

Crossing to the closest fire, Elinta warmed her hands by the growing flames.

"You are up early," Ciar said, appearing beside her.

"I'm used to it." She shrugged. "I used to get up early for work."

"The healer," he said, nodding.

"Yeah." She smiled, aware how useless her job was to them, but Ciar returned the smile kindly.

"You must miss your home."

"I do." She rubbed her arms, trying not to think of her brother.

"Someday you may return there." He touched her shoulder and left her by the fire alone with her thoughts while the rest of the Asali rose for the day.

Elinta sat with Lorrin, Ciar, and Raisa over their morning meal, the last they would have together. Despite only knowing them for such a short time, she was going to miss them and the stability they offered. They'd given her a reprieve, a break from whatever it was that she now found herself in the middle of, and now she was going to leave all that behind in a massive step. She was going to be right under the noses of the royal family, hiding in plain sight. She didn't have it in her to pretend to be excited to leave. Conversation flowed around her, but she only offered vague nods in response. Beside her, Raisa's eyes locked on hers and the woman smiled knowingly, concern in her eyes.

"Eiran, why don't you get the bag?" Raisa called to her son. He and Laira were kicking a small ball by the entrance. Eiran let the ball pass him and jogged to one of the fur beds.

Elinta shot Raisa a questioning glance, but the woman ignored her as her son arrived at her side with a brown pack slung over his back.

Raisa took the pack and dumped it between them. "We've put together some supplies for you and Prince Lorrin." She opened the pack and gestured inside. Leaning over, Elinta saw it was full to the brim. "There's another set of clothes inside for you, some food and a waterskin for when you get down the mountain." Raisa nodded at the prince. "Lorrin arrived with supplies of his own so, apart from the food, most of this is for you."

"Thank you," Elinta said warmly.

She took the pack and plopped it in her lap. With it, her possessions had just more than doubled. She choked back a half laugh-half sob, but she pushed away the lingering sadness and a new sense of determination filled her. No more self-pity now. She'd had her fill. It was time to accept her situation and move on.

"Are you OK?" Raisa asked, taking her hand.

"Yes." She was … or she would be, one day soon.

Raisa gave her hand a squeeze and turned back to her son. "Go get those jobs done before Elinta has to leave."

Eiran nodded enthusiastically and hurried off. Elinta and Raisa both turned their attention to Ciar's conversation with Lorrin.

"I am sorry we could not offer more information on the Asali who was seen among your people."

That's right. She'd forgotten the prince had mentioned that. It *was* a little odd. They hadn't been among humans since their friendship dissolved and all trading stopped. Since the Eggslaying. She sighed. So much had changed because of that.

"That's OK." Lorrin ran a hand through his hair. "I'd still like to speak to your council about it and Zhayra, but I can wait for more information before going to Calaza Forest."

"Calaza?" Elinta stammered. He wanted to go to Liyarna, the Green City?

"I've got to talk to the council eventually," Lorrin said, "but it won't be for a while."

"OK." Did that mean she would go too? If he wanted to tell them about Zhayra, maybe they'd both go with him. She couldn't stay in the palace forever. But he couldn't be going there just because of some Asali walking around human towns and a dragon showing up. Maybe it was about renewing the alliance too.

Lorrin sighed and addressed the group. "We should leave soon. I'd like to get to the base of the mountains by tomorrow, or as close as we can."

It would be quicker to fly, but she didn't mention it and neither did he. She recalled the conversation they'd had about flying, how she'd said she didn't like it, but it wasn't entirely true. She liked the idea of it, but she didn't want to try it again in the near future. The memory of their long trip and her aching muscles was still too fresh, and she really would prefer a way to keep herself on the dragon if she ever slipped. An absurd picture of Zhayra in a massive saddle crossed her mind and she fought a laugh.

"I'm ready when you are," she said, hugging the pack in her lap.

Ciar nodded, piling his empty plate on theirs. "We're sorry to see you all go. You have given us a lot to think about."

"Thank you for helping me." She ran her hand across her thigh. "And for healing my leg." She shook her head. She couldn't wrap her head around it. Healing a wound like that. She'd love to see them do it.

"You are welcome to come back to see us whenever you like. We won't be here in the cave, but we'll find you." How they'd find her was beyond her, but she appreciated the offer anyway.

"Thank you."

"Now," Ciar clapped his hands, "Prince Lorrin is right. It's time for you to go."

Rising to their feet, Ciar and Raisa led them from the cave. Eiran and Laira called their farewells after them and Elinta waved goodbye, slinging her pack onto her back. Lorrin stooped to grab his own backpack from where it sat against the wall and they left the cave, cold air biting at their faces as they emerged. Zhayra was waiting for them outside, her amber eyes locking on Elinta instantly.

"Time to go," she told the dragon.

Raisa stepped forward and wrapped Elinta in a hug. *"Ayzulla,* Elinta. May the sun continue to shine on you."

Unsure what to say in response, she settled on, "You too."

Raisa's smile told her it was the right response. She said goodbye to Ciar while the prince said his farewells with Raisa, using Asalin.

"Thank you, again."

Ciar smiled. "I hope to see you again sometime, Elinta. I think I may be correct in saying you have quite the future ahead of you." He turned his light eyes onto Zhayra. *"Ayzulla,* Zhayra. You have given us much hope. Like Elinta and Lorrin, you are welcome back whenever you desire."

Elinta chuckled at the rush of happiness she felt in Zhayra. "Thank you," Elinta said for the dragon.

"Ready?" Lorrin asked, hitching his bag onto his back. Elinta nodded. "All right." He set off, the Asali cave at his back.

"See you later?" Elinta said to Zhayra. She wasn't sure what the dragon was going to do. If she would follow them or just fly above them, but as she followed the prince, Zhayra walked after them, amused. For every step that Zhayra took, Elinta had to take six steps, smaller than usual because of the snow. The dragon was sure to grow bored with walking soon, but for the moment the three of them walked together.

"I don't think we'll make it to my horse tomorrow, but we'll be quite close," Lorrin said, a few minutes later and half a pace ahead of her. Far below them was a forest, though Elinta couldn't make out what type the trees were. It was just a grey-green blur from where they stood. From her trip up with Zhayra, she remembered it stretched across the base of the mountains as well as on the level ground. If they walked all day, they'd probably make it into the tree line by dusk.

"Will we camp in the forest?" She stumbled in a deep patch of snow.

Lorrin reached out a steadying hand to her shoulder, then nodded.

"I have a spare blanket for you in my bag. The Asali furs would get too hot below the snowline, and you've got their clothes as well." He tightened the scarf around his neck.

"I forgot it was spring," she said, dumbly.

The mountain was so cold, she'd started to think it was winter. Zhayra let out a soft rumble and leapt into the air, snow loosening from her scales and drifting down on them. Lorrin stopped in his tracks, turning a questioning face to Elinta.

"I guess she's bored." She shrugged.

The dragon had been disappointed when she'd realised Elinta would walk down the mountain, but a spark of hope remained. She was sure the dragon would try to get her to fly again soon. Elinta watched Zhayra soar above them, moving a little distance ahead and then circling back. She looked like a massive bird of prey, graceful and beautiful against the blue sky.

"What did you say to Raisa and Ciar?" she asked the prince abruptly, her curiosity getting the better of her. He'd said something to them in Asalin. "It almost sounded like a blessing or something."

Lorrin looked up in surprise. "*Zetayn nalliyan ayn palla kli ayn karn mai ti,*" he said. "It's a blessing their people use at partings. Raisa used it for you in the common tongue." He paused. "I'm not sure where it came from though."

"Huh," Elinta said, still impressed that the prince knew so much about the Asali. She supposed the royals still knew a lot about them, in case they ever had to interact. The language sounded beautiful, sort of rolling off the tongue. It would have been nice to hear more of it. Elinta ran the blessing phrase over in her mind but soon lost the wording.

They reached a steep series of large rocks going down the mountain, and they paused at the top for a drink of water from their packs. The cold water hit Elinta's throat, causing her to cough and her eyes to water. Zhayra landed beside her, forming a deep rut and splattering snow around her. The dragon locked her eyes on Elinta as her coughing finally subsided.

"What?" she gasped.

Lorrin looked up from his pack quizzically. Zhayra looked from Elinta to the rocks they were about to tackle and then back again, her exasperation clear through their bond.

"Oh, no. I don't mind climbing down," Elinta said, putting her water away just for an excuse not to look at the dragon. Besides, Lorrin still had to climb down since Zhayra wasn't offering him a ride.

The dragon snorted and launched away, landing at the bottom of the rocks in only a couple of seconds. She settled down as though to nap, clearly expecting them to be awhile.

Lorrin laughed in amazement. "I think I just witnessed an argument between a girl and a dragon."

"Possibly," she admitted, then gestured at the rocks. "Ready?"

"Ready."

They scrambled, slid, and climbed their way down the large rocks and boulders. At times, Lorrin called back warnings, or helped her slide down, but she didn't need much help. She was only a couple inches shorter than him, so they had nearly the same reach, and he picked the easiest and safest route down, never over-extending. Zhayra had twisted her neck around to watch them descend the rocks. She was clearly exasperated, but also concerned. Her eyes locked on them as they dropped from one rock to another or leapt from boulder to boulder. Elinta smiled at the dragon who huffed at the gesture. Finally, they reached the bottom, slightly out of breath and having gained a few scrapes. Small, scraggly shrubs dotted the landscape around them, thrusting through the snow or at the base of cracking rock showing through the ground.

They pushed on, the landscape an unchanging blank slate of snow with rocks dotted about. Stopping for lunch when the sun was high in the sky, they sat on a pile of rock jutting from the snow. Raisa had packed a small amount of the savoury loaf for them, so Elinta pulled it out of her pack, and they shared it.

"Have you been to Nevira before?" Lorrin asked, taking a bite of his part of the loaf.

Elinta shook her head.

"It's a huge city," Lorrin said, eyes growing distant. "The palace is at the centre with the rest of the city spread around it."

"I've been to Culmar once," she offered, thinking of the bustling trading city by the sea. "But we didn't stop in Nevira on the way there." She paused, thinking back to the trip. "I didn't even see it." They'd gone around the capital city, rather than going through.

"It's even bigger and not as sprawling as Culmar," the prince said. "I think you'll like it."

She wasn't so sure about that. Culmar had been busy, really busy. And while she'd liked it, she'd never seen so many people before. If Nevira was busier ... She shook her head. It didn't matter. She'd made her decision.

"Do you miss your village?" Lorrin asked quietly, blue eyes locked on her face. A rush of sadness hit her, and she tried to shove it away, but the homesickness lingered.

"Yes," she said. Her own feelings of homesickness were joined by Zhayra's. She looked at the white dragon, basking in the sun beside them. How long had it been since she'd seen her own home? Elinta reached out and stroked the dragon's clawed foot.

"You'll both make it home one day. I just need to get more information...." He trailed off, frustration tainting his voice.

But Elinta was flooded with appreciation for the prince. Zhayra turned her amber eyes on Lorrin and keened softly.

"Thank you," she said, pulling her hand away from Zhayra. Raisa and Ciar had said the same thing to her. Even Lorrin had offered the thought before, but she believed him this time. He really meant it, really wanted her to be able to go home, and he hardly knew her. They ate the last of their food in silence together.

The temperature began to drop as the sun slowly descended and they drew ever closer to the tree line. The temperature dropped even further once they slipped under the trees— tall, thin things that stuck up through the snow like towers looking for warmth— but as they walked it started to grow warmer. Their breath still came as vapour on the air, but the snow layer beneath them was steadily growing thinner and slushier. Water soaked through Elinta's boots, and they squeaked with every step. Zhayra was able to walk with them, slipping between the trees and stepping over small bushes.

Just before dusk, they set up camp in the forest. The Asali clothing she wore kept Elinta warm, but Lorrin lit a fire for their meal before setting up a platform by the flames to keep him off the snow. Elinta built a similar platform for herself while Lorrin took care of the food and spent the night curled against Zhayra, hardly needing the blanket Lorrin gave her.

In the morning they continued on, a mindless trek through the forest, only stopping for lunch and the occasional drink of water. That night, they camped in the dry forest, having left the snow behind them in the morning. Lorrin detailed the rest of their trip to Nevira over another meal of *rellaesi*. They'd reach Donlee early the next morning to pick up his horse. From the village they'd cut straight down to Lake Lusinata, then to Nevira, arriving at the palace within ten days. The trip would take a little longer since they had to ride together, but it would be better than walking. When they'd finished their meal, they settled down to sleep. Once again, Elinta slept curled under her blanket next to Zhayra, the prince by the fire and soaking up the heat. She slept all night, pressed against the dragon's side.

At dawn, Elinta and Lorrin shared a quick meal, covered the ashes of the fire, and set off into the cool morning once again. Zhayra walked along behind them, her tail inches above the ground and still as stone. She'd already knocked a tree down with a distracted swipe of her tail; now she moved with extra caution. An hour into their walk, they glimpsed smoke rising above the trees before them and the low hum of voices drifted through the forest.

"We'll go to the other end of the village. You and Zhayra can wait for me in the trees while I fetch my horse," Lorrin said in a low voice, leading them in a wide circle away from the village. "I won't be long."

He left Elinta and a squished Zhayra sitting far off the road.

"What do you think?" she asked, turning to Zhayra. "Do you think things could really change?"

The dragon surprised Elinta by lowering her massive head lightly onto Elinta's stretched out legs and completely covering them. Hope spread through Zhayra. She took that as a yes. A hopeful yes. Elinta ran her hand along part of the dragon's cheek-bone and along one of the three finger-length spines near her jaw, ending in a sharp tip.

"I don't know," she mumbled, thinking of her father's reaction to seeing her with the dragon, of the rest of Kethmere trying to kill Zhayra. But then, there was Lorrin, the crown prince of Eldras. Surely if his feelings could change, so could everyone else's. With a sigh, she had to admit one thing to herself; her father wouldn't change. She was alone now. Just as she had the thought, hoofbeats floated through the air.

Zhayra didn't flinch, and her emotions didn't shift, so she was sure it was the prince returning with his horse. The dragon didn't raise her head until Lorrin appeared through the trees ahead of them, sitting comfortably on the back of a bay gelding. He drew the horse to a halt still some distance from them when it shied nervously, ears flicking.

"He won't come any closer to Zhayra," Lorrin called apologetically.

Nodding, Elinta jumped to her feet. Zhayra couldn't stay with them. The trees were too close together where they were to fly through, so she'd have to follow behind them on foot for some time. "Can you walk through here for a while until you can fly?"

Zhayra grumbled and stood, shifting her wings.

"Thank you," Elinta said, smiling to placate the dragon as she crossed to the prince and the gelding.

Zhayra's only response was a snort.

The bay was a gorgeous animal with a lean, muscular body and three white socks. He was a well-bred animal, and her first thought turned to Blaine. She hoped he made it to Culmar. Maybe she'd see him there when she was done in Nevira.

"Tie your bag opposite mine," Lorrin said, gesturing behind him.

The prince's backpack was already tied off at the saddle, a dark-stained leather with small engravings along the seams. Elinta dropped her backpack and stripped off her warm jacket, but there wasn't enough room for it in the bag, so she tied it at her waist. After tying the pack to the bay's saddle, she pulled herself up behind the prince with his helping hand and rested her hands on his hips. He smelt like wood smoke and the sweet scent of the forest, and she wondered whether she did too. The prince nudged the gelding into a trot and out onto the village road, still under the trees. There was only one other traveller on the road, heading in the opposite direction to them and going into Donlee. Luckily, Zhayra was too deep in the forest to be seen.

Though she couldn't see her, Elinta could feel Zhayra as she walked along parallel to them, easily keeping up with the horse's gentle trot, hidden from the road by the trees. Soon the dragon soared above them, and whatever height she was at, Elinta could still feel her. When they broke for lunch, she stared contemplatively at the dragon soaring over them in lazy circles while the horse grazed beside them. She hadn't been able to feel Zhayra's emotions without touching her back in the forest near Kethmere, now, distance didn't seem to be affecting them at all. How far did they have to be from each other before they lost contact? Would that even happen now?

"What are you thinking about?"

Elinta started at the prince's voice. "Sorry." She grinned sheepishly. "I'm just not used to it yet."

Lorrin followed her gaze up to where Zhayra continued to fly above them in lazy circles. "No. I think that could take some time."

She knew he wasn't just talking about her. He'd said something similar when they'd watched Eiran and Laira climbing on Zhayra. Lorrin didn't seem as nervous around her, but there were times where she'd caught him staring in wonder at the dragon.

"What's it like?" Lorrin said, eyes dropping back to her. "Being able to feel her emotions?"

Elinta thought long about how to answer him. *What does it feel like?* The dragon's emotions didn't feel like her own. Their feelings were separate from each other, that much was clear. When Zhayra was nervous, Elinta didn't feel nervous. She felt Zhayra *being* nervous.

"It's like …" she started, then paused. "It's like a door's been opened between us. I can feel her emotions, but they're not mine … and they don't change mine," she finished, raising her eyebrows, hoping it made sense.

"A door," he mumbled. "Can she feel *your* emotions?" Lorrin glanced back at Zhayra.

"Yes." Until now, she hadn't really thought about it, but she was sure the dragon could. How else had she known when she was in trouble with the mountain cat that night Lorrin and Ciar had found them? She must have felt her fear. Doors were two-way, weren't they?

A flicker of amazement passed over the prince's face again.

Elinta searched for something else to say but was at a loss. What was there to say to a prince? What was OK to say? She didn't want to pry, but most of her questions would be seen that way. She wanted to ask more about his trip to see Ciar, whether it had gone as he'd hoped, except for the part of bringing a girl and a dragon home of course. How much Asalin did he know? Would he be in trouble for sneaking out to see the Asali? But even Galen had had a limit of acceptable questions. She wondered whether the young man before her did too. Giving up, Elinta resigned herself to idle small talk while they finished their meals.

An hour after they'd first stopped, Lorrin and Elinta climbed back on the horse and continued on with Zhayra flying high above them and hidden by the tree canopy. They moved off the road and onto a smaller path, altering the bay between a walk and a trot. They continued this way for most of the day, occasionally dismounting to give the horse named Bentley, or 'Ben,' a rest. Lorrin didn't want to exhaust the poor animal when they both needed to ride it for the next several days.

Familiar herbs and even some fungi lined the path, and Elinta had to stop herself from asking Lorrin to stop so she could collect them. She felt silly for the urge and berated herself, but the habit had been ingrained in her. She didn't need to collect medicinal plants anymore. Not in the way that she used to.

They spent another night under the trees and continued in the morning. The next three days passed in much the same manner, and they only saw a couple other travellers on their way to and from outlying villages. There were several roads that split off towards such villages, but Elinta and Lorrin ignored them. With Zhayra with them and the prince travelling without any guards, they thought it better to stay away from any built-up places.

Lorrin was friendly and always open to talk. He seemed to understand that she didn't want to talk about her home, but Elinta wasn't sure what else to talk about with him. She did remember to ask him about the healing ability of the Asali, but he didn't know any more than she did, which was next to nothing. How could they have forgotten something so huge about their former allies? How much else had been lost over the years? *It's a wonder he even knows some of their language.*

On their fourth day since leaving Donlee behind them, Elinta and Lorrin dismounted Bentley, planning to walk for a while to give the gelding a rest. She was thinking longingly of a bath as she tried to make out Zhayra through the thick canopy above them, but only caught glimpses of the dragon. Just as the trees grew even closer together above them, Elinta felt a spike of alarm from Zhayra and stopped in her tracks.

"Lorrin, something's wro—"

Two unkept men appeared on the road ahead of them. One brandished a sword while the other drew a dagger from inside a long, ragged coat. Twisting, Elinta saw another man appear on the edge of the path behind them. He jumped into the middle of the path, his large frame blocking their way, sword at his hip. Lorrin's hand dropped to the hilt of his own weapon.

"Hello," he called, dropping the horse's reins to free both his hands. The bay didn't move.

"Hello," the man on the left called back in a low, hoarse voice.

The man beside him grinned, showing yellowed teeth. The two looked so similar, with the same stick-thin frames and leering faces, they had to be brothers.

Elinta shifted nervously, very aware of how unarmed and inexperienced she was.

"What can I do for you?" the prince called, voice pleasant and even. Elinta couldn't see her, but Zhayra's worry sat heavily in her mind, just like her own. There was no room for the dragon to land. It was just her and Lorrin against these men and she wouldn't be any use against them. She healed wounds, not caused them.

"What you got in them bags?" the first man said, tilting his head towards the bags hanging from Bentley's saddle.

"We don't have anything of value, just some food and blankets," Lorrin said. "We don't want any trouble."

"Where you headed?" The second man spat on the ground beside him, his threadbare coat billowing in a gentle breeze. Elinta could almost taste the tension in the air.

"The capital," Lorrin said. "I have family there."

Elinta wrung a corner of her shirt around her finger.

"Nevira?" the first man said, grinning widely. "Are you sure you got family there?"

The prince nodded, his hand still loose on his sword's hilt.

"I think he's lying to us, Jed. It'll be trading day in Nevira soon. I think thems got wares to sell." The man on the right swept his dark hair from his grimy face. His brother nodded, eyes never leaving them.

Elinta's heart thundered in her chest, and she checked whether the man behind them had moved. He stood stock still in the centre of the path, eyes locked on her, sword still in its sheath. She turned back to the other men, but now she could feel the man's eyes boring into the back of her skull. She shivered as Lorrin shook his head fiercely.

"We're on our way to visit my sister," he said so confidently that if Elinta didn't know the prince was an only child, she would have believed him.

But the man on the left, Jed, still didn't buy it.

"You've b'n mighty quiet, love. Why don't you tell us what you've got in the bags?" He smiled grotesquely at her.

"Just some food," she stammered. "My cousin just gave birth," she added, hoping to make Lorrin's lie more believable. "She needs help around the house while her husband's away."

"I'm sick of this," the other man snarled. "Throw us the bags and we'll see for ourselves."

Lorrin hesitated, clearly unsure what to do, but he turned and began untying his bag from the saddle. He threw it to the men, who snatched it up greedily. They pulled open the pack and rifled inside. Anger reddened their faces the longer they searched. Lorrin tugged at Elinta's shirt while the men looked away and swapped places with her, putting her right next to the horse. He caught her eyes, then looked at the horse's reins dangling beside them. His meaning was clear. If things didn't go well, he wanted her to mount the horse and get away.

Elinta reached trembling hands towards the reins just as the two men looked up.

"What is this?" Jed said, shaking his straw-like hair from his eyes.

"Food," Lorrin said evenly. "Blankets."

Jed let the bag drop to his feet. If possible, his brother's face reddened further, and he brandished his dagger at them. "Throw us the other bag."

"It's exactly the same."

The man took a step forward, Jed close behind him. "Empty your pockets."

Lorrin shook his head. Elinta fought to keep her breaths shallow, her eyes on the men ahead of them. Lorrin was taking command of the situation. He was forcing their hand now, rather than later. She knew, despite her hope, that they wouldn't have given up on finding something of value on them. It was clear from the way they didn't believe their story of Lorrin's sister waiting for them in Nevira. But they didn't have anything of value on them. At least, she didn't. Surely the prince wouldn't have thrown them his bag if he didn't either?

The yellow-toothed man frowned. "Thought you weren' looking for trouble?"

"I'm not, but you seem set on it," Lorrin said quietly.

Elinta's hand tightened on the bay's reins. Could she do it? Leave him here? A deep rumble like thunder sounded overhead. Zhayra. But the two men didn't seem to notice anything strange about the noise, like the fact the sky was clear and without a cloud in sight.

"Throw us the sword. We need somethin' for this waste of time," Jed said, but his brother continued towards them.

"No." Lorrin's word broke whatever restraint the two men had left, and they charged. Lorrin immediately stepped away from Elinta and the horse. He had just enough time to shout for her to go before the two men were upon him. Elinta swung up into the saddle, shifting the reins in her hands. The horse didn't move under her, perfectly at ease in the conflict. He was more than a simple travelling horse.

Lorrin knocked Jed's sword aside and darted inside his brother's reach, burying his blade a few inches into the man's thigh. He pulled away, leaving the man grunting in pain, and parried another clumsy attack from Jed.

"Hey!"

Elinta startled. She'd forgotten the man behind them. He was closing in on her in long, confident strides. Stupidly, his sword was still in its sheath, but she was unarmed. Elinta's fingers twitched on the bay's reins, and she hoped she was right about the horse. Because she had an idea, and she wouldn't have tried it if the man's sword was out. Just as he drew alongside the horse's rump, Elinta dug her left heel into its side, shifted her seat and pulled on the right reign. The horse swung around instantly, driving its shoulder into the man, and knocking him clean off his feet with a loud whoosh as the air left his lungs.

Not pausing to give the man a chance to rise, Elinta completed the turn, forcing the horse to tread on the man. He screamed as its hooves drove into his chest. She backed the horse up, its ears flicking between the man in front of them and its master still fighting the straw-haired Jed, but it didn't shy. The other man had dropped his dagger and dragged himself off the path, hands pressed against the wound in his leg.

Zhayra growled and the sound of her wingbeats grew louder, but there was no way through the trees above them, not without hurting herself. A growing panic now mingled with her worry. Elinta fought to control her own emotions, to somehow let the dragon know she was OK, but adrenaline was running through her veins. She just hoped the dragon wouldn't try breaking through the canopy.

A loud clang drew her attention back to Lorrin, one eye still on the man before her in the dirt clutching at his chest and wheezing. The prince was on the attack and Jed could hardly keep a solid defence. Sweat was pouring down his face. Lorrin's blade nicked the man's arm, leg, and cheek as he stumbled backwards, only just managing to stop any serious wounds. The prince was an experienced swordsman while his opponent clearly relied on intimidation more than skill. Jed was sloppy; every move looked like an effort. With a resounding thud, the man's sword flew from his hand and landed on the other side of the path among the leaf litter.

The prince stood over the would-be bandit, the tip of his sword against his bare throat.

"Hey!" Jed gasped, eyes darting to Lorrin's sword. "I thought youse didn't want trouble."

"We didn't," Lorrin said, voice hard, his breathing fast with adrenaline.

Elinta checked on the man with the injured leg, but he hadn't moved, and the man she'd trampled didn't look likely to move on his own for a long time. She switched her eyes back to Lorrin. He was backing away to Jed's discarded sword.

He picked it up, his own weapon still trained on the man, and tucked it under his arm. "We're going on our way. I suggest you get your men some help."

"You can't leave us!" Jed shouted.

"I can." The prince backed away from the man still sprawled on the ground, picking up his pack. He threw Jed's sword deeper into the surrounding forest, sheathed his own sword and jumped up behind Elinta. He didn't bother tying his pack beside hers.

"Wait!" Jed shouted. "I know you, don' I?"

"Let's go," Lorrin said quietly in her ear.

She didn't need to be told twice. She squeezed her legs into the gelding's sides and urged him into a canter. Jed's calls echoed after them.

"Are you OK?" Elinta asked, keeping her eyes on the path and her mind away from his hand at her waist.

"He didn't even nick me," the prince said in disbelief, his breathing slowly evening. "Are you?"

"Fine," she said, pressing her legs to keep the gelding in a canter.

Soon the three men were long behind them, and Elinta dropped the horse down to a walk. "Can we find somewhere for Zhayra to land soon?" she asked, switching the reins to one hand.

"Is she OK?"

"Just worried."

"There should be somewhere up ahead," Lorrin said after a pause. "Off the path a little way."

Elinta kept the horse in a walk, giving it a much-needed rest. Sweat had formed along its sides. She gave the animal a comforting pat, amazed at how well it had done.

"On the right," Lorrin said, gesturing to a place where the trees started to thin. Elinta directed the horse towards it. They didn't stop until the path was no longer in view. Zhayra landed immediately beside them with a rush of air, startling the gelding.

Lorrin slipped from the horse first and took the reins from her as she dismounted. Zhayra grumbled and stretched her long neck out to look her in the eye.

"I'm fine," Elinta said, but the dragon's emotions were shifting from worry to annoyance. She hadn't liked not being able to help them. "We're both fine," Elinta said, gesturing at the prince.

Zhayra snorted and held her eye for a moment longer. She knew what the dragon wanted. She wanted them to fly together again. But that would leave the prince alone. Besides, it seemed she was safe enough with him. Finally, the dragon pulled her head away and blew a gust of hot breath over her.

"Thanks," Elinta said.

"I didn't know you could ride like that," Lorrin said, coming to stand beside her. Bentley was tied further back in the trees, grazing on some grass. Elinta thought about what she'd done and shrugged. It had been a simple turn, though she knew her father's horses would never have done it with the man beside them.

"My father breeds horses." She didn't want to think about him right now, but she continued, "He's a farrier too. I've been riding as long as I can remember."

"Well, thank you," the prince said, placing his hand on her shoulder.

She shook her head. "Thank you. From both of us." She gestured to Zhayra.

The dragon was looking at the prince with grateful eyes. She somehow knew what had happened on the path below her, hidden as they had been from the trees.

"We should keep going. It's still a few hours until dusk and I want us to get to Lake Lusinata tomorrow afternoon." He chuckled.

"What?" Elinta frowned at the out-of-place sound. What was funny?

Lorrin shook his head. "It's just the name. *Lusinata* is Asalin for lake."

"It's called Lake Lake?" she said in disbelief.

Lorrin just nodded, a smile lighting his face, and went to untie the horse.

Elinta spent the rest of the day's ride thinking over the attack. Even though she'd taken one of the men out, she couldn't deny that if the horse hadn't been there, or even trained, she wouldn't have been of any use. If they were attacked again, she doubted circumstances would allow for the same move. And who was to say that Zhayra would be able to help next time?

She was useless. Sitting behind the prince again, she thought through her options. Sure, once they reached Nevira she'd be safer, but what about after that? And what if Nevira *wasn't* safe for her, just like it wasn't safe for Zhayra? She hated the feeling settling over her. That she couldn't help anyone. That, if anything, she'd be a burden. No. She needed to learn how to defend herself so the next time something like that happened, she could *do* something. And she knew just the person to ask.

Zhayra curled up by the edge of the clearing they'd set up camp in, leaving space for Elinta between her and the small fire Lorrin had lit to cook their *rellaesi* in. The prince prodded at the roots as they cooked. Taking a couple of steadying breaths, Elinta braced herself to talk to the prince. She was sure he'd see the reason in what she wanted, but she hated to ask something of him. Something more, anyway.

"Lorrin?" she started hesitantly.

"Mm?" He added another log to the fire.

"I've been thinking...."

He looked up at her tone.

"What is it?"

"Would you teach me how to defend myself?" she asked in a rush.

He didn't say anything straight away. Which was good, right?

"I could do that," he said, thoughtfully, "but we'll be in Nevira in two or three days."

"You don't have to once we get there," she said hurriedly, though she hoped he'd keep teaching her. Three days wasn't very long.

He smiled. "We'll see what it's like when we get back. We have a lot to do. But in the meantime, we can start tomorrow at the lake."

Elinta grinned broadly and knew that if Zhayra could smile, she would too, because the dragon suddenly felt very at ease.

CHAPTER NINE

I T WAS MIDAFTERNOON BY the time they reached Lake Lusinata. They'd long left any paths or roads behind and emerged
from the trees to find the lake stretched out before them. It was
bigger than the one where Elinta had found Zhayra, and there
was no one in sight. The closest town or village was a day's hard
riding from them, so they set up camp in the surrounding tree
line. Lorrin unsaddled the gelding and let him graze, lead rope
slung over his shoulder.

"All right," Lorrin said, rolling up his sleeves. They'd long
abandoned their jackets in the hot spring air and sweat beaded

on their skin. "Let's go down in the open and we'll look at some basics."

He led her down to the lake, where the sun reflected off its clear surface. As they walked, Elinta caught a glimpse of a straight scar across his forearm. He'd clearly had it for a while. The colour had faded, but she could tell it would have been painful when it happened. She'd seen a lot of cuts like that in Kethmere from training accidents with Jareth's men or the occasional slip when someone was cooking. It'd been caused by a blade. How had the prince gotten it?

Elinta's stomach knotted in anticipation when they reached the lake and Lorrin turned to face her, the water lapping at the shore a few metres to his right.

"Can you show me a fist?" he asked.

Elinta made a fist, thumbs tucked on the outside of her fingers, and showed him.

"Good." He held out a hand, palm towards her. "Hit me."

She did.

"Again."

Elinta punched the palm of his hand again. Then again.

"OK," he said, his hand dropping slightly as he talked. "Hit with the first two knuckles, otherwise you'll hurt yourself."

He raised his hand again. Frowning in concentration, Elinta punched again.

"Good." He smiled. "If you ever need to punch or kick anyone, aim for here," he pointed at his nose, then between his legs and finally to his knees, "then run. Until you can take someone, it's the best thing to do."

He had her punch his hands again for several more minutes, then switched to practicing kicks at the side of his knees without actually hitting him. He gave her advice, too. Twisting her hip in the kicks and punches would give her more power. If she got the chance, she could punch and then kick before running away. He told her a punch to the jaw was good too, but a punch to the nose would make an attacker's eyes water. After an hour of practice, they trailed back to their camp, grinning, where Zhayra waited patiently.

"I'm going to see if there's anything to trap around here. It'd be nice if we could have some meat tomorrow."

"OK," Elinta said, piling some tinder and kindling together. Lorrin left the camp, sword still hanging at his hip. Elinta drew out a flint and steel from her bag and set to work lighting the campfire. Zhayra watched her as she worked.

"Can't dragons breathe fire?" she asked. Sparks shot from the flint, but they didn't take. Dragons could, that much was known, but was it possible to control a stream that fine for lighting a small campfire? Zhayra made no clear response but stood, shook her body, and stretched out her legs. With another strike of the steel, a small flame lit in the tinder. Adding more kindling and larger sticks, Elinta watched as Zhayra walked away from the camp.

"Where are you going?" she asked, distracted by the fire.

Heat was heavy in the air and sweat started dripping from her forehead within minutes, but they needed the hot coals to cook over tonight. Zhayra kept walking, going directly to the lake. She didn't stop on the shore but slipped into the water and out into the deeper parts of the lake.

"Huh," she said, watching Zhayra's tail slither through the surface of the water. Elinta loaded up the fire with some logs, then trailed down to the cooler air by the lake to watch Zhayra swim. Her movements reminded her of a snake gliding through the water. Occasionally, Elinta caught glimpses of the dragon's legs pushing her along. Zhayra turned, her nose and eyes above the water, the sun glinting off her horns, and locked eyes with her. Elinta smiled at the sight. Something about a dragon swimming was both fascinating and funny to her.

Zhayra dove under the clear water, then reappeared further out in the lake. Elinta looked down at her dirty clothes. A swim would be nice…. The air was hot and sweat clung to her face and clothes. She could have her clothes washed and hanging by the fire and be in her other set before Lorrin returned. Elinta slipped off her shoes and, toes sinking into the sandy mud, walked out into the lake fully clothed. Zhayra twisted in the water and slowly swam back towards her, stopping a few metres out, water dripping from her head and neck.

"I'm coming." She laughed, feeling the dragon's growing excitement.

Her feet left the bottom of the lake, and she swam awkwardly out to Zhayra. She hadn't swum in a long time. Other than the lake, there weren't many opportunities in Kethmere, and that had been too far from town to go to regularly. She'd swum in it once or twice, looking for an aquatic plant Galen had mentioned, but had never gone very deep. When she reached Zhayra, Elinta treaded water, pressing a steadying hand against the dragon's shoulder.

The dragon twisted and swam further out. Elinta allowed the dragon's smooth white scales to slide under her fingers. When her tail slipped into her hands, Zhayra stopped and looked back, mischief lighting her eyes. Elinta tilted her head, guessing what the dragon was thinking, and closed her hands around the tail. Zhayra slithered on through the water, towing Elinta along behind her. Elinta glided through the cool water, a huge grin on her face.

Zhayra slipped under the water and Elinta drew in a deep breath and allowed herself to be pulled down with her. She blinked her eyes open in the clear water and watched plants pass under her, sliding against her bare feet and grabbing at her pants. Just as her lungs started to burn, Zhayra drew them back to the surface, flinging Elinta up with a thrust of her tail so she burst through the surface. Sucking in deep breaths, Elinta released the dragon's tail and floated on her back in a patch of sunlight, staring at the bright blue sky above them. She felt Zhayra move away and dive beneath the water again, causing it to ripple and lap gently against her body. Elinta waited for the dragon to come up for air, but she stayed under. After another moment waiting, Elinta straightened her body and trod water. "Zhayra?"

A burst of humour. Elinta glanced down and laughed. The huge form of the dragon hovered directly below her, sunlight and water playing off her gleaming scales. Zhayra rose slowly beside her, her head breaking through the water and spraying mist from her nose. As the dragon drew level to her knees, Elinta slipped onto her back. Zhayra's excitement grew, and she leapt through the water, sending spray back into Elinta's face. They dove and jumped and floated through the water, and everything around them died away. Elinta's laughter rang out over the shining lake. For the first time, she just enjoyed being with Zhayra and sharing whatever it was that they shared without worry hanging over them.

When the heat had left the air, Zhayra swam back to the shore, water cascading from her scales as she emerged from the water. Elinta's clothes clung to her body and water poured down her face from where her hair stuck to her skin, but she was grinning. In the shallows, she slid from Zhayra's back and landed with a splash, sending water over both of them. Head down, she ran up to their camp while Zhayra shook the water from her scales. Hopefully, she still had time to change before—She looked up and saw the prince sitting by the fire, grinning.

"Uh." She stopped awkwardly, dripping water everywhere. "How long have you been back?" How long had she been swimming with Zhayra?

"Not long," Lorrin said, putting some *rellaesi* in the coals of the fire. "You two looked like you were having fun."

Elinta grinned and trudged over to her bag in search of dry clothes. Now that Lorrin was back, she'd just have to get changed somewhere else. As she rifled around inside, Zhayra bounded up to the camp, spraying water all over the place, and settled down beside her. Elinta laughed at the playful dragon, and Lorrin joined in.

"She seems happy," he said, jabbing at the coals of the fire.

"She is," Elinta said, finally tugging her clothes from her bag. She looked around for somewhere to change and her eyes settled on Zhayra's bulk. Shrugging, she slipped behind the dragon, putting her between her and Lorrin, pulled off her wet clothes, and slipped into the dry ones. They were exactly the same as the other set, but they felt wonderful after the wet clinginess of the ones she'd been wearing.

"I'll check the snares in the morning," Lorrin said as Elinta hung her wet clothes on a low hanging tree branch.

Elinta joined him at the fire, and they talked and laughed while their food cooked. After dinner, Elinta settled in next to Zhayra, tugged her blanket up around her shoulders and went straight to sleep, happier than she'd been in a long time.

Two days later, Elinta, Lorrin, and Zhayra were on the last part of their journey. The prince expected them to arrive in Nevira by midday. At breakfast (a meal of cooked rabbit that Lorrin had snared), they decided to fabricate a reason for Elinta being in Nevira and, more specifically, the palace. Lorrin thought the best idea was to say she was coming to Nevira to learn from a teacher there in the new year, but she wanted to get settled in before she started in four months' time. They'd tell whoever asked that Lorrin, who had run into her on the road and who knows the teacher, had offered her a place to stay in the meantime. He'd also help give her a head start on her studies since he'd learnt under the same man.

Elinta frowned. "But won't someone just ask him?"

"They might," Lorrin shrugged, "but Ford probably wouldn't outright deny it if he knows you're connected to me. He'd come introduce himself and ask what was going on."

"Really?" Elinta's eyebrows rose, but then a thought occurred to her. She'd certainly be suspicious of anyone making such claims … unless someone involved had a history. "Is Ford used to jokes or something? Or do you usually use him as excuses?"

"My friend and I have been caught in a prank or two over the years." Lorrin grinned sheepishly.

Elinta laughed. The prince was a *prankster?*

"He's a bad influence," he added hurriedly, but she didn't believe it. "But Ford would trust that I'd have a reason for lying about this. He'd know it wasn't a joke."

"OK, so if anyone asks, I'm there to learn under Ford …?"

"Mayes," Lorrin supplied. "And I offered to help you. Since Ford teaches history, no one will wonder why we're spending so much time in the palace library, and that's where we'll be looking for information on the dragons."

"What happens if Ford does come looking for me?"

Lorrin waved her concern aside. "He doesn't live in the palace, so it's unlikely to be any time soon, and I'll talk to him if he does." Obviously seeing her alarm, he added hurriedly, "I won't say anything about Zhayra. Ford's a good man, and he won't press."

Elinta chewed at her meat thoughtfully. There were a few holes in the plan, but Lorrin seemed confident in the idea. If she ever did see Ford, maybe he wouldn't ask what was really going on, but she doubted it. Still, this excuse gave her four months in Nevira without having to answer any awkward questions.

After their small meal, they mounted Bentley again and continued on the last leg of their journey, alternating between a trot and a walk. It became more difficult for Zhayra to stay near them due to lack of cover, so she flew high in the sky, looking like a huge bird among the clouds while Elinta and Lorrin rode south on the main northern road to Nevira. Before the sun had reached its peak, Lorrin turned off the main road and headed slightly to the west.

"Where are we going?" Elinta asked, looking back at the road that would have taken them straight to the capital.

"There are some woods near the Afonlin River that Zhayra can hide in. It's about an hour's ride from the city."

"Oh." Elinta's heart sank. She'd forgotten Zhayra wouldn't be coming with her. Well, maybe not forgotten, but the moment had come much sooner than she'd expected. Above them, Zhayra's distant form shifted to follow them, a sinking in her own stomach.

Sooner than she'd have liked, they were plunging into the woods. Zhayra landed behind them, and slithered under the canopy, her heavy steps shaking the branches of the smaller trees.

"Doesn't anyone come here?" Elinta asked, loosening her grip on the prince as he dropped Ben into a walk.

"Not really. There's nowhere to cross the Afonlin here. Everyone goes further down to the bridge. With any luck, she won't have to hide from anyone."

"What about hunters?"

Lorrin shook his head. "No one was allowed to hunt here for a long time, and most people still don't out of tradition. If anyone comes, they won't go deep enough to see her."

They rode further into the woods before Lorrin drew the horse to a halt. Elinta slid to the ground and reluctantly faced Zhayra.

"I'll visit you whenever I can," she told the dragon, crossing the distance between them.

So much had changed between them in the past few days. Zhayra keened quietly. With a final rub of the dragon's muzzle, she turned back to Lorrin and swung up behind him, heart heavy. Now, so close to the city, she hoped they'd made the right decision.

"You can take Ben whenever you want to see her," Lorrin offered, "but be careful."

"Thank you," she murmured as he turned the horse and broke into a trot.

They left Zhayra behind them, but the dragon's emotions continued with her.

At midday, Nevira finally came into view and Elinta forgot the heaviness in her heart for a moment. The city was huge, bigger than anything she'd ever seen. Watch towers stood at the edges of the city, looking out to the north. No doubt there were more to the south, east, and west that she couldn't see from the road. They rode through the outer reaches of the city at a gentle trot along a large, cobbled road made of white stones. Carts and other riders going to various places within the city moved alongside them. Men and women walked along the left edge of the road, some carrying goods, others seemingly out for a walk in the sunshine. She glimpsed a guard milling about the road. He wore the uniform grey jacket and black pants of Jareth's old uniform, but she wasn't sure if he was on duty or not. As the traffic built up, Lorrin drew Bentley back into a walk and turned onto another road.

"This will take us straight to the palace," he said over his shoulder. "But we need to stop and get you some clothes. Human clothes."

She started. Human clothes. She'd stopped thinking of her clothing as Asali somewhere along the way. But he was right. She could hardly turn up at the palace dressed the way she was when they were going to lie about where she'd come from. Her reply was lost among the sights of the city though. Shops, mostly made of a stone slightly darker than the road and displaying various trinkets and wares, lined the road. There were jewellery stores with necklaces displayed in the windows, bakeries that smelt of cinnamon and bread, cakes on display, and clothing stores with dresses and formal attire lining their windows. Lorrin passed all of these by, leading them deeper into the city, until finally the buildings opened ahead of them into a large square bustling with people.

Prince Lorrin stopped the horse outside the square and gestured for her to hop off. He slipped from the saddle after her and dug some coins from his bag.

"Jed was right," Lorrin said, referencing one of the men who'd tried to rob them. "Trading day was soon. Although, it usually lasts until Saturday so ..." He shrugged, probably meaning it wasn't hard for the man to be right. "Horses aren't allowed in the square. Do you think you'll be able to find us once you get some clothes?"

Elinta was still facing the square and her mouth had dropped open. She nodded mutely as Lorrin dropped the coins in her hand. The trading square was *amazing*. There were stalls everywhere.

"OK." He laughed, gesturing towards the square.

She took a step, then turned back, remembering herself. "Thanks for the coins."

"Just don't get lost." He laughed again.

Walking into the square, Elinta doubted she could promise that. It was busier than the docks at Culmar had been on market day in the summer, and she really had gotten lost that time. Stalls filled the square, forming aisles and aisles full of people so that she only caught glimpses of the white stone under their trampling feet. She plunged into the throng, eyes wide.

There were stalls selling bread, cakes and muffins, stalls selling candy, and still others selling fruit. She saw jewellery, horse tack, kitchen wares and cloth. At the first stall she found selling clothes, Elinta stopped to have a look. Ignoring the dresses, she picked out a green short-sleeved shirt and a pair of long, black pants.

"Do you have somewhere I can change?" she asked after paying the stall owner, a plump woman with greying hair who gestured to a curtain against the back wall.

"Thank you." Elinta slipped into the little room and changed out of her furred Asali clothing and into the cotton shirt and the pants.

She bundled up her old clothing, already missing the feel of the furs and the strange fabric, and pushed her way back into the crowd. Retracing her steps, she started back towards the prince on the edge of the square, stopping occasionally to gawk at the assortment of wares for sale. There was just so much here. The Kethmere shops and stalls were nothing in comparison with the small part of the city she'd seen so far. Elinta only bumped into one person before she made it out of the square, but she breathed a sigh of relief when she handed Lorrin the change.

"What did you think?" he asked her as she stuffed her old clothes into her backpack, now nearly empty of food.

"It's busy." She glanced back at the trading square, torn between wonder and dread. She was lucky she'd only gone a few stalls in, otherwise she was sure she'd have gotten lost among the countless people.

"It is," he agreed.

It was too crowded around the square to ride, so they left the market on foot, Ben trailing behind them by the reins. Once back on the main street, they mounted again and continued on, keeping the horse at a walk. People called out greetings to the prince as they passed.

Ten minutes later, Elinta caught her first view of the Neviran palace and, not for the first time that day, her jaw dropped.

CHAPTER
TEN

*N*O WONDER IT'S CALLED *the White Palace*, Elinta thought, staring up at the building. The stone facade was pure white, not quite the same as the stones passing under them, but fainter yet somehow clearer and more beautiful. She counted four levels to the main building, but there was a high tower on the left and right of it. A low barred wall bordered the palace. She gawked at the intricate silver gate as they passed through it and into a stone courtyard. Lorrin steered Bentley towards a smaller building to their left, which she guessed was the stables, though it looked nothing like her father's. It was a light grey stone building, and the cobbled stone of the courtyard continued inside. As soon as they'd halted outside a stall and dropped lightly to the ground, a young boy came out of a side room.

"Can I do that for you, Your Highness?" the boy asked in a high voice, a smile beaming from under his dark eyes.

Elinta almost started at the use of the prince's title. She'd become used to calling him by his name. Would she have to use his title here?

"That's all right, Jae. I think I've got it today," Lorrin said, slipping the saddle from Ben's back.

"OK." The boy disappeared back into the room.

Elinta frowned. She was pretty sure the boy had dropped the title then. What did that mean? When were you supposed to use their title?

Elinta grabbed a brush from the bucket hanging on the outside of the stall and helped the prince brush the horse down before he led him into the stall. Closing the door behind him, Lorrin hung the bridle beside the saddle on a curved bar sticking out of the wall by the stall and led her back into the courtyard after they both shouldered their backpacks.

"I'll have to let someone know I'm back," Lorrin said, "but I was hoping we could go to the library and look at those books."

Elinta nodded, feeling a thrill at the idea of reading about the dragons, and opened her mouth to ask what she'd do while he was talking to whoever he needed to talk to, presumably his parents, when a voice interrupted.

"Oi!"

Elinta looked up to see a young man standing at the top of the stairs to the palace. He wore a collared grey jacket with simple red shoulder lapels and black pants. A sword hung in a black sheath at his belt. He was a soldier of some kind, a guard. The boy grinned at the prince and trotted down the stairs. "You're late!"

A smile broke across the prince's face. "Record timing, Niles. I haven't even been back ten minutes."

Niles ruffled his dirty blond hair, which was a few inches long, straight, and it somehow looked good despite his apparent lack of styling. "You were meant to be back days ago. What's a guy gonna do when his mate's missing?" His brown eyes shone as he pulled the prince in for a friendly hug. "I've been so bored around here."

Elinta watched on from beside Lorrin. The two boys were exactly the same height and she guessed about the same age. Niles pulled away from Lorrin and turned his bright smile on her. He had a small white scar on the right of his bottom lip that stretched with the gesture.

"Hello," he said, reaching out a hand, "and who are you?" His eyes flickered between her and Lorrin.

"Elinta," she said, taking his hand.

"I ran into her on the road, and she needed a ride," Lorrin said, using their practiced story. "She's going to join Ford next year."

Niles's eyebrows rose. "Ah, another history lover."

Elinta nodded, and Niles looked pointedly between her and Lorrin again.

"No, Niles," Lorrin said. "She's a friend."

Elinta's cheeks heated as she realised what Niles was getting at.

"Well," Niles said, drawing the word out and turning back to the prince, "you might want to hide. Your parents have been worried and General Nash? Well, she's not happy."

Lorrin's smile dropped and as if on cue, a woman appeared on the steps where Niles had been only moments before.

"Lorrin Rey!" She had the same blue eyes as Lorrin, and they matched the simple strap lapels on the shoulder of her jacket. It was similar to Niles's but black and, coupled with the lapels, showed that she wasn't just an officer but a general. General Nash, Elinta assumed.

"That's my cue to leave," Niles yelped and disappeared. Elinta watched his retreating form and wondered whether she should follow him, but the woman's attention seemed to be entirely on the prince. General Nash descended the stairs, her sword bouncing against her leg with each step.

"Hello, Aunt Jaida." Lorrin tried to muster a smile.

The woman was his aunt? Elinta looked between them. Other than their eyes, there weren't any obvious shared features. But she still got the general impression they were related.

The woman's eyes narrowed. "Where have you been that you gave my soldiers the slip?"

Lorrin glanced around, making sure no one was close enough to hear, but there were only a couple other people in the court, and they were too far away.

"I er ... went somewhere they weren't allowed," Lorrin carefully said.

General Nash's brow furrowed.

"Somewhere snowy," he added.

Elinta watched the interaction carefully. Clearly, he trusted his aunt to hint about the Asali even if it was a vague hint.

The general's expression cleared. "I see. How did it go?"

"It could have been better," Lorrin shrugged, "but it could have been worse."

"Well, don't do it again." She paused, then added, "Or if you do, take Niles with you."

Lorrin smiled. "Will do." He turned to Elinta, and his aunt followed his gaze. "This is Elinta. Ford's going to take her on next year. I'm helping her study in advance."

"It's nice to meet you, Elinta. I saw Niles around here before; I hope he and my nephew haven't given you too much trouble yet." The woman smiled, lighting up her whole face.

"No, ma'am." Although she suspected that wouldn't be the case for long. Niles certainly gave the impression of mischief, and he and Lorrin definitely seemed to have a reputation.

"Good." The general nodded, then turned back to Lorrin. "You better get inside and see your parents."

"I know. I've got to make a stop by the library first."

General Nash sighed. "Don't be long. I don't want to have to come looking for you."

"Don't worry, Aunt Jaida." He winked.

Nash sighed again. "The twins are inside. I'm sure they'd like to see their favourite cousin when he's got the time, too."

"I'll go see them soon."

Nash nodded in response, then took her leave, striding up the steps and back into the palace.

Elinta didn't know what to say in the wake of Lorrin's aunt and friend.

Clearing his throat, the prince turned to her with a grin. "Well, two down, two to go."

Elinta just nodded. His aunt had been somewhat intimidating, but she liked the woman, and she could tell she was fond of her nephew. A feeling she was certain was mutual. And Niles? Well, he seemed all right.

"Come on, we'll go see what we can find in the library quickly. Then I'll go tell my parents about the Asali."

⚜ ⚜ ⚜

The library was humongous. It was a high-ceilinged room, with rows and rows of shelves lining every spare inch of the room, so that Elinta couldn't stand with straightened arms between them.

"Wow," she whispered.

There were so *many* books. Zhayra's emotions shifted to curiosity, surely in response to the changes in Elinta. Her heart sank. Like the rest of the city and the palace, she couldn't share this with Zhayra. But maybe one day she could.

"Over here." Lorrin touched her shoulder and hurried to the far right-hand corner of the room.

Elinta followed after him, passing the only other person she could see in the room, an elderly librarian with grey hair and keen green eyes. The man sat behind a desk by the doors, sorting through a pile of books. Lorrin waved at the man, but he didn't seem to notice. Elinta mumbled a hello on her way past, but he didn't respond. Shrugging, Elinta stopped next to the prince, who was pulling a small book down from the shelf. *A History of Human-Asali Relations: a Summary.*

"This is one of the only books we have left that mentions the dragons," Lorrin said, opening it towards the back and flicking through to find the right page. "Hardly any have been written since the slaying. We just don't have the information."

Elinta frowned at the title. What did that have to do with dragons? But there was one event involving both their races and the dragons that she could think of.

"Here," Lorrin said, flattening out a page.

Bending over the book beside him, she read a small subtitle. *The End of an Alliance and The Start of Peace; The Eggslaying.* Elinta skimmed the following paragraphs. It contained mostly the same information she'd been told since childhood. How the dragons had killed the crown prince and in retaliation his father, King Cenric, had led an attack against the dragons by sneaking into their breeding cave in the Ash Mountains, slaying the female watcher and destroying all the eggs inside. The dragons had abandoned the mountains and left Eldras. Reports from the following days stated the dragons had settled on a series of islands off the south coast, inaccessible to humans. No one had been near the islands since, and King Cenric later died of his wounds. He was succeeded by his brother who started the celebrations of the Eggslaying the following year.

But one section gave her pause.

'Upon slaying the female watching over the dragon eggs, King Cenric took as prize three scales, the size of a coin. These scales, as of publication 3763, are kept in the White Palace of Nevira.'

The book then went on to summarise how the event had been the end of the Eldrasian friendship with the Asali. Elinta reread the section.

"Are they still here?" she asked quietly, thinking back to Zhayra's white scale that she'd pocketed back in the forest by Kethmere. What had happened to it?

"Yes," Lorrin said, his eyes flickering as he stared at the page.

"What colour was she?" Rumours had said the dragon had been blue or green, but Elinta couldn't stop picturing Zhayra as the female guarding those eggs and being killed for something she hadn't done. For simply being in the wrong place at the wrong time. She wanted the image out of her mind.

"Blue," the prince said, looking up from the book. "I'll show them to you sometime. No one's supposed to see them, but you can."

"Thank you." Elinta straightened, her mind jumping ahead and completely changing topic. "What are you going to tell the king and queen?" she asked before she could change her mind.

"I'd rather wait until we know more, but I can't delay seeing them, and they'll need to know what I was doing," he said. "I'll have to tell them where I've been and why." He paused. "And I'm going to ask them to reopen talks with the Asali because ... maybe the Eggslaying wasn't as simple as we think. The Asali teach that the dragons were sentient, and now we know they're right."

Elinta felt her eyebrows raise. He was really going to tell them about the dragons, but she couldn't help wondering if he was right. It was a bit early to bring it up with them.

Lorrin frowned and ran a hand through his hair as he took in her expression. "I don't know if they'll listen. I don't think anyone's going to believe the dragons were—aren't," he corrected, "animals. But I can at least bring some attention to the idea. We'll keep looking for information on the dragons, and hopefully we'll find something that will change their minds."

She nodded, and they turned back to the book, reading the paragraph through for the third time.

"What happened to him?" Elinta asked. "The prince? How did he die?"

The stories and songs never actually said what happened to him or *why*. No, that wasn't entirely true. She'd heard five different versions of how the prince died, but no one seemed to know the real cause or reason behind it. Everyone said he was innocent, that the attack was unprovoked. But she didn't know if she believed it anymore. There had to have been a reason for the dragon to kill Prince Tristan.

Lorrin shook his head. "I don't know. None of the history books say, and King Cenric never made an entry for the day that it happened. His last entry was a short sentence saying he was leaving to attack the dragons for what they'd done."

"Do you think it really was unprovoked?" she asked quietly.

Sighing heavily, Lorrin stared down at the book for a long moment. "I don't know. But ..." He glanced at her. "It is possible that it was."

Elinta searched his eyes uncertainly, but there was no accusation there. He was looking for answers just as much as she was. But surely ... surely, he was wrong. Zhayra would never do that.

Lorrin watched all her thoughts cross her face. "There could be bad dragons, Elinta. Even if they're sentient."

"I know," she whispered, but she shook her head at the same time. She wanted to defend this dragon, a dragon she'd never met and knew nothing about, but she didn't want to push Lorrin away, not when he'd already done so much, already changed his own views.

"Come on," he said, closing the book and returning it to its place on the shelf.

Elinta froze. "Where are we going?"

"To see my parents," he said, grinning.

Her stomach dropped. Oh, no. That's not what he'd said earlier. She wasn't ready to meet the king and queen. She didn't want to meet them, or anyone really. The fewer people who knew she was here, the better. Not to mention she hadn't had a proper bath in … too long. At least she had fresh clothes on.

"It'll be fine," Lorrin said gently, reading her silence. "Ford takes on students all the time. They won't doubt you."

Her eyes widened. "I hadn't thought of that."

What if the king and queen realised that she was lying about her reasons for being there? And if they didn't believe Lorrin about the dragons, then she could really be in trouble if they doubted her story.

Lorrin placed his hands on her shoulders. "It'll be fine. Just come in with me, and I'll introduce you since they'll know I came back with you. Then I'll speak with them alone and get an idea of where they stand."

"OK," she said, but her voice sounded strangled. With a reassuring smile, Lorrin led her out of the library but just as they were passing the open door of the next room, an excited squeal sounded from within.

Lorrin grinned.

"My parents might have to wait another minute or two," he said right before a blurred figure raced out of the room and latched onto him. A bright face under a set of blonde curls smiled up at him right as another figure crashed into him and attached to Lorrin's other side. Jaida's twins.

"We've been waiting for you!" the young boy said, staring up at Lorrin through a mess of brown hair. His eyes were bright blue, just like his sister's. They looked several years younger than Tully though old enough to have done a couple years of basic learning.

"Have you?" Lorrin said, gaining fierce nods in response. "Do you want to meet my friend?"

The twins pulled away from him and stared curiously at Elinta as though just noticing her.

"Hi." Elinta waved. The girl let go of Lorrin and strode up to her, beaming. Her brother followed close behind.

"I'm Cassia," the girl said, holding out her hand. *Cassia, like the flower.* Elinta smiled and took the girl's hand.

"I'm Elinta."

Cassia ran straight back to Lorrin as soon as Elinta released her hand and practically pounced on him with another hug.

The boy took her place and bowed. Elinta tried not to chuckle in surprise as the boy straightened and said, "I'm Aiden."

"Hello Aiden," she said back.

"All right, you two." Lorrin put a hand on Cassia's head. "We've got to go see my parents."

"Oh," Cassia said, turning wide eyes on Elinta. "Are you in trouble?"

"Cassie!" Lorrin admonished his cousin, but Elinta's face had already heated.

After Lorrin untangled himself from Cassia, the two said their goodbyes and Elinta followed Lorrin back through the palace, retracing their steps from earlier. Even after having seen it all before, she still found herself amazed by the halls and rooms they passed, and she even managed not to feel too nervous about the upcoming meeting.

The inside of the palace was the same stunning white as the outside, though the floor was a pale grey stone laid in squares. The walls were topped with cornices of intricate patterns that she wanted to study forever. They passed down the set of stairs they'd ascended earlier and Lorrin led her towards the centre of the main floor where he paused outside a massive set of double doors bearing the symbol of the royal family. The blossom of the scarlet crown, a tiny red flower of delicate petals sitting upright and resembling a crown, glimmered in the light streaming through a nearby window. Thin spindles of gold were inlaid in the stem of the flower. Guards stood at attention on either side of the door, wearing the same uniform as Niles. *The throne room*, Elinta thought. Sending a reassuring smile her way, Lorrin pushed open the doors and pulled her inside.

Elinta's eyes landed on Lorrin's aunt, General Nash, first. The woman stood on the bottom step of a low dais where two thrones sat, talking comfortably with their occupants.

General Nash turned as they walked through the door, which Lorrin closed behind them. "Lorrin. I was just wondering whether to come and fetch you."

"No need, Aunt Jaida," the prince said easily, but Elinta was hardly paying attention to them. Her eyes were glued to the two people behind the general: King Aldon and Queen Mira. Lorrin had his father's eyes, but the king's hair was a lighter brown that fell down near his face and his slightly lighter beard. A thin, golden band sat on his neatly combed hair. His shoulders were wide, and though he was sitting, it was clear he was tall and solidly built even if he carried a couple extra kilograms. He watched them enter with intelligent, but kind eyes.

"Lorrin!" The queen's soft features lit up as soon as her green eyes landed on her son. Her long hair was dark brown, nearly as dark as her son's, and pulled away from her face. A dainty gold and silver band sat upon her head.

Lorrin led the way further into the room. Elinta fell into step behind him, forcing her legs to carry her towards the king and queen. She tried to school her features. *Why am I so nervous?*

she berated herself. They had no reason to suspect her. No way to know she'd been with a dragon. But her treacherous heart wouldn't listen and pounded in her chest. If they wanted, these people could have her killed. But, if anything, their gaze was kind and curious when they surveyed her.

"Your aunt was assuring us that you had returned and were indeed planning on seeing us," the king said, turning his stern gaze on his son, but his voice softened. "Despite your letter, we were worried when your guard came back without you."

Elinta fiddled with the hem of her shirt, wondering whether she could creep from the room without notice.

"I'm sorry," Lorrin said, flashing an apologetic smile. "I had an important trip to make in the mountains," he said vaguely, but his parent's eyes lit with understanding.

For their plan to work, Lorrin had to act like Elinta didn't know anything about his trip when they were around other people. All Elinta was supposed to know about was his trip to Tremass to see Lord Mayor Harlan and nothing more. The king's questioning gaze flickered to Elinta at his son's words, clearly wondering how she was involved and what she knew. She thought there was a hint of suspicion behind his eyes. Lorrin followed his father's stare. All hope of sneaking out was now gone.

"This is Elinta. I met her on the road back from Donlee."

Elinta smiled nervously. Lorrin's father and mother seemed more confused by his explanation and looked at her curiously. *Oh*, Elinta thought, staring into their eyes, and flashing back to their conversation with Niles, *they think we're together too.*

Lorrin clearly had the same realisation and added pointedly, "She was walking. It's a long trip, and we were both going the same way, and I had Bentley." When their expressions mostly cleared, he continued, "Elinta's going to be training under Ford. I thought I'd help her out."

Elinta breathed a sigh of relief when he'd finished, especially because his parents and his aunt seemed to have accepted his explanation without a problem. If they'd quizzed her further, she wasn't sure she'd be able to lie convincingly. *Convincing people I'm not dating the prince was not a problem I was expecting,* she thought, looking at Lorrin. Not that he wasn't handsome, and he'd been beyond kind to her. She focused once again on not revealing Zhayra.

"That is a long way to walk," the queen said, looking around her son at her.

"Yes, Your Majesty," she forced out. It would have taken her a month to walk that distance if she'd actually been going to. Thinking on her toes, she added, "I'd hoped to find a horse along the way, but none were available. I'm grateful to your son for his help."

"Do you have any accommodation in Nevira? If I remember correctly, Ford doesn't start his students until the second month of the year. That's still several months away."

Elinta began to respond, but she didn't really know what to say. Lorrin had told her she could stay in the palace.

"I thought she could stay here until she moves to Ford's place. It'll be easier for me to help her," Lorrin jumped in, saving Elinta.

"Of course, you're welcome to stay," the king said almost dismissively. He clearly had something else on his mind. "I'm afraid you must excuse us, Elinta. It's been much longer than planned since we saw our son and it seems there's much to discuss," he said, not unkindly. The queen nodded in agreement.

"Wait in the hall for me," Lorrin said quietly to her, a flash of nerves shining in his eyes for the first time. "I won't be long."

There wasn't anywhere to sit in the hall outside the throne room, so Elinta leaned against the wall opposite the huge double doors and replayed the brief conversation she'd witnessed with the king and queen. It had gone well, all things considered. There'd been no hint of Zhayra at all, which meant they were both safe. She turned her thoughts properly to the dragon, wondering what she was doing, she seemed ... bored. Her emotions were flat, neither high nor low. She wished she could be with the dragon.

"Hey El." Elinta jumped and pushed off from the wall, turning to see the prince's friend, Niles, striding down the hall towards her. El? "How long's he been in there? Is it time for a rescue attempt?"

"Not long." She couldn't tell if he was joking or not. Niles rested an elbow against the wall, his hand against his head, and stared at her.

"So," he said, "hungry?"

Actually, she was. She and Lorrin had skipped lunch since they'd arrived in Nevira at midday. She still had her backpack with her, but the only food inside was a small amount of uncooked *rellaes*. Elinta nodded slowly.

Niles gave her a winning smile. "Good, so am I. What say we three head down to the kitchen for some food just as soon as Lor's done?"

"Sure," she said, smiling in return. For a moment she'd wondered why Niles had asked her to join them for a meal. He was so friendly that it was hard to read him, but maybe he just wanted to include her for Lorrin's sake?

Her eyes settled on the red lapels of his jacket. She didn't know what the colour meant. The grey of the jacket meant he wasn't an officer, but the red lapels? Though she'd seen several others walking around the palace with the same uniform, she'd seen several without the red as well. Niles followed her eyes.

"What does it mean?" she asked. "The red?"

"And here I thought you must like a man in uniform." He pouted, then grinned. "It means I'm stationed here. At the palace. Anyone dressed like me but without the red is from the city or somewhere else."

Elinta nodded but decided against asking him any more questions.

A minute later the doors to the throne room opened, saving her from having to think of something to say to Niles. Lorrin didn't seem surprised at the sight of his friend waiting for him. Elinta gave him a questioning look. Lorrin's shoulders dropped slightly, and he shook his head in response to her unasked question. His parents weren't going to seek out the Asali. Elinta's heart squeezed, and she grabbed hold of Zhayra's steady emotions, finding comfort in the dragon. *What now?*

"Food?" Niles asked, oblivious to their silent conversation.

"Food," Lorrin agreed.

CHAPTER ELEVEN

"A ND THIS IS WHERE you'll be staying," Lorrin said, pushing open a door for her. He'd spent the afternoon showing her around the palace before finally taking her to the third floor where her room was. The floor housed the royal family's rooms, the council room, and the guest rooms for when important people from around the country visited. Why she was staying on the third floor, Elinta didn't know, but Lorrin had assured her it was all right, saying it'd be easier for them to meet up and discuss their plans for the future. Whatever those were going to be.

Now, with dusk falling outside, Elinta stepped ahead of the prince and into the room. She inhaled a sharp breath. The room was at least double the size of her room back home. A large queen-sized bed sat against the centre of the left wall with thin silk curtains draped around it. A door to the left led to a bathroom and a fire crackled in the right wall, a beautiful wooden chair sat beside it.

"The window looks out over the front gate and the courtyard." Lorrin gestured to the large window inlaid in the opposite wall. The sill was engraved with the same flower as on the throne room doors: the scarlet crown.

"Thank you," Elinta said, gazing around the room in awe. There was a large built-in wardrobe to her right, near the fire, but she dropped her backpack by the bed. Since she only had the two sets of clothes from the Asali, which she couldn't wear around the palace, and the ones she wore now, there was no need to unpack it.

"I'll make sure you're able to get some more clothes," Lorrin said. "I'll send the tailor by tomorrow and you can work something out."

She spun on her heel to face him.

"You can't wear that every day," he said pointedly, misreading the look on her face. He was right, but she had been going to say that just one other set of clothes would do, and perhaps something she could wear to bed. But she didn't argue the point.

"Thanks," she said again, overwhelmed with gratitude. Lorrin had done so much for her already.

"Did you want to come down for dinner? Or I can have something sent up?"

Suddenly feeling very tired, Elinta stared longingly at her new bed. "Could I have it up here tonight?" she asked hesitantly.

"Of course." He smiled. "One of the servants will bring it up for you soon. Goodnight." He turned to leave the room.

"Lorrin," she called.

"Yes?" he said, twisting to face her again.

"What happens now?" she asked, thinking of his parents' decision not to pursue a renewal of the treaty with the Asali. He understood immediately.

"They were more concerned about me sneaking off again," he confessed. "My father wasn't interested in anything Ciar said. But we'll keep looking for information; hopefully something will come up that they can't ignore," he said, unable to hide his disappointment. "Then I'll try talking to them again."

She nodded.

After saying goodnight again, he backed out of the room, closing the door, and leaving her alone. Elinta stood in the centre of the room and slowly turned on the spot, taking it all in. Her eyes landed on the door to the bathroom. She could really do with a bath.

Crossing the room, Elinta held her breath as she pushed open the door and smiled.

"Yes," she whispered.

A large, clawed bath sat in the corner just waiting for her. She turned on the taps, making sure the water was hot, and waited for the tub to fill. She didn't even want to think what was involved in heating enough water for the palace. Her own home had a very limited supply, and they often heated water on the fire instead of using it from the tap. However, the palace did it, she was thankful.

Once she'd filled the deep bath, Elinta undressed and climbed in, sinking gratefully into the hot water. It'd been over two weeks since the last warm bath she'd had and, after scrubbing herself clean with a luxurious perfumed soap, she rested her head against the tub and closed her eyes. She ran a finger along the new scars on her thigh, still marvelling at how she'd got them. Finally alone though, it wasn't long before her thoughts turned to home again despite all her intentions not to think about Kethmere anymore.

But she couldn't help it. What was Blaine doing? How was he? Were the villagers treating him well even though he was related to a traitor? And mostly, she wondered whether he really would follow his dream and go to Culmar even if it meant their father would be alone. A stab of guilt bit at her. What if he never left Kethmere because of her? She longed to write him a letter, but they'd both be safer if he never heard from her again. Someone could find out, and then what? Blaine could be in even worse trouble.

She submerged her head, scrunching her eyes up against the water's heat and the thoughts of her family. When she re-emerged gasping, she turned her thoughts to Zhayra and the dragon's emotions. She'd continued to feel her throughout the day even though they were so far apart, and she was thankful for it. She didn't feel so alone with the dragon there.

It had been so quiet in the woods where they'd left Zhayra, the dragon had probably scared all the birds away. It would be alive with crickets now though. She could almost hear their drone ebbing and swelling. Elinta sat up with a splash. She *could* hear them. And the gentle trickle of running water. She scanned the bathroom, checking the taps at the sink. They weren't dripping. *Maybe the tub's leaking?* Elinta craned to see around the bathtub, but there was no water on the floor or anywhere other than in the bath with her. Certainly, there weren't any crickets in the room, but they were so loud it sounded like they were right next to her.

Elinta climbed out of the bath, spilling water over the floor as she wrapped a fluffy towel around herself. She cocked her head, listening intently. But now everything was quiet. The steady drone of the crickets had stopped, and the trickling of water was gone. Frowning, she walked around the room, stopping occasionally to listen. But other than the sound of her own footsteps and the water dripping from her and onto the floor, there was nothing. No crickets and still no trickle of water like a river. Had she imagined it?

She waited a moment longer, still dripping water on the grey tiles of the bathroom floor, but nothing happened. *Is it possible?* Elinta tried to think whether anything similar had happened since she'd met the dragon, but she knew it hadn't. They only shared emotions and that dream about Zhayra and the dragon islands. Still, it didn't fit. *I'm just tired. I must have imagined it.* Sighing heavily, Elinta ran a hand through her wet, stringy hair and let the water out of the bath. Drying off, she slipped back into her clothes from the trading square and ran her fingers through the knots in her hair.

Stomach growling, she went back into the main room to wait for her meal, only to find a tray already waiting for her on the chair by the fire. She cast a quick look around the room, but whoever had dropped it off was gone. Picking up the tray, she sat in the chair, enjoying the heat of the fire on her bare feet, and looked at the bowl. It was full of a thick stew, with gravy and spices added for flavour. Chunks of meat and vegetables floated around in the bowl, and she scooped up a mouthful. It was divine, made even better by the fact she'd eaten mostly *rellaesi* for the past several days. Elinta gulped the stew down.

Unsure what to do with the empty bowl and tray, she left them on the chair, intending to find someone in the morning to ask about it. She still didn't know what she was meant to be doing tomorrow, other than the tailor dropping by, but finding herself with a full belly and a lovely room, for the moment she didn't mind not knowing.

Elinta climbed into bed, sinking into the soft mattress with a long sigh and, after sending Zhayra and Blaine a silent goodnight, she closed her eyes and drifted off to sleep.

𖤘𖤘𖤘

Light streamed in from the window and a warm beam of sunshine landed on her face. Elinta was extra aware of her connection to Zhayra as soon as she woke, though she wasn't sure that it hadn't been there when she was asleep. She hadn't seen the dragon since they'd parted yesterday morning, and she wanted to know she was OK. Elinta studied the dragon through their connection. Her emotions felt fine. No pang of sadness or worry. Thinking of the dragon, Elinta remembered the sounds she thought she'd heard the night before in the bathroom when she'd been thinking of Zhayra. She mentally shrugged. Imagination was a weird thing.

With a groan, Elinta rolled onto her back and pried open her eyes. She'd forgotten to pull the curtains closed around the bed before going to sleep, and she looked around the room, taking it all in once again. Things had certainly changed for her; whether for good or ill, she wasn't entirely sure. Now she was in the palace; she'd have to be careful. If someone saw through her thin explanations and lies for being there....

A light knock sounded on the door before it opened enough for a woman, in her early twenties, to stick her head through the gap.

"Ah, you're awake." She pushed open the door and bustled inside with a silver tray of food. "Here you go."

The woman brought the tray over to her before tucking her dark hair behind her ear and starting a new fire to warm the room. Elinta stared at the woman, open mouthed, unsure what to say. The woman was undoubtedly the maid Lorrin had mentioned, but her manner had thrown her off.

Maybe we're not meant to talk? Elinta wondered, staring at the woman.

The maid looked up, realising Elinta wasn't eating, and registered the open confusion on her face.

"Oh! I've done it again, haven't I?" Her green eyes sparkled. "It's so rare that we get entirely new people on this floor. It's always cousins and aunts and uncles and close friends, and I never have to introduce myself!"

"Oh," Elinta said, blushing.

"I'm Neva," she said with a laugh. "And you're Elinta, aren't you?"

"Yes," she choked out.

This young woman was so expressive. Elinta wasn't sure if she found it intimidating or comforting. Elinta settled on it being a bit of both when the woman started pottering about the room again. Finally turning her eyes to the tray Neva had brought, she found a fresh roll that looked slightly sweet and twisted into a knot, a small dollop of butter and three different jams to choose from. She ate with relish, finding the roll the perfect balance between sweet and savoury.

"How long have you worked here?" Elinta asked Neva between bites of the roll.

"Oh, about seven years, I think," Neva said without pausing as she swept near the fireplace. "I was fifteen when I started here."

She took another bite of her toast. "Really?" That would make the woman six years her senior.

"It's a lovely place to work. Everyone here is so kind. Well, not *everyone*. Mrs Triggs can get a bit funny when she's stressed, but then who doesn't? So, I suppose everyone here *is* kind."

Elinta hardly had time to acknowledge Neva's words before the woman continued on, telling her about the time a friend of the queen's had brought her family with her to stay at the palace for a month, and Mrs. Triggs had fluttered about the castle in a mess because the party had arrived with one more person than expected and not enough rooms had been made up for them.

"Poor thing was so red in the face, she looked like she was going to have some kind of episode. She didn't, thank goodness, but I'm sure she was close to it."

There was a tug of amusement from Zhayra, startling Elinta. What was the dragon up to? Had she felt ... whatever it was Elinta was now feeling and reacted to that? *This is confusing.*

The maid continued talking, and Elinta suspected the woman would eventually ask about her trip with the prince. If rumours of them travelling together had spread, Neva was sure to know and even surer to ask, judging by her constant talking.

But Neva soon scooped up the tray Elinta had left on the chair from her meal the night before, then apparently seeing she'd finished with her breakfast, took that tray as well. "All done then?"

"Yes, thank you."

Neva nodded and walked straight out the door.

"Bye?" Elinta stared at the door the maid had closed behind her. What an ... odd woman. But she found she liked her, and it seemed that no one was wondering why she was there. After all, her and Lorrin's story about Ford was a seemingly legitimate reason for her to be in Nevira and even to be in the palace.

With that in mind, Elinta climbed out of bed and straightened her rumpled clothing. She slipped into the bathroom to freshen up, then stood uncertainly by the fire. She didn't have any more clothes. What was she supposed to do now? As if in answer to her thought, there was another knock on her door.

She pulled it open, expecting to see Lorrin or Neva, but it was a middle-aged woman in a fine shirt and silk pants, her blonde hair tied back in a bun.

"Hello," Elinta said, staring at the notebook, pen, and tape measure in the woman's hands.

"Good morning," the woman said, stepping inside as soon as Elinta moved from the doorway. "My name is Kalla. I'm the head tailor for the palace. Now, Prince Lorrin asked me to stop by. He said your luggage was lost on the road and you don't have any clothes?"

Elinta nodded, glad that Lorrin had thought up a reason for her lack of belongings, since she didn't know what she would have said if asked.

"All right. Let's get some measurements."

The woman spent the next several minutes taking notes of Elinta's measurements, checking her arm length, leg length and width, her hips, her torso, her chest. On and on it went. Elinta couldn't see why she couldn't just go down to the trading square and buy some clothes there, but she thought Kalla might be offended by the idea, so she kept it to herself. Kalla seemed proud of her job.

"Turn," the tailor said, twisting Elinta's body so her left side was to the woman. She wrapped the tape around Elinta's thigh.

"There," Kalla said, making one last annotation on her notebook and rolling up the tape. "What you're wearing will have to do you for now, but I'll have some clothes to you by the end of the day. Your gowns won't be with you until the week they're needed."

"Gowns?" She frowned. What gowns?

Kalla fixed her with a confused stare. "Yes, your gowns. I'm told you'll be with us until you start with Mr. Mayes in the new year."

Elinta continued to frown. What did that have to do with gowns?

Kalla let out an exasperated sigh. "The king's birthday is fast approaching, child. Not to mention you'll likely be with us for the Eggslaying festivities in January since Mr. Mayes won't want you until February. You can't very well go to such events dressed like that." Kalla pointed at her rumpled clothing. "Especially as a guest of the prince."

Elinta ran a self-conscious hand over a large crease by her hip.

"Oh." She was invited to the king's birthday?

"Yes." Kalla then repeated, "Gowns."

There was another knock on the door, causing Elinta to jump. She desperately hoped it was Lorrin and not someone else coming to poke and prod at her. Kalla opened the door for her, but Elinta couldn't see who it was around the woman's figure. The tailor gave a quick bow of her head. "Your Highness."

"Good morning, Kalla. We can come back if you're not done?" came the prince's questioning voice. Elinta nearly sighed with relief.

"No need, Your Highness. I've just finished." Kalla looked back at Elinta. "I'll see you again soon." With another bow to Lorrin, the tailor slipped out the door.

A rush of air left her once the woman was gone. Between her and Neva, Elinta had hardly had any time to collect herself. A light chuckle sounded from the door and Lorrin stepped into the room, Niles's bright face appeared behind him in the doorway.

"Kalla's not that bad," Lorrin said, obviously seeing her relieved expression. His clothes seemed a little tidier today, a bit more formal, but somehow, he still managed to seem casual. She smoothed out another wrinkle in her shirt.

"No, I know. It's just ..." she trailed off awkwardly, but Lorrin seemed to understand anyway. It was a lot to take in. Everything. And she'd been awake for barely an hour and already things were moving along quickly. Gowns, though? She shoved the thought away.

Niles pushed his way into the room. "He's lying. She *is* that bad. We've come to rescue you!" He was wearing the same outfit as when she'd last seen him, the high collared grey uniform jacket with the red shoulder lapels and dark pants. Hadn't he said something about rescuing the prince from his parents the day before?

"Thanks?" she said, raising an eyebrow.

"Can we go now?" Niles bounced on his toes. Lorrin cocked an eyebrow at his friend but turned back to her.

"Since you haven't seen much of Nevira, I thought you might like to see the city today?"

"We," Niles corrected, and Lorrin shook his head.

"I'd love to," Elinta interrupted, seeing Niles about to argue further. It'd be nice to get out of the palace. Although she hadn't even been there a full day, she already needed some space. Even if that meant Niles came too. And they could always go to the library tomorrow.

"Let's go." Niles pivoted on his heel and left the room.

Elinta stared after him and a startled laugh escaped her. He was just so odd. Lorrin gestured for her to go ahead of him, then closed the door behind them.

The city was amazing. Even going down the same streets they'd walked on and ridden through the day before, Elinta was impressed. Lorrin and Niles led her back to the trading square where the market was still set up and booming with people.

"Don't get lost," Lorrin said, repeating his words from yesterday as they plunged into the crowd. But he and Niles stayed close beside her as they made their way among the stalls, going further in than she'd gone before. They stopped occasionally to look through stalls and to chat with the owners. Everyone, naturally, knew the prince, but they even seemed highly familiar with Niles. The more time she spent with the two, the more she realised that her suspicions had been correct. They did seem to have a reputation, Niles in particular. He flattered every woman he saw, especially a plump woman in her early thirties who owned a stall selling small cakes. He came away with three slices of chocolate cake, one for each of them, and a huge smile on his face. The cake melted in her mouth.

After seeing the way he spoke and charmed other women, Elinta found herself a little more comfortable around Niles. He did it in a playful manner and though they enjoyed it, no one seemed to take him too seriously. He wasn't inappropriate and he flattered himself as much as he did the women when he spoke to them. By the time they were ready to leave the market to go further into the city, Elinta had decided to do the same as the others and not read into anything he said.

Elinta took one last glance back at the bustling crowd in the square as they left and stopped in her tracks. The close-knit bodies had parted for a moment, revealing a strange, cloaked figure. Not an inch of the person's skin was visible, though he wasn't facing her way, she could see that even his face was hidden in the depths of the cloak. Something about the way the person held themselves told her it was a man. There were a number of reasons a person could dress like that, the most likely being some form of sickness, but the sight filled her with a deep sense of foreboding that she couldn't explain.

"Lorrin." She turned to the prince.

He was walking towards her as though just realising she'd stopped. "What is it?"

"Over there," she said, spinning back around to point. But the cloaked figure was gone. She frowned. "Never mind," she mumbled.

Lorrin would probably have explained away the strange attire of the man anyway. Maybe he *was* sick. But he hadn't been stooped, and his gait had been strong. Shaking her head at her own jumpiness, she followed Lorrin and Niles from the square.

They had lunch in the large bakery off the main road that she'd seen the day before. It was almost filled to the brim with patrons, some sitting down over a meal and others ordering breads, cakes, and pies. Her mouth had started watering before they'd even entered the building. A small, skinny man from behind the long L-shaped counter called out a greeting and told them to take a seat wherever they liked, he'd be with them in a moment.

"That's Merton Alvey, the owner," Lorrin said, pulling out a seat for her. She ignored Niles's sad expression and took the seat. Niles seemed disappointed Lorrin had got there first.

"His wife is the one who gave us cake," Niles said, leaning in conspiratorially and sending a glance Merton's way as the man headed towards them. Niles sat back in his chair, wiping the smile from his face, just as the man arrived.

"What can I get for you, Your Highness?"

Elinta hid a smile. He had flour all through his thin moustache, so much so that if the hair on his head wasn't brown, she'd have thought the man had gone prematurely grey.

"Three of the usual, Merton. And I think I've bought enough of your pies that you can call me Lorrin."

Merton smiled but shook his head. "Afraid not, Your Highness. I guess you'll have to keep coming back." The man glanced around the table with a smile, but his eyes narrowed when he saw Niles's face. He was trying, and failing, to look innocent. Elinta watched the man curiously.

"You've been charming my wife again, haven't you?"

"No, sir." Niles shook his head, but Merton cocked an eyebrow. "Yes, sir."

A large grin broke out across the man's face, dislodging flour from his moustache.

"That woman is too good a baker for her own good." Merton shook a wooden spoon in Niles's face. Elinta had no idea where it had come from. The spoon hadn't been in his hand a moment ago. Niles smiled and winked at Elinta as the man twisted to face her. "You're doing very well putting up with him." Merton gestured with his head at Niles, who gave him an affronted look.

"Yes. I know," Elinta agreed without a moment's thought.

Niles put a hand to his heart in mock offence, and she and Lorrin laughed while Merton left to get their order ready. The three of them fell into comfortable silence, and Elinta took the opportunity to look around the bakery. Several glass displays were set under the counter, with the shorter leg of the 'L', the part facing them, containing savory rolls and loaves of bread covered in herbs and spices. At a table nearby, a man and a woman shared a large meat and herb pie while a boy at a corner table was practically inhaling a slice of cake. All around them were people eating and ordering breads, pies, and cakes. It all set her mouth watering again.

"Here you go." Merton appeared beside their table balancing three plates and placed one in front of each of them. They each held a large pie, with crispy golden pastry and a sprinkle of herbs across the top. Elinta took in a deep breath of the scent of warm pastry, meat, and herbs through her nose and picked up the cutlery beside her plate.

"You're the best," Niles said, sighing happily as he picked up a knife and fork.

Elinta nodded her agreement, sure the pie was going to be delicious. Lorrin handed Merton a few coins. The bell at the counter rang and the baker was off again.

By the time Elinta was ready for her first bite of the pie, Niles was already halfway through his. She blew on the meat and pastry and stuck it in her mouth. A burst of flavour in the meat of sharp herbs mixed with a soft sauce hit her. She followed Niles's and Lorrin's examples and dug in. Their silence was broken only by Niles's exclamations of delight as the three of them shovelled food into their mouths. She could definitely understand why the two of them came here. The pie was delicious.

"That was good," Niles said, leaning back in his chair and smacking his lips.

Elinta nodded, putting her cutlery down on the plate.

"I'm gonna get one for the road," Niles said, springing from his chair and hurrying to the counter.

Lorrin laughed and finished the last bite of his pie. Elinta twisted to face him. Now was the perfect time to talk to him, with Niles out of hearing range. She'd been thinking about it all day but hadn't had a chance to speak with him. Now was the time, before she could get too worried about bothering him.

"Would—" she started, then changed her mind. "Could you still teach me to fight?" They'd talked about it days ago when she'd first asked him, and he'd said he might be able to continue in Nevira if he had time, but he hadn't brought it up again.

Lorrin looked at her in surprise, and she realised exactly what she'd said. At Lake Lusinata, she'd asked him to teach her to 'defend' herself, but this time she'd said, 'fight.' But that didn't seem to be what had surprised Lorrin.

"Of course. I thought you'd want some time to settle in, but we can start whenever you're ready."

"I ... I don't want anyone to know about it. I don't want to draw any attention to myself." *Or Zhayra,* she mentally added, thinking about the dragon waiting for her in the woods. Surely it would be considered strange if a history student started learning to use a sword.

"Yeah, I think that's probably a good idea." Lorrin watched Niles as he ordered something from Merton. "When do you want to start?"

"Tonight." The word was through her lips before she could stop herself. She didn't mean to rush him, but she just wanted to get over the feeling of helplessness. She wanted to know how to defend herself properly. She wanted to be capable. To fight. Especially if her life was going to continue being the way it was now for a while yet. Zhayra was a magnet for trouble, and she was alone for the first time in her life.

"OK." A smile broke out across Lorrin's face. "You're serious about this." It was a question, but a statement at the same time.

Elinta nodded but before she could say anything else, Niles appeared at their table, a bag in hand.

"What did you get?" she asked him curiously, staring at the bag. Niles clutched it tighter to himself.

"Cake."

"Of course, you did," Lorrin muttered, pushing back his chair. "Ready to go? There's more to see."

Elinta jumped to her feet and followed the boys out of the bakery, ready to see the rest of the city.

꧁꧂ ꧁꧂ ꧁꧂

After dinner that night, Lorrin dropped by her room to take her somewhere they could train. True to her word, Kalla had sent some clothes up to her room, which Elinta found waiting for her on her bed. From these, she'd changed into a loose pair of pants that looked easy to move in and a grey cotton shirt. Now, she walked beside Lorrin as he led her down the hall outside her room.

"Where are we going?" she asked, eyes roaming the artwork strung along the walls showing previous royals, their families, or locations across Eldras. She recognised the White Mountains in one painting, their peaks hiding in a low cloud line.

"There's a couple of private rooms we use for training on this floor. I thought we'd go there instead of the more public ones on the top floor." That sounded good to her.

A few minutes later, Lorrin was leading her into a private room off a small corridor that connected to the main one on that side of the palace. It was slightly bigger than her bedroom and someone had covered the stone floor in mats that sunk ever-so-slightly under her feet as she walked in. A door sat in the wall in the corner, which she supposed led to a storage room.

"Here we are," Lorrin said, stretching out his arms.

Nerves tugged at her stomach, a feeling that was instantly mirrored by Zhayra. Not for the first time, she wondered how the dragon was doing by herself and whether she was just responding to Elinta's emotions, or something was happening where she was to make her feel that way too. If only there was some way to tell. *Something else to practice,* Elinta thought, then looked around the room again.

"It's great," she said to Lorrin, thinking how empty the little corridor had been. The likelihood of someone walking in on them was slim. Lorrin rolled up his sleeves and gestured for her to move into the centre of the room.

"Let's go over what we've already done first, and we'll go from there," he said, holding up his hands as a target. Elinta punched his palms in time to his count, then swapped to a jab-punch combination. Occasionally, he corrected her stance or told her to turn her hip into it more, but already she could see improvement since that first session by the lake. She grinned and immediately felt Zhayra's mood lighten, once more mirroring her, confirming the dragon did respond to her.

They moved on to some kicks, and her grin widened as Lorrin taught her more variations. She loved it. After an hour, Lorrin told her to stop and jogged over to the other door. He ducked into the room beyond, and she tilted her head, wondering what was in there. Her question was answered when he emerged again, a wooden sword in his hand.

She watched him part in anticipation, part dread. Surely, she wasn't ready for that? She'd hardly thought about training with a sword, even if she'd secretly hoped he'd teach her some basics.

"All right." He held the sword out to her, and the light caught on a small leather loop under its crossbars. "Put this on your belt."

Frowning, she took the wooden sword from him. It was surprisingly heavy, and she slipped it over her belt. Lorrin smiled at her confusion.

"It's to help you get used to the weight of it." He patted the sword at his own hip. "Otherwise, it can throw off your weight. My first teacher made me walk around with one for weeks before he even allowed me to use it." He laughed, lighting up his face.

Lorrin clapped his hands and raised them in front of him again. "Let's start over."

Elinta punched his fist and saw what he meant immediately. The weight dragged on her hip, and she felt the way her body sat differently with it there, the way she had to move differently to accommodate it.

"See?" Lorrin said.

She nodded and punched again. And on it went for another half hour until sweat had beaded on her forehead and her muscles were starting to ache. A deep satisfaction had settled over her in a way she hadn't known since the early days of her apprenticeship when things were still new to her, and she learnt every day.

Lorrin finally put the wooden sword away, and they crossed the room to peer through the door to see if it was OK for them to leave. Elinta stood behind the prince, listening.

"Wait," he murmured, and carefully closed the door. "Shae just turned into the corridor."

"Shae?

"An advisor."

"Will she come in here?" Elinta breathed. What would they say if she found them? There wasn't anywhere to hide other than the storage room, and odds were that's where a person would look. Elinta's breath quickened.

"I don't think so," he said.

They waited in silence, but it was hard to know what the woman was doing. They couldn't hear anything in the corridor with the door closed. After one long minute, Lorrin opened the door a crack again and checked for any sign of the woman.

"Empty," he said after a moment, and opened the door fully. Breathing a sigh of relief, Elinta followed him.

"That was close," she said as Lorrin walked her to her room.

"It shouldn't happen again," Lorrin said with a frown. "It's usually pretty quiet there."

"Thank you for tonight," Elinta said outside her door.

"You're welcome. I'll see you tomorrow," he said, then paused as he turned to go. "I always go for a run in the mornings," he said, watching her face. "You're welcome to join me, if you want."

Elinta smiled and nodded. "Yeah, that would be great."

"OK. See you in the morning," he said and left her outside her door. She watched his back as he walked down the long hall, grateful for his willingness to spend time with her, grateful for his friendship and happy to have something to do to help fill her time with.

That night as she lay in bed with nothing to distract her again, her thoughts turned back to Zhayra. She'd have to visit the dragon soon. It'd already been a couple days since they saw each other last and a heaviness was sitting in her heart, a heaviness she felt in Zhayra too. Somewhere along the way, they'd become so used to each other that being apart was hard. She found she was grateful for that friendship too. Tomorrow. She'd visit her tomorrow.

CHAPTER
TWELVE

E LINTA ROSE EARLY IN the morning and pulled on the pants she'd worn training with Lorrin and grabbed a shirt from the wardrobe where she'd packed all her new clothes away. She pulled on her old boots, ignoring the new ones in her wardrobe for fear of blisters. Not knowing when Lorrin would come by to collect her for their run, she sat on her bed and waited. If only there was a way she could tell Zhayra she'd be visiting her in the afternoon. They could only communicate so much through their emotions; it was like a guessing game. But she'd see her soon, so it didn't matter too much.

A knock sounded at her door. Sliding off her bed, Elinta hurried to the door to find Lorrin ready and waiting for her. He wore a light cotton shirt with short sleeves and a pair of loose pants sitting over his boots. His eyes travelled over her own outfit. "Ready?"

"Yep." She closed the door behind her, and they made their way to the bottom floor. She fought the urge to ask him about his plans with the Asali as they walked. She couldn't afford for someone to overhear her. The area around the front of the palace was clear of any buildings or structures so that anyone approaching could be seen well before they reached the gate. Elinta assumed it was the same all the way around the palace since it was in the centre of the city, but when Lorrin led her to a small door on the south side of the building, she wondered whether this was true. Where exactly did he run in the mornings? He couldn't just run through the city, could he?

He pushed open the door and a gentle breeze brushed against her face. Peering around him, Elinta saw a garden. A beautiful garden with manicured grass and tall trees, trimmed hedges, and flower after flower. She recognised some of them from her work with Galen, while others were purely pretty to look at, and others still she didn't recognise at all. It was all protected by a stone wall.

"You run in the palace garden?" she said in surprise.

Lorrin laughed. "I do. There's not really anywhere else to go. I used to run the halls when I was a kid, but that didn't work out."

She trod softly through the door, the grass spongy under her feet, and looked around in awe. Her eyes landed on the first patch of scarlet crown she'd ever seen. The little flower grew in small clumps, each plant only supporting five to six flowers on their long stems. For generations only the royal family were allowed to grow them, and people still kept to the tradition today.

Making a mental note to come back and look around later, she faced Lorrin again. "Where do we start?"

Without another word, Lorrin broke into a jog along the right wall and Elinta hurried to catch up, studying the plants around them as they went.

"I have a few things to do today," Lorrin said after they'd been jogging in silence for several minutes. "I won't be able to see you until dinner."

Elinta's stomach sank. She'd thought he would be free today. It was the weekend, but he had spent yesterday with her. Elinta hadn't really thought she might be left alone in the palace. She should have known he'd have other things to do than search books with her.

"That's OK," she said, her voice bouncing as her feet hit the ground. "I ... I'll go to the library for a little while. There should be something there to help with your parents. And I thought I could see Zhayra today?"

He'd offered her the use of his horse before, but she wanted to make sure the offer still stood.

"You can take Bentley if you want. I won't need him today."

"Thank you," she said.

Lorrin upped the pace, breaking into a run. Elinta lengthened her strides and ran beside him.

They alternated between a run and a jog for the next forty-five minutes and though Lorrin ran beside her the entire way, and even walked with her for a couple minutes before pushing her back into a jog, she was sure he had dropped his usual pace so she could keep up. As it was, she was puffing hard when they finally came to a stop and stretched out their legs. She'd never thought of herself as unfit since she walked so much around Kethmere collecting and delivering medicines, but running with Lorrin had shown her she wasn't entirely fit either.

"Want to join me again tomorrow?" Lorrin said, his breathing only slightly faster than normal. Her own breaths were still heaving.

"Yeah," she said, surprising herself. "Yeah, I do."

After a quick scrub and change, where Elinta noticed Neva had dropped by to light the fire and take her washing, Elinta met Lorrin in the main dining hall with Niles, who'd come to the palace early. The three of them ate breakfast together, sitting on a bench at one of the long tables. Apparently, the royal family had a private room where they could eat, but when his parents were busy with work, Lorrin liked to sit with Niles, who was up for a free meal whenever he could get one.

Elinta found herself watching the two of them again while they ate breakfast opposite her. Niles didn't live in the palace; she'd found out when they'd shown her around the city. He'd pointed down one of the roads not far from the palace and told her he lived down there with his father. But, for the amount of time he spent in the palace between his work as a guard and his friendship with the prince, he might as well live there.

"What?" Niles asked, spoon halfway to his mouth. He'd caught her staring at them. "I know I'm attractive, but there's no need to stare."

Elinta choked on the sip of water she'd just taken, and Niles cracked a knowing smile.

"No, I was just wondering how you two met," she said.

Niles frowned. "You don't think I'm attractive?"

Rolling his eyes, Lorrin elbowed his friend and answered her question, saving her from replying. "Niles's father is one of our top generals. He's always around and he used to bring Niles with him as a kid." Lorrin shrugged. "We spent a lot of time together, grew up together. There weren't a lot of kids in the palace."

"Oi! You make it sound like you just got stuck with me," Niles said, spoon still hanging in the air.

"I did," Lorrin said with a wide grin.

Niles's eyes narrowed at the prince. "Maybe I'm the one who got stuck with you." He put the spoon to his mouth and ate in silence, frowning comically at Lorrin. The prince just shrugged.

Elinta fought a laugh and asked, "How long have you known each other?"

"Fifteen years?" Niles said, drawing the words out.

Lorrin nodded thoughtfully. "Yeah, that sounds right."

Elinta's eyebrows rose. "You would have been toddlers." That explained their brotherly bond.

"Nah, I wasn't a toddler. Unlike him." Niles gestured to Lorrin with his head. "You should have seen him, running around in his nappy, food all over him." He shook his head at the memory.

"Niles," Lorrin said in exasperation, "you're only a year older than me."

"It's enough, Lor. It's enough."

Lorrin tactfully changed the subject. "Do you remember how to get to the library?" he asked Elinta.

"I think so," she said. It was on the second floor, on the east of the building.

"All right. I've got to get going." Lorrin stood. "See you both at dinner," he said, and left the hall.

"Well, as entertaining as the library sounds," Niles said, pushing back his empty bowl. "I'm on duty in ten minutes. I better go, El."

She watched him leave, realising the nickname he'd given her was going to stick, but she didn't mind. It'd feel strange if they used the shortening of her name that her brother used. 'Lin' wouldn't seem right coming from Niles or even Lorrin. No, she liked 'El.'

Other people within the hall started to leave as well. It seemed as good a time as any to head to the library. She didn't know what she'd find there, or even what to look for, but she didn't have anything else to do until she'd go see Zhayra. Elinta retraced her steps to the main staircase and hurried up to the second floor, her eyes wandering over the paintings and cornices as she went. She had to follow the exact route that Lorrin had taken her the day they'd arrived, but eventually she found the library.

The librarian was nowhere to be seen, so Elinta went straight to the shelf Lorrin had taken her to and searched for the book he'd shown her, something about Asali relations. There! She pulled the tiny book down from the shelf. Carrying it to a chair by a nearby window, she sat down and flicked open the book. Information on the Asali was so hard to come by, and she wanted to learn more about them, but looking at the small book in her hands, she wondered just how much there was on them. She shrugged and started at the first page, *Appearances and Origins.*

> *'First contact with the Asali is believed to have oc-curred in the year 400 between Edwin Coombs, an ancestor of the human royal house of Rey, though a silversmith at the time, and a warrior of the Asali. Edwin named her as Lila. Lila led Edwin to the Asali city of Liyarna in Calaza Forest, also known as the Green City, where he met the first king of the Asali; Asa Elliar. It was the beginning of a tenta-tive alliance that wasn't officially recognised with a physical treaty until many hundreds of years later. The details of the alliance changed over the years, such that by the dissolution of the treaty in 3667, it was in its eighth form.'*

Elinta read on, inhaling the information within the short book. She found herself reading every page, every little detail she could, but there wasn't much. Just a description of the basic appearance of the Asali, which she'd already observed: grey or silver eyes, a white, ovular pupil and luminescent skin. There was no mention of their healing abilities. Most of the book simply covered the changes to the treaty over the years and detailed which towns and villages traded with the Asali.

There was a small note at the bottom of one page showing that trading with the Asali in the White Mountains began in 3500, but no one knew how long they'd been there or whether they were a group that had split off from the Green City or come from somewhere else. She read over the paragraph on the Eggslaying again and found she'd reached the end of the book. No ... there was one more page, one line, almost like it was tacked on at the end as an afterthought, though it was clearly a part of the book and not added at a later date.

> *'Traditionally ruled by a monarch, with the death of King Riah Elliar and the disappearance and suspected death of his son (name unknown) in 3667, the Asali are now ruled by a council.'*

3667 ... the same year as the Eggslaying. What happened to them? Elinta closed the book, resigned that if the prince's name was unknown, she'd probably never know more than what was in the book. There just wasn't enough information available.

She stared at the front cover for a moment then returned the book to its place. What she really needed was something about the human prince that had died. If they could find something in the account that suggested the dragon hadn't been entirely at fault ... She jumped to her feet. Surely, there were records of *how* he died. Elinta wove her way through the bookcases, searching for a section on the royal family or even a history for the year of the Eggslaying. The closest she could find was *Unforgettable Deaths: Meaningful, Impactful, and Downright Strange.*

She opened the cover and her eyes landed on the first entry. A strangled laugh of horror and humour left her.

'1492—Palmer Arthurson—killed after an apple fell on his head causing him to stumble into the path of a crazed stallion.'
After a moment of doubt whether this book would have what she wanted, Elinta continued to flick through the pages until she found what she was looking for. *'3667—Tristan Rey—killed by a dragon. His death led to the Eggslaying, now marked by the biggest celebrated event on the calendar.'*

There was nothing else with the entry.

Slipping the book back on its shelf, Elinta continued her search, looking for anything on dragons, Asali, or the Eggslaying but there wasn't much to find. Mostly, there were one sentence mentions, a word here or there, but nothing that she didn't already know. She couldn't even find a mention about the healing ability of the Asali, and she mentally kicked herself for not asking Raisa or Ciar more about it while she'd been with them.

Her stomach had started to rumble, and she wondered what time it was, but kept looking through the shelves, her curiosity piqued by so many books. Finally, needing a break from her search, she pulled an encyclopedia of local medicinal plants from the shelf, huddled in a corner, and read. It was calming to read something so familiar, something so normal to her. She ran her fingers over the diagrams of flowers, roots, and trees. Elinta read page after page of information and tried not to wonder whether Galen had replaced her in the three weeks she'd been gone. Hours passed, but she drank up the information, lost in the comfort of her old life.

"There you are."

Elinta jumped, dropping the book onto the floor.

Niles laughed as she ducked to pick it up, her heart still thumping in her chest.

"Have you been here all day?" he asked, perching on the sill of the window beside her.

"Uh," Elinta caught sight of the darkening sky outside. *What time is it?* "I think so." Lunch must have been hours ago. It looked like it was almost dinner time now.

Niles shook his head. "You must be reading something good," he said, tilting his head to read the cover. "Medicinal plants? I thought you were into history?"

"I am," Elinta stammered, ignoring the urge to hide the book. "I just ... this looked interesting," she said, cringing.

Niles seemed to accept her words though and shrugged.

"You hungry? I'm starving and we've been looking for you for a while now. Lorrin just ducked back to check if we'd missed you and you'd returned to your room."

"Sorry, I guess I just got carried away."

"No worries," he said, waving aside her apology. "Let's go. Lor can find us in the dining hall."

He grabbed her hand before she could protest and pulled her from the chair. Realising she still had the book in her hand, she dropped it into the chair, hoping the librarian wouldn't be angry. Niles didn't look like he'd stop his trip to the dining hall for anything, least of all for her to put a book back on its shelf.

After dinner, Elinta made sure Lorrin was still OK with her borrowing Bentley and took the horse out in the dim light of dusk to see Zhayra. She'd considered just going tomorrow, but she desperately wanted to see the dragon. Just through the borders of the wood, Zhayra's emotions shifted immediately into excitement. Somehow, she knew Elinta was coming. Bentley was still a little nervous around Zhayra, so when she thought she was close to where they'd left the dragon, she dismounted and tied him to a tree. Hardly able to contain her excitement, she broke into a run as soon as she caught a glimpse of white gleaming in the moonlight.

"Zhayra!" she called, a smile breaking out across her face.

The dragon rumbled in pleasure and rose to meet her, her face coming into view a moment later.

"I've missed you," Elinta said, running her hand along the dragon's muzzle. She had, too. Sure, she'd felt Zhayra's emotions the whole time they'd been apart, but it wasn't the same as being together. Actually, physically *seeing* each other. Zhayra settled into a crouch, and she sat against the dragon's front foot, slightly reclined by the angle.

"How's it been out here, girl?" she asked as Zhayra grumbled and settled her head next to her. She patted the dragon's cheek, causing her to close her eyes in pleasure.

Elinta said nothing for a moment, wondering how bored the dragon had been by herself. So much had happened to Elinta, but so little would have happened for the dragon out here.

"I had a busy day yesterday," she finally said, running her hand over the dragon's muzzle. "Lorrin and Niles showed me the city."

She launched into a summary of her day, which quickly turned into a step-by-step description of everything that had happened, starting with Neva and Kalla and ending with her training session with Lorrin. She even told the dragon about their run in the palace gardens that morning. Zhayra listened with interest, her emotions shifting to humour as she described some of Lorrin and Niles's antics.

It felt nice to have someone to talk to and tell everything she'd been experiencing. Lorrin was great, and even Niles, but she still didn't know them well enough to talk to the way she felt she could with Zhayra. It was a strange thought, but the dragon had become her closest friend.

"I haven't found much about the Eggslaying," Elinta said, finally reaching the topic she both dreaded and looked forward to discussing, "or the Asali. There's just ... nothing." She sighed and Zhayra's stomach sank.

"We're going to need something big to convince his parents, Zhayra," Elinta said, thinking of the king and queen. They were upholding over a century's worth of tradition. "I thought if there was something in the accounts of how Prince Tristan died that showed the dragon wasn't as responsible as everyone thinks, then they might at least consider it, but there's nothing."

She paused. She didn't even know that the dragon wasn't responsible. But it didn't seem right. Zhayra wouldn't attack without a reason. Surely the dragon that killed Tristan hadn't.

Elinta stared at Zhayra for a long moment. "Do you think Tristan was innocent?"

Zhayra lifted her head and held Elinta's eye but made no clear response. Her emotions were unclear. Maybe Zhayra didn't know either. Or maybe it wasn't as simple as only one of them being responsible. Perhaps Lorrin hadn't been completely wrong when he'd suggested there could be bad dragons, just as she wasn't completely right.

"I guess it's not that easy?"

Zhayra blinked. Elinta sighed again. But if the royal family did have some evidence that showed the death of the prince was more complicated than it seemed, then Lorrin would have told her, and maybe things wouldn't be as they were with the festival. No. She doubted she would find anything about the prince. She needed to look for something else.

Elinta looked up at the sky and the fading light. Judging that an hour had passed since she'd sat down with Zhayra, Elinta stood and brushed off her pants.

"I should head back," she said, checking that Bentley was still where she'd left him. "I'll come back as soon as I can."

She patted Zhayra one last time. The dragon gently nudged her, causing her to stumble. With a sad smile, she twisted and picked her way back through the wood to Bentley, untied his reins, mounted, and rode back to the palace by the light of the moon.

♨♨♨

The next day Neva woke her up, pulling the curtain back on the window and smiling brightly. "Good morning," she said, placing a tray with a mug and a jug of milk beside her bed.

Elinta groaned and squinted against the light. "Neva?"

"I brought you some coffee to start off the day. Have you had coffee from the palace before? It's absolutely delicious," she said, moving to the fire and poking the flames to life.

Elinta pushed her arms under her and grabbed the steaming cup. She'd had coffee a few times back home, but it was always too bitter for her, even with milk. Blaine said it was the variety, but she'd never been sure. Pouring some milk into the cup, she took a tentative sip.

"That is good," she said, taking another sip of the slightly nutty drink. A faint bitterness still underlined it, but it was much better than the drinks she'd had in Kethmere. She actually liked this one.

"I told you it was good," Neva said, with a smile. "Now, Prince Lorrin said he'd be dropping by this morning to take you somewhere. Isn't that exciting?"

Lorrin was taking her somewhere?

"He's always been kind to me," Neva continued. "He's always kind to everyone, you know? Even Mrs. Triggs. Anyway, I'll bring you some breakfast and, in the meantime, you need to get dressed."

"Thank you." Elinta was at a loss for words in the face of Neva's constant talking. The young woman hardly seemed to pause for breath. The maid smiled again and left the room, closing the door behind her.

Gulping down the last of her coffee, Elinta flipped the covers off her bed and padded over to her wardrobe, her nightgown falling just past her knees. She peered at the clothes hanging inside. Unsure what she'd need depending on where Lorrin took her, she slipped into the pants she'd bought at the market and a comfortable shirt. She didn't grab a jacket, since it looked like it'd be another warm day. It was now October, and spring had well and truly arrived. Slipping into the bathroom, she washed her face and came back into the main room just as Neva arrived with a tray of food for her.

"Here you go," the maid said, putting the plate down on the chair by the fire. "I'll drop by and pick the tray up later. Lorrin will be here soon so don't take too long."

And just like that, Neva was gone again.

Shaking her head in amusement, Elinta took the tray and carried it over to the bay window where she sat on the wide sill. Working her way through the toast waiting for her, she watched people moving about in the courtyard below. A little figure darted out of the stables (Jae, she presumed), and took the reins of a horse from its rider. The boy and horse disappeared into the stables.

She hadn't seen him when she'd taken Bentley the night before; he'd probably been sent home long before she'd left. No doubt like his master since she hadn't seen him either.

Just as Elinta finished her toast, there was a knock at the door.

"Just a minute!" she called, racing into the bathroom to run a hand through her hair and brush her teeth. She ran back to the door, stumbling in the process, and swung it open to see Lorrin, patiently waiting for her.

"Hello," she said, slightly breathless.

"Hello. I asked Neva to get you up this morning...?" He glanced over her shoulder into the room. She wondered if he could tell she'd only just gotten up.

"Yes," she said. "She said you were taking me somewhere?"

"Yeah, are you ready?"

Glancing at her bare feet, she grabbed her shoes from beside the wardrobe and pulled them on.

"Yep," she said, walking out of the room and closing the door behind her. "Where are we going?"

"A secret room," he said with a teasing smile.

Hmm, no morning run? "What do you mean?"

"Come on, I'll show you."

Lorrin led her down the hall in the opposite direction they normally went, towards his rooms and his parents'. It was still early in the morning and the hall was surprisingly empty.

"We have a private room where we store certain valuables," he said, drawing Elinta's attention away from the paintings lining the walls that she hadn't seen before. She nodded, wondering where this was going.

He led her further down the hall and she peered at the various doors they passed, wondering who they belonged to, which one was his. After a while, he opened a door on his right and led her inside, closing the door behind her. She looked around in surprise. The room looked like any normal office. There was a desk on the opposite wall with a tapestry hanging behind it that stretched from the floor to the ceiling. Full bookshelves lined the wall on their left, and a fire danced in the right wall. A man stood by one of the shelves, placing a large book back on the shelf.

"Alexander," Lorrin said, nodding his head in greeting.

"Your Highness." The man bowed his head, his grey speckled hair falling over his blue eyes.

"We won't be long." Lorrin walked around the desk and gestured for Elinta to join him.

Frowning, she followed him and stood staring at the tapestry, all too aware of the man by the bookshelves. Why were they in this man's office? The tapestry was nothing particularly magnificent though it may have been when it was first made. It showed a lone hunter stalking a herd of deer in a forest. The hunter crouched behind a large tree, peering around the trunk, and lining up a shot with his bow on a young fawn separate from the group. The colours had faded though, and the edges of the tapestry were frayed.

"Wha—" she started, but at that moment, Lorrin reached out and moved the tapestry aside, revealing an archway. *Oh, secret room.*

The prince ducked through the arch and led her up the staircase just peeking through on the other side. It took them up another level and let them out at a thick wooden door.

"Alexander is the guard for this room," Lorrin said. "Everyone thinks he merely reads over minor laws and announcements, but his real job is making sure no one gets up here."

He fit a small key in the lock and pushed open the door. They stepped into a long, thin room. A couple small shelves decorated the walls, displaying a mix of old books, jewellery, and armour. Right at the opposite end of the room was a small square display case, and Lorrin was leading her straight to it.

Heart pounding, realisation slowly hit her as she drew closer to the case. Lorrin had promised to take her to see something very valuable the day they'd arrived, and there they were, sitting on a red velvet cloth, gleaming in a light she didn't know the source of. There weren't any windows in there, or open flames, but the room was bright as day. If she looked around, she thought she might find the reason for it, but her eyes were glued to the case, glued to those three blue objects inside. Dragon scales.

Lorrin dropped back behind her, but she hardly noticed as her feet carried her the last of the way. The three scales that King

Cenric had taken as prize after the Eggslaying. After he killed the guardian dragon. After he destroyed an entire clutch and sent the dragons fleeing from Eldras. They were right there.

The scales were beautiful, a deep navy blue, smooth and gleaming. They were smaller than her palm, smaller than the scales on Zhayra's back, but no bigger than the ones on her lower legs, even those near her neck. Where had these ones come from?

Lorrin gently placed a hand on her shoulder.

"Are you OK?" he whispered.

Raising a hand to her cheek, she brushed aside the tear she hadn't been able to hold back.

"Yes," she said, though she wasn't really sure. "I wish I knew what really happened."

Lorrin squeezed her shoulder. "Me too," he said quietly.

Sniffing, she twisted to look at the rest of the room.

"How old is all this?" she asked, taking in the stiff paged, yellowing books, the pieces of armour with scratches crisscrossing the metal that didn't quite shine, and the jewellery that didn't fit the style of the last several decades.

"It's all over a hundred years old. Some is a lot older." He gestured at a ceremonial helmet resting on a stand nearby, several small jewels lining the brow. "That's over three hundred years old, I think." His tone was light, but his eyes seemed heavy.

She gawped at the items surrounding her, but the scales drew her back. They were so different to Zhayra's perfectly white scales, but the deep colour suited them. She tried to picture the dragon they'd belonged to, but the image tugged at her heart. How many dragons were left now? Had they ever recovered from the Eggslaying?

Lorrin stood by her as she stared at the scales for a long time.

"Come on," he said eventually, gently taking her hand and leading her from the room.

CHAPTER
THIRTEEN

W HEN FRIDAY CAME, ELINTA had been at the palace for
a week, researching and training every day and spending
her free time with Lorrin and Niles. She found herself leaving her
room with Lorrin, who'd dropped by to pick her up on the way
down to lunch. The door had only just clicked shut behind them
when a voice she didn't recognise sounded from right beside her.

"So, you're Elinta?"

She whirled around, nearly jumping out of her skin, and found
herself face to face with a man in his mid-thirties, with dark hair
and dark, intelligent eyes. He was looking at her intently, studying
her face. She gulped.

"Ford," Lorrin said, a note of guilt seeping into his voice. "I didn't know you'd be around today."

"No. It was a last-minute decision," he said, his eyes not leaving Elinta. "The queen was kind enough to inform me that my new student had arrived early. I thought I'd better come meet her."

His eyes finally left Elinta and focused on the prince who stood behind her. *Wait.* This was Ford Mayes? The man they'd lied about her coming to learn under? He looked so young, much younger than she'd thought he'd be. He couldn't be older than thirty-six, or thirty-seven at most, and he was shorter than Lorrin.

"Yes … perhaps you'd like to come inside?" Lorrin opened the door to Elinta's room, and she turned mechanically to follow the prince inside. She could feel Ford's dark eyes boring into her skull as he followed them into her room.

"I assume you're going to tell me what you're up to, Your Highness?" Ford said, his voice calm.

Elinta sat tentatively on the edge of her bed, her eyes glued to the man. What would happen to her if he refused to help them?

Lorrin's eyes flickered to her as he crossed the room, picked up her chair by the fire and came back with it. Putting it down by the bed, he gestured for Ford to take a seat and then joined Elinta on the bed. As he sat, her ears popped, and she worked her jaw to ease the feeling.

Somewhere between Elinta turning around to see Ford and walking into the room, Zhayra's own emotions had jumped into overdrive, reacting to Elinta's intense surprise and nerves. The dragon's worry was a knot in her stomach. Elinta fought to calm herself, to somehow let Zhayra know she was OK, but her palms were sweaty, and her heart pounded in her ears. Lorrin had made it sound like meeting Ford wasn't likely to happen any time soon, or even at all. Yet she'd only been at the palace for a *week* and here he was.

She thought back to what Lorrin had said about the man before her. Didn't he say that Ford would probably just come and introduce himself if he ever found out about her, ask what was going on? And Ford had done exactly that. She just hoped the rest of what Lorrin had said was true, that the man trusted him and wouldn't press.

"Elinta's here for something else," Lorrin started. "Something we're not ready to talk to my parents about yet."

Ford's eyebrows rose. "Something to do with the mountain Asali? I assume things went well since you were gone for so long."

Elinta's own eyebrows rose in surprise. He knew about that, too?

Lorrin hesitated and then nodded. "I met her there."

"I see." Ford turned his thoughtful eyes back to her. "So, you needed a reason for her to be here without arousing any suspicion."

It wasn't a question, but Elinta saw Lorrin nod from the corner of her eye.

"Ford," Lorrin said. The man raised an eyebrow again. "Have you heard anything about an Asali near human settlements?"

"No more than you have, no doubt," Ford said, seemingly unsurprised by the question.

"And what about ... what about a dragon?" he stammered.

Ford's eyebrows didn't move this time, but Elinta nearly choked at the question. He was dancing a little too closely to letting on why she was really there.

Ford's eyes flickered to her and then back to Lorrin. "There were whispers of a dragon a couple months ago, but nothing that can be confirmed and nothing since then."

Then Lorrin asked a question that both shocked her and had her waiting in desperation for a response. "Do you know anything *more,*" he said, pointedly emphasising the word, "about the dragons?"

"More?" Ford sat back in his chair, interest lighting in his eyes. "Many believe that the dragons were a race of their own," he said carefully. "There are stories of dragons bonding with Asali many hundreds of years ago. It is said the pair could communicate in ways the Asali had never been able to before."

Was it her imagination, or did he look at her when he said that?

"Is there anything else?" she choked out, trying to hide her interest, but he'd already said more than Ciar had told her. She had to know if there was more.

Ford cocked his head.

"They tell stories of one of their own, bonded to a dragon who left them to live among the dragons in the White Mountains. They say he forgot his own language and became one with the dragons. He hardly recognised his own people when they searched for him." He shrugged. "I can't tell you if that's true, but even we had stories many years ago of dragons and humans showing some kind of bond."

Elinta's heart stuttered. "He forgot his own language?"

Ford nodded.

"Was that common?" she asked before she could stop herself. Would that happen to her? Zhayra seemed filled with interest as Elinta's own emotions twisted and changed with every passing second.

"I know only of the one story," Ford said, tilting his head.

Elinta clamped her mouth shut to prevent herself from asking any more questions. She didn't like the way the man kept looking at her.

But where did he get this information? Lorrin said there were hardly any books remaining on the dragons, and even the books she'd found on the Asali in the library had failed to mention anything remotely similar to what Ford described now, to what she was experiencing.

Lorrin cleared his throat. "Thank you. You've given us something to think about."

"No doubt," Ford said, his voice still perfectly even.

There was a long moment of silence where Elinta shifted, nervously folding her hands in her lap. The knot in Zhayra's stomach had loosened a little, but she was still worried, still feeling the nerves knotted in Elinta's own stomach. It didn't help that Elinta wasn't sure what to think of this man and everything he'd said. Could someone really forget their own language, their own race? And the dragons ... they had actually been another race! Like them or the Asali.

"I'm leaving the city once I'm done here. I don't know how long I'll be gone," Ford said, apparently satisfied with the explanation Lorrin had given about Elinta. "Don't get into any trouble while I'm gone." A flicker of amusement lit his eyes but was gone when he looked at Elinta and stood. "If anyone asks whether you will be learning under me, I will confirm it. Though, if you are still around when February begins, I do not know what you'll be able to say then."

"Thank you," she whispered, her voice catching in her throat.

She couldn't believe this man was so willing to go along with their lie, to help her when he knew hardly anything about her. As for February, she hoped she and Lorrin would have some kind of plan in place by then and would be implementing it. Hadn't he talked about seeing the Asali council? Maybe by then, if Lorrin didn't mind, she'd be there since things weren't going well with the king and queen. She shook her head, marvelling once again at how much her life had changed.

She refocused on the conversation happening around her.

"Thank you, Ford." Lorrin clapped his hand to Ford's forearm.

"Whatever you're up to, be careful," Ford said, turned on his heel, and left the room.

Elinta exhaled a long breath and slumped in relief as soon as the door closed.

Lorrin smiled. "Well, the hardest part is behind us now."

"He trusts you," she said, staring at the door as if she could still see the man.

"He'll keep his word. He won't tell anyone."

"I know." Ford had certainly seemed sincere, in both his promise and his trust of Lorrin. "How does he know so much about the dragons? And the Asali? I couldn't find anything even remotely similar to all that anywhere."

Lorrin shrugged. "I don't know. I actually don't know much about him." When she didn't respond, he added hurriedly, "But I've known him a long time. We can trust him."

They sat in silence for another long moment, before Lorrin jumped to his feet and pulled her to hers. "Let's go to lunch then, before we miss it."

She followed him out of her room, amazed that someone so mysterious was allowed into the palace and around the royal family. Who was Ford Mayes?

Elinta ate her meal mostly in silence. Zhayra's worry had dissipated by the time she'd arrived at the dining hall, but she wanted to see the dragon and tell her everything that had happened and reassure her she was OK. Her mind was alive with questions and thoughts. The dragons had been, or were, the third race of Eldras! She tried to picture them making laws or something, but the idea seemed ridiculous. Just as she and Lorrin finished their meals, a messenger ran through the hall and straight to the prince's side. The lanky man bent to whisper in Lorrin's ear.

"When?" Lorrin said. His eyes had widened in alarm, but he kept his voice even.

"No more than an hour ago," the man said, his voice still low but not low enough to stop his words from carrying to her.

"Thank you. I'll be there in a moment." The messenger nodded and hurried from the room again. Elinta looked at Lorrin curiously, unsure whether to ask what had happened. She didn't need to. Lorrin leant over and whispered in her ear. "The scales are gone."

Elinta took a sharp breath. "What?" she breathed.

"No one knows what's happened. Alexander is dead."

She pictured the man she'd only seen briefly in the office below the secret room containing the scales and other valuables. He was dead?

"But ... it's the middle of the day?" Who could have snuck into the room and not be seen in broad daylight?

"I know. I have to see my parents." He pushed away from the table. "I'll talk to you later."

She was still nodding as he walked away. Why would someone steal the dragon scales? What could someone want with them? Her thoughts jumped to Ford. Maybe he would know why someone would take them? He seemed to know a lot about the dragons. She paused. Would he have known about the scales? For that matter, how many people did? If no one was supposed to know where they were, then surely only a select few did. But it didn't matter, Ford had probably already left on his trip, and they didn't know when he'd be back, so there was no use asking him.

She stared at her empty plate for a long time, picturing the blue scales in the hidden room, trying to imagine what the dragon they'd belonged to must have looked like. Who'd known about the room?

CHAPTER
FOURTEEN

E LINTA WAS WANDERING THE hall by her room when Lorrin found her. It had taken all her willpower not to stop by Alexander's office to see for herself that he was gone. She'd only met the man once, but the idea that he was gone, that the scales were gone, didn't sit well with her. But it was the thought that Lorrin might not have told anyone other than Alexander himself that she would be seeing the hidden room, and whoever was there now would find her presence suspicious, that stopped her. She had no reason to go there, and every reason not to draw attention to herself.

Now, she stood in front of a painting of King Cenric, studying the man's eyes, trying to understand what had led him to the decisions he'd made. Wondering at the anger that must have made him kill the blue dragon and the eggs she'd guarded. Was he responsible for the change in the way they saw dragons today? Was he the reason that all accounts of them had practically disappeared so that they seemed little more than animals? Or was it something that had happened gradually over the years?

"Elinta?" Lorrin's voice cracked through her thoughts.

"Hmm?" she said, dragging her eyes away from the man who'd changed the world. "Sorry!"

Her eyes landed on the prince. Lorrin glanced at the portrait she'd been staring at, and a flicker of something she couldn't quite identify crossed his face.

"How did it go?" she asked.

Lorrin looked around, his eyes landing on the maids walking the halls.

"Come with me," he said, striding down the hall and around the corner. She took one last look at the portrait of King Cenric and hurried after Lorrin. He pushed open a door down the hall on the left and walked inside. She hesitated in the doorway before following him and took her first look at his rooms. They'd walked into his office, a small room with a desk in the corner and a set of chairs placed before it for meetings. A full bookshelf sat against the left wall. He had a neat stack of papers on the desk, a map of Eldras on the right wall next to another door, and light trickled in from a window in the back wall. It looked like any normal, functional office.

"In here." Lorrin walked straight across the room to the other door and led her through to his bedroom.

The door they'd come through was the only entrance into his room that she could see. The only other door was cracked open and led to a white bathroom. Elinta looked around the room curiously. His bed was against the opposite wall, neatly made and draped in a heavy grey blanket. A white rug lay spread across the floor beside it, lighting the dullness of the floor. Her feet carried her to a set of shelves against the wall to her right, filled with more books and a few rolls of parchment. Beside an old ring sat a knife sheathed in black leather with three small sapphires in an arrow at the tip.

"We'll have some warning if anyone comes looking for me here."

She whirled around to see Lorrin sitting on the sill of the inlaid, bay window opposite a carved wooden chair.

"It's nice," she said, taking another look at the room. There was a fireplace next to the door they'd entered; a book was left open on the carved mantle. She spotted a wardrobe by his bed, similar to hers, but inlaid with golden, swirled patterns, with the door ajar and an inch of fabric poking out on the floor. She trailed over to Lorrin and sat on the edge of the chair. "What happened?"

Lorrin sighed, running a hand down his face. "We don't know. We don't know how they got up there and they didn't take anything other than the scales once they did."

"Was anyone else killed?" she whispered, thinking of Alexander. Did he have a family waiting for him?

"No," he said softly.

"What would someone want with the scales?" she asked. "*Who* would want them?"

He shrugged. "Only a handful of people knew about the room, and all were accounted for at the time of the theft. Beyond that, my parents think it was a human, but they don't know who or why."

"Do you think it was?" she asked after a long moment. She could see why one of the Asali might want them. They'd broken the alliance between their races over the Eggslaying, wasn't it possible that they'd try to take the scales if they learnt where they were? The scales were a symbol of that victory after all, and the Asali still disagreed with the killings.

"I don't know," Lorrin said, looking out the window and over the low wall bordering the palace and over the city. "It's possible it was an Asali. Do you remember I said there's been one wandering around human settlements? Maybe he's been looking for something? But my parents don't think it would be him. They think if the Asali wanted the scales, they would have gone looking for them by now."

"Is anyone going to go looking for them?" Elinta asked.

"We're sending out some men. If the thief wants to sell them, then they'll pop up soon, but if not ..."

He didn't need to finish the sentence. If the thief didn't plan on selling them, then there was no way to find them. A lone person could easily disappear.

She nodded, and they fell into silence. Who would they send after the scales? It seemed there were about to be a lot more people who knew about them then there was before. And what if it was an Asali that took them? It was then that a vague memory surfaced. Of a hooded figure in the crowd the day she'd arrived in Nevira.

"Lorrin," she said hesitantly. "I saw someone in the city the day we arrived." She tried her best to describe the hooded figure, and the uncomfortable feeling it had given her. But there wasn't much to say. She hadn't even seen the person's face.

Lorrin frowned. "It's odd, but it could have been anyone. There are a lot of reasons people might cover themselves. If they'd been in the palace, there might be something to it ... but out in the city?

"I know," Elinta said, feeling like she hadn't really needed to mention it. Even if a part of her still wondered about the person. She returned to their earlier conversation. "Do you still want to go to the council? We could ask them about the scales."

"We?" Lorrin looked back at her, surprised.

They hadn't really talked much about what they'd do after visiting the palace, but now she realised that it might be good for her to visit the Asali. There didn't seem to be much here for her to learn anymore, and the Asali were sure to know more than she could ever find.

"We," she confirmed. "You need to talk to them about mending things between our people, and maybe they can tell me, us, more about the dragons. Whatever we learn might help with your parents."

Lorrin seemed to consider what she'd said for a moment before he nodded. "You have a point." He smiled. "I guess we're going to see the Asali together."

"OK," she said, almost surprised he'd agreed. "When do we go?"

He shook his head and ran a hand through his hair. "Not yet. Humans aren't welcome in the Green City anymore. They might let you in because of Zhayra, but I'm not sure she'd be able to get in there. I don't know what the canopy is like."

"What do *you* need to get in?" she asked, dismissing the problem of Zhayra moving through the forest for the moment.

"I-I don't know," he stammered. "We still don't know why Zhayra's here or where the missing Asali from the White Mountains have gone. They might be going to Liyarna, or they could be up to something else. I think we just need to see if anything comes up about the scales. The men could be searching for weeks. They've been given until the end of January." He glanced out the window before looking at her again. "And I'd have to go at a time when I'd be least missed ... if that's possible. It's my father's birthday next month. We can see how things are going then. If any of the men have returned," he said. "Maybe I can try talking to my father again too. I'll sneak out again if I have to, but I'd prefer to have his blessing."

It was the first time she'd see him so unsure, and it was partly her fault. Her presence, with Zhayra, had changed things for him. It had changed his plans and, no doubt, so much that he had believed about Eldras. Before he'd met Zhayra in the White Mountains, he'd believed what their people said about dragons.

She ran over his words again in her mind. It wasn't much of a plan; it wasn't really a plan at all, but she didn't have any better ideas. If the men returned with news about the scales though, preferably before January, it could really help them with the king or even the Asali. And if Lorrin needed to be in Nevira for his father's birthday, then they'd have to go afterwards anyway. Besides, as long as they were at the palace, Lorrin could continue to train her. At the very least, she'd learn how to fight and defend herself while she was here.

"OK," she said finally.

They sat in silence for a long moment. Elinta's mind was whirling, thinking through what was happening and all the things that she still needed to learn. Lorrin was already spending so much time teaching her, but there was still something else he might be able to do, if he had the time. She was loath to ask him for more help, but she didn't have anyone else to ask and she needed to learn.

"Would you teach me Asalin? Before we go to the council?" she said, and this time he didn't seem all that surprised by her question. "I heard you speaking to Ciar in their language when we left, and I haven't found anything in the library on the language."

"No, you wouldn't. It's not public knowledge. I'm not fluent," he said modestly, "but I could teach you some of the basics when I have the time."

"Thank you."

He stood, straightening out his shirt. "I'll walk you back to your room."

✤✤✤

"Good!" Lorrin said. "Now follow through with the block."

Elinta moved the wooden sword diagonally across her body. After sparring with her for a little while that night, Lorrin had finally asked her to draw the training sword from her hip and started running her through some basic stances. She still had a long way to go with her hand-to-hand, but he thought it was time to start her on the sword as well. She had no objections.

"Back to one," he said, moving his own sword into the position. She moved the sword into an overhead block.

"Two," he said.

They both moved.

"Three."

On it went until her arms were shaking with the effort of holding the heavy sword, and then they kept on going.

Her body had toned since they'd started training together at night and running in the morning, but using the sword was completely different to the sparring they'd been doing. Her forearms and shoulders were aching by the time the prince finally stepped back and let her lower the sword. She groaned, nearly dropping the weapon.

"Don't worry, your arms will get used to it pretty quickly."

"I hope so." She shook out her arms. Her muscles felt like jelly. And her feet were aching. She'd been wearing in her new boots, and while they hadn't given her any blisters, they were still uncomfortable after a couple hours. She now regretted turning them down occasionally for her old boots.

"I'll put this away," Lorrin said, taking pity on her and prying the sword from her stiff hand.

"Thanks." While he walked away, she windmilled her arms to loosen her shoulders.

"So," he said, reappearing from the storage room, "my mother wants to have morning tea with you tomorrow."

She spluttered. "What?"

She'd seen the queen a couple of times since meeting her in the throne room, but they'd hardly spoken. They certainly hadn't shared a meal together.

Lorrin laughed. "It's just morning tea." He paused, a teasing glint coming into his eye. "She's asked me about you a few times."

"Why?" She frowned. What would the queen want to know about her?

"Probably still thinks we're together," he said.

"Togeth—" she started, then she realised what he meant. "Oh. Do you think?"

"No." He laughed. "You looked really nervous. I couldn't miss a chance to tease you."

She shook her head. "Niles is a bad influence on you," she said, giving him a shove, but she was smiling.

"She likes to meet with people who are staying at the palace. See how they're going, get to know them a bit. That's all."

That didn't sound too bad. Certainly better than trying to explain to the queen that she wasn't dating his son. For a moment, she wondered which would be worse: talking to the queen about her friendship with Lorrin or her connection to Zhayra. She shook her head.

"What do I say if she asks where I'm from?" she asked. She hadn't even told *Lorrin* where she was from. At first, when she met him, it was because she hadn't entirely trusted him, but lately she just hadn't wanted to talk about her home. About her family. Maybe now was the time.

Lorrin seemed to think about her question for a moment, unaware of the tangent her thoughts had taken. "The day we got back, I already implied you're from Donlee. It's probably best if you stick to that story."

Nodding, she rubbed at her arms. "Thank you for helping me so much."

She looked at him in disbelief. She'd thanked him a lot since they'd met, but he'd helped her so much and he'd asked nothing of her in return. Even inviting her to the palace had so far been more to her benefit than his. She took a deep breath and plunged on.

"I don't know why I haven't told you before now. It's not that important ..." she said, shaking her head slightly.

Lorrin searched her face.

She cleared her throat. "Um, I'm from Kethmere."

Lorrin smiled softly. "Kethmere. I'd like to see it one day."

Elinta swallowed heavily and just nodded.

"I'm glad that I can help you, Elinta."

"I'm glad too." She gave him a shove, returning to their earlier lightness. "Let's go, it's getting late," she said.

Lorrin let her change the subject and followed her out of the private training room, laughing.

Elinta woke early the next morning, nerves knotting in her stomach again. She'd never been this nervous so often. It wasn't a nice feeling, but Zhayra somehow seemed to know she wasn't in any danger, as her own feelings seemed quite steady.

She climbed out of bed and looked through the clothes in her wardrobe. What were you supposed to wear when you met with a queen? She thought back to the simple pants and shirt she'd been wearing when she first arrived and saw the queen and king in the throne room. Anything was better than that. Kalla had sent her a couple of dresses with the clothes she'd given her, so Elinta pulled these out and laid them on her bed. One was a deep green colour that would fall halfway to her ankles and covered her shoulders. It had a silver sash across the middle to tie at the back. The other dress was similar in style to something she'd wear at home, except it was pink, a colour too light to wear in Galen's garden or in the forest without getting filthy.

Coming to her decision, she slipped into the green dress. Her run with Lorrin had been cancelled so he could attend a meeting about the missing scales. They had some finer details to arrange with the men they were sending out. Elinta went into the bathroom to tidy up. She wasn't meeting the queen for a few hours, but after breakfast she wanted to go to the library again and browse through some books. She'd go straight to the queen from there. Ready, she headed down to breakfast to find Niles.

"Oi! El!" Niles called as soon as she entered the dining hall. He was sitting at one of the tables in the centre of the room. He grinned when she caught sight of him. Amazingly, none of the other people in the hall had even looked up at Niles's voice. They were so used to him that they didn't even seem to notice he'd shouted.

She weaved her way through the tables, smoothing out her dress, and sat opposite him.

"Good morning," she said, lifting the lid off a tray and grabbing two pieces of toast and jam from the plates lining the centre of the table. Breakfasts were set up like a buffet at the palace, whereas you could choose between two or three meals at lunch and dinner.

Elinta chewed at her food thoughtfully, sending Niles furtive glances when he was busy with his own food. This was the first time she'd properly seen him since the scales were stolen, other than a very rushed dinner last night. Did he know about the scales and what happened to Alexander? She sighed. She'd have to ask Lorrin what Niles knew. Even if he could never know more about her, maybe he could still help. She took another bite of her toast.

Niles smiled. "You're pretty quiet this morning."

"Oh," Elinta said. "I was just thinking."

"Lor tells me you're having tea with his mum," Niles said, cutting off a bite of his eggs on toast.

"I am," she said, fully anticipating a teasing comment from him, but he surprised her.

"Do you know where you're going?"

She hesitated. Lorrin had shown her around most of the palace when she'd first arrived, including the rooms the queen used to meet with people. They were on the lower floor somewhere. "Um ... kind of."

"I'll take you. Where can I meet you?" Niles said, finishing his food and loading more onto his plate.

"Thanks. I was going to go to the library this morning," she said.

He grunted acknowledgment around his mouthful of food. She shook her head, watching the mountain on his plate disappear.

Zhayra's stomach jumped, the feeling making Elinta's own twist. What was the dragon doing? Was she OK? She focused on the dragon's body, waiting for any other feelings from the dragon. What did a stomach jump mean? Not for the first time, Elinta felt frustration rise in her. This bond was confusing.

A hand waved in front of her face. "You OK?"

"Huh?" Elinta said, still focusing on the dragon. Had someone found her out there?

"El?"

"Yeah?" she said, snapping back to herself and finding Niles staring at her.

"You OK? You zoned out a little there. What were you thinking about? You were mumbling."

Elinta's eyes widened. "I was?"

"Yeah." Niles looked at her expectantly.

"Uh, I was just thinking about something Ford said," she stammered. "Before he left."

"Oh. He must have you pretty busy then." He was still frowning, but his expression had mostly cleared. What had she mumbled?

"Yeah. Yeah, it's been busy." She shoved another bite of food into her mouth so she wouldn't have to answer any more questions.

Niles didn't say anything more, but she couldn't help the feeling settling over her. What would have happened if Niles had found out about Zhayra? How close had she come to revealing herself? Zhayra's emotions had relaxed. She could have been revealed for nothing.

🔥🔥🔥

"Woah, you really are here." Niles sat heavily on a windowsill beside her in the library. The previous awkwardness between them was gone. "I thought you would have read all of them the other day, you were here so long."

"Nearly," she said, closing her book. She'd been looking for clues to why a person would want dragon scales. But, frustratingly, just as there was little information on dragons, there was none on scales. Maybe they'd been stolen for the historical value? Sighing, she put the book back on the shelf. The librarian hadn't said anything about the book she hadn't put away the first time Niles had come looking for her, but she thought she'd caught him glaring at her the next time she'd dropped by.

"Ready to go?" Niles asked, pushing himself to his feet.

"No?" she said, her stomach knotting.

"Ah, don't worry." He waved a dismissive hand. "Mira is great. She's pretty quiet but once you get to know her, she's real sweet. Just don't zone out, hey?"

Ignoring his playful jab, Elinta's eyebrows rose. Did he call the queen by her name to her face? She didn't know the queen, but something told her Niles had probably started using her name without her permission and she'd just accepted it. It seemed like something he would do.

"Let's go," she said, heading for the exit.

Niles hurried to catch up with her. "I thought you didn't know where you were going!"

"I don't."

"Well then, miss." He held out his arm to her. "Let me escort you."

Laughing, she looped her arm through his.

"Where to?" Niles said, straightening.

"The queen, please, sir."

"This way, miss." He led her downstairs to the first level, and they wove their way towards the south side of the building, past the throne room and several public rooms. Niles greeted nearly every person they passed though there was one he greeted with particular fervour.

"Good morning, Shae!" Niles yelled as a small, slightly rounded woman appeared at the other end of the hall.

The woman's green eyes slid right over Elinta and narrowed as they landed on Niles. "That's *Advisor* Shae to you, soldier."

Elinta frowned, a memory tugging at her. She'd heard that name before ... she was sure Lorrin had mentioned the woman.

"Please call me Niles, Shae. There's no need to pretend you don't like me. I know your true feelings." Niles winked.

Elinta thought she heard a guard chuckle as they passed him in the hall. Shae's face darkened and her lips tightened into a grim line.

"Who is this?" she said, finally looking at Elinta.

"Ah, don't be jealous, Shae. She's just a friend. This is Elinta." Shae tilted her head. "Prince Lorrin's new friend?"

Elinta nodded, then realised where she knew the woman's name from. The advisor had nearly stumbled upon her and Lorrin training.

"Hmm," the woman said, stared at her a moment longer, then walked by them in silence, her back rigid.

"I'll see you later," Niles called over his shoulder as they turned down another hall. Elinta looked around at her familiar surroundings. They were near the gardens she and Lorrin ran in.

"Is she really an advisor?" Elinta whispered, looking over her shoulder even though the woman was now out of sight. Had he really antagonised the woman?

Niles glanced at her, catching the note of worry in her tone. "Oh, don't worry. Shae thinks a little too highly of herself 'cause she advises King Aldon and Queen Mira."

"But if she's an advisor ..." Elinta trailed off. Wasn't she important?

Niles shrugged, jostling her arm still looped in his. "My dad's an advisor and so is General Nash. Shae just wishes she had a title of her own, so she tries to get everyone to call her advisor, but it's not a rank."

"Your dad's an advisor?" Even though they'd spent a lot of time together since she'd arrived in Nevira, she didn't know much about his family other than his father was a general.

"Mm hmm."

"What is it?"

Niles smiled broadly. "I've just had a wonderful idea! Oh, Shae's gonna hate me."

Elinta's eyes widened. "A prank?"

Niles hadn't done anything that she knew of since she'd arrived, but both he and Lorrin had a reputation for causing trouble. Shae didn't seem like the kind of person to forgive a prank.

Niles nodded and stopped them outside a door before Elinta could try and dissuade him from whatever he was planning. "Here we are."

Her trip with Niles had distracted her so well from thinking about the queen that she couldn't help herself; Elinta's shoulders slumped when she saw the door. "Already?"

He dropped her arm and patted her shoulder. "Seriously, El. There's nothing to worry about."

Before she could respond, he reached out, knocked on the door, and disappeared back up the hall. He had a spring in his step. Whatever it was he was planning, he was definitely on his way to do it now.

The small wooden door opened inwards, revealing a middle-aged woman. "Elinta?"

"Yes?"

"Come in," she said, moving aside to let Elinta into the room and revealing the queen.

Lorrin's mother sat on a padded seat by a window overlooking the gardens, a little sketchbook and pencil on the small, rounded table in front of her. Another similar chair sat to the side across from her. The room was small but styled beautifully with a mixture of soft and bold colours that complemented the white walls and grey floors.

"Elinta." The queen smiled softly in greeting, putting her sketchbook and pencils on the floor beside her. Elinta was surprised to find the queen drawing by the gardens, something so similar to what she had done countless times over the years, both for herself and for Galen.

She smiled awkwardly, unsure whether to curtsy or bow. She hadn't when they'd met before, and no one had told her to since and she'd forgotten to ask. After a brief pause, Elinta decided formality was best and hurriedly curtsied. The queen smiled.

"Please, come and sit." Queen Mira gestured to the seat opposite her. Her dark brown hair was pulled away from her face today and tied in an intricate knot at the base of her head.

"Thank you, Your Majesty." Crossing the room, Elinta sat in the chair and nervously smoothed out her dress. "It's a lovely view," she said, looking out the massive windows and into the garden.

"I find it can be quite relaxing," the queen said, following Elinta's gaze.

Elinta mumbled her agreement. It was probably a good thing she and Lorrin ran in the early morning. Two people running around the garden would probably ruin the effect for anyone trying to relax by a window.

"I'm sorry for not inviting you to tea earlier," the queen said, turning back to her. "It's been quite busy around here."

"Oh," she said in surprise. "I-I wasn't expecting an invitation, Your Majesty." She paused, then realised she might have sounded ungrateful. "Thank you," she added hurriedly.

The maid who'd opened the door to Elinta appeared with a tray of biscuits, a teapot, and two cups painted with the royal flower. She poured the tea and then disappeared through a side door. It was just the two of them in the room now. There weren't even any guards.

"How has your stay been?" The queen took a sip of the tea.

"Great." Elinta swallowed nervously but was put somewhat at ease by the kindness shining in the queen's green eyes. "Lorrin's been helping me in the library. I've been learning a lot, Your Majesty."

She shoved at the guilt lining her stomach and hoped her lies and half-truths were convincing. Blaine had always been able to see right through her when she lied, but she hadn't needed to in so long. Now it seemed as though all she could do was lie by omission or directly.

The queen paused for a moment, and Elinta could see her debating whether to say something. The pause gave her the opportunity to take a sip of her tea in an effort to hide her nerves, which was a blend of several herbs she couldn't quite recognise. One was definitely camomile. Whatever the others were, the mix was delicious.

"You two seem close friends," Queen Mira finally said, studying her.

"We are. He's been a good friend to me," she said, and she meant it. Lorrin was the closest friend she had, perhaps next to Zhayra, though she doubted her relationship with the dragon could be compared to anything else. It occurred to her that maybe Lorrin had been right when he'd teased her last night about the queen thinking they were together, but she seemed to accept her response.

Taking another sip of her tea, Elinta was unsure what to say and whether she was supposed to say anything. Too late she realised she'd forgotten to say, 'Your Majesty.'

The queen took a biscuit. "Have you seen Ford since arriving in Nevira?"

"Yes," she said, remembering that the queen had been the one to tell the man about her. "He wasn't expecting me so early." Which was mostly true. He just hadn't been expecting her at all. In retrospect, it was almost funny. If her heart hadn't been in her throat for most of the meeting, she probably would have laughed. "But I've had more time to prepare before starting under him. Thanks to your son, Your Majesty."

"Lorrin has always loved history. He's quite fond of Ford. He's a very knowledgeable man. I'm sure you'll learn much from him."

Nodding, Elinta's eyes landed on the queen's sketchbook. "Do you often sketch, Your Majesty?" she ventured.

"When I have the time, which unfortunately is rare. But the gardens are a favourite of mine."

Elinta smiled, seeing a glimpse of herself in the queen again. "I used to draw the plants at home," she said, looking out of the window at the walled garden. "I loved leaves the most."

The queen nodded. "I tend to linger on them. Tell me about your home, Elinta. Lorrin said you're from Donlee?"

Elinta's knee jerked under the table, and she was thankful she was sitting down, and the reaction was hidden from the queen. Tell her about her home or about Donlee? She took a sip of the tea again to buy herself some time. "It's a small village at the base of the White Mountains," she said, trying to remember as much about the town as she could. "It's strange being here. I'm not used to so many people."

"Do you have any family?"

Elinta felt as though the breath had been knocked out of her. Yes, she wanted to say, a father who hates me and a brother whose dreams I've squashed. Or no, no, she didn't.

The queen noticed her hesitation. "You didn't leave on the best terms?"

"No." Elinta deflated. "No, I didn't."

"Is that why you came to the city so early?" Queen Mira tilted her head slightly, concern in her eyes. "I confess I was confused at your arrival."

"Y-yes." Elinta latched onto the excuse. If it stopped people paying attention to her, she could live with them knowing things weren't well at home.

The queen gave her a small smile. "Time and distance can heal most wounds. Any parent would miss their child after so long apart."

Not her father. "Thank you, Your Majesty."

They talked for a long time, finding each other quite similar in many ways and yet quite different in others. Elinta found that the queen was a very quiet-natured woman, but just as Niles had said, she was a lovely person. She spoke fondly of her husband and son and seemed genuinely interested in Elinta. After an hour, the maid reappeared and gave the queen a small nod.

"I'm afraid we must end our tea here," the queen said, checking a small clock on the wall above the doors Elinta had entered through. "I have another meeting to attend very soon. I've enjoyed your company, perhaps we can meet again soon?"

"I would like that, Your Majesty."

Queen Mira smiled. "When it's just us and my family, you don't need to use my form of address anymore, Elinta."

"Thank you." She nodded, trying to hide her relief. She was sure she'd forgotten to address the queen properly at least a dozen times throughout their morning tea, and she was sure to forget in the future. At least it wouldn't matter too much if it was just them.

She took her leave of the queen, thanking her again, and wandered slowly back to her room, wondering what Niles had gotten up to while she was with the queen.

CHAPTER
FIFTEEN

L ORRIN CONTINUED ELINTA'S TRAINING with the wooden sword again that night, showing her through various stances for attacks and blocks.

"Did Niles get into trouble?" Elinta asked as they paused for a drink of water. As it turned out, Niles hadn't pulled his prank on Shae until just after they'd finished dinner that night and Elinta had missed the entire thing.

"Not really," Lorrin said with a smile. "Shae wasn't impressed, but everyone else seemed to enjoy it. I think a few people were even jealous."

Elinta shook her head, trying to imagine the scene. Niles had, according to palace gossip, serenaded the advisor in the dining hall. He'd called it "tonight's entertainment," and sang old love songs to her. Elinta had to hand it to Niles; it was a more harmless prank than she'd expected. And she almost wished she'd seen it.

"All right," Lorrin said, putting his glass down and jogging across to the storage room. "Let's try something different."

Elinta pulled the sword from her hip again, feeling the muscles in her arms and shoulders twinge at the movement. When Lorrin reappeared with a wooden sword in hand, she knew immediately what he was thinking. Standing opposite her, he raised the point of the sword and smiled.

"We're going to put some of this into action," he said, and immediately swung the sword at her.

Elinta just managed to raise hers in time to meet the strike, their wooden swords clanging loudly. Relief spread through her at the lack of force behind the blow, but as soon as their swords met, he shot his in a downward strike towards her knees. She met it too and, just barely, the next one. When he stabbed towards her side, she twisted out of the way and somehow ended up with the tip of his sword against her shoulder. He prodded her gently with the tip.

"Not bad," he said.

Elinta smiled at his praise, though she felt a tug of annoyance that she hadn't lasted longer. Noticeably, she was puffing and he wasn't. She still didn't know how his sword had come to be at her shoulder either.

"Again," Lorrin said, stepping back and waiting for her to move into position.

With a nod from her, they started again. She stuck to defending, blocking his attacks, and twirling and ducking out of the way. She was breathing shallow breaths, her muscles ached from the weight of the sword, but she felt alive. Her senses were working as they never had before, straining to keep her moving as the speed behind Lorrin's attacks picked up.

A sound from outside in the corridor distracted her for a moment. Her sword dropped an inch. Footsteps. "Ow!" She gasped in shock as Lorrin's sword caught her hand, but she turned to stare at the door.

"Are you al—"

"Someone's coming." Even as she said it, the footsteps stopped outside the room, and the door opened.

"Niles," she breathed, lowering her sword.

Niles stood in the doorway, his uniform slightly rumpled after the day, looking between them with open confusion. His hair was messier than usual, as if he'd just ruffled it.

"Er ... hi," he said. "I was looking for Lor, figured since he wasn't in his room he might be here."

Elinta looked at Lorrin. He lowered his own wooden sword and ran a hand over his face. He seemed unsure what to say. When she thought about it, without revealing why she really was learning to fight, there wasn't any other reason good enough for them not to have told Niles.

"So ... training, huh?" Niles said, looking between them with a confused frown.

Elinta jumped in before Lorrin could respond, not wanting to come between their friendship. Thinking quickly, she said the first thing that came to mind.

"We were attacked on the road back from Donlee," she said, mind racing. Out of the corner of her eye, she saw Lorrin glance curiously at her. "I couldn't help Lorrin fight them, so I asked him to help me learn to defend myself so that I'll be OK if it ever happens again."

Niles nodded, his face clearing for a moment before he looked accusingly at Lorrin. "You were attacked on the road?"

"Just some guys looking to make some money," Lorrin said, trying to placate his friend.

"I didn't want anyone to know," Elinta continued before Niles could say any more, and slightly louder than she'd intended. "I'm here to learn from Ford, and I thought it might seem strange if I started learning all this." She gestured vaguely at the sword dangling in her grip.

Niles blinked, taking it all in his stride. "Well, now that I know about these secret, nighttime rendezvous, you might consider inviting me along. Lor and I are about even in fighting, but we've learnt very different styles, so we'd teach very differently. What do you think? I bet I can teach better than the prince here." Niles smiled at her expectantly.

Rendezvous? But she thought over the rest of what he'd said and had to agree he had a point. Niles clearly had to be good with a blade, and his fists, if he was stationed at the palace. Besides, he was handling the situation really well, and she hated that she'd been hiding so much from him. She looked at Lorrin to see what he thought, but he wasn't giving anything away. If anything, he seemed to be *studying* her. It was entirely her decision.

"OK," she said, turning back to her newest friend, a smile breaking out across her face. "That would be great."

"Good, because swordplay actually requires finesse, and Lorrin is strongly lacking. I was just being kind when I said we were even." He strode across the room, took the sword from her hand, gave it to Lorrin, and shoved him out of the way. Elinta looked at him in surprise; she'd thought he'd meant to spar with her.

Niles grinned, cracked his knuckles and raised his fists. "Show me what this dope has taught you with your fists first."

Lorrin shook his head, a smile tugging at his lips, and stepped out of the way. One look at his face showed he was happy for Niles to be involved though, and Elinta felt relieved she'd avoided causing a falling out between the two friends.

"Ready?" Niles asked.

Taking a deep breath, Elinta raised her own fists and nodded. Niles charged and panic lit in her chest at the sight. She desperately hoped he was going to pull his punches. When she dodged his first attack, a jab at her face, she knew she'd made the right decision in accepting his offer. His approach was very different to Lorrin's. Their training would complement each other's well.

Elinta blocked a punch and struck out at Niles. He easily knocked her fist aside. And back and forth it went. She blocked and ducked and tried her best to attack whenever she could. Niles's fists made contact with her several times but, just as she'd hoped, he was kind enough to pull his punches. That didn't mean she wasn't going to have a bruise or two in the morning, but they'd be no worse than the odd one she'd gained from Lorrin, just more in number. She just hoped that her fortune continued, and no one asked where the defensive bruises on her forearms were from.

Niles ended the fight when he grabbed her arm, pulled her in with a twirl so her back was against him and slid his arm around her neck. Lorrin had taught her how to escape the hold, but Niles released her before she could move.

"Not bad," he said.

"Thanks." Elinta crossed back to the water and took a big gulp, her chest heaving. She hadn't done this much sparring with hand-to-hand, or the sword, in one night before.

"How long have you two been training?" Niles asked Lorrin, while Elinta took another drink of water.

"Tonight?"

Niles grunted in affirmation.

"Two hours. We were going to finish up soon."

Elinta nearly sighed with relief. Her arms were aching like never before. She downed the last of her water while Niles finished asking about their training.

"I can drop by whenever I'm not on duty," Niles said. "If that's still OK with you both?" he added, turning to Elinta as she joined them again.

"Sounds good to me," Lorrin said, and Elinta agreed.

"Sweet," he said, clapping his hands together. "See you guys tomorrow then." He pivoted and headed for the door.

"Niles," Elinta called after him. He turned at the door, his hand on the knob. "I'm sorry I didn't tell you."

Niles waved a hand. "No problem, El." He left them to pack up the gear they had out, closing the door behind him.

Elinta walked with Lorrin to the storage room as he put the swords away. "Do you think he's OK?" she asked, thinking of Niles's confusion when he'd found them training.

"Yeah," he said. "That was good thinking, telling him about Jed."

She shrugged. "It's mostly true. I don't want to lie to him any more than we have to."

"Yeah," he said with a heavy sigh.

She ducked to pick up the empty pitcher of water and the cups from beside the door as they went out into the corridor. Niles was nowhere to be seen, and the palace seemed to be empty, just as it usually was in that part of the palace at night. The maids and other staff finished on the third floor by nine o'clock. It was now just after ten.

After a minute of walking, Lorrin broke the silence. "Before … just before Niles came in. Did you hear him?" he asked hesitantly.

Elinta started in surprise. She'd entirely forgotten about that, with her concern about Niles learning what was happening and then agreeing to help train her.

"I did," she said, thinking back. She'd heard him walking in the corridor.

Lorrin shook his head. "How? I didn't even know he was there until he opened the door."

"I don't know," she said, at a loss for how to explain it. But then she remembered another time she'd thought she'd heard something strange. "Not long after we got to the palace, I was thinking about Zhayra, and I heard the woods where she was. The crickets chirping and the river running. It was like I was right there. I thought I was imagining it." She pulled Lorrin to a halt. "Do you think this is a part of ... of whatever it is Zhayra and I share?"

"I don't know," he stammered. "I wish there was more information on this, but I don't see what other explanation there could be." He shook his head. "This is amazing."

Elinta smiled, glad he believed her and didn't think she was going mad. "I don't know how I did it though, tonight or the last time."

"If it's already happened twice. It'll probably happen again," he said slowly. "There's got to be some kind of pattern explaining why it happens when it does."

She thought about it for a moment but couldn't see what possible connection there could be. The first time she'd been in the bath thinking about Zhayra, the second she'd been fighting Lorrin. The two experiences were entirely different. The best explanation she could think of for hearing the woods was that she'd heard through Zhayra, like how she could feel the dragon's emotions, but the second time it had been her own ears but ... better. Neither seemed like something she could knowingly replicate. Her hearing had never changed when fighting Lorrin before, nor had anything happened while relaxing in the bath since that first time.

"Maybe I'll know what it is next time," she said, frowning.

Lorrin mumbled in agreement, and they stopped outside her room. "I'll see you tomorrow."

"Good night." She slipped inside her room and looked hesitantly towards the door to her bathroom. It was already over a week since she'd visited Zhayra, and she wanted to make sure the dragon was OK. Not to mention, she was sure the dragon had caught the way her emotions had jumped between several different and contrasting emotions within the last hour. Zhayra probably wanted to make sure *she* was OK too. Lorrin had said she was free to borrow Bentley whenever she wanted, and there was no better time to sneak out than night. Crossing her room, she pulled a jacket from her wardrobe and, without another thought, made her way down to the stables.

A lamp shone by the doors and another two lit the line of stalls, but the stableboy, Jae, was nowhere to be seen nor his master whom she still hadn't met. Shrugging, she grabbed Lorrin's tack, glad there wasn't anyone to ask her what she was up to, and crossed to Ben's stall. The gelding nickered in greeting as she entered and rubbed him down.

"Want to go for a ride?" she murmured, throwing the saddle blanket across his back. "It's been a little while, hasn't it?"

Tacked up, she led Bentley from the stall, grabbing one of the enclosed lamps as she went, and out the palace gates. The guard ignored her as she passed through and as long as she was back before the gates closed at midnight, he wouldn't bother her when she returned. It suited her quite well. She'd just have to be quick tonight.

Once on the main road that she and Lorrin had ridden into the city, Elinta slipped into the saddle and with the lantern in one hand and the reins in the other, she urged Bentley into a trot. She closed her eyes to the feel of the wind rushing over her face and through her hair. Opening her eyes, she grinned and turned him towards the woods where Zhayra waited for her, moving by the light of the moon and the circle of light the lantern provided.

When they ducked into the darkness under the trees of the woods nearly an hour later, she slid from the saddle and guided Bentley by the light of the lantern, picking her way through the undergrowth. It was awkward to move through the darkness, but it was better than making the trip during the day when she didn't have a good excuse and people would notice she was gone. Just like the last time she'd visited, Elinta felt Zhayra's growing excitement before she even saw the dragon. She stopped to tie Bentley to a tree.

"I won't be long," she whispered to him, patting his neck.

Weaving her way deeper into the forest, the dragon's bulk came into view and Elinta stumbled in her hurry to reach her.

"Zhayra," she called softly, catching sight of the dragon's eyes gleaming in the darkness.

"Hello girl," Elinta said, throwing her arms around her large chest.

She sat down in front of the dragon. Zhayra rested her massive head on and over her lap and legs. A deep contentment settled over them both as Elinta started to fill her in on all that had happened since she'd seen her last; meeting Ford, the dragon scales going missing, her morning tea with the queen, and Niles finding out about her training with Lorrin. There was a lot to cover.

"… he was really good about it," Elinta said, coming to the end of her story about Niles. "He's going to help me too. I wish—"

Zhayra's head left her lap, and a startled growl escaped her throat.

"What?" Elinta gasped, twisting to follow the dragon's gaze.

The beam of the lantern only reached a few metres around them, but it was enough to see the outline of a familiar figure in the shadows just beyond its reach.

Her breath left her. Her mouth opened and closed.

"Niles?" she choked, experiencing an odd déjà vu from earlier in the day. Niles stumbled into the very edge of the ring of light, his face completely colourless and his wide eyes locked on Zhayra.

"Want to explain to me what's going on?" Niles said, his voice surprisingly firm.

She shivered at the anger in his face, the hardness in his eyes. He'd heard her talking to the dragon. Could see them comfortably sitting together. She swallowed heavily.

"I-I," she stuttered, a rising panic taking over.

"I can explain," she said desperately.

Her mind was already flying back to the last time someone had found her and Zhayra together under some trees. Though now it was night, and there was no lake nearby, she felt as though she was reliving it. They'd been too caught up in each other again to notice someone sneaking up on them. It wouldn't have surprised her if an army of angry people appeared behind Niles.

The dragon rumbled, sensing her distress, and shifted in place. If it was possible, Niles's face paled even further, his hands hung loosely by his sides. His sword probably wouldn't damage Zhayra, and he knew it, unlike the villagers from her home who'd brought bows and pitchforks among other weapons. Normal steel couldn't do as much damage as *illayas*. She cleared her throat.

"It's OK, Zhayra. It's Niles," Elinta mumbled to the dragon and shakily pushed herself to her feet. Where did she begin? How was she supposed to explain all this to Niles? All she could do was hope he'd at least hear her out. Let her tell him what was happening.

"This is Zhayra," she said, gesturing at the dragon and taking a hesitant step towards him. "She's the real reason I'm here."

Niles gulped.

"What do you mean?" he asked, anger making his voice sharp.

She fought the urge to flinch away and pushed on. This had to be hard for him, harder than it had been for Lorrin when he'd first met them. At least he'd been surrounded by the Asali who could explain to him how things really were. She didn't know nearly so much herself, only what her experiences had taught her.

"I—Lorrin and the Asali found us in the White Mountains. He's offered to help us," she gushed.

Niles's face shifted in surprise at the mention of the prince, but the tension in his body didn't ease.

"She's not what you think, Niles. She's *aware*," she said desperately. She had to make him see.

"Aware?" he repeated, rubbing his palms on his pants.

How would Ciar explain it? "The dragons aren't animals. They're sentient ... more like another race," she said.

Niles frowned. "And Lorrin knows about this?"

"Yes."

"The dragon can understand us?"

"Yes." She nodded, watching his face intently.

He ran a hand across his face, his eyes flickering between her and Zhayra. "I don't—I don't understand."

"It's OK," she said, moving closer to him. "What do you want to know?"

She tried to keep her face as honest and open as possible. It was the least she owed him. To explain what he was seeing. She realised now that she couldn't lose his friendship. He was one of the best parts of her day, of her time in Nevira, and she didn't want him to turn his back on her, on them. Zhayra didn't move, but she could feel the dragon's gaze on her, the nerves clenched in her massive gut. Zhayra knew what Niles meant to her.

"That's a dragon," Niles stuttered. She nodded, too scared to laugh at the obviousness of his statement. "What's it doing here?"

"I don't know," she said, frowning. She thought back to the sadness and worry Zhayra had felt when she'd asked her why she was in Eldras. Of all the questions, he had to ask one she couldn't answer. A flicker of doubt crossed Niles's face.

"She crashed in a storm, and I treated some cuts on her wings," she explained, reaching out to him as if the gesture would convince him. "I don't know where she came from or where she was going."

His frown deepened. "Treated?"

There's so much he doesn't know. She took a steadying breath. "I was an apprentice to a healer in my village."

"What about Ford? Aren't you going to be learning under him?" He paused, his eyes slid from hers to the ground and then back up. "Are you even from Donlee?"

"Could we maybe sit down?" she asked, seeing a long night of explaining ahead of her. She didn't wait for his response and sat down opposite him, her fingers automatically tugging at the grass under her. Niles's eyes didn't leave Zhayra as he mirrored her movements and sat, crossing his legs under him.

Elinta gathered her thoughts and launched into as detailed an explanation as she could about how she'd found Zhayra, the attack by the villagers on them, the trip to the White Mountains including Lorrin's offer to help her, and his hopes of fixing things with the Asali as well as for the dragons, or more specifically, Zhayra. When she got to the part about the bond that seemed to exist between her and the dragon, Niles's eyes widened.

"What do you mean you can feel her emotions? What does that even mean?"

She thought back to what she'd told Lorrin on the road from Donlee all those weeks ago and repeated something similar to Niles now. "I can feel her emotions within her. It's mostly just an awareness, but I can also feel the way anger boils her blood, the way her nerves curl her stomach sometimes. If I couldn't feel those things, I would still just *know* how she was feeling."

Niles laughed incredulously. She took it as a good sign. His eyes slipped back to Zhayra, who was still crouched behind her.

"What's she feeling now?" he asked.

"She's worried," Elinta said, focusing in on the dragon's emotions. "Scared."

"Of what?" His eyebrows rose in surprise.

"You," she answered honestly. Just like her, Zhayra was scared of what Niles would do, though with every second that passed without him panicking, she could feel both of them calming.

"Really?" he asked, his eyes flicking back to her. His expression turned serious as he studied her. "You don't need to worry about me saying anything."

"Thank you." A flood of overwhelming gratitude and relief hit her, and Zhayra's own tension eased, as Niles took her hand.

"So, you can't go home?" he asked quietly.

"No." She shook her head. "None of them would take me back," she said quietly. "Except my brother, but he'd be the only one."

"You have a brother?" He cocked his head in surprise.

"Yeah." Her throat clogged just thinking about Blaine. She swallowed heavily.

"You'll see him again one day," Niles said, squeezing her hand. "Maybe I can meet him."

She smiled. "I think he'd like you."

"Are you kidding? Who wouldn't like me?"

A startled laugh escaped her. She studied him. His face was still pale, but his brown eyes were sparkling and that more than anything convinced her he was all right.

"Niles," she started.

"Hmm?"

"How did you find us? Did you follow me?"

"Oh." He released her hand and rubbed the back of his neck, grinning sheepishly. "I saw you take Bentley. I wondered where you were going so late with Lorrin's horse." He laughed. "I didn't think you'd be sneaking out to see a dragon."

"Yeah, that would have been a shock."

"You have no idea." He sighed. "So, what's the plan now?"

"What do you mean?" She started tugging at the grass by her knee.

"You said Lorrin's trying to help. What's the plan?"

"I ... we're going to see the Asali council soon." She shrugged. "And he's trying to find a way to get through to his parents."

"That's not really a plan," Niles said, cocking an eyebrow. "A rough idea at best, but more like some hopes and dreams."

"I suppose." She sighed. "He tried talking to his parents when we got back from the White Mountains, but they weren't convinced. We're going to try and see the council in Liyarna instead and see if they can help, but I think we're mostly waiting to hear more about the dragon scales that were stolen before we do anything."

Niles nodded. "Still sketchy, but it's something I guess."

"What do you think?"

"Based on what you've said, the Asali are probably the best way to go. Things might be easier with them on your side." Niles looked back at Zhayra again as though realising something. "Is this why you want to learn to fight?"

"What I said earlier was true, about being attacked on the road," she said, and Niles's face darkened at the mention of the bandits. "But it's also because of this. I'm kind of expecting more trouble as long as Zhayra and I are together."

She expected him to ask whether she had to stay with Zhayra, and she had her answer ready, but Niles didn't say anything. He simply nodded, accepting what she'd said. He was usually such a light-hearted person, but tonight he'd shown a more serious side. She was beyond thankful for the way he'd listened to everything she'd said, considering it all and coming to his own conclusions.

"Thank you," she said again.

He smiled in return. "So, what now?"

"Now?" She grinned, jumping to her feet. "I'll introduce you to Zhayra."

"What?" His eyes widened comically and what little colour that had returned to his face disappeared.

"Yeah," she said, grabbing his hand and dragging him to his feet. Zhayra had let them talk for some time, but she sensed the dragon was growing impatient. She wanted to meet Niles properly, and Elinta was all for it.

"Uhhh." Niles laughed nervously. "Are you sure about this?"

"Yep." She gave his arm a hard tug and led him over to the dragon whose amber eyes were fixed on his brown ones.

Elinta brought them to a stop right in front of Zhayra's face. "Zhayra, this is Niles. Niles," she yanked on his arm to bring him forward another step, "this is Zhayra."

"Hello," Niles said, faintly. Humour bubbled up inside the dragon. With a wink at Zhayra, Elinta pulled Niles's hand forward. "What are you doing?" He looked from her to his hand and back.

"It's fine." She laughed and dropped his hand onto the scales of Zhayra's nose.

Niles laughed nervously. "She's so smooth." He slowly moved his hand down Zhayra's muzzle.

"She likes to be patted along her cheek," Elinta said quietly, watching the wonder play across Niles's face.

He glanced nervously her way.

"Go on," she said, giving him a gentle shove.

He stepped sideways, closer to Zhayra, and reached his hand out to rub the dragon's cheek. Zhayra's eyes closed in pleasure. This time Niles smiled without any nerves tainting his face.

"She's amazing," he whispered.

"Yeah," she said, and Zhayra opened her eyes to look at her. "She is."

Niles ran his hand along Zhayra's face, then stepped back and looked at the dimming lamp that Elinta had left behind them.

"It's getting late and that'll be out of oil soon. We should get back to the city."

Elinta nodded. She wasn't sure what the time was, but she had a feeling she'd been out for too long already.

After saying goodbye to Zhayra, Elinta picked up the lantern and walked back through the trees with Niles to Bentley. There was another horse tied near him, the one that Niles must have followed her on.

"I'll still help you," Niles said, untying his horse's reins. "Training," he added when she frowned in confusion.

"Thank you." She hugged him. "Thank you for listening."

"Of course." His arms slipped around her, and he gave her a squeeze. "I knew you liked me," he said, pulling back and winking at her. "This just proves it. Wait until I tell Lorrin you hugged me."

Rolling her eyes, she took Bentley's reins and mounted the gelding. "He'd never believe you anyway. We all know you're deluded."

"Deluded?" he said, slipping into the saddle of his own horse. "That's just cruel."

She smiled and nudged Bentley into a walk. Niles hurried to catch up with her.

"Are there any other secrets I need to know?" Niles said. "Twice in one day is a bit much for me, you know. I'd like some warning next time. You're not madly in love with me, are you?"

"No." Elinta laughed, switching to hold Bentley's reins with one hand. "No. That's about it."

"Good." He sounded genuinely relieved.

Once they'd left Zhayra behind, Elinta's eyes grew heavy but strangely, she didn't feel tired. There was too much adrenaline running through her body, mingling with an overwhelming sense of relief. The trip back to the city seemed to pass quicker than ever, but as the palace came into view, Elinta was hit with a sinking feeling.

"Niles," she said, as they drew nearer to the street he lived on.

"Yeah?"

"I think the gate's closed," she said, looking at him worriedly.

He craned his neck to see the palace gate, then looked up at the moon. "I think it's been closed for a while." He saw her face and waved a hand. "Don't worry, I'll talk to the guard."

"OK," she said, trying not to sound too concerned. She mentally kicked herself for taking so long in the woods, but she couldn't have helped it. She'd needed to tell Niles everything, and that had taken time. A lot of it.

They finally came to a halt in front of the closed gate and a shadowed figure appeared.

"Gate's closed," came its deep voice.

"Aaric, is that you?" Niles called lightly.

The man stepped into the light of Elinta's lantern. "Niles?" The man sighed. "What is it this time? If this is about that singing thing you did in the dining hall ..."

Niles grinned. "Oh, I don't need to go in. My friend here is staying on the third floor and needs to come inside before she's missed."

Niles pointed at Elinta with his thumb. She knew the third floor was specifically for the royal family and important visitors. Elinta had been confused when she found she'd be staying there, but now she was grateful.

Aaric turned thoughtful green eyes on her. "I've seen you around."

Elinta nodded, finally recognising the man. She'd seen the guard a couple of times during her stay at the palace.

"Don't you know the gates close at midnight?" Aaric said, his voice annoyed more than anything else.

Niles cut in before she could respond. "She's a tad forgetful. Just this once, could you let her in? Won't happen again though, man."

Aaric sighed again and stepped out of view. A moment later, the left gate started to move.

Relieved, Elinta leant over in the saddle to give Niles another quick hug.

"Thank you," she said, "for everything."

"Oh, this just proves it," Niles said, eyes twinkling. "I have to tell Lorrin now."

"Goodnight, Niles," she said, dismounting and leading Bentley through the gate.

"Goodnight, my love," he called after her.

She was sure she heard him laughing as she crossed the courtyard. Aaric closed the gate with another loud sigh.

Despite not getting into bed until the early hours of the morning, when Elinta woke, she felt lighter than she ever had. There were two people in her life now that knew all about her and Zhayra and who had decided to stick by her. The idea of not having to hide anything from Niles anymore practically caused her to float. She changed into her running clothes and had to stop herself from skipping her way down to the gardens to meet Lorrin for their morning run.

"You seem particularly happy this morning," Lorrin said as they started their run at an even pace along the track worn by their feet.

"I had an interesting night," she said, voice bouncing in time with her gait.

Lorrin frowned. As far as he knew, she'd gone straight to bed when he'd left her by her room after training the night before.

"I paid a visit to a friend," she said, purposely cryptic in case anyone heard them.

"How was she?"

"Good. Except I wasn't the only one that visited her."

Lorrin tripped on his feet and nearly landed in a bed of bright red flowers. "What?"

"Niles followed me out last night."

"Niles?" Lorrin spluttered, his face draining of colour. "What happened?"

"It's OK." Elinta stopped beside him and smiled reassuringly. "I told him everything. He took it really well."

A gush of air escaped him. "Really?"

"Really. He still wants to help too."

Lorrin smiled. "He's a good mate," he said proudly.

"He is," she said, running off.

Lorrin hurried to follow her. "And your friend? Did they get along?"

"Once the initial shock went away." She laughed, the light of day helping her forget the panic of the night before.

Lorrin laughed too, and they finished their run in companionable silence. It seemed as though a weight had been lifted from Lorrin's shoulders as well. As they left the gardens and headed towards the dining hall for breakfast, Lorrin interrupted the quiet.

"Preparations for the ball for my father's birthday are starting today. We probably won't see much of each other during the days until it's over." He grimaced apologetically.

She paused in surprise. The king's birthday wasn't for another month at least, but she shrugged. There must be a lot to do then. "That's OK. I'm sure I can find something to pass the time." There had been many days where she only saw him at mealtimes or when they trained, so she'd already had to entertain herself before, since Niles was usually on duty as well. Lorrin nodded a greeting to one of the uniformed soldiers that passed them.

"Is Niles on today?" she asked, thinking of the way he'd promised to help her despite the paleness of his face.

"He doesn't start until after lunch. Although," he cocked his head, "he never misses a chance for a meal, so I'm sure we'll see him at lunch."

CHAPTER
SIXTEEN

E LINTA HURRIED DOWN THE steps from the third floor, a
new sketchbook and pencils in her arms. Queen Mira had
sent them to her the day before so she could take a break from her
supposed research for Ford, and they'd sketched together in the
afternoon. But, with Niles and Lorrin busy again, she wanted to
go sit in the gardens and finally draw the scarlet crowns. She was
halfway down the stairs when three guards strode past, their eyes
fixed ahead as they went up to the third floor. Elinta stopped to
watch them go. There'd been more guards around since Alexander's death and the theft of the scales. But the additional soldiers
seemed kind of pointless to her. The thief had got what they'd

wanted. Or maybe that was just her discomfort speaking. The men made her even more aware of the secret she was hiding. She almost felt silly going to the gardens now.

"Is there a reason you're blocking the staircase?"

Elinta turned towards the voice, finding the advisor she'd passed with Niles just days before, a few stairs below her.

Shae.

"I—" she stammered. "I'm sorry." Elinta glanced around. She was hardly blocking the staircase. In fact, she thought she could easily spread her arms to either side and there would be room to spare. And the guards had just walked easily past her.

Mentally shrugging, Elinta tentatively took a step down, but Shae didn't move.

"You heard about Alexander," she said, her small eyes scanning Elinta. Her brown hair was tied back into a strict ponytail, tugging at the corners of her round face.

"Yes," Elinta said. Word had spread throughout the palace that Alexander had died, though no one seemed to know how. The cause hadn't been confirmed by the royals. Elinta didn't like the way the woman was looking at her, so she added, "Do you know what happened to him?"

Shae's head tilted. "Yes, and we will stop the person who did it."

Elinta paused. The woman had just told her Alexander was murdered. Something no one but a select few seemed to know.

Shae was still staring at her.

"He was killed?" Elinta said, a beat too late.

"Yes."

"That's awful." She sidestepped. "I should get going." She gestured at the sketchbook she held and went down another step.

"Of course," Shae said, but she didn't move. "If you should hear anything about what happened, if you *know* anything, it would be within your interests to come forward."

Elinta stared at her. "I don't know anything." She cringed as she said it. It was the kind of denial someone who did know something would say. But she didn't know what'd happened to the man, just why it'd happened.

"No." Shae cocked her head. "It was nice seeing you again."

"Uh, you too, Shae."

Shae's face darkened, and Elinta felt her eyes widen. The woman really did want people to call her advisor.

"Bye!" Elinta hurried down the steps, forcing herself not to look back at the woman who she knew instinctively was watching her go.

When she arrived in the garden, Elinta couldn't pull her mind away from her strange encounter with the advisor. The woman had acted so oddly, almost as though she'd been testing Elinta. She bit her lip. Maybe the woman just didn't like her because of Niles and the prank he'd pulled. After all, she'd been there when he'd decided to do it, just after running into Shae. But it seemed such a harmless thing. Anyone else would have laughed along with Niles, she was sure of it.

Elinta stared at the patch of scarlet crown in front of her and opened her sketchbook. She didn't have any real reason to worry about Shae yet. She'd just have to be careful around the woman and watch what she said. More than usual, anyway. Elinta pulled out a pencil and got to work, trying not to let the advisor spoil her day. But Shae remained in the back of her mind.

When Monday arrived, Elinta finally ventured down into the city by herself. Both Lorrin and Niles were busy again for the day, and she could hardly spend all her spare time with the queen either. When she told Lorrin of her plans at breakfast, he gave her coins to buy lunch in the city and encouraged her to make a day of it. They'd hardly spent any time together, and he was clearly feeling guilty. But Elinta didn't mind. She was enjoying her time at the palace more than she ever thought she would, and though she looked forward to their trip to Liyarna, she found she wasn't entirely in a hurry for it either. If Zhayra had been allowed in the city, she would have been perfectly happy.

Tying her hair back and hitching her backpack over her shoulder, Elinta set off into the city streets, letting her feet guide her. It was a warm day with the sun reflecting off the stone streets, but there was a gentle breeze to cool her bare arms. She'd seen most of the city during her trips with Lorrin and Niles, but she still found herself gawping at the many sights around her. Nevira was so different to her home, so different to what she remembered of Culmar, that everywhere she looked she was amazed anew.

Even though the markets weren't open, she went down to the trading square. She'd never seen it empty of stalls before and marvelled at how big the area seemed even with all the foot-traffic. She gazed around the square and her jaw dropped when her eyes landed on a cream-coloured statue in its centre. Somehow, she'd missed the human shaped, and sized, statue on her previous visits to the square.

She meandered through the square, glancing around the rest of the space in case there was something else she'd missed, but there weren't any other statues. She approached it from the back, but it was clearly the figure of a man in an elegant coat dipping down to the ground. Slipping around to the front of the statue, she looked up into its face and her heart stopped in her chest.

"King Cenric." Her voice shook and her eyes suddenly grew heavy. She was looking, once again, at the man responsible for the banishment of the dragons. It felt like this man was everywhere. Zhayra's emotions had shifted into a deep sadness, tainted by an anger rising in her throat as soon as Elinta had looked at the statue. Was it possible the dragon somehow knew what she was looking at? King Cenric had been carved in a magnanimous pose as though he really was their saviour, and he knew it. Her stomach curled. How different her views on this man had become in the past few weeks.

"Elinta."

She whirled around and found herself face to face with Ford Mayes, just as she had the day they'd met.

"Ford. Hi," she said, her voice rising in surprise. He was wearing a light shirt, revealing surprisingly muscular arms.

"Are you alright?" he asked, frowning down at her. She rubbed at her watery eyes, wondering whether they were as red as they felt, and nodded.

"Yes." She sniffed. "Sorry, I wasn't expecting to see you."

"I've only just returned," he said, glancing between her and the statue of the king behind her thoughtfully.

"Did you have a good trip?" she asked, not sure what else to say to the man.

He smiled gently. "Yes."

Elinta shifted uncomfortably. Now that she wasn't looking at it anymore, she wanted to get away from the statue of King Cenric, but she didn't want to be rude to the man that had kindly agreed to cover for her. Thinking of the king prompted a memory.

She lowered her voice, making sure there was no chance of them being overheard.

"Did you hear about the dragon scales?" she asked, sure this man at least knew they existed.

One of his eyebrows rose. "I did."

She took a deep breath and plunged on. Lorrin would want to know the same things as she did. "Do you know who'd want to take them?"

"No," he paused, "but I'm sure we'll hear from them again."

"Why?"

"Will you walk with me?" he asked, his dark eyes searching her face.

"Sure," she said, adjusting her backpack and hesitantly following him out of the east side of the square.

"Whoever it is went through a lot of trouble to get into the palace for the scales," he said, when she drew alongside him. "Someone with that kind of motivation will hardly settle just for the scales."

"What do you mean?" she asked, quickening her pace to keep up with him.

"There are other trinkets that may appeal to someone interested in old artifacts," he said in a low voice. He didn't say anymore but led her further into the city. She recognised several of the buildings they passed, but she'd spent most of her time on her previous visits around the major parts of the city and along the main road. Once they left the road they were on, she'd probably lose track of where they were. *Where are we going?* she wondered.

An elderly man was walking slowly on the other side of the road, heading towards them. Elinta waited for him to pass before she continued to quiz Ford.

"Do you think the thief will sell the scales?" she asked, once the old man was out of earshot.

Ford was silent for a moment. "No," he said finally. "I believe they mean to keep them."

Elinta's stomach sank at the idea. That would mean the men sent out to look for them would return empty handed, and Elinta and Lorrin's cause wouldn't be helped by the tragedy. But there was no real way to know without the men actually returning, and that wouldn't be for at least several more weeks, even months. And all that time could be a waste.

"This way," Ford said, interrupting her thoughts and turning down another street. Hardly a hundred metres on, he turned again, and Elinta's fears were realised. She'd need him to take her back to the market square if she was going to find her way back to the palace. Even though it loomed over a large part of the city, the winding streets made it hard to reach.

They stopped outside a small building made of a dark grey stone. Small pots full of herbs, medicinal and culinary, hung from the windows and lay sprawled by the front door.

"Please come inside. I have something that might interest you." Ford disappeared inside and Elinta hesitantly followed him into his home. She blinked as her eyes adjusted to the dim light of the entryway, and the simple room came into view.

Ford stood in the far corner of the main room, looking through one of the many shelves filled to overflowing with books and scrolls lining the walls. A table stood in the centre of the room, covered in papers, pencils, and pens. It was all completely at odds with the rest of the main room, which was clean and ordered. A sink was tucked into the corner of the room, and to her left were two doors, one at least had to lead to a bedroom.

"Here we go," Ford said, pulling a scroll down from a shelf and turning back to her. "I know you're not really my student, but this might interest you."

Elinta took the paper from his outstretched hand and gawked at the little image smiling up at her from beside the seal. A black dragon, wings spread in flight, stared back at her.

"Where did you get this?" she asked without thinking. In all her time in the library, she'd never found a book solely on the dragons. In fact, she was sure she'd read everything there on the topic. She was too surprised for a moment to think about the reasons behind him giving it to her.

Ford smiled as though satisfied with something he saw in her. "I'd appreciate it if no one saw you with this except perhaps Prince Lorrin. Whilst my position allows me access to resources others don't have, I'd prefer it if this wasn't advertised."

"But," she stammered, "why give it to me?"

He didn't know about Zhayra. He couldn't know.

"Am I wrong in assuming you might find it informative?"

She stared down at the little dragon for a long moment, then looked back up into his dark, knowing eyes. "No."

"Good." He led her back to the door. "Return it to me when you're finished with it."

"Thank you," she said, still wondering what he must suspect about her to give her a scroll on dragons. She and Lorrin hadn't revealed that much to him, had they?

"There is one more thing," Ford said.

Elinta looked up from tucking the scroll inside her backpack.

"Shae has been asking questions about you."

Elinta's eyes widened. *The advisor?* "What do you mean?"

"She thinks you might have *other* reasons for being in Nevira. Don't worry," he added, seeing her face pale. "As far as she can tell, you are my student."

"Thank you." But what had made the woman so suspicious of her? She thought back to the last time she'd seen the woman and the way she'd stared at her. The way she'd insinuated Elinta knew more than she should. More than she did. What did Shae think she'd done?

"Be careful, Elinta," the historian said, stepping out into the fresh air. "I'll take you back to the square."

That night Elinta lay curled in bed, propped up against her pillows and pouring over the scroll Ford had given her by the light of a lantern. Her mind had been on nothing but the scroll since she'd returned, and she'd paid for it at her lesson with Lorrin and Niles by receiving several new bruises. She couldn't help it though; she was desperate to know what Ford had given her.

There were only two small paragraphs inside, one in Asalin and the translated text below it in the common tongue. That small paragraph contained more than she'd been able to find on the dragons in all her time searching the library. The first few words were unintelligible, but she could just make out the rest.

> '... zearla lurai ngaran *greeted me to my immense surprise and brought me before their queen. I was fortunate enough to have arrived during their breeding season and was allowed a glimpse of the cave where their eggs are watched over. Though I cannot communicate with them, I expect my brief stay here as your representative will yield much insight into their ways.'*

She read over the words several times before putting the scroll aside. There was so much in the scroll to unpack, but it still didn't tell her anything about the emotion sharing she was experiencing. She repeated the opening words, *'zearla lurai ngaran.'* Hadn't Ciar called her *'Zearla lurai'?* What did it mean? She re-read the rest of the paragraph. It sounded like the Asali had sent some kind of ambassador to the dragons. Had this person written any other reports to the Asali king? Where were these now? But what she found most interesting was the dragons were ruled by a queen!

Beyond a doubt, this scroll confirmed what Ciar had told her and what she had seen herself in Zhayra. The dragons were sentient to the point that they had a society. Structure. They had a queen and needed ambassadors, or something similar. They really were the third race.

I have to show Lorrin! Maybe this was exactly what they needed to convince the king and queen of what Lorrin had tried to tell them when they'd arrived at the palace so many weeks ago.

Throwing back the covers of her bed, she quickly changed out of her nightgown and into the dress she'd discarded at the end of her bed.

She picked up the scroll and stared at it for a long moment. Certain she wasn't technically supposed to have it in her possession, she pulled a jacket on over her dress and tucked the scroll inside and out of sight. It was an odd look, but it was late in the night, and she doubted she'd run into anyone between her room and Lorrin's.

Ducking out of her room, she hurried down the corridor, glad she'd been there before. She found the door to his office easily and gently knocked. Then, wondering whether he'd hear her knock from his room, she lifted her hand to knock harder when the door opened.

"Elinta?" Lorrin stood before her, barefoot and in the same clothes he'd worn to their training session, but slightly more crumpled.

"Hi." She shifted uneasily, suddenly aware just how late it was. "I know it's late, but I wanted to show you something."

"Sure," he said, stepping aside to let her enter. She glanced around the office, noting his shoes by the door and the paperwork spread across his desk.

"Are you still working?" she asked, gaping at the amount of work he had.

"Yeah." He rubbed the back of his neck. "I had to put it off today."

"Oh. I can come back tomorrow?" she offered though she secretly hoped he'd refuse.

"No, it's OK." He smiled and gestured for her to take a seat at his desk. Rather than returning to his own chair, he sat in the one beside her. "What did you want to show me?"

Elinta pulled the scroll from inside her jacket and held it out to him.

"I thought this might help us," she said, barely able to contain her excitement. Lorrin cast her a curious glance before opening the scroll and reading the contents. She watched in anticipation as his eyes slid over the words inside. When he reached the end, he read it through again.

"A queen?" he said in wonder.

Elinta nodded. "It looks like it's written by an ambassador or something, don't you think?"

He nodded slowly. "This is amazing." He looked up at her. "Where did you get this?"

She hesitated a moment before replying, but Ford had told her it was OK for Lorrin to know, so she told him where she'd gotten it. She didn't mention her many questions as to why he'd given it to her. Ford knew they had questions about the dragons, but why give the scroll to her and not directly to Lorrin?

Lorrin chuckled. "Why am I not surprised?" he muttered, then turned back to the scroll, perusing the contents again. A shadow of doubt crossed his face.

"What is it?" she asked, just above a whisper.

"I don't think my parents would accept this," he said. "What did Ford say?"

She ran over their conversation again in her head. "That it might interest me and not to show it to anyone, except you," she admitted. "Why wouldn't your parents accept this? It shows what you've been saying all along!"

"I know." He sighed. "As far as I can tell from what I can read, the translation is accurate, but we can't prove it's a credible source. And," he sat back in his chair, "I don't know that they'd accept the written word of the Asali on this any more than they accepted Ciar's. I don't think they're going to throw over a century's worth of beliefs away for something like this."

Elinta desperately tried to find a way around what he was saying, but no matter how she looked at it, she knew he was right. "I guess that explains why Ford told me not to show anyone else."

"Yeah." He put the scroll down on his desk and looked her in the eye. "I'm sorry we're not getting anywhere with this."

"It's OK. I didn't think it would be easy." She averted her eyes, then looked back at him. "I—I just want to be safe," she whispered, voicing the truth that had been stirring in her mind for some time. Lorrin seemed confused by her words, but she wasn't finished. "I want to be with Zhayra, but I miss home, and I know that I can never go back there even if things work out here."

Her thoughts lingered on Shae. Things had been going so well for her in Nevira until now. Had the woman asked anyone else about her?

Lorrin took her hand. "What makes you say that?"

"My father," she said, shaking away her thoughts of Shae and all too easily recalling the expression on her father's face when she'd left with Zhayra. "He didn't need to say anything for me to be able to tell. He'll never change his mind on the dragons."

She didn't mention that she'd no longer have a master to learn from either. Even if he had the room, she doubted Galen would want her back. She was certain it was him who'd told the village about Zhayra in the first place. And he'd been there to see the results.

Lorrin opened his mouth to respond, but she interrupted him, shaking her head. "I'm sorry. I didn't mean to give you more of my problems."

"No, it's OK. I don't mind." He smiled, squeezing her hand.

"So," she said, slipping her hand from his and grabbing the scroll, "I guess we're back to square one."

"I guess," he said, following her gaze to the paper.

"Oh!" she said, her eyes catching on the first few legible words in the scroll. "Do you know what *'zearla lurai ngaran'* means?"

Lorrin had given her a couple small lessons on Asali, mostly teaching her greetings, farewells, the common blessing, and the proper pronunciation of them. She wasn't familiar with any of the three words from Lorrin's lessons but thought she knew what 'zearla' meant, or at least she had when among the Asali. They'd all whispered it when they saw Zhayra. Unaware of her trailing thoughts, Lorrin read the words aloud.

"No," he said, frowning over the paper. "*Lurai* is their word for friend, but I'm not sure about the others. Didn't Ciar call you *Zearla lurai*?"

She nodded.

"Huh," was all Lorrin could say.

"*Lurai,*" she repeated, "I thought *zearla* might mean dragon."

"Dragon friend," he said, smiling at her. "That certainly fits. I wonder what *ngaran* means then? It sounds a little like their words for husband and wife, but that doesn't make sense."

She laughed. "We're definitely not married."

"No," Lorrin agreed, stifling a yawn.

They sat in silence for a while, both pondering the scroll, but when Lorrin yawned again Elinta came back to herself.

"I should go. It's really late," she said, casting an apologetic look towards the papers Lorrin still had strewn across his desk.

"I can make it up tomorrow," Lorrin said, following her gaze. Rolling up the scroll, he handed it back to her. "Thanks for showing me this. I can't believe they had a queen!" he said with wonder.

"I wish I could ask Zhayra about it," she said, voicing a desire that had crossed her mind more than once. Things would be so much better if they could talk to each other.

Lorrin agreed and showed her out, wishing her a goodnight. As she left, he called down the hall after her. "El?"

"Yeah?" she said, turning.

"You're welcome to come by whenever you need to talk. Even if it's late."

"Thank you." She smiled. Waving goodnight, she padded down the hall back to her room. She dreamt of dragons that night.

The next few weeks passed in much the same way as the past week had. Elinta kept searching for answers but found none. The palace grew busier by the day with preparations for the king's birthday fully underway. Lorrin was detained with work even more than usual and had to drop back his help with her training to three nights a week. As a result, she had four one-on-one sessions with Niles a week, who then went home early on the other nights. The arrangement suited Elinta just fine, and she soon found she could train a full hour with the wooden sword without her arms aching. In fact, her arms had become quite toned from the constant workout.

Niles had been right the night he'd offered to help her train. He did have a different style of fighting and teaching than Lorrin's, and she excelled under their different methods. She'd only won once against Niles, and not at all against Lorrin, and she was certain the win was a fluke. But it was progress.

Through all of this, Elinta snuck out of the palace at night once a week to see Zhayra. She would have gone more often if she wasn't worried about drawing attention to herself. As it was, several of the guards recognised her on sight when she left the palace. Neither Lorrin nor Niles joined her on the trips as their nights were often full between juggling their duties and helping her train, so she had Zhayra all to herself.

CHAPTER SEVENTEEN

"U P YOU GET, MISS! You'll be late for your run with the prince," Neva said, bustling into the room and drawing back the curtains from the window.

The sunlight streamed inside and Elinta blinked fiercely against the light.

"It's going to be a busy day!" the maid said, hurrying about the room. "Kalla will be by for one last fitting straight after breakfast, but she hardly ever gets anything wrong, so I expect it won't take very long. The ball starts at seven tonight, so make sure you've got plenty of time to get ready."

As usual, Elinta hardly had a moment to speak a word to the maid.

"Will you be needing my help getting ready tonight?"

Elinta nodded, hoping to at least indicate her acceptance of the offer before the maid continued talking, but she managed to thank her as well.

"I'll come by at five and we'll get you ready." Neva jumped in excitement, her green eyes sparkling. "You're going to have so much fun!"

Elinta nodded hesitantly. She hoped she'd have fun, but ...

"Neva?" Elinta said uncertainly.

"Yes?"

"Aren't I going to be a little out of place?" Elinta asked, picturing a room full of dancing advisors and generals. She was just ... Elinta. And to the palace, she was just a history student. "I'm not important," she added, seeing the maid's frown.

Neva waved aside her concerns. "Oh, don't worry. The ballroom will be full of people who aren't connected to the royal family like the officials and their families are. Besides, the whole city will be celebrating as well."

She wasn't sure whether that made her feel better or not.

🔥🔥🔥

"It looks lovely!" Neva shrieked beside her, causing Elinta to flinch.

Elinta laughed and ran a hand down the front of the dress. She'd spent the day hiding out of the way in the palace gardens but had returned to her room in time to meet the maid.

"It's amazing," Elinta agreed.

Kalla had dropped the dress off sometime during the day and though she never would have picked it for herself, Elinta couldn't get over just how beautiful it was. Neva had spent the last two hours doing Elinta's hair and makeup and helping her into the dress. The ball was due to start any minute.

Elinta grabbed the other woman's hand. "Thank you, Neva."

"Oh! It was my pleasure." Neva jumped up and down. "You have to tell me all about it tomorrow!"

"I will." Elinta chuckled. It was so good to have Neva, someone who could help her and could talk with her about the ball. Niles and Lorrin didn't seem like the kind of people to talk to about that kind of thing.

She glanced towards the bathroom door, wondering if she'd have time to quickly look at herself in the mirror before the boys arrived.

There was a knock on the door and Neva squealed again.

"That's them," Elinta said, turning away from the bathroom, suddenly a mess of nerves and excitement. She was going to her first proper ball!

"All right then, time to go." Neva swept open the door and shoved her through, almost straight into Lorrin. Niles stood beside him.

"Wow." Niles looked her up and down. "You clean up good."

"Thanks," she said. "You don't look bad yourself."

Which was an understatement. Niles cleaned up *really* well. His blond hair was still messy but could be called neat for him. He wore a formal version of his uniform, red shoulder lapels and all, except the smooth grey jacket folded across itself and was held with small silver buttons. His sword was at his hip in its usual simple scabbard, but it complemented the look.

Niles nudged Lorrin with his elbow in what she assumed he thought was a movement she wouldn't notice. Elinta turned her eyes to Lorrin a moment before he was able to collect himself. He'd been gaping at her. She ran a hand consciously over her dress again and spoke before he could.

"You look …" She took in the suit he was wearing, the vest peeking through underneath his jacket and the sword at his hip in an elegantly decorated scabbard. "Good," she finished, but she wasn't sure that was the word she'd been looking for.

"You look beautiful," he said in response. "That dress … Kalla outdid herself."

Elinta agreed, and the three stood there a moment awkwardly. She found it hard to keep her eyes away from Lorrin and the way the vest brought out the colour in his eyes.

"Let's go." Niles clapped his hands together and Lorrin offered her his arm, which Elinta took with a smile.

Niles appeared on her other side and took her free arm in his. The boys led her down to the ballroom on the first floor. She had to let go of Niles on the way down the stairs to hold up the hem of her dress, but grabbed his arm again, much to his satisfaction, once they reached the bottom.

She caught her first proper glimpse of herself in a mirror as they rounded a corner and sent a silent thanks to Neva again because there was no way she could have done what the maid had with her hair or makeup. And the *dress*. The dress really was beautiful. It was light blue-grey in colour, made of an incredibly thin, silk-like material that became twice layered and covered with a delicate lace from just above her hips and reaching down to her feet. The top had a V-shaped neckline with a deep-grey beaded section across her middle. Thick ribbon, tied at her shoulders, held the dress in place. The same ribbon, secured in a criss-cross pattern that Neva had both adored and condemned, ran up the back.

Elinta's blonde hair was pulled back in an elegant bun with wisps left out to frame her face. She desperately hoped she wasn't overdressed, but the dress was so beautiful that she almost didn't care. For a moment, she felt like any normal girl, not one hiding a dragon.

The large open doors of the ballroom came into view. Two guards stood at attention on either side, but people moved through them unchallenged. When the guards caught sight of Lorrin, they nodded respectfully.

"At ease, boys," Niles said with a grin.

Lorrin hardly seemed to react to his friend's antics, and Elinta's eyes were on the doors to the ballroom, her ears glued to the music drifting out.

She stopped, awestruck as they reached the doorway, unsure where to look first. The room was full of people, most of them dancing to a soft tune the band was playing to her left, on the other side of the huge room. But it was the room itself that caught her attention, stretching away to her left and right. Large, indented arched windows lined the opposite wall, reaching nearly all the way to the high vaulted ceiling. They were bigger than any windows she'd ever seen before. Beautiful engraved sills surrounded the glass panes and framed both the windows and the view of the shadowed grounds. Her eyes flitted up the glass to the curved ceiling where large paintings stared down at her, framed by intricate golden webbing, coming together in the centre, and forming simple circles at the base of seven huge, crystal chandeliers. Elinta stared at each one for several long moments. They had three levels, each larger than the previous until it ended with large crystal jewels dangling below, reflecting the light above and around them.

A light chuckle sounded beside her. "Do you want to go inside?"

"Please!" Niles answered for her.

Elinta ignored Niles and switched her gaze to Lorrin. He was watching her with a sparkle in his eyes. "It's ..." She searched for the right word. It was beautiful, it was extravagant, it was... "Huge." She frowned. "And beautiful."

"It is," Lorrin said, his eyes not leaving her.

"So, can we go in?" Niles said, hardly listening and eyes glued to a table of food set against the wall to their right.

Nodding, she followed Niles inside since she'd unconsciously let go of them both while she'd been staring at the ballroom.

"Niles," Lorrin called from beside her with a sigh, but he was smiling. "We have to see my parents first."

Niles's shoulders slumped, and he turned his back on the food. "I know."

"Wait, we do?" Elinta asked, eyes darting between her friends. She'd spent a lot of time with Queen Mira though not at any formal events and had occasionally seen the king around but not enough to make her feel totally at ease with approaching them in the ballroom.

"It's customary to present yourself to the king and queen at certain events," Lorrin explained and struck out towards the other side of the room.

Elinta trailed after him and Niles dejectedly joined her right as she caught sight of the king and queen. The king wore a formal military suit decorated with gold patterns along the collar and shoulders, even the buttons were made of gold. His sword was in an extravagant sheath, but it was the simple silver-blue band on his brow that caught her attention.

"Is that *illayas*?" she breathed, eyes locked on the crown.

"It is," Lorrin said, dropping back to walk with her and Niles. "It was a gift from the Asali centuries ago."

"But ... he's wearing it," she stammered. She'd thought the Asali were practically a taboo subject in the palace since so little information on them existed and the king and queen refused to mend ties.

"That's usually what you do with a crown." Niles laughed.

She slapped his arm. "You know what I mean." She paused. "Don't you?"

Niles rubbed at his arm in mock pain, but she knew she'd barely even touched him.

"Things might not be going well between our people, but *illayas* is extremely valuable, and the gift was given in a time of peace," Lorrin said with a slight shrug.

Elinta considered this and nodded. She supposed it made sense. When she thought about it, all of the *illayas* among their people was technically from the Asali since they were the only ones who had discovered how to shape it. If anything, she supposed it was even more valuable since their friendship had ended and the dragons had left. Now they were unlikely to ever get more.

"Lorrin, there you are," King Aldon said, pulling his son into a hug. The queen smiled and kissed him on the cheek.

"You look beautiful," Elinta heard him say to his mother.

Niles nodded a bow and greeted both, also complimenting the queen on her stunning dress. Elinta repeated the greetings to both of them, shifting awkwardly under the king's gaze. She'd hardly seen him since she'd first arrived in Nevira and though he seemed kind, she was uncomfortably aware of her link to Zhayra while under his gaze. She managed to wish him a happy birthday before moving to stand in front of the queen. Elinta couldn't help complimenting Mira on her dress as well, a deep red that hugged her figure before spreading out at her waist and falling to the ground. When the queen twisted, she could see the back fell down in a large V, stopping halfway down her back. Her hair was half down with intricate braids pulling it back, and it was framed by a delicate crown on her head.

"You look lovely, Elinta," Queen Mira said quietly in response.

Elinta curtsied, turning to take her leave of the queen, and found Shae directly behind her.

"Shae," Elinta said, throwing her hands up to stop them colliding. The woman had placed herself strategically, so Elinta had no choice but to speak with her.

Her beady eyes swept over Elinta, noticeably landing on a bruise on her forearm. She had a moment to be thankful Niles hadn't given her any fresh ones in their training last night.

"That is a nasty bruise," Shae said though the bruise was a faint yellow. "Where did you get it?"

Elinta lowered her arms, her answer ready. She'd planned her excuses the very first night she'd trained. "I tripped in the hall outside my room a couple days ago."

"And bruised your forearm?"

"I'm really clumsy." Elinta felt Lorrin stiffen behind her, still in conversation with his mother.

"Really?" the advisor said.

Elinta swallowed heavily. She knew what the woman was getting at. Bruised forearms were common defensive wounds. Elinta had seen them a hundred times working with Galen, particularly after Jareth's training nights. But why wouldn't Shae drop it? A small bruise was hardly cause for suspicion. And why was she so interested in her? This was only the second time they'd actually spoken, yet the woman had treated her strangely right from the beginning. What had she done? Sweat began to bead on her forehead.

"Oh, Shae, leave the poor girl." Queen Mira laughed, moving to stand beside her. Lorrin joined them as well, his face unreadable. "Elinta's a little clumsy. Why, she tripped just a couple days ago on her way out of my tea rooms! She's lucky she doesn't have more bruises."

Elinta nearly sighed in relief, but a snicker from Niles distracted her and she discreetly elbowed him. Shae's beady eyes lingered on Elinta a moment longer before she nodded a bow to the queen and Lorrin, and left, a slight waddle in her hips.

Elinta, Lorrin, and Niles took their leave of the king and queen but stopped only a few metres away. She could still feel Shae's eyes on her.

"That was weird, hey?" Niles muttered. Elinta and Lorrin both nodded. "Oi." He turned to Elinta, a wide grin spreading across his face. "Since when are you so clumsy? You're gonna have to do a demonstration for us."

Niles laughed as Elinta jokingly glared at him. He'd never let her forget that.

"I have to finish greeting everyone, but I'll catch up with you two later," Lorrin said and joined his parents again. She thought she saw him glance at Shae. But otherwise, it seemed the queen's defence of Elinta had been enough to push Shae from his mind as he didn't look at the advisor again, and Elinta tried to do the same. It was her first ball, and the woman's strange attentions wouldn't ruin it.

Elinta gazed after Lorrin in mild confusion though, but when someone else arrived to greet the king, queen, and him as well, she felt silly. Of course, Lorrin wouldn't be able to spend the whole night with her and Niles; he was the prince.

"Hungry?" Niles asked.

"Yes."

"Would you like some help getting there?" Niles reached for her arm, and she batted him away.

"I'm never going to live this down, am I?" she said, but she was thankful for his attempts to distract her from Shae.

"No. Never."

She followed him to the food, careful to stay out of the way of the couples dancing and tried the first thing Niles recommended; a soft biscuit dotted with chocolate pieces and a caramel centre. The sweetness burst into her mouth, and she couldn't help closing her eyes in pleasure.

The dance floor was steadily filling with more and more couples as the band smoothly transitioned through songs of various tempo. Elinta watched the couples dancing, occasionally checking to see how Lorrin was doing, but he was always talking with someone. She couldn't stop her eyes from drifting up above the twirling couples and towards the painted ceiling and the chandeliers. *How do people paint so intricately on a ceiling?*

Niles cleared his throat and she turned to see his hand held out towards her. "May I have this dance, miss?"

"Um … sure," she said. He frowned at her lack of enthusiasm. "I haven't danced in a long time."

Niles waved her concern aside. "All you need is a good partner and, fortunately, I am just that."

"You're incredibly modest too." She laughed, taking his hand.

"Now you're getting it," he said, leading her towards the other couples just as a new song began.

She put her hand on his shoulder as he took her waist and led her around the floor, effortlessly following the same steps as those around them.

"You're not so bad," he said, gracefully dropping her into a dip.

"It's all you," she said in complete honesty. She wasn't at all familiar with the dance and had already trod on his foot twice.

"Bet you're glad I didn't give you any new bruises while training last night," he said, eyeing the one on her arm that Shae had noticed.

"A little." She paused as he twisted her away then pulled her back. "But I would have liked to return some of those bruises."

He laughed, continuing to lead her around the room. "You are getting better. Might have to start you on a real sword soon." He saw the alarm flash across her face. "Dulled, of course. I don't wanna lose a limb."

"Good," she said and returned to his earlier compliment on her skill. "I have two very good teachers."

The song finished and another began. Niles easily led her through the new moves.

"I didn't know you were such a good dancer," she said, just managing not to stand on his toe.

"I've been to a lot of these." He shrugged. "When your father's a general and an advisor to the king *and* your best mate is the prince, you always seem to be at some kind of function."

"Is your father here tonight?" She hadn't met General Sonnen yet and was curious to see if they were anything alike. Niles had a lot of mischief in him; maybe he'd gotten it from his father.

"He'll be here soon," he said.

She lapsed into silence as they moved through some more complicated moves.

When the song ended, Lorrin appeared behind Niles and tapped him on the shoulder.

"My turn," he said with a grin.

Niles frowned. "Go find yourself some other pretty girl," he said, but released Elinta anyway. "If this man bothers you too much, just call for me." He beelined for the buffet table, throwing them a wink over his shoulder.

Shaking her head at Niles, Elinta placed her hand in Lorrin's and her other on his shoulder just as another, slower song started. Elinta didn't speak for the first minute as she focused all her attention on not stepping on his feet, watching her own as they moved.

"You know," Lorrin said, "it's easier if you look up."

"I know," Elinta said, glancing up and finding Lorrin's eyes locked on her face. "But I don't want to stand on you."

Lorrin smiled. "I'm sure I can take it. I'd much rather be looking at your face than your head even if I have to suffer."

Elinta laughed and forced herself to keep her head up, just as she'd done with Niles.

"There," Lorrin said a moment later. "Not so bad?"

Elinta stood on his foot. "I'm sorry." She laughed, leaning into him to hide her flushed cheeks. "I think you spoke too soon."

Lorrin laughed and Elinta pulled back just as he led her through a graceful spin and a couple of more complicated moves.

She had to admit that if Niles had been a good dancer, Lorrin was incredible. If only she wasn't so nervous.

"You've given me worse in training," he said to her, continuing their conversation once she was back in place before him.

Elinta cocked her head. "I suppose. But we'll wait and see if it bruises first."

The song came to its end, and the musicians seamlessly moved onto another song.

"Have you been to many balls?" Lorrin asked, continuing to lead her around the floor.

She shook her head. "I don't think there's ever been one in Kethmere."

"I couldn't tell." Lorrin smiled. "You really do look beautiful tonight, El."

"Thank you." She blushed. They finished the dance in silence.

"I think I need a drink," Elinta said, stepping away from Lorrin as the music faded. Her cheeks still felt warm.

"Good idea."

They left the dance floor to find Niles and the drinks table. As it turned out, they were both in the same place.

"Here you go." Niles handed them both a glass of pink liquid. Gratefully taking a sip, Elinta tasted a fizzy mix of berries. Thirsty, she guzzled it down.

"I'm thinking about asking Shae to dance," Niles said, and Elinta choked on her drink.

"No! Not tonight," she said, once her coughing had subsided. She didn't want to give Shae any more reasons to dislike her. Not that she knew the supposed reason she had *now*. But if Niles teased her tonight, she had a feeling Shae's dislike of *her* would deepen too.

Niles's eyebrows rose in surprise.

Lorrin glanced at her with narrowed eyes.

"Just," Elinta stammered, aware she hadn't told them everything, "Shae's been a little weird tonight. I don't think it's a good idea."

"OK." Niles shrugged, but he looked a little disappointed.

"Your father's arrived," Lorrin said to Niles, glancing towards the door.

"And your aunt," Niles said.

Eagerly following Lorrin's gaze, Elinta saw a man with combed, shoulder-length greying brown hair enter the room and instantly saw his resemblance to Niles, particularly in his eyes. He wore a similar uniform to Niles, but the jacket was black and didn't fold over itself. His general's colours were on his shoulders. Elinta almost didn't recognise Lorrin's aunt, General Nash, entering behind him arm in arm with a man she assumed was her husband. General Nash was also in the colours of her rank but in a dress that fit snug against her figure and her hair hung loose about her face. Their twin children followed behind them, also arm in arm. The large group, including General Sonnen, crossed the room to greet the royals.

Elinta reached for another glass of the drink Niles had handed her. The twins plunged into the crowd as soon as they'd greeted their aunt and uncle, and she lost sight of them within seconds. Elinta locked eyes with General Nash as the woman turned away from speaking with her brother and smiled at her. Returning the smile, General Nash allowed her husband to lead her to the dance floor. Elinta found the sight completely at odds with the view she'd formed of the woman through their short meetings, but she enjoyed watching her twirl across the floor. Like Lorrin and Niles, she would have grown up going to balls like this one.

"Your Highness," a gruff voice interrupted her thoughts, and she focused on the man that had just approached them. "Son," General Sonnen said to Niles, gripping his son's forearm, before fixing his eyes on her. Faint lines from years in the sunshine and hard work streaked his face, yet he seemed younger than her own father. "You must be Elinta," he said. "I've heard a lot about you."

"It's good to meet you, General," she stammered, caught slightly off guard. What had he heard about her? She shot Niles a look.

"All good things," Niles hurriedly assured her.

The general didn't confirm or deny his son's words. "I hope you enjoy the night," he said to the three of them before nodding to Lorrin and turning away. As he left them, Elinta caught sight of a scar twisting from behind his left ear and down his neck.

So that was the man who'd raised Niles. She looked between her friend and the general's disappearing figure. They seemed so different. Like hers, Niles's mother had died when he was young, and he hardly ever spoke of her. Maybe he didn't have many memories of her. Elinta had been lucky to have Blaine around to tell her stories of their mother. Had General Sonnen kept his wife's memory alive? How had the father and son become so different?

"Another dance?" Niles said, holding out his hand again and shaking her from her thoughts.

"Maybe the next one?" she said, sipping at her drink again. She was still thirsty from all the dances she'd already had. Niles shrugged and grabbed a slice of cake from the table beside them.

"You tried this, Lor?" he said through a mouthful.

"No." Lorrin eagerly took a slice while Elinta returned to surveying the room.

She hardly knew anyone there, though she recognised several officials and soldiers she'd seen around the palace over the past several weeks. The king and queen had joined the dancers on the floor, and she watched them for a moment before watching the band play for a while. She was determined to drink in as much of the ball as she could, fully intending on keeping her promise of telling Neva all about it, and even Zhayra. She'd told the dragon about the approaching ball at her last visit and had felt Zhayra's excitement for her throughout the day. She entertained herself for a moment with the absurd idea of somehow getting Zhayra into the room and couldn't help a wide smile breaking out across her face at the thought.

"What?" Lorrin said.

She shook her head. "Nothing. Just something silly."

Lorrin cocked his head, but his eyes drifted past her, and he smiled.

"Ford," he said in greeting, and Elinta felt herself stiffen for a moment before she turned to face him. She hadn't forgotten her questions about the man and why he'd given her information on the dragons, but he'd been nothing but nice to her, if somewhat reserved. Eyes suddenly feeling heavy, she tried to blink the sensation away, but it clung on. She shook herself. She couldn't be tired already, could she?

"Lorrin." Ford greeted the prince with a smile, nodded at Niles, who was still eating, and turned his gaze on Elinta.

"Enjoying yourself?" he asked.

"Yes," she said, smiling despite the slight pressure in her eyes. "Have you been here long?" she asked, taking in his suit. It was deep green, so dark as to be almost black, perfectly complementing his dark hair and eyes. She would have thought the historian would be out of place at a ball, but he looked entirely comfortable.

"No," he said quietly. "I was running a little late."

He studied her eyes for a moment, then seemingly happy with whatever he found there, he inquired whether she'd found the item he'd loaned her to her satisfaction. Elinta startled. It had been weeks since he'd given her the scroll and since she'd returned it. He'd been busy that day and unable to talk to her, and she'd completely forgotten about it since.

Lorrin listened with interest while Niles appeared not to care as he stood over the food table, but she knew he was listening. Whilst she hadn't told him where the scroll had come from, not wanting to keep more from him, she had told him *about* it.

"Yes. I wondered ..." she said hesitantly. "... who the author was?"

A slight smile crossed his face. He seemed surprised but pleased with the question. "A teacher."

"Teacher?" She frowned. Thinking back to the small, translated paragraph, she was even more puzzled. She'd been sure an ambassador had written it.

"Not what you expected?" Ford asked.

She shook her head.

"When was it written?" she asked, curiosity bubbling inside her.

"During a time from which not much survives among our people," he said cryptically. "Have a good night." He nodded at Lorrin. "Your Highness." And turned back into the crowd.

"He's a mysterious fellow," Niles said, turning around.

Elinta couldn't help but agree.

"Do you think he knows?" she asked, looking to Lorrin, and noticing at the same time that the heaviness in her eyes had lessened. The prince frowned; his eyes glued to Ford's back.

"I don't know," he finally said, lowering his voice. "We did ask him about the dragons though."

That was true. Maybe that was why Ford had supplied her with the scroll, but she couldn't help wondering whether that really was it. She couldn't shake the memory of the way he'd looked at her, both today and in the past, with such ... knowledge and understanding. But there was no way he could know. No, it must just be that he was acting based on what they'd told him.

"Ah," Lorrin said, looking into the crowd.

Elinta followed his eyes to Cassia, who had fixed him with a smile that spread from one ear to the other.

"I'm afraid I owe a dance to another young lady," he said, excusing himself to weave through the crowd and offer his hand to his cousin, who giddily accepted. Elinta grinned as Lorrin pulled the girl onto his feet and carried her around the room to the music.

The girl's twin brother appeared in front of her, drawing her attention away from Lorrin.

Niles gave her a nudge.

"You're popular tonight. Look at this fine gentleman," he said.

"Can I dance with you?" Aiden said, his brown hair slicked back and making his bright blue eyes brighter than ever. She realised now that he'd inherited his father's eyes.

"Can I dance with *you?*" she said back and earned a blush in response accompanied by a nod.

Aiden hesitantly took her hand and gave her a tug towards the dance floor. She handed her half-empty glass to Niles and followed the boy. Elinta found her eyes drifting unconsciously towards Lorrin every few seconds and had to force herself to concentrate. She, thankfully, managed not to stand on Aidan's feet as they danced, not straying far from their place. When the song ended and another began, she danced again with the boy, earning a wide grin in response.

Niles danced the same song with a girl Elinta had seen standing next to one of the officers earlier, and every single time Elinta caught a glimpse of them, Niles was busy chatting to the girl. Elinta grinned. No doubt he was flattering both of them.

Elinta danced again several times with Niles and Lorrin during the night, and even spoke briefly with the queen and General Nash. She met the general's husband, Stanford, a tan man with stunningly blue eyes who'd just returned from Culmar on business. He was held in high regard as one of the best blacksmiths in Nevira, but she found him extremely humble when she asked him about his work.

When the night ended, Elinta tiredly returned to her room, escorted by Lorrin and Niles once again.

"Well, good night," Niles said cheerfully, and went back downstairs to return home.

Elinta watched him go before turning back to Lorrin. His gaze held hers.

"Good night," he said softly, a small smile on his face.

"Good night," she said.

Why were her cheeks heating? She hurried into her room but, unable to stop herself, she peeked through a crack in her door and watched Lorrin as he returned to his room, a small smile on her face.

CHAPTER EIGHTEEN

A WEEK LATER, NILES had lived up to his promise, and he and Lorrin had started Elinta with a real sword. It was blunt and unable to pierce the skin, but Elinta loved it. They decided to throw her right into it and paired her up against Lorrin, who had a similar sword, in a sparring match and she marvelled at both how similar and different it was compared to her wooden sword.

They danced around the room, blocking, stabbing, and slashing at each other, always careful to pull their hits enough not to cause serious damage, but Elinta came away with more than one bruise. To her delight though, so did Lorrin. As they walked out of the room and back towards her own, the boys were both congratulating her on particular moves or advising why ones didn't work. But she was looking with pride on the bruise forming just above the scar on Lorrin's forearm. She could look on it without any guilt. Though Niles had given her more bruises courtesy of their different training methods, Lorrin had given her plenty over the couple of months they'd been training too. Every single one she gave him in return was a triumph.

"Where did you get that?" she asked as soon as Niles took a breath, gesturing at the scar on Lorrin's arm.

"That," Lorrin said with a pointed glance at Niles that didn't really carry any weight, "is why we're using a blunt sword."

"I consider it a permanent mark of my superior swordsmanship. Hey!" Niles said, spinning around to look at her and walking backwards. "I should have pointed that out when I applied for this job."

"Job?" she asked, giving him a look of fake hurt.

"Er ..." He cleared his throat. "Privilege?"

"That's better," she said, nodding. "So, how'd it happen?"

"We were training, decided real swords would be fun," Lorrin said with a laugh. "We did pretty well, though. First time using them unsupervised."

"Pretty well?" Niles exclaimed. "I kicked butt. Yours."

Lorrin grinned at his friend.

"How old were you two?"

Lorrin cocked his head. "Eight?"

Niles nodded.

"Eight?" she said, shaking her head. It was a wonder they hadn't seriously hurt themselves.

"Hey, we still on for tomorrow?" Niles asked, still walking backwards.

"Yeah," she said, casting a questioning glance at Lorrin.

"I'll be there," the prince said, unrolling his sleeves.

"Awesome," Niles said. "Looking forward to Zhayra not eating me."

Elinta laughed. "She's looking forward to *seeing* you."

"That never gets old." Niles shook his head, staring at her with wide eyes. "What's she feeling right now?"

"Tired," she said through a yawn.

"OK, so that wasn't convincing," Niles said, crossing his arms, but just at that moment his shoe caught on the rug, and he stumbled backwards, straight towards a display case of vases. Lorrin leapt forward and just managed to grab him by his shirt before he hit the breakable collection.

"Phew." Niles clapped Lorrin on the shoulder once he was back on his feet. "The generals and your mum all would have killed me at the same time for breaking that."

Elinta smiled at the phrasing. The generals was what he called his father and Lorrin's aunt.

"I—" Elinta began, but someone cut across her.

"What's happening here?"

Elinta's heart sank. Shae stepped out from inside a room directly beside them. Elinta stepped backwards, putting Niles and Lorrin in front of her, not wanting to draw the woman's attention.

"Everything's alright, Shae," Lorrin said lightly.

"The rug tried to trip me," Niles said.

"I see," the woman said, but then she saw Elinta. Her gaze locked on her, and Elinta fought to keep herself from squirming under it.

"It's quite late," Shae said, her eyes still fixed on Elinta.

There was a question in her words that made Elinta glance at Lorrin. Other than his parents and his aunt, no one had really questioned the prince. And while she didn't think he was the kind of person to get angry about something so small, it was unusual.

Shae was being careful not to ask them outright, but the question was there. What were they doing? What was *Elinta* doing?

"Yes," Lorrin said, deftly avoiding it. "If you'll excuse us, Shae, we were just finishing for the night."

Shae tore her eyes from Elinta with noticeable effort, recognising the clear dismissal. "With someone on the loose killing our guards and stealing precious objects," she said, eyes flicking back to Elinta, "you need to be more careful, Your Highness." Shae bowed her head and disappeared down the hall.

Lorrin and Niles stared after her in surprise.

"What was that about?" Niles said.

"Me," Elinta said.

Niles turned in surprise, but Lorrin understood first, likely remembering Shae questioning the bruise on her arm at the ball.

"She's been asking questions about me." Elinta hadn't told either of them how the advisor had asked Ford about her, but now seemed to be the right time. "She asked Ford if I really was his student when he got back from his trip. And ... she's been strange around me."

"Why?" Lorrin said. "You haven't done anything to make anyone suspicious."

"I don't know." Elinta shook her head. Other than slipping out to see Zhayra, which no one but Lorrin and Niles knew about, she'd been going about her days normally. She went to the library regularly, just like she would if she were really a history student. And Ford had confirmed he was going to teach her. So, what was it about her that had made Shae stop and look so closely? All she knew was she didn't want to be caught alone with the woman again.

"Maybe it's not you," Niles said, rubbing his chin. "I mean, it is you, but just because you're with us. She wants to make sure you won't cause any trouble."

"I don't think so," she said, thinking of the way the woman had looked at her while talking of Alexander's death. Had the boys been unaware of it?

Silence settled between them.

"I'll keep an eye on her," Lorrin said, frowning. "She hasn't brought you up with the rest of the council, so maybe Niles is right. She's watching you to watch us."

Elinta didn't respond. They continued down the hall in silence until they reached her room.

Saying goodnight, Elinta slipped inside for a quick rinse and then collapsed on the bed. But she dreamt of Shae that night. Of the woman finding her with Zhayra and leading an army of the villagers from Kethmere against them. Lorrin's parents cheered from the side.

🔥🔥🔥

At breakfast in the morning, sitting by herself, Elinta was shocked to realise that people were already talking about the next big event: the Eggslaying in the new year. Her stomach sank at the excited chatter around her. December was only a day away, which meant the Eggslaying was in less than eight weeks, and she still didn't know when they'd be going to the Asali. The men the king had sent out to find the scales still hadn't returned. She spooned at her food despondently. Maybe it wasn't worth waiting around any longer. That was what they were all planning on talking about today. Lorrin had suggested they go and see Zhayra while they talked it through so the dragon was involved. Elinta smiled at the memory of that moment, and the moment she'd told Zhayra. Gratitude had abounded on both sides of their bond.

She ate the last of her food and hurried to meet Lorrin and Niles, who'd both had business to attend before they left. Walking down to the stables, she greeted the stableboy, Jae, who'd already saddled Bentley, Niles's horse, very creatively named Horse, and a black palace mare.

"Thank you," she said as the boy ran from the stables on an errand.

Lorrin and Niles arrived a moment later and began tying some bags to their saddles.

"Do you think Shae will wonder what we're doing?" Elinta asked Lorrin quietly, thinking of her dream.

"Why would she? We're just going for a ride." He winked.

Elinta smiled appreciatively. But she saw the flicker of anger in his eyes at the mention of the woman.

"Right," Niles said, clapping his hands together. "Ready to go?"

A couple minutes later, the three of them were leaving the palace behind and making their way to Zhayra who waited expectantly for them in the woods.

When Zhayra came into view, Elinta could hardly contain her excitement long enough to successfully tie off the mare. Niles pushed her out of the way and finished tying the reins, allowing her to run the last of the way to the dragon, who had dropped to a crouch with her tail swinging softly in excitement behind her. Laughing at the sight, Elinta threw her arms around the dragon's chest. It had been too long since they'd last seen each other.

"Hello," she whispered.

Zhayra lowered her head over her shoulder to rest against her back, almost as though she was hugging her in return.

"Do I have to do that?" Niles asked.

"No," she said, pulling away from Zhayra and turning to face Niles. He hadn't seen Zhayra since the night he'd followed her into the woods and received the surprise of his life. His face had definitely paled by a shade, but not nearly as much as the last time.

Lorrin didn't hesitate in greeting Zhayra verbally, and Niles hurried to do the same before the three of them sat where they were. Elinta had her back against Zhayra's chest, and Niles and Lorrin sat opposite them.

Comparing Lorrin to Niles, Elinta realised just how comfortable he'd become around Zhayra. While Niles was noticeably less afraid of the dragon, he was obviously still uncomfortable in her presence, but Lorrin seemed totally at ease.

Lorrin stretched his legs out in front of him with a sigh and dived right into the reason they were there.

"I don't know what to say," he said. "My father's birthday has come and gone, and we still haven't learnt anything more. I'd hoped some of the spies would be back by now, but none have returned. Their deadline is the Eggslaying festival though, so there's still time."

"I've learnt a lot," Niles added, "but I was a little late to the party so ..."

"What are we going to do?" Elinta asked.

She didn't want to be around for the festival, but then, if the men returned with news of the scales, it'd be best if they were there. If only she and the boys could have helped in the investigation, but they couldn't from the palace.

"There's not much we can do." Lorrin shrugged apologetically. "Until we find out more information or something else happens, I don't think the council will speak to us."

"Couldn't I just fly in on Zhayra and ask nicely?" Elinta said, absently tugging at the grass in front of her.

Zhayra hummed in pleasure at the use of the word flying, but Elinta pointedly ignored her. Time had lessened her aversion to flying, but not by much. Sure, maybe she just needed practice, but it probably wasn't a good idea to go flying on a dragon right next to the capital city. And she still didn't have a way to make sure she stayed on.

Niles laughed. "I like that plan, but something tells me it wouldn't work."

"So, we just wait?" Elinta asked, looking between them.

They both hesitantly nodded.

"I'm meant to be starting with Ford in only two months. What am I going to do if we're still here?" she said, feeling the weight of all her lies closing in. Her time at Nevira had been wonderful, but now February was looming over her.

"We'll work something out, and the men should be back by then," Lorrin said, but she could sense his impatience was similar to hers. His own plans for communication between their people and the Asali were being delayed too. "Ford could be right. If someone went to all the trouble to take the dragon scales, they must be up to *something*. Surely, they'll turn up again soon."

Elinta found it strange that they were hoping for something to happen, something that would most likely be bad. But it would open doors, doors that were firmly closed right now.

"What would someone want with scales?" Niles asked, repeating the question they'd often mulled over.

Elinta in turn repeated the same conclusion they'd always come to. "It must be the historical value behind them. They're a symbol." She stopped and tilted her head back to look up at Zhayra. "I haven't seen you shed any scales in a while."

The dragon twisted her head and looked down at her with one eye but didn't make a sound in response.

She turned to find the boys grinning at her.

"What?" she asked, but they both shook their heads.

Elinta mulled it all over in her mind. *Could we stay longer?* Zhayra certainly seemed safe out here, but she worried that someone might stumble upon her by accident. Although, with Zhayra's heightened senses, that was unlikely. She focused in on Zhayra's emotions and tried to work out what the dragon was feeling. She still didn't know why the dragon was in Eldras, but whatever it was, it didn't seem to be stopping her from staying out here. And Shae ... Well, unless she directly followed Elinta out one night to see Zhayra, she couldn't cause them any real problems. Even if Elinta did lose sleep over the woman. Just to be sure though, she asked the dragon what she thought about hanging around a bit longer, and she seemed content with the idea.

"Oh, are you doing the thing?" Niles asked, looking excitedly between her and Zhayra.

"Yes," she said, rolling her eyes with a smile.

"So, we staying?"

"Yeah, we're staying."

"I'll let you both know as soon as we hear anything about the scales. But in the meantime, we'll keep on doing what we're doing," Lorrin said, leaning back on his hands. "And I can give you some of the exercises I used to do for Asalin if you want."

"Thanks." While she was competent in greetings and other basic phrases, she wouldn't say she even had a basic understanding of the language yet. Trying to wrap her head around the way tenses and ownerships changed a sentence was just plain confusing.

Lorrin nudged Niles, and the two shared a long look. Lorrin whispered something and Niles nodded.

"What?" Elinta asked, glancing between the two. Zhayra picked up whatever they were talking about and grunted softly. To Elinta, it sounded like approval.

The boys stood and Lorrin weaved his way back through the trees to Bentley, where he pulled something long and wrapped in paper from underneath his saddlebags. She hadn't even noticed when he'd put it there. Immediately she had an inkling of what it was.

Niles grinned at her as Lorrin joined them again.

"We thought it was time," Niles said, pointing at the package. She tilted her head. "Is that ... what I think it is?"

"Possibly." Lorrin stepped forward and held it out to her. "Here."

She took it from him, and her suspicions were confirmed just by the feel of it. Peeling back the paper, she found a sword in a simple leather sheath. Her mouth dropped open.

"Thank you. But ..." So many thoughts were running through her head. "Can I even wear it?" They'd kept her training a secret for a number of reasons, but wouldn't it be equally odd if she just started wearing a sword around the palace after these months without one?

Lorrin seemed to think about it a moment, then shook his head. "Maybe wait another week or two, once you've had some more time with the metal training blade, but I don't think anyone will really question it. A lot of frequent or long-term visitors to the palace have some kind of blade, and if you start wearing one people will just assume I approved it. Which I have." Seeing her hesitation, he added, "Besides, we already told everyone that you lost your belongings on the way here from Donlee, so no one actually knows that you couldn't use a sword when you got here. Don't worry about Shae."

Lost for words, she merely nodded and pulled the blade from its sheath. It was a simple weapon without decoration or flair, but that didn't matter. Slightly worn leather bound the handle, but the blade itself was in perfect condition.

"It's my old blade," Lorrin said, "I hope you don't mind. The sheath is new."

The idea that it had been his meant more than a new blade in her mind. "It's perfect," she said, eyeing the blade with a smile.

"Good. Let's practice," Lorrin said, and both boys drew their weapons.

The three of them moved through a series of stances, practicing offense and defence in a line under the trees.

Zhayra watched on intently, her amber eyes almost glowing with pride. But when the sun slipped beneath the trees and hit her, the dragon curled up on her side and closed her eyes, soaking up the warmth.

Elinta's new blade was no heavier than the dulled one they'd had her using or the wooden weapon she'd started on, so when they finished moving through the stances her arms were no more sore than usual. Which actually wasn't very much anymore. Elinta ducked away for a drink and Niles turned to Lorrin, sword raised, grin across his face and cocked an eyebrow.

"Is that a challenge?" Lorrin asked, turning his weapon on his friend.

"Maybe," Niles said, then plunged forward with the blade, slipping his front foot forward as he did.

Lorrin easily deflected with a flick of his sword, and it was on. The two leapt back and forth, ducking, weaving, and striking in a beautiful dance that left Elinta amazed by the control they exhibited. Neither of them gained a single cut. They always pulled back before making contact or struck each other with the flat of the blade, and they made it look effortless.

All she could think of were two things; she had a long way to go in her own training, and that they were right. They were almost evenly matched.

The two boys laughed and joked as they moved around each other, jabbing both verbally and physically in a good-natured way. She was grinning almost as widely as they were when they finally broke apart, sweat beading their foreheads.

"I'm starved. It's gotta be lunch time by now." Niles shielded his eyes and searched the sky for the sun. "Close enough," he said with a shrug and jogged back through the trees to retrieve the food while Lorrin sheathed his sword.

Turning to see how Zhayra was doing, Elinta let out a quiet, amused laugh. Curled up as she was, twisted slightly on to her back with her chin nearly facing upwards, she looked like a cat. Elinta scratched at the dragon's exposed chin, getting a low rumble of pleasure in response.

"Yeah, that is just so bizarre," Niles said from behind her.

Elinta twisted with a grin, still scratching the dragon's chin. Niles looked on with a fascinated smile and even Lorrin mimicked the expression.

"Still getting used to it?" she asked, and they both nodded. With a smile, Elinta realised that for the first time, she was truly comfortable with it. Nothing seemed odd to her anymore about Zhayra. She didn't find it strange to pat the dragon, sit with her, or talk to her. It wasn't even strange to sense her feelings or to know the dragon could do it right back.

Still grinning, she sat with the boys over a meal of sandwiches and coffee they'd kept warm in a special container. Elinta stirred some honey into her coffee before taking an appreciative sip.

"Has anything else happened with the hearing thing?" Lorrin asked her, pausing from his meal.

Elinta shook her head, remembering the two strange occurrences he was referencing. Nothing had happened since then, but she'd decided just to wait and see if it ever did. Since she didn't know how it happened and therefore couldn't make it happen, it seemed like the best course of action.

"No," she said, taking a bite of her sandwich.

"That's too bad. Imagine the stuff we could get up to with super-hearing," Niles said around a mouthful of food.

They all lapsed into silence, thinking about the possibilities. Eavesdropping didn't really appeal to Elinta. But Niles had mischief in his eyes that told her he could think of several reasons to do it, and they probably all had to do with pranks.

They were happily chatting about what they would do in the city for the rest of the day, when another horse appeared on the road, riding towards them. Something about the shape of the figure made Elinta's skin crawl before she could even make out its features.

"Is that Shae?" Niles asked, turning back to glance at them.

Elinta nodded.

"Is she following you now?"

Elinta swallowed heavily. "I-I don't know." What would have happened if the woman had stumbled upon them with Zhayra? Her stomach tightened.

Lorrin's voice was tight when he spoke. "We've been on a ride to show you the countryside. You were sick of the city."

"What?" Elinta asked, but Shae was now too close for them to speak any further. Instead, she adjusted her saddlebags to cover her new sword.

Shae looked the peak of discomfort sitting atop the large chestnut she jerkily steered their way.

"Shae," Lorrin greeted. There was some effort behind the friendliness in his voice.

"Your Highness," Shae said, dragging the horse to a stop with a heavy hand.

Elinta only just stopped herself from a cutting remark that the horse clearly had a soft mouth. Only a slight pressure on the reins would have done the job.

"Such a lovely day for a ride," the advisor said. Her false smile wavered as her small eyes landed on Elinta. "When I heard the three of you had gone for a ride, I thought it was a fantastic idea. I didn't realise you'd come this way. How nice to run into you."

"I didn't realise you were a horsewoman, Shae. I would have invited you along." Lorrin did a much better job of hiding the falseness of his words than Shae.

"It's a new interest of mine. Might I ask where you've been? I'm not familiar with riding areas out this way, Your Highness."

Elinta's eyebrows rose at the woman's lack of any attempt to hide her true intentions, but Lorrin smiled.

"Of course." He twisted slightly in the saddle to point back up the road. "Follow the road for another kilometre, and you'll see a small path heading off to the east. It leads to a hill that overlooks the city. We've just had lunch there ourselves."

"It's great," Niles said. "You'll love it, Shae. Lots of flowers."

Elinta nodded along.

Shae smiled tightly. "Thank you, I'll ..." Her words died off as her eyes landed on Elinta's saddlebags. The hilt of her new sword was sticking out. "I didn't know you were skilled with a sword, Elinta. I've not seen you carrying one around the palace."

The woman's face remained light, but Elinta could see the suspicion darkening her eyes again. The woman was surely thinking of Alexander and the scales.

Elinta swallowed. "No—I—"

She cleared her throat to try again, but Lorrin spoke up.

"Surely, you've heard how Elinta lost her things on the journey from Donlee?" He gestured at Elinta. "This is her replacement for the one that was lost."

"I see ... now is not the time for swords to be in the palace, Your Highness."

Niles opened his mouth to respond, but Lorrin stopped him. The prince's tone was level as he responded. "As my personal guest in the palace, Elinta is welcome to have one. I assure you; she can be trusted with it. Now, if you'll excuse us, I have some work to attend to."

Lorrin nudged Bentley into a trot before Shae could respond, and the three quickly left her behind, not bothering to see if she would follow Lorrin's directions. Somehow, Elinta didn't think she would. Lorrin and Niles shared a tense look. Suddenly, waiting for the king's men to return didn't seem so simple anymore.

Two weeks later, Elinta found herself sitting across from the queen in the tea rooms. She shifted nervously, infinitely aware of her son's old sword that now hung at her hip. Her run-ins with Shae had left her tense, and she'd been doing her best to avoid the woman. If she'd known Mira was going to invite her to lunch, she would have left the sword behind in her room. But the queen had seen her out in the gardens again and called her inside. Elinta shifted again. She'd been wearing the sword for a couple days now, and whilst no one had asked her about it, she'd received a couple interested stares from the familiar faces of palace regulars.

Now, the queen sat across from her, kindly chatting about the day and the business of the week when she finally broached the subject Elinta had been expecting since she walked in.

"How do you like my son's old sword?" the queen asked, her expression unreadable.

Elinta smiled. "It's a great blade. It was very kind of him to give it to me."

The queen nodded. "It was the first blade that he ever owned. Until then, he'd only used practice blades."

The queen paused as though thinking about whether to say any more.

"My son is very fond of you," the queen said finally, and Elinta's stomach clenched. "I don't mean to pry, Elinta," she said, looking very awkward and just meeting her eyes. "I certainly don't have anything against you, but, well, I'm a mother ... I hope you'll excuse me. Are you two dating?"

Elinta felt her eyes widen.

"No," she spluttered, possibly a little too quickly. "Not at all." She added, "He's been a great friend to me, but that's all."

She tried to keep her mind from their dances the night of the ball.

Queen Mira smiled. "Perhaps Niles?"

"Oh, no." She laughed and Mira seemed to relax, probably realising her questions hadn't offended Elinta. They'd talked a lot together, but never anything so personal, or awkward. "I love Niles, but not in that way."

"Those two get into a lot of trouble together." The queen smiled affectionately. "I'm glad they have you around."

If you only knew ... Elinta tried to school her face so that the thought didn't cross her face. If only the queen knew what they were really up to, she wouldn't think so.

Elinta saw an opportunity to ask about Shae, and took it, not stopping to allow herself to back out.

"Mira," she said, "do you know why Shae doesn't like Niles?"

Mira pursed her lips, lowering her teacup. "I suspect she doesn't appreciate his sense of humour. He's not serious enough for her."

"But he is serious. When it matters," Elinta said, thinking of the moment Niles had met Zhayra.

The queen nodded. "Yes. He is. But Shae ... Shae takes things gravely. She's worked hard to be where she is. To her, there's no room for anything but work." Mira cocked her head. "Why do you ask, dear?"

Elinta paused. "She just ... doesn't seem to like me either."

Mira smiled gently. "She doesn't like many people. It's no fault of your own. Now," she said, "have you heard from Ford yet with a starting date?"

"No." Elinta took a sip of her own tea to gain time to collect her thoughts. "Lorrin thought he might wait until the new year," she said, belatedly realising that technically meant she could *hear* from him tomorrow.

Mira frowned over her teacup. "I'm sure he'll get back to you soon, dear. Have you seen him recently?"

"Just at the king's birthday ball," she said, honestly. "But he didn't say anything about it."

The conversation drifted off and away from areas that made Elinta desperately worried about slipping up. She asked the queen whether she'd completed any new drawings and how her father was. Mira had grown up in the palace as the daughter of one of the previous king's advisors. The queen had happily shared how she and King Aldon had grown up together. They'd married the year before Aldon was crowned.

"What are your plans tonight, Elinta?" the queen asked. As she'd just remembered, it was New Year's Eve. It was traditional for families to gather together over a meal lit by candles to reflect over the year that had been and the year that was coming. At midnight, when the year ticked over into the next, the candles were blown out, and new ones were lit to symbolise the end of the old and the beginning of the new.

"I'm just going to turn in early," she heard herself saying.

Mira paused, studying her over her teacup. "Are you sure? You're welcome to join us."

Overcome by gratitude, Elinta took a moment to respond. "That's very kind. Thank you, Mira. I don't want to intrude. I'm very tired, anyway."

But that night, Elinta crept out under the stars and welcomed the new year in with Zhayra in the warm summer night air. She stayed late, risking not being allowed back into the palace until dawn, just so they could light their own candle together. When she returned, the guard opened the gate anyway and wished her a happy new year.

CHAPTER NINETEEN

"E LINTA, MAY I HAVE a word with you?" Ford said, meeting Elinta outside the dining hall after dinner one day. It was a week out from the Eggslaying and Elinta had been counting down the days with nothing short of dread. She couldn't imagine celebrating it at all, let alone in the capital city where celebrations were set to be the biggest. Added to that was her lie about Ford and the lessons she was supposed to take with him. And Shae. Always Shae. Now she looked at Ford in concern.

"Yes," she said.

"Lorrin," Ford said, looking over Elinta's shoulder, "perhaps you'd like to come too?"

Elinta twisted to find Lorrin leaving the hall. He stopped beside her and nodded quizzically. "We can use my office if you need."

Ford nodded, and they moved up the stairs, the historian a few paces ahead of them.

"The last of the men returned today," Lorrin said, leaning into Elinta to avoid anyone but Ford hearing.

Elinta glanced at Lorrin in surprise. The men sent out to look for the scales had been returning in trickles for the last two days. "Have you heard anything?"

Lorrin shook his head. "We're having a meeting tonight in the council chambers. Come to my room at nine. Niles will be there too."

Elinta nodded and fixed her eyes on Ford's back. The historian didn't say anything about their exchange, and she suspected he was going to pretend he'd heard nothing. Even though Lorrin hadn't tried to hide his words from him.

A moment later, Ford opened the door to Lorrin's office, and the three ducked inside. They'd barely sat down, with Ford leaning against the desk, when there was a knock on the door. Lorrin grinned.

"That'll be Niles," he said, and sure enough, when he opened the door, Niles was waiting.

"He knows I know, right?" Niles said, looking from Lorrin to Ford. "You know I know, right?"

Lorrin turned and cocked his head at Ford.

"Come in," the man said, seemingly unsurprised by Niles's arrival.

"Great," he said, hurrying inside.

Elinta waited in silence for the historian to tell her why he wanted to speak with her though she suspected she knew the reason.

"I don't want to know the details, but what are your plans?" Ford said, fixing Elinta with his dark eyes. "This lie won't hold on much longer."

Elinta exchanged a glance with Lorrin. If the last of the men had finally arrived, and they'd soon know what they'd learnt, then Elinta and the boys would be on their way to Liyarna soon. She felt a thrill of nerves that was quickly met with interest from Zhayra.

"We won't be here when February comes," she finally said, confident in that much at least.

"Good," he said, pushing off from the desk. "Don't tell me where you're going."

Elinta nodded though she suspected he knew. At least this way, he could deny any knowledge of their plans when she failed to turn up for her lessons, and the prince and his best friend disappeared.

"Thank you for your help," Elinta said.

The corner of Ford's mouth twitched, almost into a smile. "I hope your journey goes as you hope."

And with that, he left.

Elinta, Lorrin, and Niles sat in silence.

"Well," Niles said, jumping to his feet. "What say we sneak in a training session now before this council meeting tonight?"

"Sounds good," Elinta and Lorrin said at the same time.

Two and a half hours later, Elinta and Niles were inside an inner room of the council chambers. Apparently, it was Shae's old office space, but she preferred to work in one of the rooms near General Nash's and General Sonnen's offices, so the room wasn't currently being used. Lorrin had snuck them in a half hour before the meeting was due to start, and she and Niles were waiting for the first sign of someone entering the main room.

"So," Niles said in a low voice, "what are your intentions with my best friend?"

"What?" Elinta spluttered, completely blindsided by the question.

Niles cocked an eyebrow. "You know you two have great chemistry, right? I saw you two dancing at the ball."

"I danced with you too," she said, avoiding his question.

It was bad enough that Queen Mira had asked her about Lorrin, and now Niles? Elinta's ears popped, and she shook her head to clear the feeling.

"I'm flattered, El," Niles said, "but we both know this is more of a sibling relationship."

Elinta sighed. "Niles, now's not the time."

She really, really didn't want to think about this now. There was too much going on, too much about to happen to analyse, or acknowledge, whether she did or didn't have feelings for Lorrin.

"Fine," he said, "but we both know something's there."

Elinta opened her mouth to respond when a voice drifted in from the outer room. Her eyes widened and she and Niles hurried to put an ear to the door, squishing together in the tight space.

"Reynard," came the king's voice.

Elinta cocked an eyebrow at Niles.

"My father," he mouthed.

Oh, she thought. General Sonnen responded in greeting to the king. Elinta listened with excitement, part of her aware that Zhayra was missing out. She'd have to tell the dragon everything she learnt later. There were several minutes of mixed voices where Elinta couldn't tell what was being said as everyone arrived. Since the advisors paused to welcome him, she heard the moment Lorrin arrived. She even heard Shae's half-hearted greeting of the prince.

"As you are all aware," General Nash's voice drifted through the door when the others had quietened, "the last of our spies has returned."

This statement was met with a silence in which Elinta imagined the other people in the room nodding.

"Unfortunately, nothing could be discovered about the scales."

"Impossible!" came Shae's indignant reply.

"It seems you were right, General Nash. The thief had no interest in selling the scales," General Sonnen's gruff voice rose above Shae's.

"Then they're as good as lost," Queen Mira said.

"We'll continue the search for them," King Aldon said, "but there's no knowing where they are."

"Perhaps they never left the palace," Shae said.

Elinta frowned, pressing closer to the door.

"You believe the thief is someone close to us?" King Aldon said.

There was a silence in which Elinta imagined Shae nodding.

"I assume you have some suspicions?" King Aldon asked.

Elinta felt the blood drain from her face as a terrible thought occurred to her.

Lorrin's voice rose sharply above Shae's reply. "We've already dismissed everyone who knew about them as a suspect. Unless you would like to accuse someone in this room, Shae, I think we can safely say the scales are gone."

"Why would someone steal the scales only to remain in the very place they took them from?" General Nash said.

"I merely meant to ensure there is no one *else* we should be looking at. For example, someone close to the royals."

Elinta's heart skipped a beat.

"If you mean to accuse someone, say it," Lorrin growled.

"Very well. Has anyone looked into Elinta? The girl did arrive not long before the scales were stolen, she's close to the prince and carries a weapon."

Silence descended in the room.

"Elinta?" Queen Mira said.

"Elinta is only here for her lessons with Ford. As for the weapon, she has it because she can use it. I gave it to her." Lorrin's voice was tight.

"And the defensive bruises on her arms?"

"Skill with a blade has to be maintained. We practice with Niles regularly."

"Shae," King Aldon said, "do you have any real evidence against the girl?"

There was a pause. "No."

"Does the girl know about the scales?" General Sonnen asked, curiosity tinging his voice more than anything else.

"She does, but only because of her interest in history. Elinta didn't have time to tell anyone about them before they were stolen. She was with me."

"But she could know—" Shae began.

"Enough," King Aldon said firmly. "There's no need for this to proceed any further,"

Shae didn't say any more.

"What about the Asali that's been seen around our settlements? Did they hear anything about him?" Lorrin asked the silence, his tone still sharp.

Elinta silently thanked him for drawing their attention elsewhere. She *was* close to the royals after all, and in a prime position to learn of the scales. Shae wasn't wrong to suspect Elinta knew of them.

But Elinta listened intently for the council's response to Lorrin's question. She'd momentarily forgotten about the Asali, and it was something they could raise with the Liyarnan's council.

"There's been no more reports," General Nash said. There was a pause. "There was something else."

"Yes?" came King Aldon's voice.

"Rumours of a dragon seen in a village several months ago have spread through the south."

Elinta clamped a hand down on her mouth. Niles placed a steadying hand on her shoulder.

"Were there any other sightings?"

"No."

Elinta waited with bated breath to hear what the king would say. She should have known word would reach Nevira about Zhayra eventually. But she'd hoped it wouldn't.

"It doesn't—" Lorrin started but someone cut across him.

"They're probably just aftershocks of the previous sighting," Shae said, sounding disinterested. "We all know how fruitless that turned out to be. The dragons will never return."

Niles's hand dropped from Elinta's shoulder, and he turned his shocked face towards her.

"Shae?" he mouthed.

Elinta nodded slowly. Shae had just potentially saved her and Zhayra. Right after trying to accuse her of stealing the scales. A laugh bubbled up in her throat, but she hurriedly swallowed it.

"You are all in agreement?"

There was a chorus of yeses.

The room fell silent, and Elinta exchanged a glance with Niles. What did all this mean for them then? There was no use waiting around in Nevira any longer. There was nothing left to learn. The scales were gone. They could strike out for the Calaza as soon as they were ready. Elinta secretly hoped it would be before the Eggslaying, but she doubted Lorrin would be able to sneak away before then. He was already in more and more demand as the day drew closer.

The conversation within the room slowly shifted away from the scales and Alexander's murder. Elinta and Niles, losing interest, moved away from the door, and settled on the edge of Shae's old desk to wait for Lorrin to let them out after the meeting. Elinta was glad for the meeting happening in the other room because it meant that Niles couldn't reopen their earlier conversation about Lorrin, and she could focus on what they'd just learnt.

The council room had been quiet for some time when Lorrin finally came for them. In the dark of Shae's old office, they finalised their plans. They'd leave in the week after the Eggslaying since Lorrin couldn't get away before then. Elinta's heart sank at the idea of attending the festival, but then it'd only be days after that before they finally, *finally* went to see the council about Zhayra and a treaty. But not once did Lorrin mention his parents, and Elinta studied him in surprise. Treaties were two ways, and it seemed he still hadn't spoken with the king and queen about it or the dragons.

"What about your parents?" Elinta said. "Are you going to try talking to them again?"

Lorrin paused. "No."

"Why?" Elinta said, glancing at Niles. "We need them." She couldn't stop the edge from creeping into her voice. He'd said he wanted to talk to his father again, hadn't he?

"I know," Lorrin said, sighing, "but they're not going to listen."

"But—"

"They might after we've been to Liyarna," Niles interjected, looking between them.

Lorrin nodded.

Elinta stared at them both, ready to argue though she didn't really know why, but paused when Lorrin caught her eye. He understood. He knew her need for the dragons to be vindicated. For her to have the possibility of being safe with Zhayra. If he thought this was the only way, then it was. She deflated.

Besides, she found she was ready to go to Liyarna now. Her time at the palace had been better than she could have imagined, but she was ready to move on. She missed Zhayra, and she hated the way she was hiding right in front of the king and especially the queen who had been particularly kind to her. And now, with Shae's accusation out in the open, the royals might unconsciously pay more attention to her. She might even have to drop back her visits to Zhayra. No, it was time to go. And if that meant convincing the king and queen had to wait, then so be it.

In the dim light, Lorrin nodded, silently acknowledging her acceptance.

CHAPTER TWENTY

"HERE IT IS," KALLA said, popping a large box down on her bed. It was early afternoon and Elinta had been trying to put off acknowledging what day it was ever since she'd rolled out of bed.

"Thank you," Elinta said, trying to force a happy tone as she looked at the box containing her gown for the Eggslaying festivities. They were set to start in two hours' time and run until nine o'clock and she wasn't ready for it. She'd never be ready for it ever again.

Kalla opened the box to reveal a soft green fabric, light and airy. "You shouldn't need any help with it."

"Thank you," she said again, finding it hard to look at the woman. She wore a dress of brilliant orange that hurt Elinta's eyes and yet suited the tailor.

"Enjoy the festivities," Kalla said with the first hint of excitement Elinta had ever seen in her.

With that, the woman turned on her heel and left. Elinta stared at the dress despondently for a long time and tried to rally herself, but it didn't help that she had a direct line to Zhayra's emotions which closely resembled hers: a deep sadness that wouldn't go away. Elinta studied the emotions for a moment and realised what it was they were both feeling. They were mourning. They were both mourning for the dragons. *If Father saw me now ...*

Shaking herself, she pulled the dress from its box and couldn't entirely stop a small smile from lifting her lips. It was a beautiful dress, but it was the wrong colour. Black and sombre would have been better. Not this bright thing that screamed summer and happiness. Somehow, it suited both the day part of the festivities and the night though not entirely an evening gown.

She held it against her body and walked into the bathroom to look at it. Once again, Kalla had done a great job. Unlike the gown she'd worn to the king's ball, this one-layered dress fell midway down her calves with sweet sleeves to cover her shoulders and a ribbon across her midriff. The entire thing was a faint green.

With a small sigh, she put the dress aside and started to get ready by herself. Neva had offered to help her again, but Elinta had waved the offer aside. She didn't think she could deal with the maid's excessive excitement today and besides, the woman had her own preparations for the day.

Putting on a simple layer of makeup, Elinta wondered how long she'd have to stay at the celebrations. Surely, she didn't have to stay for the entire thing? But then, someone was sure to notice if she left, and if she didn't attend ... that would almost be suspicious. Who wouldn't attend the biggest celebration of the year?

The only bright side she could see to the afternoon was that she could spend it with Lorrin and Niles. But they both had to be involved in the whole night.

Her makeup done, and leaving her sword on her bed, Elinta changed into the dress. Finding a pair of small heels at the bottom of the box, she slipped them on and returned to the bathroom. She decided to leave her hair down and wasted away the remaining time by sitting on her bed and wishing she could speak to Zhayra. But she didn't have the right words to make the dragon feel better even if they could talk. She didn't even have the right ones for herself. She was a traitor to her people, but she didn't care. What broke her heart was the fact that no one thought it was wrong to celebrate the Eggslaying.

There was a soft knock at her door.

"Elinta?" Lorrin's voice drifted through the door.

Elinta startled. Was she late? They'd arranged to meet with Niles at the bottom of the stairs on the first floor, where they'd all go together to the festival.

"Coming," she called, her voice sounding strained. Clearing her throat, she jumped to her feet and hurried to the door, but Lorrin twisted the handle and gently opened it before she reached it.

"Are you alright?" he asked, stepping inside.

Elinta's eyes lingered on his suit. She reached out, tentatively touching his chest. The suit was black as was the vest underneath. The mourning colour. "Elinta?"

"I'm fine," she said, trying to muster a smile and pulling her hand away. "I lost track of time."

"I'm sorry," he said softly.

"Why?" she asked, startled.

He looked away from her. When his eyes returned to hers, they were full of sadness and regret.

"The Eggslaying," he said, "I'm sorry it's still happening. That we're here for it."

She smiled and took his hand, giving it a gentle squeeze.

"Thank you," she said softly. "But it's OK. You didn't promise me the world would change in only a couple months."

He chuckled, but the sound was half-hearted. "It would've been nice though."

"It would have," she agreed with a laugh.

But she could still see the regret there. It touched her that he cared so much about her and Zhayra that his views had changed so much. That he seemed to look forward to the Eggslaying about as much as she did. He needed to know how much it meant to her.

"You've done so much already," she whispered. "I'm so grateful for it. If we've been here longer than we thought we would, I'm grateful for that too."

He squeezed her hand in response. "You look lovely, by the way."

She grinned, glancing down at her dress. "Kalla is amazing."

"She is," Lorrin agreed, "but it's not just the dress." Heat flooded her cheeks, but before she could think of what to say, he offered her his arm. "Niles is waiting for us; we'd better get moving before he comes looking."

He led her downstairs, telling her about the trouble he and Niles had gotten into at the Eggslaying festival when he was seven. They'd tried to pull a prank on the king and queen, involving a bucket of flour, which had backfired.

"General Sonnen and my aunt found us hiding in one of the fourth-floor rooms," he said, laughing. "We had to wash dishes in the kitchen for a week after that."

Elinta was still laughing when they joined Niles, and at seeing his face, her laughs redoubled.

"What?" he asked, looking down at his uniform. "Is there something wrong?"

"No." She shook her head, tears in her eyes. "Nothing at all."

Niles stared deep into her face, then turned narrowed eyes on Lorrin. "You told her the story, didn't you?"

Lorrin tried to hide his smile by looking at his feet, but it didn't work.

"You did!"

"I did." Lorrin grinned. "As you can see," he pointed at her, "it was well received."

"I'll have you know, Lorrin was equally involved in it. He likes to downplay his role, but he was there too!" Niles said, trying and failing not to smile.

"Of course," Elinta said. "I'm just imagining you covered in flour and trying to worm your way out of trouble. A taste of your own medicine." Another chuckle escaped her. She could just picture them in their excitement knocking the door the bucket of flour was balanced on and gaining a face-full of it themselves instead of the king and queen.

Shaking his head, but laughing too, Niles gestured for them all to move into the throne room. "It's about to start."

After slipping her arm from Lorrin's, the two fell into step beside Niles and entered the throne room where several dozen people already waited.

The king and queen stood in front of their thrones and when the king's gaze locked with Lorrin's, he raised a goblet before him. "On this day of days, let us not forget the loss that set these legendary events into motion. Today, we begin by remembering Prince Tristan, beloved and only son of King Cenric, the Dragonslayer. His death is still felt today." He paused while the room filled with murmurs of agreement. "And though we celebrate King Cenric's deeds, let us not forget that he also was a casualty of the war with the dragons." He took a long drink from the goblet, then put it aside. "Let the celebrations begin!"

Cheers spread throughout the room and people instantly began streaming through the large doors. Niles grabbed her hand before she could get separated from them and gently pulled her out of the way.

Flattening against the wall in the throne room, she turned to both boys in surprise. "Where's everyone going?"

"Most are going out into the streets, a few into the ballroom," Niles said, raising his voice over the people bustling around them.

"Where are we going?" Elinta asked, watching as the last of the people trickled out of the room.

"I'm expected on the main road," Lorrin said. "We watch the procession before coming back for the celebrations. Niles usually comes with us; you can too." He glanced at his parents. They still stood by the thrones as a small group of guards entered the room, led by the generals and Shae.

"We're ready for you," General Nash said, glancing around the now mostly empty room, at the king and queen and then at their small group against the wall.

Shae stared at Elinta for a long moment before turning away.

"Thank you, Jaida," King Aldon said, offering his wife his arm and descending the stair before their thrones.

General Sonnen turned his brown eyes to the three of them and gestured with his head for them to join the main group. They pushed away from the wall and fell into step behind the king and queen. The generals and the guards moved into place behind them. Elinta's breath stuttered in her chest when she saw the clip securing Mira's hair. It was a beautiful silver dragon, wings spread in flight. The sight tugged at her heart.

Niles nudged his shoulder against hers, and she gave him a tentative smile. He raised his eyebrows in question, seeing if she was OK, and she gave a slight nod. Then they were moving. Leaving the throne room behind them, the group walked through the front doors of the palace, through the gates and down on to the main road. Men, women, and children already lined the city streets. Those that had come from the palace ahead of them were now mingling with the crowd. Elinta caught sight of Merton Alvey, the owner of their favourite bakery, standing with his wife further down the road as someone stepped aside. Their faces were both alight with excitement. Somewhere among the crowd were General Nash's children with their father too. The idea of their young faces shining with glee at such an event caused her stomach to curl.

"The procession starts at the outskirts of the city and ends here," Lorrin said quietly. "We won't see them for several minutes, but we'll be able to hear them soon."

Sure enough, within minutes, the sound of drums reached her, pounding out a familiar tune. "The Ballad of the Slain." Traditionally it was the first of the songs performed during the celebrations. It told the story of King Cenric's grief and rage, the fulfillment of his revenge and the lasting peace it brought despite his own death. Elinta closed her eyes to the sound for a moment, centring herself before the words began. Opening them once more, she watched the crowd around her and lining the streets teem with growing excitement. Kids were darting across the road, pushing between people, and jumping up and down in an effort to find a better vantage point before the parade reached them. Where once she'd have found it cute, now it was sickening to Elinta. Lorrin's fingers brushed hers. She fought the urge to hold on to him in front of so many people, his family included.

The singing started, rising above the drone of excited voices, and keeping time to the drums. The crowd joined in, shouting the story of King Cenric's revenge for all to hear. Even the group of royals and advisors that surrounded her joined in the song. Not a person in the city wouldn't be able to hear it, and she was the only one that wished she couldn't.

No, a glance at Niles and Lorrin told her she wasn't the only one. Neither sang along to the ballad, and though their expressions remained perfectly schooled to hide their emotions, she knew the real reason they didn't sing, and it gave her the strength to face the road again. Straightening her spine, she waited for the procession to appear in the distance and tried not to focus on the words surrounding her.

The drums grew louder and louder and they drew closer and were soon joined by the pounding of countless feet dancing, marching and running up the paved road. The tone of the ballad changed. It became more angry, urgent, and then the procession appeared between the buildings, led by a blue dragon. Elinta's breath caught in her chest.

She couldn't make out the details of the large puppet, but rather caught sight of a figure running around the dragon. A glint of sunlight caught on the sword in his hand and the crown on his head. They were drawing near the end of the ballad, and the fake King Cenric ducked, spun, and stabbed his way around the dragon. The drums dropped away, the singers stopped, and the crowd fell into silence as Cenric's solo began. He lowered his sword and ran ahead of the dragon, and his voice arose in a long, clear note of anguish.

The dragon ran after him, causing the king to launch into a desperate, fast-paced verse of both anticipation and the joy of the hunt. The dragon's vicious face finally came into focus, ducking and weaving as it chased the king. A terrible, almost comic, grimace twisted her face, and she let out a fearsome roar when Cenric paused to rally himself for the final fight.

The fake king stopped metres from King Aldon and his party, turned to face the dragon, and let out a fierce shout of challenge that stopped the beast in its tracks. King Cenric cried his challenge again, lifting his sword high above his head. The people lining the streets repeated the yell so loudly that Elinta clapped her hands over her ears. She watched in horrified fascination as the dragon, enraged by the shouts, charged at Cenric. He lowered his sword and held it before him, ready for the kill.

A moment before it happened, she realised what the actors intended and tore her eyes away, unable to watch as the king impaled the puppet dragon on his sword. She wished she could block out the yells and cheers of triumph raised around her, but not even the sound of her heart breaking could drown it out. Unable to watch anymore, Elinta slipped away from the group. Everyone was focused on the display before them, and she disappeared unnoticed into the crowd, her heart set on one thing. She had to get out of there. She had to get away from them all. Had to see Zhayra. Zhayra whose own heart was broken, whose heart ached for her and for herself. Zhayra, who she knew instinctively, was waiting for her. *This is wrong. This is wrong. This is wrong!* her mind screamed.

Elinta ducked and weaved through the crowds lining the main road and broke through onto a parallel road. Grinning faces turned to her, faces painted to look like the dead dragon. Children ran around with fake swords. Smaller dragon puppets lay discarded on the city street around her, some with people standing over them, others left behind in the frenzy of excitement. Is this what she'd been like? Was her brother now celebrating the Eggslaying in Kethmere, knowing that his sister was with a dragon?

Bile rose in her throat, and she ducked another street over, unable to stomach the faces around her. The road was empty and breaking into a run, she hurried from the city, aching for the sounds behind her to fade, but even when the city was far behind her, she could still hear the shouts and screams of victory.

Zhayra met her at the edge of the forest. How the dragon knew she was coming, she didn't know, but she was grateful. She didn't know how long she'd been walking, but the sun was steadily going down and dusk was only just around the corner. Niles and Lorrin had to be worrying about her, but she couldn't find it in herself to feel any guilt. All her energy was focused on trying not to remember what she'd witnessed in the city.

Zhayra took one look at the dried tracks of the tears on her face and let out one long, low keen that captured the brokenness of both their hearts. Stumbling forward, Elinta rested her face against Zhayra's and let the dam of her tears break open again.

"I should go," Elinta murmured to Zhayra, watching the changing colours of the sky. She'd missed dinner, and it'd be dark soon. She had to get back to the palace. If only she'd thought to bring a horse. The trip back on foot would mean the festival would be nearly over by the time she returned. She looked despondently at her aching feet and the heels she was wearing and longed for her boots. Her feet were going to be so sore by the time she got back to the palace.

Zhayra grumbled her displeasure at the idea of her walking home. Elinta had to agree that she'd much rather have her sword with her for such a trip, but she had to get back before she was missed. She was one of the prince's closest friends and people saw her with him every day. If she wasn't with him now, someone would notice. Someone probably *had* noticed. And she could guess who it would be. Elinta mentally kicked herself as she thought of the advisor, but it was too late now to change it, and she wasn't sure if she wanted to. She never would have been able to face the rest of the celebrations after the procession. She'd needed

Zhayra, and Zhayra had needed her too. She'd been where she should have been all along.

With a sigh, Elinta struggled to her feet from where she'd been sitting between the dragon's front feet, her back against one and her feet against the other.

"I'll be OK," she assured the dragon, now standing. "I can look after myself now."

But she knew the ball of nerves in her stomach gave her away. Zhayra's amber eyes stared into hers, so she voiced her previous thoughts on why she needed to get back to the palace. She couldn't put their trip to Liyarna in jeopardy.

The dragon blinked.

"I have to go, Zhayra," she said again.

She gave the dragon one last hug and twisted on her heel. She had a long walk ahead of her, and she needed to get started now if she wanted any chance of getting back before the festival ended. But that seemed entirely unlikely. It had to be at least seven o'clock. The festival was set to end by nine. If she'd had Bentley, she would have been there well within time, but on foot …

Once she was back on the road, Elinta broke into a jog, immensely thankful that she'd been running with Lorrin every morning for months. She didn't know what she was going to do once the sun disappeared below the horizon and cast the world into darkness, but the sky was clear of clouds and there'd been a half-moon the night before. With any luck, there'd be enough light for her tonight to make out the road.

Her dress flapping in the wind, Elinta pushed herself into a run and watched as the shadowed landscape grew ever darker. Her eyes were still heavy, but she didn't feel like crying anymore. She was done with that. Their trip to see the Asali was less than a week away, and she would spend that remaining time acting as though nothing was wrong while she planned what she was going to say to the council. *I have to convince them. They have to help us.*

Elinta dropped back to a walk for several minutes to catch her breath and slipped out of her shoes, holding them in one hand, before jogging on. The road was mostly smooth, but she preferred the pain from treading on the odd rock over the steady ache the shoes gave her. She maintained this pattern, jogging for ten minutes before dropping back to walk for five. Her body was pumping with the adrenaline of the day, of her flight from the city and even her time with Zhayra in the woods, but she needed to save her strength.

After only thirty minutes, the sun had nearly dropped below the horizon, and Elinta had to watch the ground in front of her so she wouldn't trip on dips and rocks hidden by the failing light. Ahead of her and far in the distance, lights from the city shone bright. The festival still had at least another hour to go officially, but it'd never finished on time at Kethmere. She doubted a city as big as Nevira would finish by then either.

Dropping back to a walk again and eyes glued to the ground, Elinta drank in the night air, beyond thankful that summer was now in full force, and she wasn't suffering for wearing only a dress at night. The exercise was keeping her warm too, but she was now desperately hungry and thirsty. That was when she heard the steady drum of hooves on the road ahead of her, her head whipped up at the sound and she saw a figure on a horse, carrying a lantern and coming towards her. Before she could decide what to do, the horse had stopped beside her and she found herself face to face with a familiar bay.

"Elinta?" Lorrin jumped down from the saddle and pulled her into a hug. "Are you OK? We've been looking everywhere for you."

"I'm sorry," she said into his suit. "I just needed to get out of there."

He pulled back and looked her over, making sure she was OK. His eyes lingered on her bare feet, before returning to her face.

"You should have told us where you were going. Or taken a horse!"

She nodded, then realised exactly who it was she was looking at. "Wait. What are you doing out here? You're supposed to be at the festival!"

"I am," he said, "but I had to find you. Niles is covering for me."

"We'd better go," she said, slipping her shoes back on and not wanting to know how Niles was explaining their absence. He gestured for her to climb into the saddle before handing her the lantern and jumping up behind her. Lorrin took the reins and pushed Bentley into a trot.

"I'm sorry I worried you," she said after a moment, touched that he'd noticed her missing and gone looking for her.

"I'm sorry you had to see all that," he said in return.

Her stomach growled loudly, getting a chuckle out of Lorrin.

"I don't have any food with me, but are you thirsty?"

"Yes."

"There's some water in the bag," he said, gesturing to the saddlebag propped in front of her. She slipped her hand into the bag and pulled out the bottle, downing several large gulps before putting it back inside the bag. How long had it been since she'd last had a drink?

"Are you alright?" Lorrin asked again when she'd finished.

"I am," she said honestly. Her time with Zhayra had eased her tumultuous emotions, and her run on the road had been strangely cathartic. She could face the rest of the festival now.

"And Zhayra?" he said quietly.

"She's fine too." She rested her free hand on the saddle pommel, unsure where to put it. "I'm sorry," she said again.

"Don't be. You don't have to stay for the last of it."

"No, it's OK. I should be there." Elinta owed it to the dragons to be there, to be the person keeping their memory alive even as others degraded it. She'd had her time to collect herself; now was the time to finish the night out.

Bentley broke into a canter and the city lights steadily drew closer. They'd be back in time for the end of the festival, and maybe she'd be able to get some food before heading to bed. Night had fallen properly before they reached the outskirts of the city, but the silver light of the moon lit the last of their way. Elinta adjusted the lantern so that the light streamed directly in front of them just as a shadow passed in front of the moon. She frowned, there were no clouds in the sky but whatever it was cleared, and the light returned.

When they reached the city, the streets were still teeming with people, but the main road had cleared significantly, and they were able to ride straight through to the palace. Lorrin dismounted first, kindly helping Elinta down so she could keep her dress from riding up. She could still feel the ghost of his hands on her hips once he'd placed her on the ground. In the stables, Lorrin whispered something to Jae before handing over the reins, taking Elinta's hand and hurrying into the palace.

Once inside, he dropped her hand and turned to her. "Niles is waiting for us in the ballroom. I'll let him know you're back if you want to go freshen up before coming in?"

That was probably a good idea, she thought, looking down at her dress. It had held up very well through her trip to the woods, but she couldn't say the same about her windswept hair or her makeup which she knew must have smudged across her face. She nodded, reaching out to brush some dust from his suit before hurrying up to her room on the third floor. Once inside, she brushed out her hair and pulled it up into a simple ponytail before she cleaned her face and reapplied a light layer of makeup. Her shoes were a little dirty, so she cleaned them as best as she could, thankful that they hid her dirty feet from sight. Satisfied that she looked perfectly acceptable, and exponentially glad that her eyes weren't red or her face puffy, she hurried back downstairs. She checked on Zhayra's emotions one last time and, satisfied that the dragon was OK, slipped into the ballroom.

It was a completely different picture to the king's ball. The same band played a jovial tune and rows of people danced in time to it, their faces alight with joy. Others milled around tables of food and drink set against the wall to her right and the wall at the end of the room. Dragon puppets danced around the room, operated by people hiding under them in groups of two. One of them was being chased by a gang of giggling children no older than five years old waving fake swords. Elinta searched the crowd for Lorrin or Niles, but she instead found a set of curious eyes. Ford raised an eyebrow as her eyes locked with his, open question spread across his face. Mustering as big a smile as she could, which she feared wasn't big enough, she waved, then returned to searching the room. Ford's eyes didn't leave her, and she hoped he couldn't guess where she'd been.

But Ford's eyes weren't the only ones on her. Shae, her hair pulled back tightly into a bun, stared openly at her from across the room. The woman hadn't given up her dislike or apparent suspicion of Elinta since she'd been shot down in the council meeting. Unsure what else to do, Elinta waved at her too, then kept searching for the boys, trying not to panic under the woman's gaze.

There! She weaved her way through the milling crowd and around the closest table, then crossed the last of the way to the table at the far end of the room.

"Ah, there she is!" Niles called, turning his face away from General Nash to wink pointedly at her. "You're looking a lot better. Whatever it was didn't last very long then."

"No," she said, coming to a stop between him and Lorrin and nodding along. "I'm sorry I missed so much of the night."

General Nash smiled sympathetically at her. "What horrible timing. We weren't sure where you'd disappeared off to."

"Remember that time I was sick at Mira's birthday party?" Niles said, saving her from replying. "That was awful! I think it was something I ate earlier in the day."

"Yes," General Nash said, frowning. "Or maybe it was *everything* you ate. I'd rather we didn't have a repeat of that. Well," she said to Elinta, "I'm glad you're feeling better. Try to enjoy what's left of the night."

Elinta forced another smile as the woman left the three of them standing around the table. Hardly a second passed before she was enveloped in a hug.

"Next time you run away, please tell someone," Niles said in her ear.

"Doesn't that defeat the purpose of running away?" she asked, returning the hug.

"Oh, ha ha. You've been around us way too long," he said, pulling back to look her in the eye. "I'm serious, though. You gave us a heart attack."

Her stomach growled again, and concern instantly flittered across his face. "When was the last time you ate?" he said, voice rising.

"Erm ... lunch?" she said, fully aware of his views on food. Anytime was a good time to eat, and three meals a day wasn't nearly enough.

"Get yourself over to that table and eat, young lady!" He turned her around and gave her a shove towards the table, sharing an exasperated look with Lorrin.

Elinta stood with Lorrin and Niles, grazing from the table and chatting about anything other than what was happening around them. The food, as usual, was divine.

"Thank you," she said when the boys finished filling her in on their search for her. She gained two happy grins in return.

"So, we still on tonight?" Niles asked.

"Shh!" Elinta said, pausing as she raised a glass to her lips and looking around for Shae, but the advisor was still on the other side of the room.

Niles rose his eyebrows at her.

"Sorry," she said.

Lorrin had revealed that they trained regularly, but Elinta didn't want Shae to know that the sessions were every night. They often talked of Zhayra then.

She refocused on Niles.

"Training," she said. She'd assumed they weren't going to tonight as did Lorrin by the surprise on his face. "Yeah ... but no dummy tonight." She wanted to spar properly, the way she'd seen them do several times before.

"Woah, just as long as you're not venting those pent-up emotions on us," Niles said, reaching for another muffin.

"Sounds good to me," Lorrin said, but she wasn't sure if he meant training without the dummy or the part about emotions.

Soon the band was packing up, and the crowd began to thin. Unbelievably, the festival really was ending at nine o'clock ... at least in the palace.

"We'll meet in the usual place in thirty minutes, OK?" Lorrin said, leaving them to join his parents in farewelling the more important guests.

Niles and Elinta parted ways, and she returned to her room to change into her training clothes. She carefully laid the green dress aside on her bed and the heels at the foot. She slipped into her boots, the ones Kalla had given her when she'd first arrived, with an audible sigh of relief. The inner padding felt wonderful on her sore feet. Not bothering to wash her face of the makeup, she tied her sword at her waist and went to their training room early.

Aside from the addition of the affectionately named dummy, Geoffrey, that stood in the centre and slightly to the left of the room, the space hadn't changed since they'd started using it, except Geoffrey wasn't the original one anymore. The one that she strode towards now was the second that Niles and Lorrin had sourced for her.

Elinta drew her sword and practiced a few strikes against him, hitting the knee in a sweeping motion, coming downwards on the head, then the shoulder, thrusting the sword into Geoffrey's material torso. Stepping back, she sheathed her blade and dropped to sit on the cushioned floor, stretching out her muscles in anticipation for the upcoming sparring session.

Who would fight her? Both Niles and Lorrin would be coming for their session, so it could go either way. Maybe she'd fight both of them, one after the other, like she had before with the wooden sword. It didn't cross her mind that she'd fight both of them at the same time though she wanted to be able to one day. How her goals had changed! At first, she'd just wanted to know how to defend herself in case she ever got into trouble; now she wanted to be able to fight two people at once and those people were the prince and a palace guard.

"You're early." Lorrin's voice sounded behind her, and she twisted in a stretch to see him entering, Niles close behind. They'd both changed out of their formalwear and into their usual training clothes.

"I was ready early; thought I may as well wait here." She pushed her feet under her and faced them.

"Ready?" Lorrin asked.

She only managed to nod before he pounced. Elinta met his blade mid-strike with a parry, a grunt of surprise escaping her, but Lorrin advanced in a series of attacks that forced her to stay on the defence. She told herself there was nothing different between this and fighting with the wooden swords or the blunt blade, and it helped her a little. And she knew he'd pull any attack that broke through her defence. So, she ducked, dodged, and parried his attacks, looking for an opening. He'd stepped up their training to make it harder on her, but whenever there was an opening, she took it. He blocked every one of her attacks.

Niles stood off to the side, watching with open enthusiasm, a commentary of gasps and whistles following every move they made. Occasionally, he praised her defence or lamented when Lorrin blocked one of her attacks, but he didn't offer any advice. This one was up to her, and she was glad for it.

It was Elinta who made first contact in their sparring, and Niles yelled in delight. She'd stepped to the side of one of Lorrin's attacks, feigned a strike towards his side before twisting around behind him, and just managing to tap the flat of her blade against his thigh before he pushed the blade away.

"Good!" he said, grinning.

They danced on. Back and forth. Blocking and attacking. Sweat beading on her forehead, breath coming quick, but she hardly noticed. She tapped Lorrin again on his arm. He returned with a tap to her shoulder one minute later. He pulled a blow back just before stabbing into her hip. She did the same to his chest.

It's just like the wood, she told herself over and over, determined not to scare herself out of fighting well. Lorrin finally ended the fight by rapping her on the back of the head, lightly, with the flat of his blade.

Panting, Elinta lowered her sword and pushed a strand of hair away from her face.

"That. Was. Great!" Niles clapped his hands together. "Right. Let's unpack it."

They spent the next hour going over the fight, repeating moves and working on areas that needed improvement. Niles and Lorrin took turns going over particular attacks and defences with her, correcting each other as much as they corrected her. All the while, Elinta made sure to stop and check on Zhayra occasionally, making sure the dragon's emotions hadn't returned to the way they'd been earlier in the day. Like her though, Zhayra seemed to have picked up after her visit.

"All right, I think that's it," Lorrin said, slipping his sword back into its sheath. Elinta and Niles both copied the movement.

"Tomorrow night?" she asked, looking between them.

"Definitely. You didn't think you'd get away without fighting me, did you?" Niles said.

She grinned. "I hoped not."

"Will you help me move him back?" Niles asked Lorrin, pointing towards Geoffrey, whom they'd moved during their practice.

"Sure."

Elinta yawned loudly despite the energy running through her muscles.

"You don't need to hang around," Niles said to her while Lorrin moved back to the door to slip his shoes back on. "We won't be long."

Even though her body was still zapping with adrenaline, she nodded gratefully. After such a long day, her bathtub was calling to her. She yawned again.

"See you in the morning," she said, waving over her shoulder at them.

"Goodnight, El," they both called as she closed the door behind her.

A smile on her sweaty face, Elinta tugged out her hair tie, which had already released a large portion of her hair and pulled it all back up into a ponytail. She was just a few metres down the main corridor when a figure appeared in front of her, standing directly beside a light. The city had long ago quietened, and she'd expected the rest of the palace to be deserted by now, especially the part she was in, since there were no living quarters nearby. But she wasn't entirely surprised that not everyone had turned in for the night yet. The festival may have ended, but it was still a holiday.

She opened her mouth to call out a greeting to the man just as the figure stepped away from the lantern. The words died on her lips. White pupils shone in the shadowy light and the glowing figure smiled. "My, this is a surprise."

CHAPTER
TWENTY-ONE

H IS EYES WERE WRONG. That was all she could think as the man drew near her, and he came fully into view. He was stunning. With tanned, glowing skin, black hair, and a perfect face, he was the most handsome Asali she'd seen. But his eyes. His eyes were wrong, and the sight filled her with unease. Her own eyes wouldn't leave them. Not because the pupils glowed or because they were white. That was normal. But because they were slitted so much that they reminded her of Zhayra's. And his irises ... where every other Asali she'd ever seen had eyes a shade of white, grey, or silver, this man's were red. No. *Maroon.*

"What were the chances of running into you?" he said, his voice soft yet piercing in the silence. He spoke with the same lilting accent as Eiran and Laira, and though it was likely not his real age, physically he looked to be in his early twenties. Yet his accent was much stronger than the other adult Asali she knew.

Elinta frowned. Repeated his words over in her head. It almost sounded like he knew her, but he couldn't. She'd never seen him before. She would have remembered his unusual eyes if he'd been among Ciar's people. The man smirked at her confusion, and she was struck again by his good looks. Tearing her eyes from his face and downwards, she finally saw the armour he wore.

"Is that—" she choked, "is that dragon scales?"

All of a sudden, her eyes felt heavy again. Why did that keep happening?

The man wore an armour that fit his lean form perfectly from his wrists down to his ankles. It moved easily with his every movement and matched the colour of his eyes, deep maroon. The armour was made entirely of overlapping scales the size of a coin. Spread across his chest, in an arc, were three blue scales. Elinta gasped.

"You were the one who took them," she whispered, staring at the scales that had disappeared months ago without a trace. "You killed Alexander."

He was a murderer. Her sword-hand twitched, but she didn't dare reach for her weapon; the man was armed and covered in armour near impenetrable to steel. *Lorrin, Niles, please hurry.* She kept her face pointed straight at him, but all her hope was in the training room she'd just left behind and the two people inside it.

The man smiled indulgently at her and cocked his head.

"Have you been here this entire time?" he asked, his eyes narrowing.

"What?" She tore her eyes from the sheathed dagger at his belt and back to his dragon-like eyes.

"It never occurred to me that she might have used the *zearla lurai ngaran* on you. Yet here you are." He took another step towards her. "Where is the dragon?"

Her heart jumped a beat. He *knew.*

She tried desperately to school her features, but she wasn't sure what had crossed her face. "What dragon?"

Under her blank exterior, Elinta's mind was racing. How did this man know about Zhayra? And what did he mean that Zhayra had *used* something on her? Was she the reason they could sense each other?

Feeling Zhayra's emotions coiling in the dragon's stomach, Elinta refocused and tried to steady her own. The last thing she needed was to make Zhayra panic because of her own fear. Because what if the dragon came *looking* for her? And came face to face with this man?

He tsked her. "Do you honestly think to fool me?" His eyes glinted in the light of the lanterns lining the hallway. "Where are my manners?" He paused and smirked. "You are Elinta Ferran of Kethmere." She gasped. How did he—? "I am Mazen of Liyarna. You have something I want, Elinta."

"How do you know me?" she asked, her thoughts flying to her brother and father. This man knew where she was from. *Please be OK,* she thought desperately. The man had already killed at least one person ... what if? *No, don't even think it.*

"Quite by accident, I assure you," the man said. "I was following a white dragon, and I learnt about you."

"You went to Kethmere." She closed her eyes. "Why are you after Zhayra?"

She wasn't surprised when he didn't answer her question.

"Tell me, Elinta," he said instead, her name sounding strange in his mouth. "Did you enjoy the festival? No?" he said, catching sight of the hurt she couldn't hide.

"I didn't think so," Mazen crooned, stepping forwards again so there were only a couple of metres between them. *Lorrin, please hurry!* "Does the prince know your secret, Elinta? Does he know about Zhayra?"

She stiffened, forced her eyes not to leave him and betray her by looking over her shoulder at the corridor she'd left. The corridor where she hoped Lorrin would appear any second in with Niles. But it didn't matter.

"He's not coming," Mazen said, his voice ringing with fake sympathy. "He and Niles are busy sparring."

He laughed at the horror spreading through her.

"How?" she whispered. How did he know? How could he know? He couldn't. He couldn't know. This man couldn't know where she'd just come from and who she'd been with … or what they were doing now. And yet he did. She had to keep him talking until they came out. *I can't take him alone,* she thought, *even if he wasn't wearing that armour, I couldn't do it.* She didn't even question if it would come to that.

"Do you really think he'll stand by you when he finds out?" Mazen asked.

"He already knows," Elinta spat back, unable to hide the truth.

Mazen's eyebrows rose, and a startled chuckle left him. "You told the prince?"

She nodded.

"You're a fool if you believe you're safe here. How long until he tells someone else? How long before Zhayra's scales take the place of hers?" He pointed to one of the blue scales on his chest. "Did you know they still have it?" His face darkened. "The sword that killed her."

Elinta's eyes widened, and her heart stuttered in her chest. She'd never considered what had happened to the sword. Why hadn't Lorrin told her about it like he'd told her about the scales? Elinta shook her head. *He'd never hurt her.* "It doesn't matter. Lorrin won't tell anyone."

"Come with me, Elinta," Mazen said. "You're not safe here. Take me to Zhayra, and we can leave."

"What do you want with Zhayra?" she asked again, ignoring his words. Dread weighed her down. *Who is this man?*

"I want you to be safe," he said again, his voice like honey. He was jumping around so much, his tone shifting constantly, it was confusing. What was he trying to do? Whatever it was, she wasn't fooled.

"And Alexander?" she asked, balling her fists. "Did you want him to be safe?"

"No." He laughed. With a heavy sigh, he pulled the dagger from his belt. Elinta gaped at the blue metal glinting in the light of the lanterns. His dagger was made of *illayas.* Pure *illayas.* "Enough of this. I came here for the prince, but you are a prize indeed."

He lunged.

Elinta stumbled backwards, desperately grabbing at her sword and nearly flinging it across the room in her hurry to unsheathe it.

Mazen's maroon eyes sparkled.

"Ah, but can you use it?"

He lunged again, aiming the dagger straight for her heart. Elinta spun aside, trying to get some room between her and the Asali, but he continued to advance. Illar's words flew back to her mind from the shadows of the White Mountains, when they'd knelt over the *rellaes* in the ground. *Our race is naturally more agile than yours. We have faster reflexes and are stronger.* Her eyes widened. Right in front of her was the very proof of his statement.

Mazen moved with unnatural speed. Even though she had the longer reach with her sword, he moved faster than she ever could and was clearly an expert. His armour didn't even seem to slow him down. All she could do was try to block each blow as it came. There was no room for her to return the attack. All her thought and energy were on blocking the next stab, the next strike. But even if she could have attacked him, only his hands and face were left uncovered by the scale armour.

Within the first minute, his blade had caught her along her forearm in a shallow gash. His beautiful face twisted in pleasure, but he didn't let up and came at her again with the dagger in a vicious attack.

Elinta was already gasping, desperately aware of her shortcomings and resenting the fact that she'd just finished hours of training with Lorrin and Niles. She was already vastly outmatched without her tired muscles weighing her down, and the difference showed. Her arms shook as Mazen brought down a blow upon her that forced her to her knees. She looked up into his face, sweat streaming into her eyes. Mazen smiled.

When his dagger whipped out and down towards her neck, Elinta could do nothing but throw herself to the side and roll away, somehow managing to keep hold of her sword. Mazen's dark chuckle followed her, and she had the distinct feeling he was merely playing with her. She came to a stop near the wall, fear clutching at her stomach. The only reason she was alive was because Mazen wasn't done with her yet. He could move faster than this. He could kill her in an instant.

"Where is Zhayra?" Mazen asked calmly.

Shaking her head, Elinta jumped to her feet.

"I won't tell you," she said breathily.

Mazen's face darkened and he struck again. Elinta had hardly met his next strike when the dagger was flashing through the air towards her leg. Moving to parry the blade, his vastly superior reflexes outdid her. In the blink of an eye his blade stopped, twisted, and darted towards her abdomen. Just managing to twist her body in time, Elinta stopped the blade from plunging into her but couldn't prevent it from slicing across her hip.

"Argh," she cried out, but didn't dare lower her sword.

"Where is Zhayra?" Mazen repeated, but Elinta was hardly listening.

Please, Lorrin! she thought. Her breath came in heaving gasps, and her arms were sore, so sore. She didn't have long before he'd tire of asking her about Zhayra and decide to end it. She'd never tell him where the dragon was hidden. One last idea came to her. Desperately hoping she wasn't too far away, she sucked in a deep breath and screamed at the top of her voice. "LORRIN!"

She parried Mazen's next attack, but if anything, his apparent humour deepened.

"It's no use, *Zearla lurai,*" Mazen said. "Even if he comes, I've already won. *Zetayn eyan pepyan eka ayn air kli nalliyan.*"

The sombre words hung in the air between them, but Elinta didn't have time to consider them because Mazen's manner instantly changed. He was no longer playing with her, and his dagger was slicing through the air again. She threw herself to the side, gaining a precious few centimetres of space before he was on her again. She only had seconds left.

"Get away from her!" Lorrin's voice sounded from behind, and she would have sobbed in relief if not for the dagger she was still trying desperately to avoid.

Mazen easily blocked Lorrin's sweeping attack when it came from behind, aimed at his knees, but Elinta finally had a chance to attack. In a flash, Mazen parried her blade, kicking out at Lorrin at the same time. Just like that, she and Lorrin were both fighting him, and somehow the Asali blocked their every blow.

"I tire of this," Mazen said, ducking Lorrin's blade and catching Elinta with a back fist across her cheek that sent her stumbling. The three stood a moment apart, surveying each other. The Asali cocked his head as though listening. Elinta heaved in deep gasping breaths, a frown crossing her still stinging face as she watched the man. *What's he listening for?* There wasn't a single sound other than what they were causing.

"I'll be back for you," Mazen finally said, pointing his dagger at Lorrin.

"As for you," he said, turning to Elinta with another twisted smile. "It was nice to meet you. My condolences to Zhayra, but please make sure you let her know I'm coming for her."

Mazen twisted on his heel and shot back down the corridor, moving with a speed only an Asali could manage.

"Hey!" Lorrin chased after him, sword still in hand, and disappeared around a corner before Elinta could call after him.

Gasping for breath, Elinta leant against the wall and placed a shaking hand against the cut on her hip, Mazen's Asalin words echoing in her head. Her hand came away from her side bloody. Red dripped from the slash on her forearm. Her cheek ached. But she was alive. Zhayra's relief was immediate, flooding the dragon's entire body.

Pounding feet sounded from the opposite end of the corridor, and Elinta cautiously pushed herself away from the wall, raising her sword in her free hand and bracing herself. Had Mazen somehow come up behind her? A troop of figures appeared around the corner. She saw several familiar faces among them, but it was the one leading them that caught Elinta's attention.

"Niles?" He must have slipped by their group to get help while they fought.

"El! Are you OK? Where's Lorrin?" He grabbed her by the shoulders, looking her up and down. His eyes lingered on her bloodied arm and hip.

She pointed to where Lorrin had disappeared. "That way."

General Sonnen and two soldiers ran down the hall, but Lorrin reappeared a moment later.

"He's gone," Lorrin said, confusion clouding his face.

"Are you alright, Your Highness?" General Sonnen's gruff voice echoed down the hall.

"Yes," he said, waving away the concern, his eyes locked on Elinta who still had her sword in hand.

"Did you see where he went?" the general asked.

"No. I followed him down another hall, but when I came around the next corner, he was gone." He turned to one of the soldiers. "Would you please have a healer sent to my office?" he said, taking charge of the situation.

With a curt nod, the soldier disappeared.

General Nash's voice sounded from beside Elinta. She hadn't even realised the woman was standing so close to her. Her breath was still coming in puffs from adrenaline and exhaustion, and she hadn't heard the woman approach at all. "We'll escort you there."

"That was my intention." Lorrin nodded.

"Here," Niles said, tearing a strip from the hem of his shirt and tying it around Elinta's arm. She was glad to see that her hands had stopped shaking while Niles tore off more fabric and gave it to her to hold against her hip.

General Sonnen surveyed her, looking from the sword still gripped in her hand to the bruise she knew must be forming on her face. "You OK, kid?"

"I'm fine," she said, her breathing finally beginning to calm.

Niles's father watched her a moment longer, then nodded, apparently satisfied that she was OK for the moment.

"Let's go," General Nash said, ordering two of the soldiers to walk in front of the group.

Elinta slipped her sword back into its scabbard, noticing as she did that there were several small nicks along the blade. She shook her head at the memory of Mazen's *illayas* dagger. It was strong enough to damage her sword.

Niles offered her his help, but she shook her head.

"I'm OK," she said with a small smile. Nodding, he walked on one side of her, Lorrin on the other. The generals and two other guards followed behind them.

"Enough backup?" Niles asked Lorrin quietly.

"More than enough," he said, looking across Elinta. "Where did you find them?"

"They were debriefing. Apparently, they've just finished for the night. I think I ruined the afterparty."

"Thank you, Niles."

Niles was quiet for a moment. "I'd rather you didn't order me to leave either of you ever again."

"Noted," Lorrin said, but his voice was full of gratitude.

Elinta was only half listening. Zhayra was furious. Really, really furious. And it didn't help that with every passing second Elinta's adrenaline faded, and she felt the full force of her aches and pains. Particularly the gash at her hip. She pulled back the cloth and glanced at the weeping wound before covering it again. It didn't look too serious, but she definitely needed stitches and it had slashed through tender skin.

Lorrin whispered in her ear, "You'll have to tell everyone what happened. Leave out anything about Zhayra."

She nodded, dreading the thought of reliving whatever it was that just happened, but maybe it would help her straighten out her thoughts. She'd have to tell Lorrin the rest later. And ask him about King Cenric's sword. Elinta could tell Mazen's last words to her, about sending condolences to Zhayra, had confused Lorrin, but she was equally confused. *And how did he know about Zhayra? And the sword?*

One of the soldiers in front opened the door to Lorrin's office and stepped aside to allow her, Lorrin, Niles, and the generals to enter. Before closing the door, Lorrin asked one of the men in a low voice to find his parents and Shae and ask them to come to the office. The other soldiers waited outside, guarding the closed door.

A healer was already waiting inside for them, and he hurried over to Elinta.

"My, my, what's happened here?" the thin man said, pushing his glasses further up his nose.

"I'll need yarrow, calendula, or black disc fungi," she told the man, her training taking over, and eased herself into one of the seats by Lorrin's desk. "Actually," she said, looking at the cut on her forearm, "honey would do, too."

General Nash's eyebrows weren't the only ones in the room to rise, but Elinta was too tired to care. The healer threw her a shrewd look before pulling her hand and shirt away from her hip, then untying the strip of shirt from her arm.

"Hmm ... yarrow and honey, I think." The man covered the cuts again, then rifled inside the satchel slung across his body, pulling out a jar of mashed yarrow.

"It needs stitches too," the healer said, gesturing to her hip, but she wasn't at all surprised. The cut to her arm was still weeping too and would probably need some.

Niles's eyes were glued to the man as he pulled out some thread and a needle.

"Can I do it?" he asked.

Elinta punched his arm.

"No," she said, getting a grin in response.

She thought she caught General Sonnen roll his eyes at his son.

"Here." The healer handed her several flowers to chew, which would act as a minor pain relief. It wouldn't be enough to block out the pain of the cuts or the stitches, but it would dull it.

"Lean back," the medic said, and Elinta did as she was told, munching on the flowers. She tried not to look at all the people in the room watching as the man cleaned the wound and stitched her skin back together. With the flowers, she only felt a small prick as the needle glided through her.

While the man covered the wound, Lorrin turned back to their company and cut across his aunt before she could finish asking what had happened. "I'll tell you everything I know as soon as my parents arrive." He gazed at Elinta sympathetically. "But I'm afraid I don't know much."

The healer had just finished treating the cut on Elinta's arm when the king and queen entered the room. The king wore a loose shirt and pants, and the queen had pulled a dressing gown over her nightdress. Mira's eyes flittered around the room; her shoulders physically slumped in relief when she saw Lorrin unharmed. Shae's small figure appeared behind them in the doorway. Despite the heavy bags hanging under her eyes, she seemed to take in the situation quickly, her eyes darting across everyone, lingering only a moment on Elinta. The woman's beady green eyes noticeably slid right over Niles.

"What's going on?" King Aldon asked, watching the healer pull a jar from his gear and hand it to Elinta.

"Take a spoonful before bed, then tomorrow in the morning, and again before bed. Keep taking it for three days."

"Thank you," she said and watched the man bow to the royals before leaving the room.

"There's been an intruder," Lorrin told his parents, dragging his chair from behind the desk and placing it beside the other two, one of which Elinta still occupied.

No one took it.

Elinta watched on in silence, trying to ignore Zhayra's raging emotions and the pain in her body. Why had they trained for so long before finishing for the night? Her arms were aching in a way they hadn't since she'd first started using the wooden practice sword. The medicine had done little for her in that regard.

"Who?" Mira asked, her expression turning worried as she caught sight of the bandage on Elinta's forearm. The one on her hip was covered, but the queen's eyes still landed on her bloodied shirt.

Lorrin turned expectantly to Elinta and nodded for her to tell them what happened. She cleared her throat, all too aware of how many people there were in the room who didn't know about Zhayra. Who *couldn't* know. Just as Lorrin told her, Elinta left out everything about Zhayra, focusing more on Mazen's apparent original reason for being there. She didn't mention Cenric's sword either, not knowing who was supposed to know about it.

"He was after Prince Lorrin?" General Nash repeated when she'd finished.

"Yes," Elinta said, though once he'd realised who she was, all thought for Lorrin seemed to have escaped Mazen. He'd been focused on her and Zhayra after that.

"But who was he?" General Sonnen said. The lighting of Lorrin's office made the lines on Niles's father's face seem deeper. "The only name he gave was Mazen?"

She nodded.

"He said he's from Liyarna. Clearly this was a move against us!" King Aldon said, anger bending his brow.

"The king is right," Shae clipped, speaking the first words she had since arriving. The advisor had hardly looked at Elinta as she'd recounted the events of the night. But Elinta didn't mind. Mazen's appearance with the scales meant that the woman no longer suspected her. At least not of being a thief and murderer.

"He must be working for the council," Shae said.

Lorrin shook his head, thoughtfully. "I don't think so. Remember the reports of the lone Asali spotted near our towns? And Ciar and Raisa said someone unknown to them was seen in the White Mountains not long before I was there."

"You don't think he's acting on behalf of the council," General Nash said, more of a statement than a question.

Elinta was glad to see that she wasn't jumping to conclusions like the king and Shae were. Based on Ciar's words about the forest Asali, Mazen's actions didn't seem to line up with them and she didn't want them blamed for something one lone person had done. And if he wanted to hurt Zhayra ... that certainly didn't sound like something the council would approve of.

"No, I don't."

King Aldon shook his head. "Even so, we can't trust them. It's no coincidence that he meant to attack on the night of the Eggslaying. And this armour ..."

Elinta was hardly listening now. Her eyes were still heavy, and she was tired, desperately tired, now that all the adrenaline had left her body. Shae jumped in as well, but Elinta didn't bother trying to listen to the woman. Lorrin didn't respond to either of them. At least, she didn't think he did. Maybe she missed that too. But she couldn't muster the energy to make herself listen. It had been a long day, and coupled with the training session and Mazen's attack, she was exhausted. Elinta's head nodded, and she caught herself.

"Your Majesty, we should double the guard in the palace," General Sonnen said, his gruff voice piercing Elinta's tired mind. "Especially on the third floor. This man might come back to finish the job."

"Agreed," the king said. "If that's all, we can pick this up in the morning. It looks like Elinta could do with some sleep. We all could."

Eight sets of eyes landed on her and she forced herself to focus.

"Sounds good to me," she said with an embarrassed smile.

"We'll walk you back to your room," Lorrin said, gesturing to Niles.

Shae left the room with hardly a word, merely saying goodnight to Lorrin and his parents. She barely even acknowledged Generals Nash and Sonnen. *Strange woman.* The generals moved after Shae towards the door, saying their goodnights.

"Good job, kid," General Sonnen said over his shoulder.

She smiled in return, but he was already out in the hall. Niles's dad wasn't so bad. He was gruff and a little hard around the edges, but she liked him.

Lorrin assured the king and queen that he was OK, and with one last, long look at him, they returned to their set of rooms, leaving Elinta alone with her two friends.

"Ready to go?" Niles said, looking down at her.

"Please," she said, slowly rising to her feet. She felt like all her joints should have audibly creaked with the movement, and the skin pulled tight at her hip.

"Come on, old lady," Niles joked, but his voice was soft.

"I'd like to take this moment to remind you that you're older than me." At seeing Lorrin's grin, she added, "You both are."

"And neither of us are walking around like Niles's grandmother," Lorrin said, following her out of the room and down the hall.

"My grandmother is more agile than that, Lor," Niles said with a deep frown from beside her.

"Thanks guys," Elinta scoffed, her pace quickening as they neared her room and her thoughts turned to her bed.

Lorrin's grin only widened as he stepped in front and pushed open her door, leading them inside. As a group they all moved to her bed where Lorrin propped up her pillows and Niles told her to sit.

Slipping her sword from her belt and dropping the jar of medicine on the bed, she sunk gratefully onto the mattress. She didn't even care that she was still in her dirty, and bloody, training clothes. She was too tired to change. The boys climbed on the bed as well and sat at the foot of the mattress. After making her take the spoonful of medicine the healer had prescribed, the two stared at her for a long moment.

"So, what else happened?" the prince asked softly.

Niles stared expectantly, but Elinta had just remembered something, or someone.

"Zhayra!" she gasped, moving to swing her legs over the side of the bed.

"Woah. I don't think so!" Niles grabbed her legs mid-swing and dropped them back to the bed.

"Zhayra will be fine until the morning," Lorrin said. "The last thing you need is to go riding out there in the middle of the night."

"Actually, I think it's early morning," Niles corrected.

"Either way. You need to rest."

Reluctantly, Elinta agreed and settled back in the bed. She told them everything she'd left out before, all about how Mazen had known about Zhayra and her, and the *ngaran* which she was now sure meant something to do with 'bond.' She'd heard it twice now, once in the scroll from Ford and once from Mazen, and it seemed to fit. *Zearla lurai ngaran*. Literally 'dragon friend bond.' But she didn't linger on the revelation that Zhayra was responsible for it, it didn't matter to her how it had come about. Just that it was there.

She told them how he'd been to Kethmere, too. Whether that meant he'd just been to the crash site by the lake or into the village was unclear, and not knowing was weighing on her. Even though she hadn't left her family on the best of terms, she loved them dearly.

"I'm sure your family's fine," Lorrin said, seeing her worry. "We would have heard something if Mazen had been *in* the village. Just like with all the others."

"I know," she murmured, but it didn't ease her worry. She'd never been away from her family, from Blaine, for so long before.

"He knew about something else," she said quietly, watching Lorrin's face. His eyebrows rose. "He said you have King Cenric's sword."

Lorrin nodded slowly.

Niles's mouth dropped open. "You do?"

"We do," Lorrin said, looking between them. "No one's supposed to know. There's so few *illayas* swords in existence and this one ..." he trailed off. "It's hidden. I don't know how Mazen could know about it."

Elinta couldn't find it within herself to be angry at Lorrin for not telling her. She only wondered who else knew. If Niles hadn't known about it, maybe only the royal family knew. What could someone do with a sword of *illayas?* Mazen's dagger had been bad enough, but a sword? It was a good thing that no one knew about it. Elinta took another moment to be glad that Zhayra was hidden out in the woods and away from the *illayas* weapon.

"Can we just talk for a minute about that fight?" Niles said, a grin spreading across his face. "You were awesome, and I only saw a few seconds of it! I knew my training was going to make a difference."

Lorrin cleared his throat.

"Yes, yes," Niles said with a long exhale. "You helped."

"He did," Elinta said, but she didn't mean the training. She recalled the moment he'd finally appeared in the hall when she thought she was facing death and the hope he'd given her.

Lorrin met her gaze, seeing what was going through her head. "You did well to hold him off. He was a natural with that blade."

Elinta shook her head. "He was toying with me. If he'd been serious from the beginning, I wouldn't be here now."

They sat in silence, thinking over all that had happened. There was one thing that bothered her, something Mazen had said. That he'd already won, but she'd never told him where Zhayra was. And those words he'd said to her in Asalin? What did they mean?

She couldn't recall the exact phrasing, but it had left a chill in her heart. Elinta didn't say anything. Instead she watched her two friends as they reflected on the night.

Lorrin was the first to break their silence. "I think we should leave earlier than planned."

"When?" Elinta said, knowing immediately what he meant. They'd planned to leave for Liyarna within the next week, but now they actually had concrete information that the council needed to hear. They had their way in.

Lorrin hesitated. "The day after tomorrow?"

"Sounds good to me." Niles clapped his hands together.

Elinta agreed. She could do with a day to rest before they left on the cross-country journey. The Calaza was close to the western coastline of Eldras, and they were currently only a day's ride from the eastern coast.

"You can let Zhayra know tomorrow," Lorrin said, "I'm sure she'll be happy to move on."

Elinta gave a tired smile. "She will."

They'd finally get to spend more time together again. She'd missed the dragon's company beyond anything she could have imagined. Elinta's eyes began to droop, and she fought to keep them open.

"This guy's armour sounds cool," Niles said to Lorrin. "Imagine having armour made of dragon scales!" If Lorrin responded, she didn't hear it.

It was early afternoon by the time Elinta eased herself down to sit against Zhayra's massive chest. She let Zhayra's emotions wash over her: happiness, fear, concern, and love.

Sighing, Elinta rested her head back, shifting to relieve the sting in her hip. "I'm OK," she finally said.

Zhayra grumbled.

"I am," she said though her body ached. She frowned. "He knew about you, Zhayra. About us."

The dragon's stomach tightened.

"He wanted to kill you." She stroked Zhayra's leg.

A huff was her only response.

She smiled.

"And me," she admitted. "We're leaving for Liyarna tomorrow. Maybe they can tell us more about him...."

She let the sentence hang in the air between them.

Tomorrow.

Tomorrow they'd be on their way to the Asali. They could finally talk about the dragons. Maybe she'd learn more about the bond between her and Zhayra. But now, now there was something else she needed to know. Who was Mazen? And why did he want to kill them?

PRONUNCIATION GUIDE

Names:

- Ferran pronounced FEH-RAN

- Zhayra pronounced ZAY-RUH

- Ciar pronounced KEER (like 'here' with a 'k')

- Raisa pronounced RAY-SUH

- Mazen pronounced MAY-ZEN

Locations:

- Nevira pronounced NEV-EAR-RUH

- Liyarna pronounced LIE-YAR-NUH

- Calaza pronounced CUH-LAR-ZUH

Other:

- *Illayas* pronounced ILL-UH-YAS

- *Zearla lurai ngaran* pronounced ZEE-ARE-LA LER-EYE NG (like Si*ng*apore)-ARE-AN

- *Zetayn nalliyan ayn palla kli ayn karn mai ri/ti* pronounced ZEH-TAYN NULL-EE-YARN AIN PALL-UH KLEE AIN KARN MY REE/TEE. Meaning: "May (the) sun (present) continue to (present) shine on you (male/female)."

Zetayn eyan pepyan eka ayn air kli nalliyan

Four months ago, Elinta Ferran's life changed forever when she found an injured dragon, but now someone wants them both dead.

In the wake of an attack by the mysterious Asali Mazen, Elinta and her friends begin the journey to the Asali city. Elinta hopes to learn more about the man who tried to kill her, while rekindling the alliance between humans and Asali. If she succeeds, the dragons could finally return.

In the city Elinta meets Tamir, an Asali with a curious amount of knowledge of the *Zearla lurai* and Mazen. When Tamir offers to help her learn more about the bond between her and Zhayra, Elinta accepts without hesitation. But not everyone is as welcoming as Tamir. Some have questionable loyalties. And all of them know Mazen.

When Elinta's family is threatened, she must decide whether to face the exiled prince or lose them forever. But there aren't a lot of people a *Zearla lurai* can trust....

Elinta will return in 2023

ACKNOWLEDGEMENTS

Wow! I have loved writing The Dragon Healer! I'm so glad to finally be able to share it with you. There are quite a few people I need to thank for helping me get here.

Always first and most important, I have to thank God. Thank you, Papa, for carrying me through a really difficult time, and using that time to draw me back to my love of writing. I'm so glad I could make this dream a reality.

Carrie Jones, my fantastic editor! Thank you for going over my manuscript not once but twice. Your edits and feedback were fantastic! I also apologize for any errors on this page ... I left it to the last minute and you never saw it. I feel like that would bug me lol

Taire, your cover is divine. Thank you so much. It's a dream come true. I could stare at it forever.

My beta readers, you were all so amazing! My first round betas, you read something that had a lot of flaws but you saw it for the potential it had and helped me give the next round something better, so they could find more problems (*insert crying but laughing face here*). Jemma, you were my first ever beta reader, thank you for your advice and feedback, and for coming back for TEC2. Beba and Caroline, you've not only come back to TEC2 but you also read TDH for me more than once. You're all extraordinary.

My parents and brother, you never looked down on this dream. Never made me feel like it wasn't worth it. You even listened to some of my crazy story gushing. Thank you.

And lastly, thank *you*! Thank you for picking this book up. If you leave me a review, thank you thank you thank you. I can't say what it means to me that you've given this book a chance, and if you're still reading by now, I hope that means you enjoyed it!

Until next time. *Zetayn nalliyan ayn palla kli ayn karn mai ris.*

Tiani Davids grew up in Victoria reading middle-grade and young adult fantasy, a love that soon expanded to include writing. She now lives on the Far South Coast of New South Wales where she cultivates her passion for reading, writing, and all things Tolkien.

Connect with Tiani online to keep up to date on upcoming releases at:

Instagram: @tianidavids
Facebook: @authortianidavids
Website: tianidavids.com
Sign up to Tiani's newsletter on her website to keep up to date and receive exclusive content.